The Girl from Her Mirror

Becki Willis

Clear Creek Publishers

ISBN: 1500491373
ISBN 13: 9781500491376

Other Books by Becki Willis
He Kills Me, He Kills Me Not
Mirror, Mirror on Her Wall
(September 2014)

Light from Her Mirror
(November 2014)

The Girl from Her Mirror
Book One: Mirrors Don't Lie
By Becki Willis

Chapter 1

San Antonio, TX
June, 1991

The little girl stared into the mirror, studying the reflection before her with wide, intelligent eyes. Even at the tender age of three, she knew there was something monumental about this moment. Something she needed to absorb, needed to remember.

Her solemn gaze roamed over the image, taking in the tumble of wayward curls, tracing the outline of a chubby cheek, memorizing the light in the wide green eyes.

"I'll never forget you," she whispered.

Her mother stepped into the room, her body rigid. "It's time," she announced briskly.

The little girl continued to gaze into the mirror. She put her tiny hand up, palm against palm.

"I'll never forget you," she promised. "Never."

Chapter 2

Austin, TX
April, 2014

Makenna Reagan rushed through the automatic doors of the Emergency Room, desperate to find her best friend. The message left on her voice mail had been sketchy, at best; there had been an accident, and she was listed as next of kin. If she hurried, she could make it before Miss Reese went into surgery.

"I'm here to see Kenzie Reese," she told the receptionist, pushing back an unruly lock of auburn curls. "She was admitted about an hour ago."

"Have a seat. Someone will be with you shortly."

Be with her? What did that mean? Makenna nibbled on her bottom lip as she took a seat in the hard plastic chair. Why didn't they just take her straight back? Maybe Kenzie was more seriously injured than they said. Maybe…

"Ma'am? You may see your sister now." A nurse in blue scrubs motioned from the electronically controlled door she held open. Makenna scrambled to her feet, not bothering to correct the mistake. The two of them looked so much alike, everyone thought they were sisters. Being listed as next of kin only cemented the misconception.

"How is she? Is she all right?"

"Pretty banged up, but all and all, she's very fortunate. The doctor will be in to speak with you before we take her up to OR. She's been asking for you." The nurse talked as she led the way through a maze of hallways and cubicles. "Here you go," the nurse said, pulling back the curtain and revealing her very bruised and battered friend.

"Oh, Kenzie! Kenzie, are you all right?" She rushed to her friend's bedside, trying to note all her injuries at once. There was a wide bandage wrapped around her forehead, blood caked in her dark tangled hair, an angry red bruise encircling the point of her chin, scrapes and bruises and small cuts on both arms, and her left leg was heavily bandaged and elevated on a stack of pillows. Wires and tubes sprouted from her in all directions.

"Makenna. You came." This, groggily.

"Of course I came! What on earth happened?"

"Don't know. One minute I'm driving home, the next thing I know there's a car in my windshield. When I woke up, I was here. What time is it?"

Makenna glanced around for a clock. "Uhm, just after noon."

"Good, there's still time." She sounded relieved.

"Time for what?"

"My flight. It leaves at 2:35."

"You aren't going anywhere, my friend, except to the operating room."

"Not me. You."

Makenna frowned. Either she had taken a nasty knock to the head or the pain medication was making her loopy. "I'm not going with you, Kenzie. You were going on this trip by yourself. For work."

"I know. But I need you to go for me."

"Kenzie, I think you're a little confused. Why don't you just lie back and relax? Can I get you anything, do anything for you?"

"Yes."

"What? You name it. Would you like some ice chips?"

The young woman in the hospital bed shook her bed, wincing at the pain caused by the simple action. "I need you to do this for me."

"Okay, honey, what? What can I do for you?" She found a spot on her friend's arm that wasn't injured and patted it comfortingly.

"Take my place. You get on that plane."

"What? What on earth are you talking about?" Makenna drew back, her brow furrowed.

"I need you to do this for me, Makenna." Focusing her eyes on her friend with obvious effort, the injured woman spoke in a clear, strong voice. "My career depends on it. Please, take my place. Pretend you're me."

"I can't do that!" Makenna cried. "I don't know the first thing about taking pictures."

"Of course you do. Point and shoot. And you know how to do research."

"Kenzie, I think that bump on your head knocked something loose. Do you know what you're asking?"

Kenzie Reese took a deep breath, willing the pain away until she made her point. After she won the argument - which she knew she would - she would reward herself with a nice, deep sleep. Medically induced, perhaps, but numbed to the pain that radiated throughout her body.

"I'm asking you to save my shaky career. The trip is already paid for, but I maxed out my credit cards doing it. The magazine will pay me back, but only if I turn in the story. If I don't make this assignment, I'm toast. Please, Makenna. I need you to do this."

"I can't just up and leave at a moment's notice!"

"Why not? You don't have a job."

True. As of two days ago, she was 'relieved' of her duties as reporter for the *Austin Daily Newsprint*. If Kenzie weren't in her current condition, Makenna wouldn't appreciate her blunt reminder of the situation.

"Still, I can't just hop on a plane and fly off to New England for a week!"

"Why not? What's keeping you here?" she asked pointedly.

This time, she was polite enough not to remind Makenna of her new status as 'single'. Seemed when it rained, it really did pour. Within five days, Makenna had lost her boyfriend and her job. Surprisingly, the first didn't smart nearly as much as the latter.

"You, for one thing. Who's going to take care of you when you get out of here?"

"There was something about cracked ribs and a bruised spleen, plus this leg. I'll be in here a couple of days. You'll be home before I am." Her strength was fading. She closed her eyes and continued, "If not, I'll call Marci or Linda."

"I couldn't leave you at a time like this!"

"You'll be doing me a bigger favor, bigger service, by going."

"But the plane ticket is in your name . . ."

"So take my driver's license, I won't need it. Pretend you're me. We've done it before." She opened her eyes long enough to summon an impish grin.

"Fooling blind dates, job interviewers, and crazy old Professor Nolan is one thing; impersonating someone else to airport security is a federal offense!" Makenna protested. Nibbling her lip again, she added, "At least, I guess it is. Yes, I'm sure it must be. Why would you ask me to do something like that?"

"Because I'm desperate. I have to make this assignment, Kenna. My job depends on it. My financial future depends on it." She tried a new tactic. "Our apartment rent depends on it."

"But..."

"I'm stuck here with a busted leg. I'll be out of commission for who-knows-how-long. This piece can either make me or break me. Please, Kenna. The magazine will never know who gets on that plane, who takes those pictures. Please, do this for me."

Makenna hesitated, thinking of all that could go wrong with her friend's scheme. Something always did.

"Please, when have I ever asked anything of you?" At Makenna's unbelieving snort, the bruised and battered woman changed her question. "Okay, so when have you ever turned me down? And why start now, when it's so important? As your best friend, as your roommate, please, please, I'm begging you to do this for me."

Makenna shoved back a handful of curls as she leaned over the hospital bed to peer more closely at her friend. What if her wounds were more serious than she thought? Should she deny her something that was obviously so important to her? But could she leave her at such a crucial moment? Torn between wanting to go and needing to stay, she insisted, "Kenzie, it's not that simple!"

"Of course it is," Kenzie argued. "You've been saying you're stuck in a rut, that your life is too boring, too predictable. For once, do something spur-of-the-moment. Do this for both of us."

"But - But the plane leaves in two hours! I hardly have time to get to the airport, much less pack."

She was weakening, Kenzie thought with a smile. "Already done. Half your closet is in my suitcases anyway. You have just enough time to pack your own overnight bag, drop my bag with Linda to bring down here, and get to the airport."

Makenna paced the small confines of the cubicle. "But so many things could go wrong! I would have to check in with the magazine, wouldn't I?"

"By e-mail. You know my account."

"What if I need some sort of verification for something?"

"Like what? You know all my information."

It was true. Kenzie was terrible at remembering passwords and numbers; her best back-up was Makenna's uncanny memory for details. Still doubtful, she threw out a half dozen other scenarios, all of which her friend had an answer for.

"Makenna!" Kenzie finally stopped her. "It's already 12:30. If you don't leave now, my career is over. Will you do this for me, or not?"

Makenna hesitated another full thirty seconds, staring hard at her friend. She was torn between the duty to stay and the thrill of going. Kenzie was right; this was the perfect time, the perfect opportunity, to step out of her boring little box and do something completely spontaneous, all while helping her best friend. It seemed to be a win/win situation, so what did she have to lose?

Before she could answer her own question, Makenna drew a deep breath and took a leap of faith. "I have a feeling I'm going to regret this, but … all right. I will take your place this week. I will pretend to be Kenzie Reese."

If she could have managed it, Kenzie would have squealed with delight. Instead, the best she could muster was a weary smile as she closed her eyes and sighed in relief. "Thank you. I can't tell you what this means to me."

"I still feel terrible about leaving you at a time like this…"

"Don't. It's what I want." Kenzie took her hand and squeezed, her grip strong. "They put my purse on that shelf. Take my wallet. It's got everything you'll need, even cash. I stopped by the ATM just before the accident. Now get out of here, before you change your mind."

"I'll call when I land. Please, please be fine."

"I'm already better, knowing you're doing this for me." They said their goodbyes, and Makenna grabbed her friend's wallet from her purse before leaving. Just as she pulled open the curtain, Kenzie called groggily, "Oh, and I may have borrowed your new black boots."

With absolutely no time to spare, Makenna made it to the airport. Check-in went smoothly enough, but she feared hyperventilation at the security checkpoint. When she handed the TSA agent her ticket and photo ID, the woman looked first at Makenna, then at the license, then back at Makenna.

"Says here you have black hair."

Makenna grabbed a curly auburn strand and stared at it, searching for a plausible excuse. Praying she wouldn't get arrested, right then and there, she struggled to keep her voice light. "They did an amazing job, right? Who would guess this wasn't my natural color?"

The woman raised her eyebrows, still unconvinced. "Birth date?"

Without hesitating, she rattled off her friend's birth date. "2-21-88."

"Address?"

Again, she supplied it without missing a beat.

"Guess I need the name of your stylist," the security officer muttered, handing Makenna back her license. "Have a good flight."

Makenna's knees were weak as she made her way to screening. Her hands trembled as she tugged off her shoes, placed them in the plastic bin alongside her purse and Kenzie's camera case, and waited her turn through the full-body scanner. As she feared, the camera case had to be searched, costing precious minutes before she was cleared. She started down the long corridors at a fast clipped pace that soon turned into an all-out sprint. She arrived at her gate, out of breath and practically frantic, just as the first passengers were called. Her borrowed ticket granted her select boarding privileges, so she went straight to the gate.

Makenna stumbled through the boarding, hoping her breathlessness would be attributed to cutting her arrival so close. It was one of those seat-yourself flights, so she found the first empty row and plopped down by the window. As more passengers filed down the aisle, she found herself watching for someone in uniform. Any minute now, they would stop at her row and demand she come with them.

She looked at each passenger without really seeing them, scanning their faces for any sign of censure. A nun, a businessman, a grandmotherly type. Her gaze fell on one particularly nice looking man with vivid blue eyes. On some level, as their eyes met and held, her brain acknowledged how attractive he was, but she didn't have time for chemistry right now. She looked past him, to the next person. So far, so good. No one in uniform appeared.

Her line of vision was blocked as someone stopped to deposit their case into the overhead bin in front of her. She tried to see around the person, but all she could see was a torso wrapped in blue. Again, on a subconscious level, she appreciated the trim waist and well-toned abs, quite nicely defined beneath the clingy blue knit sports shirt; on a conscious level, she was slightly irritated at the man for obstructing her view.

The man fluidly swiveled into one of the seats beside her, nearest the aisle. Even with an empty seat between them, Makenna was instantly aware of his presence. He had that sort of magnetism, the kind that demanded your attention and sharpened your awareness. This was a man not easily ignored. He oozed a sense of strength and confidence, an aura of control. Even the spice of his cologne did not hide the heady musk of the man. He was of average height and weight, had average coloring, average styled hair and clothes. He was, however, anything but average. His body was in excellent shape. His muscles were lean and well sculpted. His hair was a bit more blond than brown, and clipped close to his head. The neatly trimmed box beard and mustache that ran along the firm line of his jaw and framed the generous curve of his mouth were a few shades darker than his hair and emphasized the square, handsome chisel of his face. And his eyes. There was absolutely nothing average about the clear blue depths of his eyes.

Those eyes were turned on her now, making observations of their own. Makenna smiled nervously, allowing her gaze to linger in appreciation for just a second more before she went back to scanning the aisle.

"Waiting on someone?" She knew his voice would be pleasant and mellow, even before she heard it.

"Uhm.... No." She pulled her eyes back to him, trying to focus on his question. She was so worried about getting caught using someone else's ID that she couldn't appreciate having caught this attractive man's attention. She really should relax. Other than the TSA agent, no one had even questioned her claim to be Kenzie Reese. And if she had convinced trained personnel standing only two feet away, she really had nothing to worry about. Surely.

"You keep watching the aisle. I thought maybe you were holding the seat for someone." He subtly glanced at the empty cushion between them.

"No, just people watching," she denied. "It's a good way to pass the time."

"Didn't look like you had much of a chance before boarding the plane."

"You saw that?" Makenna groaned. She knew her cheeks were now pink, an unattractive contrast to her dark auburn hair.

"I might have noticed you, racing down the corridor and skidding to a halt five feet past the gate."

His easy grin made laughing at herself so much easier. "Running a bit late today," she confessed. "I can't believe I actually made the flight."

Before he could comment, a young woman stopped in the aisle and nodded to the empty seat between them. "Taken?" she asked, hoisting a large purse more securely onto her shoulder.

With graceful economy of motion, the blue-eyed man swung from his seat to the one in question, bringing himself that much closer to Makenna. A little surge of pleasure rippled through her; he was deliberately taking the middle seat for a three-hour flight, based on their brief conversation.

After a few polite words to the newcomer, the man turned back to Makenna. She was watching the aisle again.

"You'll have to key me in on the fascination," he murmured, following her gaze. He saw only harried passengers, filing down the aisle one after another.

Instead of revealing her true reason for watching the aisle, she reverted to an old game she liked to play. "You have to imagine their story."

"Their story?"

"Sure. For instance, see the woman in gray? She looks irritated at having to go to the back of the plane. It's because she's anxious to get to Manchester. She'll have a new grand baby waiting at the airport, and wanted to be the first one off."

"And the man behind her?"

"He's in no real hurry. He's divorced. He'll just have an empty house to go home to."

As the man neared, he steadied himself by reaching for the seatback in front of them. The diamond on his shiny gold wedding band winked in the dim light.

"Okay, so sometimes I miss," Makenna admitted with a laugh.

"Oh, but I definitely agree about Grandma. And I think this young lady in red is headed to an exciting job interview, her first real job out of college," the man said, falling into the spirit of the game.

"I hear it's an impressive law firm in Boston. She's their new intern." Makenna played along with a serious expression. "And see the guy in the cowboy hat? First time to fly."

"Where's he headed?"

Makenna thought for a moment. "Nashville. It's a connecting flight, the only one he could find on short notice. His girlfriend left him in hopes of making it big in the music business. He's headed there to propose."

"Ah, a romantic at heart," he grinned, sliding her a speculative glance.

She offered a noncommittal shrug. She wasn't sure if he meant her or the cowboy. "What do you think the story is behind the man in the gray jacket?"

"Oh, he's the sky marshal."

The words were spoken in jest, but there was no mistaking Makenna's reaction. She jerked, the breath catching in her throat as her eyes darted guiltily away from the man, then flitted nervously back.

"Hey, I was only kidding," her neighbor reassured her. With curious eyes, he asked, "What's wrong? You running from the law or something?"

"Of – Of course not." She tried to muster the sound of outrage. Searching for a plausible explanation, she said, "I guess I sometimes get nervous when flying. The need for sky marshals and all…." She let her words trail off.

"Hey, I hear ya. Never know these days. But at least we know we're not in danger from Johnny Kidd up there." With his chin, he pointed to the young man coming down the aisle. "He's obviously headed home, and can't wait to get back to his girlfriend and tell her about the colleges he checked out."

"Obviously." Relaxing once again, Makenna's eyes twinkled as she teased, "Now who's the romantic?"

"Just call 'em like I see 'em," the man said with a flourishing hand movement and an easy smile.

The flight attendant came over the speaker, asking passengers to prepare for final boarding. Makenna's cell phone buzzed, alerting her to a text message from her neighbor Linda.

Still in surgery.

Will let you know when out.

Makenna's fingers flew over the keys in reply.

Please do. Hated to leave, but she insisted.

Have to turn off phone, will check msg when land.

Thanks for being there.

She deliberately led their friend to believe this had been her trip all along; no need in pulling more people into their web of deceit. As she turned off her phone and slid it into the bag resting at her feet, she noticed her seatmate sending his own last-minute message before tucking his phone away.

"So, do you fly often?" he asked.

Makenna shrugged. "Not often enough to earn any fabulous vacations, but I'm no stranger to the airlines. And you?"

"About the same."

The flight attendants were making their way down the aisle, checking to see that overhead bins were secure and seat belts were fastened. Two different attendants passed their aisle and paused, creating a fine sheen of perspiration to form on Makenna's forehead. She maintained an innocent pose, her breath clutched in her chest. Any minute now …

She did not breathe easily until the plane had been cleared for takeoff and they began to roll down the runway. If her seatmate noticed her obvious discomfort, he was polite enough not to mention it. He pulled out a magazine and began rifling through it as the plane bumped its way along the tarmac. With a shaky exhale, Makenna turned grateful eyes out the window and stared blindly at the parting view.

New worries plagued her. She had fooled the officials here in Texas, but what about the return trip? The Manchester, New Hampshire airport was smaller than the one here in Austin, but that might mean they had more time to study her identification. What if she couldn't get home? Were the fines stiffer out-of-state?

No, silly, her inner voice scolded. *A federal crime is a federal crime, regardless of the state it is committed in.*

She nibbled on her lower lip, thinking of all the things that could go wrong. Why on earth had she let Kenzie talk her into this scheme? She still had to get past the rental car company, where she would be forging her friend's signature. That would encompass insurance fraud and credit card fraud and lying-to-the-person-behind-the-counter fraud and Heaven only knew what else! Makenna's palms turned sweaty and her breathing came in short, quick puffs.

Even if she made it through the car rental, there was still the hurdle of checking into the hotel. She felt less guilty about deceiving the hotel staff, although she wasn't sure why. But then she would have to pose as her friend for the rest of the week, doing her interviews and taking her photos and remembering to introduce herself as Kenzie Reese. Basically, she had to lie to everyone she met. The upside was that no one here knew Kenzie and would ever know the difference; the downside was that she had to lie and cheat and break the law, and she had to do it all without having a nervous breakdown.

Tenting her hands over her mouth, Makenna rocked slightly in her seat, considering her options. She could get off the plane right now, before it lifted into the air. It would mean causing a stir and raising suspicions, but her conscious would be clear.

Except that she would be letting her friend down, and this was so very important to Kenzie.

Okay, so she had to stay seated. But that didn't mean she had to lie, did it? She could rent the car in her own name and check in at the hotel as herself. The room was already waiting and paid for, so it didn't matter who slept in the bed. And she could simply tell the people she interviewed that someone else was covering the story, no further explanation needed. No further lying needed.

Except, then the magazine wouldn't reimburse Kenzie. Knowing her extravagant friend, she had booked the best hotel and the fastest sports car, racking up quite a bill. And if the editors knew Kenzie didn't go on the trip and do the actual interviews herself, they might not pick up the story as promised, meaning Kenzie wouldn't be paid, at all.

She had promised her friend. Kenzie was resting easier, knowing Makenna was doing this for her. And if something horrible should go wrong in surgery, at least Makenna would know she had honored her friend's last request.

Before she got any further with her thoughts, the man beside her was talking again. "Wow, you really do get nervous flying, don't you?" he asked sympathetically.

"I'm sorry, what was that?" With an effort, Makenna pulled herself from her reverie.

"Are you all right? You look a little pale."

"No, no, I'm fine."

"No offense, but you don't look fine."

The plane was moving now, picking up speed as it rolled ever closer to lift-off. As the huge machine left the ground and vaulted into the air, Makenna drew an obvious sigh of relief. Addressing her neighbor, she went with the truth. "I'm worried about a friend of mine. She's in surgery as we speak and I couldn't be there for her."

"Ah, that's rough. Anything serious?"

"She was in a car wreck this morning. They're operating on her leg, but who knows if more is wrong with her? I feel so guilty, leaving like this."

"Did you talk to her before you left?"

"Yes. She insisted I come." *In more ways than you can imagine!*

"So there you go," the man said with a charming smile. "She understands and gives you her blessing. Stop feeling guilty."

"Easier said than done," Makenna muttered.

Makenna turned to gaze down at the city below, still dumbfounded that she was actually on the plane. She rarely did anything spontaneous. Most trips she took required weeks of planning, what with itineraries and reservations and packing and lining up all the little details. This was totally unlike her, on so many levels.

Kenzie, however, had been right about one thing: Makenna was stuck in a rut. Her life had become boring and predictable, her routine more like that of a middle-aged spinster than a twenty-six-year-old young professional. She needed an adventure, something unexpected to happen in her life. Losing her job and her boyfriend, all in one week, definitely offered the unexpected; maybe this spur-of-the-moment trip would offer the adventure. If not actual excitement, perhaps this trip would at least offer a refreshing change of pace.

"So, what's your story?" Her new friend turned the tables on the little game they had been playing. "I now know all about our fellow travelers, but not a thing about you. What adventure awaits you?"

"Job assignment."

"As in reporter?"

"Photojournalist." She was pretending to be her friend this week, so she might as well start now.

"Really?" He seemed duly impressed. "Who do you work for?"

"*Now Magazine*."

He let out an appreciative whistle. "Very impressive."

Okay, so if Kenzie were here, she would toss her head and flirt. And since she was pretending to be Kenzie...

"It'll do," she shrugged saucily. In her best sultry voice, she purred, "And you? What's your story?"

His intriguing blue eyes twinkled, picking up on the flirtatious tone. "Actually, I'm headed to the mountains for cross country training."

"Skiing?" She frowned in confusion. It was late April.

"Cycling."

"You're a cyclist?" In her brief imaginary synopsis, she had never imagined him as a cyclist. He had the physique, but cycling never crossed her mind, probably because she knew nothing about the sport.

"Not professionally," he was quick to say. "I'm participating in the Ride for the Hills Cancer Charity. I'm just getting in shape."

"Wow, that's … impressive." She hated to copy him, but it was the truth. "Going all the way to New England to practice for a charity event?"

He shrugged his nicely developed shoulders. "I had a week's vacation coming, and needed to practice for the race. Weather's so much nicer in New England than in Texas, I decided to come north."

Makenna wondered if Kenzie had packed for cooler temperatures. Surely it would have occurred to her, but with Kenzie, you never knew. She had probably been more concerned with fashion than with comfort. "Hmmm, you definitely have a point. It's supposed to be in the mid 90's by this weekend."

"Not where we're headed." Again, that fascinating twinkle, this time with a waggled brow. "In my case, it's primarily New Hampshire. What about you?"

"The same." At least, she supposed so. Kenzie had mentioned a few of her plans, but Makenna knew very little about the actual assignment and specific elements of the trip. The more she thought about this crazy scheme, the less it made sense.

He mentioned a few more of his plans, day-trips he intended to take into Vermont and the western edge of Maine, trails he had heard of in the White Mountains, places he wanted to see. Makenna made mental notes of the locations that would be of interest to her project, wondering if Kenzie had made an itinerary of her own. Knowing her impulsive friend, she suspected she already knew the answer.

As the plane banked and headed north, Makenna felt a burden lift from her shoulders. The journey had begun, and so far, no one even suspected she wasn't who she claimed to be. Maybe this crazy scheme was going to work, after all.

"Please secure your personal belongings as we prepare for descent into Manchester."

The three-hour flight had literally flown by. Makenna and the handsome blue eyed man spent the entire time chatting about everything from current movies and magazines – particularly *Now* – to tastes in music, from their home state of Texas to the undeniable lure of New England. Makenna's worries melted away as she laughed with her charming companion. He was witty and sharp, and offered the perfect distraction from her guilt-plagued conscious. By the time the flight attendant announced the current time and temperature in New Hampshire, Makenna was feeling much more optimistic about the upcoming week.

"Let's exchange phone numbers," her companion suggested as they touched down and were allowed to turn their cells back on. "Maybe we can touch base during the week, have lunch or something."

"Sounds like a plan." Makenna fiddled with her phone, finding the right screen. "By the way, what's your name?"

"Hardin. But here, let me. It's easier this way." He went to the corresponding screen on his phone and traded devices, so they could each enter their own information. As he keyed in his number, he glanced up at her. "So what's your name?"

She almost goofed. She was busy putting her friend's name alongside her own phone number, which took a fair amount of concentration. She started to answer automatically, "Ma - ." She quickly caught herself. "McKenzie, but look under the 'K's. Everyone calls me Kenzie."

"All right, Kenzie with a K." He returned her phone with a charismatic smile. "All done. Be expecting a call."

"I will." She gave him a cheeky little grin before slipping her phone into her bag.

They continued a casual conversation as they made their way down the aisle, off the plane, and toward baggage claim. When no one came rushing toward her, demanding an explanation for posing as her friend, Makenna breathed easier.

"Well, thanks for making the flight less stressful," she said, piling her bags together after retrieving them all from the carousel. His still had not arrived. "It definitely kept my mind occupied."

"No problem. I'm glad I sat on your row," he grinned. "Oops. That's mine." He nodded at the black bag tumbling onto the conveyor belt.

"Well, have a great vacation." She was reluctant to part with the handsome man, but his luggage was moving closer.

"Hey, I'll call you," he promised. He was obviously torn between lingering beside her and retrieving his bag now, without waiting for it to cycle again. He reached out to touch her hand, their fingers trailing through the air as he stepped away.

"You do that." Makenna would have offered her best smile, but he had already turned his back toward her. Puffing a breath of air from her cheeks, Makenna made her way toward Ground Transportation.

Her adventure was now underway.

Chapter 3

Thirty minutes later, Makenna pulled out of the rental car lot in a shiny red convertible. As predicted, Kenzie pre-paid for the ultimate driving experience. The car had every gadget imaginable, most of which Makenna had no clue on how to operate. But it had a full tank of gas and a navigation system, the only two things she really needed to make it to her destination. The hotel where she was booked was over an hour away, and the late afternoon sun was already setting low in the sky, casting long shadows on a day almost over.

Setting her cruise control a mile above the posted speed limit, Makenna headed toward the mountains in the distance. She stopped once for a snack and a restroom break, then jumped back on the interstate. It wasn't until after the break that she became aware of the green Chevy, traveling in the same direction she was. Amused, she realized they were playing a game of road tag, switching positions with one another as they gobbled up mileage. First she would be in the lead, then they would go around her. Before long, their lane of traffic would slow down and she would go sailing past. She never got a good look at the driver, but she knew it was a male traveling alone.

Signs along the highway informed Makenna her exit was only a few miles ahead. Knowing she was near her destination brought a smile to her lips. She looked in the rearview mirror to check what was left of her make-up. Movement caught her eye as the green sedan approached at an alarming speed. Glancing into her side mirror, Makenna moved over into the empty lane on her left. The green sedan moved behind her, its speed still too fast. It was practically on her bumper.

Trying not to panic, Makenna moved back into the right lane, belatedly noting there were no other cars in sight. When had that happened? She was so busy thinking about this impromptu trip and watching the scenery that she failed to notice the now-deserted highway.

Deserted, that is, except for the green sedan.

The sedan came alongside her, and she breathed a sigh of relief. They were simply trying to pass. When the Chevy suddenly swerved into her lane, she knew she was in trouble. The car was trying to run her off the road!

Makenna had no choice but to floor the gas pedal. She shot past the other car, but it kept pace with the convertible. Faster and faster, they raced down the road, Makenna only slightly ahead of the vehicle chasing her.

Seeing an exit up ahead, Makenna debated on taking it. Surely, the crazy driver would not follow her. She kept her speed steady until just before the exit. Without using a blinker, she whipped onto the shoulder, planning to jerk onto the exit ramp and make her escape.

But where was she escaping to? She had no idea where she was or where the road led. At the last moment, just before the green sedan could slam into her, she shot from the shoulder into the left lane, her foot to the floor. The green car followed, trying to force her off the road as it crowded into the lane with her. With two wheels on the uneven pavement of the left shoulder, Makenna struggled to maintain control of the speeding sports car. With a guardrail approaching, she knew she had to do something quickly to avoid sideswiping it. She doubted her insurance – or should it be Kenzie's? – would be very forgiving.

Makenna finally saw taillights in front of them, but she knew the other vehicles were too far ahead to notice what was happening. If she could catch up with them, perhaps she could put enough traffic between herself and the green sedan that she could get away. Praying the little sports car had the motor for it, Makenna stomped her foot on the gas and never let up.

With the green car now at least a full car length behind her, Makenna sped her way to the beckoning taillights and slid up beside a blue mini-van. Soon she had eased between it and a white Lincoln, but she could see the green sedan behind the van. Dusk made it difficult to distinguish the vehicles behind her, but she knew the shape of the green car's headlights. If she lived through this ordeal, she would be seeing those same headlights in her sleep tonight.

Feeling a little more confident with other vehicles around, Makenna eased off the accelerator. She didn't want to get ahead of the traffic and find herself alone with the green sedan again. She thought back to the beginning of the trek, trying to recall if she had done something to evoke such road rage. Had she cut the green car off? Forced him to be caught behind a slow moving eighteen-wheeler? She couldn't recall a thing. Maybe he was a really sore loser, seeing their little game of road tag as an all-out competition.

Whatever the case, the green sedan had eased its way behind her again. There was another exit coming up, the last one before she got off the interstate. Should she take it? Surely it would lead to her destination, just a few miles down the road. There was a truck in front of her, but Makenna maneuvered her way into the next lane and in front of the truck, just in time to slide onto the exit ramp. But when she saw the green Chevy move to follow, she jerked the wheel and whipped back onto the freeway. The truck blared its horn, and for a heart-stopping moment, all she could see was a blur of headlights crowding down on her bumper.

Gunning the engine, Makenna zoomed down the road, barreling away from the truck's menacing bumper. She breathed a sigh of relief as she eased into the left lane, snugly between the white Lincoln and an older model pick-up truck.

Her sense of security lasted for about two miles, when the white Lincoln was suddenly replaced by a familiar pair of headlights. The green car was back again, and following closely.

She saw her exit just ahead, but there was a steady lane of vehicles on the right, solidly between her and her chance of freedom. She looked into her rear view mirror and found the green car so close to her bumper she could hardly see its lights. There was a small gap to her right. Was it large enough for a little red sports car?

While she debated the distance, her foot eased off the accelerator uncertainly. Though slight, it was enough that she felt the brush of the green sedan's bumper clicking against hers. In a flash of surety, Makenna knew what she had to do.

With a deep breath and a quick prayer, she made her daring move. Whipping the wheel, she shot into the small gap between the vehicles on her right. Amid blaring horns, she shot straight across the lane and kept going, straight onto the exit ramp off the freeway. She knew the green sedan was unable to follow. Too many vehicles blocked its path, and the next exit was miles ahead.

Finally, she had escaped the green sedan.

Makenna gripped the steering wheel with trembling hands and slowed her speed considerably. She told herself the irate driver would go on down the road and forget his bout of road-rage, but her body did not seem to believe her. She was shaking uncontrollably now that the crisis was over. She was tempted to pull over and allow herself a breakdown, but she worried that the green car might somehow appear out of nowhere. It was best to forge ahead, to the security of her hotel.

Full darkness had fallen, enveloping the cozy little mountain village in muted shadows and twinkling lights. Makenna relaxed her grip on the wheel and forced herself to appreciate the beauty around her. The navigation device led her straight to her location, where she pulled up in the circular drive and killed the motor.

Nice place, she noted with approval. Not that Kenzie would be caught staying anywhere that garnered less than three stars. Her friend wasn't a snob, she merely had good taste.

Again, check-in went smoothly. She soon forgot about the green sedan, as new worries about duping the receptionist assailed her. It was amazing, however, how easy it was to pass herself off as her friend. Granted, the two of them did look a great deal alike, but no one, other than the TSA agent, had even questioned why her driver's license photo showed a head full of bouncy black curls instead of the gentle tumble of auburn she sported. She merely had to flash her ID, present a credit card, and claim that she was, indeed, Kenzie Reese.

She left the car where it was as she unloaded and carried her luggage to her room. Billed as a condo-style resort, there were no bellhops to help with the luggage, which was no problem for Makenna. Even though her borrowed suitcases were bulging and she was a few pounds too heavy to be called athletic, she was in good physical condition. She opened the door to her second floor room and murmured a delighted hum of approval.

She had lived in apartments smaller than this suite. A full kitchen, totally modern and stocked with the latest of every gadget, offered an eat-in granite bar with barstools. The living room yawned beyond, a large room with comfortable furnishings and a cozy corner fireplace. The bedroom with its king sized bed and ample storage pieces boasted a Jacuzzi tub in one corner and a huge bathroom larger than the one she and Kenzie now shared.

"I could totally get used to this for the week," she said aloud to the empty room. She deposited her luggage and roamed through the space opening doors and drawers, familiarizing herself with her home-away-from-home. *Well done*, *Kenzie*, she thought. *Well done*.

A sudden stab of guilt flashed through her at the thought of Kenzie. Some friend she was turning out to be! She hadn't even thought of the dear woman, lying up in a hospital bed thousands of miles away. She grabbed her phone and clicked to her messages, relieved to see one from Linda.

Out of surgery and doing fine.

Awake and flirting with cute intern.

Will keep you posted. Take care.

Makenna laughed, thinking that sounded par for her best friend. Kenzie was a natural born flirt, and men were automatically drawn to her fun, vibrant personality. While they were so alike in some areas, in others, like their flirting prowess, they were worlds apart. As Makenna typed the Austin hospital's name into the search engine on her phone, she wished she were more like her friend in that aspect. How would Kenzie have handled meeting Hardin today on the plane? Makenna had gotten his phone number, but Kenzie would probably have secured a definite date with the handsome stranger.

Maybe this week, while pretending to be her friend, Makenna could emulate some of her moves. She had certainly watched her roommate enough, flirting and toying with men's emotions, but somehow she had never been brave enough to try any of those tactics for herself. This week, however, she was pretending to be someone else, so why not act like someone else? This might be the perfect opportunity to step out of her comfortable little box and try to be more aggressive, more engaging. With a naughty jiggle of her eyebrows, Makenna decided she just might make the first move in calling the handsome blue-eyed man.

Finding the number she was looking for, Makenna dialed the hospital and asked for her friend's room number and to be connected. Kenzie answered groggily on the fourth ring.

"How are you?" Makenna asked anxiously.

"Sore. Sleepy. Are you there yet?"

"Yes, all checked in to my room. It's gorgeous, Ken, all done in creams and browns and splashes of red."

"Send me a picture."

"Are you sure you're all right? Who's been there with you?"

"Marci and Linda and your mom and Robert."

"Who's Robert?"

"This really cute intern I met. He's hot." The sleepy words lacked enthusiasm.

"Only you, my friend, would hook up with one of your doctors while having surgery!" Makenna laughed.

"He's seen me at my worst and still wants my number."

"You sound like you're still a little loopy. I have a ton of questions to ask you, but they can wait until morning. I just wanted to know you were all right."

"I'm fine."

"Okay, then I'll let you get back to sleep. I'll talk to you in the morning."

"'Kay. And Makenna?"

"Yeah?"

"Thanks again. You saved my life today."

"We'll see about that. I haven't pulled this whole thing off yet." She said goodbye, thinking of a dozen things she wanted to ask her best friend, and at least one thing she wanted to tell her, namely about a handsome stranger with the most amazing blue eyes.

Hardin. She smiled just thinking of him. She scrolled down through her phone, finding his entry. Hardin Kaczmarek. Under 'notes', he had entered 'Call me. I think you're hot.'

She laughed in glee. Take that, Derek Morton. Another man thought she was hot! And not just any man, a very handsome, exciting man. A carpenter by trade, a cyclist by choice. It made for an extremely fine, fit physique. Derek may have accused her of having ice in her veins when they stepped into the bedroom, but that hadn't been ice surging through her during the flight. Her blood had been plenty warm while talking to the handsome stranger, leading her to believe the problem may have been Derek, not her.

She and the computer analyst had dated on and off for several months. About four months ago, they had agreed to make it exclusive, but last week, he announced he had met someone new and no longer wanted to see her. While she had hardly been heart-broken, the cold dismissal had wounded her pride, more than her feelings, especially when he had gone to great lengths to detail exactly what he found lacking in their relationship. He was particularly brutal in his assessment, pointing out her faults with perverted savor.

Just days later, she lost her job. Her boss had cited much the same reasons. They were looking for someone with fresher, newer ideas. Someone exciting. Someone glamorous. He didn't say it in so many words, but one look at her replacement explained exactly what they were looking for: someone tall, buxom and blond, with a gushing smile and a bubbly brain.

Hardin Kaczmarek was exactly what her bruised ego needed. She wasn't looking for a romance, but a little innocent flirtation certainly wouldn't hurt. Even if it went beyond innocent, a little fling might be just the thing she needed to regain her confidence and get her back into the real world.

She started to call him, then decided better of it. It was getting late, and she was hungry. She still needed to move her car, and she might as well do that while she was out finding a restaurant. Tomorrow she would find a grocery store and stock the kitchen, but right now, her top priority was finding a place to eat. Maybe she would text him over her meal…

As Makenna approached the front desk, the woman asked with a pleasant smile, "May I help you?"

"I hope so. I'm starving, and I hoped you might have a suggestion on where to eat."

"We have tons of choices. What kind of food are you looking for?"

As the receptionist made suggestions, Makenna heard someone call her name. She turned around, amazed to see Hardin Kaczmarek standing behind her.

"Kenzie! Are you kidding me? We're booked in the same hotel?"

Delighted with the happy co-incidence, Makenna thought her luck just might be changing. "Apparently so," she said with a pleased smile. "Are you just checking in?"

"Yes. There was a mix-up at the car rental agency. I need something to carry my bike, and they tried giving me a tiny compact with no bike rack." He pulled a face. "Have you eaten yet?"

"No, that was what I was doing, asking for suggestions."

"If you'd care for company, give me time to check in and I'll join you."

"Sounds great." She hoped her smile didn't look as giddy as it felt. "I'll check out those brochures while I wait."

Makenna wandered over to the display of area brochures and selected a half dozen or so that caught her eye. There were ample attractions and activities to do in the region, many of which would be helpful in completing Kenzie's assignment. While she waited on Hardin, she found a chair to sit in so she could peruse the colorful flyers.

"Sorry it took so long," he said as he returned, jogging down the stairs that emptied into the foyer where she waited. He made the action look effortless. "My room's all the way at the back."

"No problem. I had plenty to keep me occupied." She held up the fistful of brochures before she slid them into her purse.

"Did you decide where you wanted to eat?"

"I think so. They recommended a little place just down the road."

When Makenna told him she was driving a convertible, he opted to let her drive. She laughed at the totally masculine response to a sports car. They found the restaurant without incident and settled into a cozy little table near the windows.

"Where are you from?" the hostess asked conversationally as she handed them their menus and slid a basket of warm bread onto the table.

"Central Texas," Hardin answered, not bothering to explain they weren't a couple.

"Oh really? That couple over there is from Texas, too. Small world, isn't it? You're welcome to help yourself to cheese and crackers, served in the bar, just through there. Your server this evening will be Neil. He'll be with you shortly."

"Thank you," Makenna smiled. She glanced at the couple sitting across the room. "Hey, I think they were on our flight," she told Hardin. "I had them pegged as celebrating their twentieth wedding anniversary. I wonder what the odds of that are, all four of us on the same plane, ending up in the same town?"

"I'd say pretty good, considering this is a popular resort town. And you're forgetting, New Hampshire is like twenty eight times smaller than Texas. The entire state could fit inside our Hill Country region." He pulled a yeasty roll apart and stuffed it into his mouth. He chewed and swallowed, continuing with his theory. "It would be about like a plane landing in Austin, and four or more of its passengers ending up in Fredericksburg. Odds would be pretty favorable."

"I guess." Makenna shrugged, reaching for a crusty slice of bread from the assorted basket. "Just seems like a huge coincidence, especially when you factor in that you and I are in the very same hotel."

"Coincidence," he allowed. He raised his water glass and tipped it against hers. Claiming her eyes with his piercing blue gaze, his voice slid over her like warm molasses. "Or fate."

Completely mesmerized, Makenna clicked her glass to his and murmured, "To fate."

Their server appeared, sporting a bottle of Chardonnay. "Compliments of the couple by the windows."

"Oh, how sweet!" Makenna beamed, looking over at their fellow Texans. She waved her appreciation, while Hardin nodded and expressed a vocal "thank you" across the room.

"I suppose we really should invite them to join us," he told her with a resigned sigh, as the waiter poured their wine.

"It looks like they are just ordering, too. Why don't we invite them to have dessert with us," Makenna suggested.

Hardin raised an approving eyebrow at her artful compromise. To the waiter, he said, "Would you be so kind as to relay the lady's wishes to the other couple? We'd like them to join us for dessert."

"Certainly, sir."

Chapter 4

"Not that I'm all that eager to share you with someone else," Hardin admitted as he pushed away his empty plate, "but I guess it's time to do the neighborly thing and invite our guests over for dessert."

Makenna wrinkled her nose in playful distaste. "I think maybe you're right."

Right on cue, the waiter appeared at their table to take away dirty dishes and re-set the table for four. Hardin moved his chair close to Makenna's. Stretching his arm along the back of her chair, he let his fingers curl against her shoulders as he whispered conspiratorially, "If they're too boring, remind me of that phone call I don't have to make."

"You're incorrigible!" Makenna admonished. Laughing, she bumped him with her shoulder, but was slow in moving away as they watched the other couple approach.

Even though Makenna had imagined the couple celebrating an anniversary, the newcomers were not a matched set. The woman was short and… round. Makenna tried to think of a kinder word of description, but none came to mind. It wasn't simply a matter of being overweight; the woman was truly spherical. A smiling round face peeked from beneath a puffy cloud of pale gold, her hair fashioned into an inflated bouffant. With little sign of a neck, her shoulders sloped downward, curling into beefy arms that hugged her bulbous body like quotation marks. The woman's mid-section was round and full, with no definable waist beneath her peach colored pantsuit. Short, bowed legs kept her low to the ground and her feet had a tendency to point inward, completing the illusion of circularity. 'Round' was the only way to adequately describe the woman.

The man with her was her polar opposite. He towered over her, tall, straight, and thin to the point of gauntness. Where her arms jutted outward, his hung straight and limp from bony shoulders. His pearl-snap western shirt, still so new it sported factory-fold creases, was a baggy fit on his angular frame. The man was all hard lines and angles, including the downward slant of his mouth.

Hardin stood during the introductions, when the newcomers identified themselves as Bob and Lisa Lewis. After a round of thank-yous and how-do-you-dos, he reclaimed his place at Makenna's side.

"I believe we may have been on the same flight," Lisa said as they settled into their seats. She had a high pitched, nasal voice that bordered on a whine. "Did you board in Austin, or was it a connecting flight?"

"We boarded there," Hardin answered for them both.

"Us, too. We live in Seguin. What about you?"

"I live in Austin," Makenna supplied.

"Gruene."

Makenna slipped her gaze to Hardin. Where had her charming dinner companion gone? The man beside her now was brief and reserved, even borderline brusque. Granted, Lisa Lewis' voice did grate on the nerves, but she could feel the tight coil of Hardin's body next to hers; something else about this couple put him on edge.

As the waiter handed them each a dessert menu, they perused the selections in silence, until Lisa declared that everything looked delicious and Bob complained he hardly had room for dessert. Lisa finally settled on an apple dumpling and her husband ordered an éclair; Makenna and Hardin elected to share the over-sized brownie a la mode.

"So what brings you two up here?" Lisa asked after the waiter moved away.

Makenna motioned for Hardin to answer first. "I'm training for the Ride for the Hills Cancer Charity."

"Ooh, you're a cyclist," she cooed in a voice intended to be sultry. Her eyes slid over Hardin with lingering appreciation, causing him to squirm. If Bob noticed, he didn't appear to be nearly as uncomfortable as the man beneath her hungry gaze was.

With obvious reluctance, the rounded woman pulled her eyes away from Hardin and settled her attention on Makenna. "And you, dear? Just along for the ride?"

"No. Actually, we aren't traveling together," Makenna explained. She felt Hardin stiffen beside her, but she was already living with enough lies; she saw no reason to complicate matters worse with yet another misconception. "I'm here on an assignment for *Now Magazine*."

"Oh, you're a reporter? How exciting! Are you writing a story?"

"I'm a photojournalist. I'm here covering a controversial new power line that's scheduled to come through the area."

"Ooh, yes, we saw the signs!" Lisa's circular head bobbed up and down, causing her full cheeks to dance merrily. She slapped the back of her hand against her husband's arm, drawing a grunt. "What did those signs say, Bob? 'Fight the Giant', or something like that?"

"Saw something like that," he agreed. Where her voice was high and lilting, his was deep and flat. "Seems they want to cut down the mountain to get power lines through."

"What side are you covering, dear? For or against?"

Makenna tried not to take offense at the question. "A good journalist doesn't choose sides, we simply report the facts."

"Oh, but you have to have an opinion!" Lisa insisted. "I understand this is a huge issue. There have been Congressional hearings and political debates and all sorts of environmental controversies surrounding it."

"You sound like you might be covering a story on it yourself," Hardin said, softening his words with the sudden appearance of his most charming smile.

"Me?" Lisa twittered. "Hardly! I'm an avid reader is all, and read all about it before we even left home." She lowered her voice, leaned in, and said in a loud, conspiratorial whisper, "And once I heard the mob was involved, I was even more intrigued!"

"The mob?" Makenna said in surprise. This was the first she had heard of that particular angle.

"Oh, yes. What was the name of that organization, Bob?" she asked, slapping her husband's arm once again. With no padding on his bones to absorb the hit, the man had to be sore. "NorthWind?"

Makenna laughed aloud at the woman's theatrics. "That's not the mob. That's a legitimate power company, operating in most of the New England and northern states."

"Oh, so you're familiar with them?"

Makenna shrugged. "I've heard the name. From what I understand, they specialize in renewable energy sources, like wind farms and solar panels."

"So you know the ties to organized crime," Lisa said, her cheeks dancing again as she nodded vigorously. "I understand the same mafia that controlled Italy's green energy efforts is now involved in this project."

"I've not heard that," Makenna said with a frown, wondering if it was something she needed to check out.

"Oh, surely you have! Surely you've heard of the Zaffino Family!"

Lisa was so insistent, and watching her so closely, that Makenna feared the other woman was on to her deception. Was that a name she *should* be aware of? In truth, it did sound vaguely familiar, but Makenna was certain she had never encountered it while covering a news story. Not that the *Austin Daily Newsprint* allowed her to cover many stories about organized crime; the most controversial of her pieces centered around corruption within the sanitation company contracted to serve the State Capitol.

Makenna was saved from answering by the arrival of dessert. "Mmm, looks delicious," she murmured, poking her fork into the gooey warm center of a colossal brownie smothered in ice cream. "Good thing we're sharing, this thing is gigantic!" She tapped Hardin's arm with her elbow, trying to draw him into the conversation.

With a devilish glint in his eyes, he looked down at his own arm, then discreetly darted a glance to Bob's arm. Understanding his playful comparison, Makenna pretended to scowl at the silent insult. Seeing his answering gaze of pure innocence, Makenna laughed out loud.

"Did we miss something, dear?" Lisa asked, her eyes much sharper than her humorous tone.

"Seeing this much chocolate just makes me giddy," Makenna improvised.

Watching as Hardin dipped his own fork into the dish and lifted it to his mouth, Lisa's hungry gaze followed his movements. "Hmmm, I may have to try that on our next visit. It does look divine." It was unclear if she was referring to the dessert or to the man, but Makenna felt Hardin shift uncomfortably in his chair. She quickly hid her own grin behind a spoonful of pure chocolate sin.

"Does your family live there in Austin, too, dear?" Lisa asked, scooping up a generous portion of her own dessert.

"No, just me."

"Hmmm. I was just thinking about a dentist I used to go to in the Highlands area, a Dr. Paul Reese. Was he by chance your father?"

"No, I don't believe I've ever heard of him."

"So what does your father do?"

The line of questioning was making Makenna uncomfortable. It wasn't merely the fact that these were questions she might not know the answer to, considering they were about her friend's family; it was the fact that a complete stranger was asking pointed questions about the Reese family to begin with. They hadn't even been mentioned in the conversation.

"You might call him a jack-of-all-trades, master of none."

"That sounds interesting. You must have moved around a lot as a child?"

"Quite a bit," Makenna agreed with a noncommittal shrug. Changing the subject, she looked at Bob. "So how is that éclair, Bob? It looks wonderful."

"Not too bad," the thin man allowed. "'Course, not too good, either."

"Not like the ones they make at Ricki's Bakery?" his wife asked sympathetically, slapping his arm yet again. To the other couple, she explained, "Ricki's is the most divine little bakery we discovered in Chicago's Little Italy. What they do with pastry is absolutely out of this world! Have you ever been there?" she asked, looking straight at Makenna.

"No, I'm afraid I've never been to Chicago."

"Oh, really?"

"Well, I've been to the airport before," she corrected. "Connecting flights and all. One time we had a five-hour layover and I actually did go out for pizza, just down the road from the airport. I'm not sure that qualifies, does it?" She looked at Hardin for clarification. Actually, she looked at him to save her from any more of Lisa's very pointed questions.

"Oh, I think it counts, especially if you're mapping out your travels. Looks good on your resume and on your social web pages when you've been a lot of places." His blue eyes were alight with mischief. He was clearly thankful she was the one in the hot seat, and not him.

"I agree!" Lisa butted in. "We love to travel, don't we, Bob?" He merely grunted as she stabbed him with her elbow. "We prefer to travel stateside than abroad, don't you? We've been to all of the Western states, skipped the Plains, and are now going for the Eastern states. So far we've been to New Jersey, New York, and now New Hampshire and Vermont. What about you, dear?"

"This is my first time to New England. I've only been as far north as Maryland before." Remembering a shoot Kenzie did along the coast of Maine, she quickly corrected herself. "I take that back. I made a very brief trip to the Maine coastline once, near the Canadian border, but it was only a one day shoot."

"So you've never been to the Granite State before?" It was the first question Bob had asked, and it came out sounding sharp.

"N-No."

At last, Hardin jumped into the conversation. "I detect a bit of an accent, Bob. Doesn't sound completely Southern. Are you from these parts originally?"

He waved off the question with the half-eaten éclair gripped in his bony fingers. "Army brat," he explained. "Lived all over. Don't share Lisa's enthusiasm for traveling, but it gives me something to do."

"You don't have a career to tie you down?"

"Made my best fortune when I sold my business a few years back. Good for the pocket book, bad for the rump. Get lazy real quick with nothing to do. We mostly travel." It was the most he had said since sitting down.

"What kind of business were you in?"

"Software." The one word answer did not encourage further discussion. "You?"

"Construction."

"And you, Lisa?" Makenna asked, more to be polite than to satisfy her curiosity.

"I'm a free-lance travel critic. This is actually a business trip," she giggled. "I get to critique the resort where we are staying, then take the whole trip off on income tax! Pretty sweet, huh?" she beamed.

"Sounds like a win-win situation," Makenna agreed. "What resort are you staying at? Is it getting a favorable review?" As she steered the conversation to a comparison of their respective resorts, they all finished their desserts.

When Bob asked if anyone would like more wine, Makenna glanced at her watch. "It really sounds tempting, but I promised Hardin we would be back in time for him to make a phone call. If we hurry back to the hotel, I get to keep my word."

"Is it that late already?" Hardin murmured, consulting his own wristwatch. He feigned a surprised whistle. "You know what they say about how time flies... I'm sorry, but I really do need to make this call, and all my information is back at the hotel." He looked appropriately apologetic.

"Oh, no, no, we understand, don't we, Bob?" Lisa assured the worried younger couple.

"Sure, sure. You go on now, and we'll get the check."

"No, of course not. Dessert was my treat."

"Already taken care of," Bob said, holding up a lean palm to stop any further argument. "You can treat next time."

"Well, then, thank you for dinner." Hardin held out his hand for a shake, as Makenna gathered up her purse and said her goodbyes to Lisa. With another glance at their watches, they hustled to the door.

Chapter 5

Monroe, Louisiana
April, 1992

The reflection in her mirror looked different today.

Short, clipped hair. Plain blue jeans, without sparkles or butterflies. A blue and orange striped t-shirt. Instead of her favorite pink sneakers, these were bright orange.

"We're going to play a little game." Her mother made the announcement as she tucked the t-shirt into the waistline of the little girl's jeans. She called it a game, but her face was somber.

"I like games!" the child said.

"And I think you'll be very good at this one. You know how you like to play in the mud and get dirty?"

The little girl nodded. "It's fun, but you always say little girls ought not to be so dirty."

"That's why you'll like this game. You like to climb on things and play outside, don't you? And you like to play with cars and trains and dump trucks?"

The little girl nodded vigorously. "Boy toys are so much better than girl toys."

"So for this new game, we're going to pretend that you *are* a boy," her mother said. "Doesn't that sound like fun?"

If she still had curls, they would have bounced all around her face in delight. Instead, her newly shorn head felt light as air as it bobbed up and down enthusiastically. "Yes!"

"We'll have to call you something different. Do you like the name Charlie?"

"Uh-huh!"

"Okay, good. Then Charlie it is. We're going to try to see how many people we can fool, by pretending you're a little boy. We'll tell people you're our son and we'll only call you Charlie and we'll buy you boy clothes and boy toys. Doesn't that sound like fun?"

"Do I get to play in the dirt and climb trees and pick up rocks?"

"Most little boys do."

"And I don't have to wear a dress anymore with the pokey stuff on the edges?"

"No more lace dresses," her mother promised.

"Can I have a dog?"

Her mother frowned. "I don't think our new apartment allows dogs."

"But I like this house!"

"We're moving, Charlie. To a nice little apartment in a very big town."

"You just called me Charlie," the little girl giggled.

"The game has already started. That's who you are now, and it's important that you don't forget. You are a little boy named Charlie now."

When her mother had gone, the little girl looked into the mirror. She thought about the game she liked to play, when she pretended to visit with the image on the other side of the glass. Did little boys play the same game?

Just in case, she put her hand up to the cool pane of glass and smiled at herself. “I have to go now. It’s been fun playing with you. And I promise, I’ll never forget you.”

Chapter 6

Well known for her penchant for making lists, Makenna had a long one started early the next morning. Before noon, a half dozen items were already checked off.

Find Grocery Store. Done. An early morning outing in town had revealed a small market with ample provisions for her week's stay. She didn't buy much, mostly snacks and fresh fruits and a case of bottled water she could pre-chill in her refrigerator, along with a couple of bottles of locally produced wine.

Call Kenzie. She waited until returning from the store to call, allowing for the time difference and Kenzie's need for a good night's rest. Her friend was much more alert this morning, and therefore in much more pain. Makenna was able to ask more questions about the assignment, but she knew her friend's attention span was waning, giving way to the painkillers the nurse administered as they were talking. Makenna was able to cross off the third item on her list, *Devise Plan of Action*, but her questions were far from over. Promising to call again later, she wished her friend a good day and hung up the phone.

Number four on the list was *Check E-Mails*. She was hoping to find a reply from one of the jobs she had applied for, but nothing popped up.

Check with Magazine for Updates. Checking into her friend's e-mail account, she skipped over everything but the messages marked from *Now*. There was nothing new, but she read old messages, hoping to learn more about the current assignment. Kenzie had been rather sketchy on details.

Before heading out the door to begin her day, Makenna completed the sixth item on her list, *Text Hardin*. She wished him a great day and mentioned what fun she had had the night before. His quick reply came just as she stepped into the hallway.

Already out enjoying the day.

Perfect practice! I had fun, too.

Maybe again tonite?

Let me know when you get back. Be safe.

A silly smile spread across her face. She knew she was acting like a schoolgirl with a new crush, but it was so gratifying to have a man find her attractive and to be genuinely interested in her. The fact that he was handsome and so physically fine did not hurt the equation one bit.

Practically licking her lips in anticipation of seeing the blue-eyed man again, Makenna shot back a reply as she took the stairs.

Sounds like a plan.

Watch out for cars!

TTYL.

She slipped her phone into her pants pocket and hoisted the back-pack over her shoulders as she stepped out into the day. It was sunny and gorgeous. Unlike Texas, there was no humidity in the air, so even though the sun was warm and bright, the light breeze whipped the heat away.

She set off on foot, deciding to take a stroll around the town and see what the culture was like. Like any resort town, the main road was congested with places to eat and places to sleep. Storefronts were bright and compelling, eager to have you step inside and spend your money. There was a good mix of sporting goods stores, general mercantiles, souvenir and gift shops, specialty shops and convenience stores, as well as businesses offering professional services, entertainment, and guided tours. Makenna snapped several wide-angle shots of the town, found a few unique services and storefronts to get a close-up picture of, and documented a few of the community's daily activities through her camera lens. She found a small eatery for lunch, visited with a few of the locals and fellow tourists, then set out for more sightseeing by foot. A stroll to the north led her along the river that flowed right along the main road into town. The shallow waters flowed over a rocky riverbed and tempted her with dozens of photo opportunities.

As she made her way back toward the hotel, pleased with the day's efforts and the exhilarating feel of walking in the fresh air and sunshine of a warm mountain afternoon, her gaze wandered over the picturesque town beyond. Gorgeous. She stopped to snap several shots with her borrowed camera.

She stopped back by the hotel and called Kenzie, hoping her friend would be more alert and could offer more insight into this assignment. Luck seemed to be on her side.

"I'm really not sure what angle you're after," Makenna admitted.

"Is it pretty up there?" Kenzie asked unexpectedly.

"Gorgeous, and I haven't even made it out of town yet."

"What do you think will happen if a major electric company comes through the area?"

"At the very least, they'll have to cut right-of-ways and clear a path for the lines."

"Now look around your room. How many things do you see that require electricity?"

"A dozen or so?" Makenna guessed, glancing around. "Four, no five lights in the kitchen, electric stove, refrigerator, microwave, coffee pot, blender, dishwasher… two lamps in the living room, ceiling fan with three lights, television, DVD player, several outlets... Wow. Guess it's more like two dozen things, just in these two rooms."

"So how do we balance the need for electricity with the need to preserve nature?" Kenzie challenged.

"I-I'm not sure."

"Most people aren't. We all want the modern conveniences, but few of us consider the true price. That's what this assignment is about."

"Hmm. That's a lot to consider, but I think I can work with that," Makenna said thoughtfully. She paused for a moment before changing gears. "Are you familiar with NorthWind Energy?"

"Aren't they the ones in charge of the project?"

"Yes, but I mean other than this project. Have you heard anything about them being involved with organized crime?"

"Organized crime?" Kenzie hooted. "I think the altitude has done things to your brain, girlfriend!"

"Hmm. It's something to think about, though. A huge multi-million dollar project, government grants and subsidies, edging out the little guy. Has good potential for the mob."

"Has potential for a good movie, maybe, but this is real-life. Stick to the plan, sister." There was a new edge to Kenzie's voice, but Makenna attributed it to the frustration of not being able to cover the story herself.

"Okay, so tell me the plan."

The two friends bounced a few ideas off one another and Makenna scribbled notes as they talked.

"You see," Kenzie said after their brainstorming session, "I knew you could do this. You might even do this better than I would."

"I don't have your talent behind the lens, but I'll give it my best shot."

"Ha-ha, you're already talking like a photographer! Best shot, get it?" Kenzie snickered on the other end.

"At least you're able to laugh about all this. Ah, Kenzie, I feel so awful for you. Surgery, recovery, a bruised spleen... Not to mention, wrecking your car."

"I think the cuts on my arms hurt almost as bad as my leg! There's hardly an inch that's not bruised. But, meeting Robert almost makes it worth the pain. He promised to come by when he gets through with his rounds."

After listening to her friend relay the intern's wonderful attributes, Makenna made a confession of her own. "You'll never believe this, but I've met someone, too."

"Already? Spill!"

"His name is Harden Kaczmarek and he actually only lives about forty-five minutes from us, around Gruene. He's got the most amazing blue eyes, and a body to die for."

"Mmm, delish! How did you meet him?"

"We sat together on the plane, actually, and exchanged phone numbers. And then, believe it or not, he's staying at this very same resort! We had dinner together last night and we've already texted this morning, planning to have dinner again tonight."

"Ooh, sounds promising! Is he a good kisser?"

"Kenzie! We just met yesterday. Besides, we said goodnight in the lobby. I didn't want him following me to my room, in case he's a pervert or something."

"I know these days it's hard to tell about people, but do me a favor, Kenna. Don't over-analyze this. Just go with your gut feeling. What's it telling you?"

"That he's a good guy. A really hot, good guy."

"Okay, and what name did you use when you met him?"

"Yours." For a moment, she felt a tinge of guilt for deceiving him.

"Okay, so as the real Kenzie Reese, I can tell you exactly what she would do, and what you should do: Go for it! This is your chance to step out of your box and swing a little. If it turns out you really like this guy, you can come clean with him once you get back home. But if not, this is the perfect opportunity to have a little vacation fling, a chance to kick up your heels and live a little. I think you should definitely go for it."

"I've been telling myself the same thing. Chances are, I'll never see him again once we get back home, so I might as well have a little fun while I'm here."

"Exactly! And if you'll dig around in my suitcase, you'll find a couple of little outfits that will be perfect at catching his attention."

"I saw one of them," Makenna said dryly. "I might also catch pneumonia."

"Oh pooh, it's not that skimpy! And you'll look great in it. Your legs are longer than mine, making it even shorter on you. But save that for tomorrow night," her friend cautioned. "Tonight you should wear the green sweater."

"The holey one you wear with that flesh-colored camisole under it?"

"Yep. They can't help but stare all night, trying to see through the holes, trying to decide if that's skin or material they see under there!" She laughed, recalling the hapless men she had teased with that very outfit. "Wear the jeans with the rhinestone pockets and the silver strapped heels. You'll have him eating out of your hand by the time the night's over. And this time, let him walk you to your door. If things are going really good, invite him in for a night-cap."

"We'll see," Makenna hedged. "You know I'm not as good at this kind of thing as you are."

"But this week you are me, remember? Just do whatever you think I would do."

"Okay, well, right now, I think you would get back to work. I'm going to poke around in the neighboring town this afternoon, and drive up into the mountains and see some of the sights. This morning I just kicked around town, got a feel for the place."

"Make sure you take a flashlight and that your phone is charged."

"Now who's being cautious?"

"Hey, you're traveling alone into the mountains. Don't take any chances."

"Believe me, I won't. And you take care of yourself, too."

She could hear the sigh through the phone. "I'm sure they'll be in here any minute, poking me with another needle. They obviously have me mistaken for a pin-cushion."

"I really am sorry, Kenzie. I wish I could be there for you."

"It's not that I don't miss you, girlfriend, because I do. But you're doing me such a huge favor by being where you are."

"Have you called your mother yet?"

Her friend's sunny demeanor slipped. "No," she admitted. "And don't you dare call her, either!"

"You really should tell your mother you've been injured, Kenzie. She would want to know."

"My mother hasn't bothered calling me in three and a half years. I could be dead, for all she knows. My father, too."

"But you aren't, Kenzie, and they are your parents." Her reproach was gentle.

"Then they should act like parents. My family isn't like yours, Makenna. Never has been, never will be. Just let it go, sister. Don't go there." There was a firmness in her voice that Makenna knew not to argue with.

The best friends had few secrets from one another and shared every aspect of their lives, except for one: Kenzie's family life. After a difficult and emotionally starved childhood, her raven-haired friend had become estranged with her parents shortly after graduating high school. The Reagan family had happily "adopted" Kenzie into their fold and given her the family she so obviously craved. Kenzie was there for every holiday and every family gathering, and she and Makenna were truly sisters, in every way other than blood.

"All right, I promise. I'm sorry I brought it up, Kenzie. Please don't let this get you down."

She heard a smile come into her friend's voice. "Well, someone just walked through the door, and already my spirits are better," she murmured into the receiver. "I've got to go now, Makenna, the doctor's here."

Makenna laughed, amazed at how quickly her friend rebounded. "Okay, okay, you talk to your handsome doctor now. Tell him to take extra good care of you."

"Oh, he will. He has an excellent bedside manner."

"You're incorrigible. I'll call you later."

"Remember to wear the green sweater."

"Yes, coach, I will." Makenna was laughing as she hit the 'end' button.

Biting on her lower lip, she jumped up from the couch and went to the closet, inspecting the sweater in question. It was knit into large, loose squares of silky yarn, offering more than just a glimpse of what lay beneath. The deep plunging neckline had a tendency to slip off the shoulder, but the billowy effect trimmed down to a snug fit over the hips. Of all the clothes she had borrowed from her friend's closet, this sweater had never been one of them. It was simply too daring, even with a camisole.

With a sigh, Makenna shoved the sweater back into the closet. There was work to be done, and she was burning daylight.

Chapter 7

Makenna didn't make it into the mountains that afternoon. When she wandered into the neighboring village, she stumbled upon a concerned citizens meeting open to the public. The focus was on the impending power company's multi-million dollar proposed expansion through the area and the threat of imminent domain to obtain the land needed to see the project through. The group welcomed Makenna's questions and was a wealth of information for her fledging project. By the time she finally left, she sported a handful of pamphlets, a head full of new ideas, and a personal invitation to the upcoming city council meeting.

The afternoon had given way to early evening, leaving her little time to dress for her dinner date with Hardin. She took a quick shower and partially blow-dried her hair, leaving it loose and free in a riot of tumbling copper curls. The jeans were tighter than she normally wore, but there was no time to try on another pair. Per Kenzie's instructions, she pulled on the flesh-covered camisole. It was woven from cotton and spiked with spandex, enough to cling to her curves and create impressive cleavage. At first glance, the body-hugging lacy undergarment appeared as bare skin beneath the holey sweater. Although a closer look confirmed she was adequately covered, Makenna felt half-naked in the borrowed outfit. She was contemplating changing clothes when she heard Hardin knock.

Praying she could pull the look off with a semblance of confidence, Makenna spritzed on cologne and applied a satin finish gloss to her lips. A look into the mirror helped bolster her self-esteem. Rimmed softly with chocolate eyeliner and plenty of mascara, her green eyes appeared larger and more intense, if not slightly seductive. Her heart shaped face glowed with just the right mix of bronzing powder and anticipation. If it was Kenzie in the mirror, she would declare her beautiful; for herself, she chose a more modest 'presentable'.

In a truly ambidextrous move, Makenna threaded a large silver loop through her left ear while securing a strappy heel onto her right foot, all while hopping her way to the door.

She was only slightly out of breath by the time she greeted him. "Hardin, hi!"

"Hi, yourself." His appreciative blue gaze slid over her. He obviously approved of the new look. His eyes slid beneath the silky loose weave of the top, just as Kenzie had predicted. Seconds before his gaze turned into a stare, Hardin managed to pull his eyes back to her face. "You look stunning."

"Thank you." She tried not to blush, but she felt the stain spreading across her cheeks. Men rarely called her stunning.

"Ready to go?"

"Let me grab my purse." She retrieved the small clutch from the nearby bar, along with her cell phone. "All set," she announced, turning back around to find Hardin's full attention on her derriere.

"Nice rhinestones," he murmured, his gaze lingering along the swell of her hip and slowly traveling upward. There was enough heat in his eyes to kindle a small fire.

That heat elevated the evening to a whole new level. Yesterday, he had looked at her with interest. Tonight, there was open desire in his amazing blue eyes. Butterflies swarmed in Makenna's stomach as he took her elbow and steered her down the long hallway toward the stairway.

Hardin drove this night, leading her to a black pick-up truck equipped with a bicycle rack. Acting the part of a true gentleman, he opened the door for her and offered his hand as she climbed into the leather seat. Between the tight jeans and three-inch heels, Makenna managed to tuck her legs into the knee space with minimal clumsiness.

There was a crisp chill to the evening air, a welcomed treat for the two Texans. When the hostess asked if they would like to be seated in the bar's lounge by the fireplace, Hardin noted the smile that dimpled Makenna's cheeks. "Yes, please," he decided for them.

They selected a pair of overstuffed arm chairs nestled together in a cozy corner near the fireplace. The flame from the hearth offered more ambiance than warmth, but Makenna was feeling plenty of heat, generated by the man whose knees touched hers. They sipped on cocktails from the bar and nibbled on crackers and cheese, recapping their days' events.

"So you never made it into the mountains today?" he asked.

"No, I got caught up in the meeting. But definitely tomorrow."

"It's gorgeous, even though half the trees are still bare. There's even snow left in some spots."

"I know, I saw some in the distance and couldn't believe it! We haven't had snow in...what? At least three years, even in the dead of winter. I can't believe they still have snow on the ground in late April."

"But the air is so invigorating. It feels great out there, riding in the sunshine and not even breaking a sweat."

"Yeah, well, some of us would," Makenna cracked.

"Do you ride?"

"Horses? Yes. Motorcycles? Yes, though not alone. Bicycles? It's been a while. A long while."

"You know what they say, once you learn, you never forget. You should come with me. We could rent you a bike and spend the day up in the mountains." His intriguing blue eyes took on an excited light.

"I'm not sure that's a good idea. I would only slow you down. It's been so long since I've even been on a bike, I might not be able to even keep my balance anymore. And even if I could, I doubt I could make it up those mountains. Downhill, yes, but up?" She laughed at the vision of herself, huffing and puffing her way up a steep slope.

"We could do the Kanc Highway. We could pack a picnic and stop at all the waterfalls, giving you plenty of breaks."

"The what?"

"The Kancamagus Highway. Locals call it the Kanc for short. There's a gorgeous 34 mile stretch running between here and Conway."

"Yes, but once we got to the end, we'd have to turn around and come back. Those 34 miles would turn into 68, and my legs muscles would turn into mush!" Makenna laughed. "I'm afraid I'm not in that good of shape, my friend."

His blue eyes traveled over her, starting with the legs in question. At five seven, her legs were already long, and the heels she wore made them seem even more so. Her hips were full and curvy, and squirmed in the chair when his heated gaze fell upon her lap. As he slowly raised his line of vision, Hardin's sharp eyes probed beneath the moss green of her sweater, lingering on her waist and her ample bosom. Even without the squeeze of spandex, she had more cleavage than most women. Tonight it was definitely on display, visible by the sweater's generous neckline. Its edge dipped low and fell off one shoulder, exposing an expanse of creamy skin to his eager eyes.

"You have an excellent shape," he murmured lowly, his eyes still caressing her. Her skin heated beneath his gaze, and her throat went suddenly dry.

Makenna knew she was no petite goddess of femininity. She was tall and curvy, but an active lifestyle and occasional visits to the gym kept her in good physical condition and her muscles toned. She was well aware of the fact that many men preferred skin and bones over her full figure, so it was always flattering to have a man appreciate her curves, particularly a man as handsome and ripped as Hardin Kaczmarek.

By the time his eyes made their way to meet hers, he was grinning. "So maybe we'll take the truck into the mountains tomorrow. You game for some sightseeing?"

He was asking for a second date, before this one was even half started. Taking it as the encouraging sign it was, Makenna felt her own silly grin spread across her face. "Sure. But let's take the convertible. We can let the top down."

A wicked light came to his eyes. "I'm all about letting the top down," he said seductively, his brazen gaze slipping to her chest. When she blushed three shades of red, all the way down to the cleavage he ogled, he threw back his head and laughed in genuine delight. At the sound, Makenna's heart did a crazy somersault and landed in her throat.

Taking mercy on her, Hardin made a suggestion. "Maybe we should get a table now, and order our dinner."

"I think that might be a good idea." Makenna scooted to the front of her chair, waiting for his move to stand. When he remained seated and merely leaned forward, she glanced at him with a confused frown.

"Before we go, there's something I've got to do," he said. She watched as he reached out and cupped his hand around her neck. He gently pulled her forward, meeting her halfway as he pressed his mouth against hers. Her heart went into another acrobatic feat as tingles radiated from her lips and overtook her brain. The kiss was over before she had the acuity to respond properly.

Hardin helped her to her feet, and she wondered if it was because he knew her knees were shaky. His hand slid along the curve of her waist as he followed closely behind her to the hostess stand. As they waited to be seated in the dining room, his hand remained warmly in place. He told her an amusing story about a friend named Travis, but her brain was still buzzing with the electricity of his kiss. She could do little more than stare at him, drinking in the sight of him in his snug fitting worn jeans, black t-shirt, and casual gray sports jacket. The neutral colors made the blue of his eyes even more striking.

Once seated, the waiter told them about the evening's specials and set a basket of bread between them before leaving.

"This pecan crusted salmon sounds delicious," Makenna said. "Hmmm. But then again, so does the asparagus chicken with the cranberry glaze."

"We could order them both, and share."

"I figured you for the baby back ribs."

"They do sound good, but I'm pretty particular about my barbecue sauce. I'm not sure a northern chef can live up to my southern expectations."

Makenna laughed. "Spoken like a true Texan. Of course, the best place to go for barbecue ribs is Daddy J-"

"Daddy Joe's, in Wimberley."

They said the words in unison, then shared a laugh.

"You too, huh?" he asked.

"Of course. You know, they opened a store in Austin, but it's just not the same. For the real thing, you gotta go to Wimberley."

"So maybe I should skip the ribs and go with the salmon," Hardin decided, closing his menu. "Now that you've got me thinking about Daddy Joe's, ribs by anyone else will just make me mad."

"I think I'll get the chicken," Makenna said. She glanced around the restaurant. "So far, so good. No sign of the Lewises."

"Good. I'm looking forward to having you to myself and learning more about you."

After ordering, Makenna sipped her wine and murmured her appreciation of the smooth vintage. "So, you were going to tell me all about yourself," she said, beating him to the punch. "Tell me more about Hardin Kaczmarek."

"I think I've already hit all the highlights. Attended Texas State University, work in the family construction business, have a house and a few acres outside of Gruene, like to hunt and fish and ride bikes of all kinds, from ten speeds to motorcycles. Not much else to tell."

"There might be one or two little details you missed. Family? Girlfriend?" She hesitated before asking a belated question. "Wife?"

He looked appropriately wounded. "Wife? Really? You think I would have kissed you if I had a wife at home?"

Makenna closed her eyes at her own stupidity. "No, no, of course not. Ignore me. Sometimes I can be…" She broke off, searching for the right word.

"Distrustful? Suspicious?" he supplied.

"Slow. I should have asked that yesterday, huh?" she said with a rueful smile. "So no wife. Is that current or past-tense?"

"Never had the pleasure of being married. And before you ask, no girlfriend. Currently, that is." His smile was disarming.

"But you do have a family, I suppose. Parents, siblings?"

"All of the above. My parents live in New Braunfels, in the same house they bought when they married forty-six years ago. They've added on so many times it's hard to pinpoint the original frame, but I guess that's part of being in construction. You construct. At least that's my dad's theory, anyway. My oldest brother, Johnathan, lives on the family property with his wife and four kids. My brother Adam will graduate from Texas A&M next year. He's studying architecture and plans to join the rest of us in the family business."

"Sisters?"

"We're a respectable German family. Of course there are more than just three boys. There're three girls, as well. Becca and her husband run the plumbing side of the construction business. They also have four kids. Maegan and Anna help my mother with interior design."

"Are they married?" She was mentally calculating how big his family must be, given all the in-laws, outlaws, and grandchildren.

"Maegan's been married for a couple of years and is expecting her first child in the fall. Anna's been dating her high school sweetheart for years now, but still no ring. She and Adam are twins, by the way."

"Your family sounds amazing. You must all get along really well."

"You might have a different opinion if you were there during the holidays or during a football game, but yeah, we're pretty tight." There was obvious affection in his voice.

"So where do you fall in the Kaczmarek family line-up?"

"I slipped in between Becca and Maegan."

"And even though there's no current girlfriend, I'm sure there's been a long line of girlfriends past?" Makenna asked as she sipped her wine.

He had the grace to look uncomfortable. "I wouldn't say an unusually long list."

"Any names that stand out from the rest?"

He laughed at her line of questioning. "Maybe a couple, but none even came close to having their last name changed. Not by me, anyway."

Makenna felt the warm glow of satisfaction at knowing he had never been engaged, much less married. Not that their relationship - should they even get to that stage – stood a chance, she reminded herself; she was lying to him, impersonating someone else. He didn't even know her real name! He thought he had kissed Kenzie Reese, not Makenna Reagan.

"So," Hardin said with a tone of decisiveness. "You now know all about me, which means it's my turn to ask the questions." He turned his intense blue gaze her way. "Tell me about Kenzie Reese."

Makenna casually crossed her arms on top of the table and took a deep breath, before launching into the story of her best friend's life. For the sake of keeping her stories straight, she decided right then to tell everything as truthfully as possible; she would simply tell it from a different perspective. "I double-majored at the University of Texas in Communications and Journalism, minoring in Photography. I landed my dream job with *Now Magazine* two years ago, as a photojournalist. I've had the pleasure of traveling all over the United States and even to Europe, Sweden, and Mexico, covering stories through my camera lens. I even get paid for it!" she quipped, using a line she often heard Kenzie say.

"But you live in Austin," he prodded.

"That's right. I share an apartment with my best friend."

"What does she do?"

"Until this week, she was a reporter with one of the local newspapers. They let her go in favor of a blond bimbo with implants." She tried to keep the bitterness from her voice, but even she could hear the disdain dripping from her words.

"I take it you and your roommate are close."

"Everyone thinks we're sisters. We look alike, talk alike, think alike. We're like one person, divided in two." It was a joke they often told, even though it was steeped in reality.

"Your real family?" he asked. Their food arrived, but after the initial distraction, he got back on track. "What does the Reese family tree look like?"

Makenna thought about her answer for a moment. After hearing him talk about his family, it was hard not to gush about her own closely-knit clan. She, too, came from a big and loving family. After having four children of their own, Madeline and Kenneth Reagan had adopted three more; a troubled pre-teen, a lost and abandoned toddler, and a special needs infant. She was quite proud of her family and enjoyed talking about them. But she was pretending to be Kenzie, and it was best to stick to the truth, as seen through her friend's eyes. "Like a lone, lonesome pine on a barren hillside," she finally said, her heart heavy for her friend.

His brows furrowed together in a frown. "Oh?"

"I'm an only child, and I'm not close to my parents. The Reagans have more or less adopted me as one of their own."

"The Reagans?"

"My roommate's family."

"So how'd you meet your roommate ... Makenna, is it?"

She nodded. It was strange, hearing her own name and pretending it was someone else. "We met the first day of college. We were in the ladies' room, washing our hands, and I looked up into the mirror and saw myself. Only I was wearing different clothes and the hair was different. Then the person beside me glanced up and I saw the same sense of recognition flash across her face." Makenna laughed as she recalled the incident. "We turned to each other and put our palms up, like we were touching a mirror. Only there was no mirror, but a real person. She said it reminded her of a game she used to play when she was little, talking to the girl from her mirror. I said I played the same game in my mirror. We chatted all the way out the door and down the hall. The next day, we discovered we had a journalism class together. By the end of the week we were fast friends; by the end of the month we were inseparable."

"You look that much alike?" he asked, cocking his head in amazement.

"It's a little freaky, actually. I'm a little taller, a couple of pounds heavier – of course!- and our coloring is different. I have auburn hair and green eyes, she has black hair and green eyes. But yeah, if you didn't know better, you'd swear we were related."

He studied her so long that she began to squirm in her seat. "What?" she finally had to ask, a nervous laugh coming through her voice.

"I was just thinking what it must be like to see you two together. Two total knockouts, side-by-side. Every guy's fantasy," he said, a playfully wicked gleam in his eyes.

Makenna hid her blush behind her wine glass. "You are definitely good for a girl's ego, Hardin Kaczmarek! Full of it, but good for the ego."

"Full of it?" he feigned hurt feelings. "I give you a sincere and heartfelt compliment, and you accuse me of being full of shit. What's a guy gotta do to catch a break?"

In response, Makenna merely laughed and rolled her eyes. She cut into her chicken as Hardin picked up the conversation.

"So you said the Reagans took you in as their own. Where are your parents?" he asked between bites of crusted fish and rice pilaf.

Makenna shrugged. "I honestly couldn't say."

"You mean, you don't know where your parents are?" he asked incredulously.

"They haven't spoken to me in three years."

"Wow, that's harsh." He looked truly stunned at her revelation. "Where were they, last you knew?"

"The last address I had was somewhere in South Carolina. Or maybe it was North." She frowned, trying to recall what Kenzie had said. Not that it mattered; that had been three years ago, and according to her friend, they rarely stayed in one place more than a couple of years at a time.

"I'm sorry to hear that." His voice was low and sincere. "It's hard for me to imagine a family that's not close. Having mine all around me can sometimes be a pain in the butt and God knows there's no such thing as keeping a secret, but I can't imagine living my life without them all up in it."

"I know what you mean."

The moment the words were out, Makenna realized her mistake. She toyed with the stem of her wine glass and tried to sound philosophical. "It is hard to imagine. I guess that's why I have adopted the Reagans. I'd much rather pretend they are my family, than my own flesh and blood."

"Has is always been that way? What was it like growing up?"

"We moved around a lot."

"What does your father do for a living?"

"You know what? I'd rather not discuss my family, if you don't mind. I'd rather discuss something pleasant." It wasn't intentional, but when she leaned forward and propped her elbows on the table, the precarious neckline of her borrowed sweater slid even further down her arm.

"And what did you have in mind?" he grinned, gaze lingering on a creamy shoulder.

"Tell me what's planned for tomorrow."

The conversation flowed smooth and easy as they discussed plans for the next day, and Makenna could not remember the last time she had enjoyed a date so much. Hardin was easy to talk to and engaged her in a two-sided conversation. It was a complete change from most of the men she had dated in the past, particularly Derek. With her former boyfriend, everything had been about him; Makenna's opinions and tastes had been of little consequence. Derek was constantly posturing, portraying himself as the fastest/brightest/best, no matter the subject. Not for the first time, Makenna wondered what she thought she had seen in him.

By the time they sampled from the other's plate and critiqued both offerings, they had discussed a dozen topics and had at least one good-natured argument. They were contemplating dessert when Hardin caught a glimpse of Bob and Lisa Lewis coming out of the bar.

"If you don't mind, let's skip dessert," he suggested. "If we hurry, we might can get out before the Lewises spot us." He caught their server's attention and asked for the check, murmuring something about a minor emergency. She hurried back with the receipt and Hardin paid in cash, telling her to keep the change.

They almost made it to the door. Makenna tucked her head and studied the wooden planks beneath her feet as she and Hardin hurried past the other couple, thinking if she didn't see them, perhaps they wouldn't see her. It was a valiant effort, but just as they reached for the handle, they heard Lisa's high-pitched whine carry across the room, "Kenzie! Hardin! Hey there, you two!"

"Oh, hi!" Makenna hoped she looked appropriately surprised as she looked their way. She wiggled her fingers in greeting, even as she threw a desperate glance over her shoulder toward Hardin.

"We'll say a quick hello and then make our escape," he whispered out of the side of his mouth, giving her waist a slight squeeze. She felt his sigh as he moved away from the door and extended a hand to the other man.

"Are you leaving?" Lisa pouted.

"Just headed out," Hardin confirmed.

"I told you we shouldn't have made that last stop!" Lisa complained to her husband, slapping him against the arm. He grunted but made no comment as she continued on. "He just had to stop at one last covered bridge! You ask me, you've seen one, you've seen them all! But I guess you like to photograph things like that, don't you, dear?" She looked at Makenna but didn't wait for her answer. "I don't suppose the new power lines will take down any of the bridges, will they? Aren't they like historical landmarks, or something?"

"I imagine they might be, so I doubt any of them are in danger," Makenna agreed.

"So did you start on your project today?"

She nodded. "'Started' being the operative word."

"I know you two must be hungry," Hardin broke in, "so we'll let you order your meal. In fact, order anything you like. I'll get this tonight."

"No, no need for that," Bob argued.

"I insist."

“Not tonight!” Lisa whined. “We’ll let you treat tomorrow night, when we can all enjoy the meal together.”

Makenna glanced at Hardin, who quickly came up with a plausible excuse. “We have plans for tomorrow. We probably won’t be back in time for supper.”

“Well, let’s try to meet here tomorrow night about this same time. If you don’t make it back, we’ll reschedule for the next night. How’s that sound?” Lisa asked brightly, peering at first one, then the other.

“Sounds like a plan,” Hardin said, sounding more enthusiastic than Makenna felt. “Have a good evening, you two.”

“Enjoy your meal,” Makenna called over her shoulder as Hardin once again ushered her toward the door.

“Did she just rope us into another dinner?” Hardin muttered as he opened the truck door for Makenna to slide inside.

“I think so.”

Groaning out loud, Hardin shut her door, then went round to the driver’s side. “I say we stay out late tomorrow night and miss dinner. I’m willing to go to bed hungry.”

“I’m sure our ears will thank you,” Makenna lamented, pounding on her earlobes to dislodge any lingering echo. “Have you ever heard a more irritating voice?”

“Only on television. What was that show with the nanny with the horrible voice? Sounds just like her, but with a Southern twang!” As he pulled out of the parking lot, he said, “Sorry about dessert.”

“I’m too stuffed for dessert, anyway. These little bits of white chocolate they give out are just right. Here, have some.”

They discussed the next day’s events as they made the short drive to the resort and then took the stairs to the second floor. Makenna nibbled nervously on her lower lip, wondering if she should invite him in for a nightcap. Kenzie would, she knew, but she wasn't certain if she was ready to push their relationship a notch further just yet.

At her door, Hardin took hold of her wrist and gently tugged her around to face him. He stepped closer, bringing his body to within a few inches of hers. "I had a really good time tonight. In spite of running into the Lewises, that was the most fun I've had on a date in ... I can't even remember when."

"Me, too," Makenna agreed. With an impish grin, she added, "It was almost perfect, right up until the end."

Hardin moved even closer, his hand still on her wrist as he gently wound her arm behind her and maneuvered her body up against his own. When she lifted her face expectantly to his, he pulled her arm forward, to wrap around his own waist. The sky blue of his eyes darkening with desire, Hardin slipped his fingers into her hair and cupped her face within his large, calloused palms.

"Then let's close the night on a perfect note," he murmured, brushing his lips against hers. He slid his mouth slowly across hers, more a tease than a kiss. He dropped a small peck at the corner of her mouth, then drug his lower lip back across hers, his breath warm and scented with chocolate and wine. Pulling her face closer against his, he increased the gentle pressure of his mouth, pressing his lips firmly into hers before he pulled slightly away and began a slow exploration of her mouth. He began by nibbling on the fullness of her lower globe, then slid the tip of his tongue over the seam of her lips, on his way to explore the curve of her upper lip. By the time his tongue returned to run along the sensuous pleat of her mouth, Makenna was tugging his hips closer, encouraging him to deepen the maddeningly slow and masterful kiss.

His tongue slipped inside the honeyed recess of her mouth, still exploring. Makenna's body tightened with unexpected desire, even as her knees sagged. When she stepped back against the wall for support, tugging him along with her, he pressed his body close against hers. He deepened the kiss, one hand tangling in the curls at the nape of her neck to keep her face bound close to his, the other hand wandering down her collarbone, down along the dipping neckline of her holey green sweater. Hardin's fingers slid down her bare shoulder, down almost to her elbow, until they found the end of her sleeve. Slipping beneath the loose weave, his fingers traveled back up the length of her arm with slow deliberation. His touch never strayed from the safety of her upper arm, but there was something completely erotic about the feel of his fingers gliding over her highly sensitive skin.

By the time the kiss ended, Makenna was breathless. She vaguely noticed he was having similar difficulty breathing, but her mind was too muddled to take clear notes. Her entire body was in over-drive, her blood humming wildly as it zipped through her veins, her heart hammering a wild pace all its own.

"Perfect," he murmured against her lips, lingering there for one more kiss. "Absolutely perfect."

"Mmm," she agreed dreamily. It was the best she could manage.

Hardin stepped back, allowing them both a chance to gather their senses. Makenna finally thought to fish in her purse for her hotel card, which Hardin took from her trembling hands and slid through the reader with ease.

"I'll see you at eight-thirty," he reminded her, leaning in for a brief kiss. Her lips lingered, then his. "I'd better go," he finally said, but his voice was rough with obvious reluctance.

"See you in the morning." She slipped quietly inside and shut the door, her legs a trembling mess.

Chapter 8

Morning sun warmed the interior of the little red sports car as it hugged the curves of the mountain highway, climbing its way to the top. The air was crisp and invigorating, almost cold, but the bright rays of sunshine held the chill at bay. Still, Makenna was thankful she wore a light jacket over her black V-necked t-shirt.

"This is amazing!" she beamed, glancing over at Hardin. "I definitely see why you came here to train for cycling. The temps here are fantastic!"

"And no humidity," he reminded her. "Although this morning it was just down-right cold, before the sun got fully up."

"You rode this morning?" she asked in surprise.

"After the workout I had yesterday, I couldn't slack off completely or I'd be too sore to move. I got in a couple of miles this morning, just to keep me limber." He craned his neck to get a better view over the edge of the mountain. "I think there's a place to pull over just up here. We could probably see pretty good from there."

It was taking them longer than normal to travel the scenic route through the White Mountains. At a moment's notice, they would whip off the side of the road to explore a rocky stream or to gaze out over a beautiful mountainside vista. With the help of tourists' maps and local input, they were finding waterfalls and overlooks and a full array of nature's beauty.

Makenna was particularly enchanted with the mountain streams, even those that did not feature a waterfall. Half a dozen times, they stopped alongside the road and scrambled down the rocky embankments for closer inspection of a clear mountain stream. They waded out on numerous boulders, standing amid the teeming waters so she could take picture after picture of the white capped currents. More than once, she was sprayed by the frosty waters or misjudged the depth of an embedded rock, getting her shoes wet.

The higher they drove up the mountain, the more snow they saw. They stopped for a snowball fight and took pictures of each other, including a selfie when he unexpectedly kissed her cheek. Makenna sent a copy to Kenzie, knowing her friend would bombard her with a hundred questions, but she was careful to keep the screen from Hardin's view. She couldn't very well have him see the name "Kenzie" on her phone, not when he thought that was *her* name.

Spotting another photo op, Makenna slowed the convertible. "I'll pull over if this car will ever get off my butt," she said, watching as a gray car came up behind them. The biggest challenge of sight-seeing was to do it amid all the other cars on the road. There was only light traffic, but it seemed each time she wanted to slow down to enjoy the view or to make an impromptu stop, there was always a vehicle behind her, such as now. "Come on, buddy, go around." She was talking to the other driver as if he could hear her.

"He's coming up awfully fast," Hardin said, glancing in the side mirror.

"Yeah, I'd better not try to make this one." With a resigned sigh, Makenna resumed her speed.

"Damn, Kenzie, I think that guy's going to run us over!"

At Hardin's startled tone, Makenna glanced into her rear view mirror. Sure enough, the car was right on her bumper. She sped up, thinking she would put a comfortable distance between them, but he kept pace with her.

"Not again!" Makenna moaned, taking a curve faster than she felt comfortable with. "Hardin, what do I do? I don't want to go this fast, but I'm afraid he's going to hit my bumper if I slow down!"

"What is that guy doing!" Hardin bellowed, turning around in the front seat of the convertible to get a better look at the vehicle behind them. The tinted front windshield offered little more than the silhouette of a single occupant, hands intent upon the wheel. Hardin waved his arm, motioning for the car to pass, but it remained steadfast on their bumper.

"What do I do?" she demanded again.

"Just keep it steady. Don't go any faster. See if he'll pass on this straightaway."

They made the curve, straightened out, but still the gray car followed close behind.

"What the —!" Hardin whirled around again, motioning wildly at the other driver. In response, the gray car tapped against their bumper, then backed slightly off.

"Not again, not again, not again!" was all Makenna could say as they were jarred forward from the contact. Hardin was more vocal, calling the man behind them vivid names and yelling at him to back off.

"There's a big curve coming up, Hardin! What do I do? I'm going too fast!"

"Ease over, half way in the other lane, as you let off the gas."

"What if a car is coming?" she cried, but did as he instructed.

"Pray that it's not. Okay, he's coming up closer again, trying to edge you over. Stay steady, right on the line… that's it… steady." As they came into the curve and saw no oncoming traffic, Hardin gave her new instructions. "Okay, move all the way into the other lane. He's going to come up fast on our right, trying to keep you in this lane. When I say, I want you to –"

"Oh my gosh, Hardin, there's a car coming up ahead! What do I do?"

The gray car pulled beside them and matched their speed, refusing to let them back in the lane. Trying to pass him would be impossible.

"Let up on the gas. It's going to be rough, but there's a drive on your left in a hundred feet. When I say, I want you to hit your brakes and swing into it. The tail-end of the car is going to fishtail, but I'll help hold it steady."

"When?" she screamed. "That car's coming closer!"

"Ready? Okay- now!"

The brakes squealed in protest as Makenna stomped down hard on them. The sports car went into a skid, the rear-end swinging wildly as Hardin predicted. "Let up on the brake!" he yelled, his hands firm on the steering wheel as he whipped it to the left, then straight, then left again.

For a heart-stopping moment, they were airborne. Makenna felt like she was watching the moment in slow motion. The on-coming car was honking its horn, slamming on brakes that squealed, still barreling straight for them as the convertible sailed over the pavement and into the small clearing of a driveway. In the other lane, the gray car sped up and away from the potential accident in progress. Bushes scraped along the sides of the little red sports car, and suddenly things switched from slow motion to utter chaos. The gravel driveway rushed up to meet them with a vengeance, jarring Makenna off the seat. If not for Hardin's strong hands still on the wheel, she would have lost complete control of the vehicle. When she came down, she bit her tongue hard enough to draw blood.

Dust swirled around them, the acrid smell of burnt rubber and asphalt hung in the air, and the car slid sideways, coming to a sharp and abrupt stop.

For a moment, neither spoke. "Did we make it?" Makenna finally asked in a weak voice.

"Barely. Damn, girl, what was that?!"

In answer, Makenna folded her arms over the steering wheel and rested her forehead there, shaking her head.

"Hey, are you okay?" This time, his voice was gentler. He touched her shoulder, forcing her to look at him. "Are you okay?" he repeated.

"I-I think so."

He cupped her face and pulled her to him for a quick, hard kiss. "You did great. You did perfect. Where'd you learn to drive like that?"

Still too shaken to speak, she merely shook her head with a clueless shrug.

"Aw, come on, don't fall apart on me now," he urged softly, gathering her to him in a gentle embrace. "You did great. You handled that like a pro."

I've had enough recent experience, her mind screamed, but her body was too weak to verbalize the thoughts. She leaned into him, absorbing his solid strength.

He gave her a few more moments to collect herself, then he set her away. "Would you like for me to drive?" he asked.

She nodded. It was against rental policy to let him drive, but then again, it was against policy for her to drive, as well; the car was in Kenzie's name.

Hardin helped her from the car, practically carrying her when her legs threatened to give way. Settling her in the passenger's seat with a gentle kiss on the forehead, he took a moment to inspect the car before he slid behind the wheel.

"Believe it or not, I only see a couple of scratches, and I think they can be buffed out before you return the car. I'm surprised we didn't flatten all four tires, as hard as we slammed down." He adjusted mirrors and gadgets, then put the car into gear. He appeared unfazed, rattling on about mufflers and airbags and things Makenna was too emotionally drained to even think about. It wasn't until they were pulling back onto the highway, headed in the same direction they had been traveling, that she roused.

"Where-Where are we going?"

"We still have a full day ahead of us."

"We're going on?" she asked weakly.

He sent her a sharp look. "Don't you want to?"

"I-I don't know. What if – What if the car is up ahead, waiting on us?"

"They're long gone by now. They were in a major hurry to get up the mountain, and for all they know, they just caused a wreck. They don't want to be anywhere near if the cops are called."

"I guess," Makenna murmured, but she was unconvinced.

"I'll make you a deal. We'll stop up here and have lunch, and see how you're feeling. If you want to call it a day after that, I'll take you back to the hotel."

A vague "Okay" was all she could muster.

They had their picnic near the crest of the mountain, at a scenic overlook that provided a magnificent view. On a clear day, it was said you could see the ocean from there.

Ocean view or not, the stone gazebo with its informative kiosk and telescope for examining the breath-taking view, along with picnic tables, made it the perfect spot for their noon meal. Best of all, they had the mountaintop all to themselves.

The solitary setting and stunning vista were all it took to settle Makenna's nerves. After taking a dozen photos, she settled down at the picnic table with Hardin to examine the prepackaged basket he had purchased. A glass of wine was the final touch needed to soothe her scattered senses.

When the meal was over and Makenna repacked the picnic basket, Hardin threw away their accumulated trash.

"All better now?" he asked, coming up from behind and resting his hands on her waist.

"Yes, much."

"We can keep going, then? I want to explore some of the covered bridges and at least one or two more waterfalls. I hear one of them is pretty spectacular."

"I think what we've seen so far has been spectacular in itself," she said, allowing him to turn her around.

"Yeah, but you ain't seen nothing yet," he murmured, slipping his hand behind her neck and pulling her forward for his kiss. He cradled her head within both hands, this kiss slow and sweet and full of promise.

Makenna locked her arms around his waist, holding him to her. She needed to be close to him. She needed to feel safe.

When he finally lifted his head, his eyes were once again clear and intensely blue. "We still have the entire afternoon to enjoy," he reminded her. Letting his gaze wander over the lips he had just kissed, his voice turned husky. "And the entire evening."

Suddenly nervous at the implied meaning, Makenna went with a teasing reply. "Yes, an entire evening to be tortured by Lisa and Bob Lewis," she said sweetly.

"Ah, woman, you are cruel. You really know how to knock a guy down." He dropped a quick kiss into her bronzed curls before he released her. "Look on the bright side. Maybe we'll have a flat and miss dinner completely."

"Better watch what you wish for!" Makenna laughed as they gathered their items and headed for the car. "I have no idea where they even hide the tire jack on this little number."

By late afternoon, they had viewed almost a dozen more mountain streams and half as many covered bridges. They crisscrossed and back-tracked, trying to make as many of the sights as possible. Concerns about the gray car faded into the shadows, as the day shone bright with sunshine and charming company.

As they trekked into the woods to see one of the waterfalls featured in their brochure, they had a brief and close encounter with a moose. Makenna wasn't sure who was more startled, herself or the moose, but she captured the moment with her camera. She couldn't wait to share the photo with Kenzie! She was practically dancing as they came out of the woods, laughing as they recalled the moment the huge shaggy beast jumped with all four feet off the ground.

"This has got to be one of the best days ever!" Makenna insisted, swinging their arms merrily. Their hands were clasped together, moving in tandem. "Of all the things we've done and seen today, the look on that moose's face has to be the best!"

Hardin laughed. He had a great laugh, deep and generous and from the soul. "That was pretty amazing. But then again, so were some of the covered bridges." He sent her a heated look.

She couldn't help but blush. She knew exactly which bridges he referred to. At the first bridge, he had stolen a kiss. At the second, they bid their time until the other tourists had wandered away, at which time there was no stealing required; Makenna gladly gave him the kiss he sought. By the fifth and final bridge, his hands had become familiar with the curve of her hip, the creamy satin of her long neck, the delicate skin along the V-neck of her tee shirt. There were all sorts of wondrous discoveries to be made in the darkened recess of an old covered bridge, and they had little to do with historical architecture.

"So where's this last waterfall you're taking me to?" she asked, artfully avoiding the subject.

"Sabbaday Falls, not too far ahead. It's a short walk back, but I hear it's worth it."

"I think we need to raid the picnic basket again, see what's left inside before we tackle another round. All this hiking is making me hungry."

"You, Kenzie Reese, are a true delight," Hardin announced, swinging her up against him as they reached the car.

"Wh-Why is that?" Makenna was left breathless. It was a combination of the sudden move, the thrill of being held close against his body, and the suffocating crush of guilt. She hated deceiving him.

"Most women would never admit they were hungry. Half of them won't even eat around a guy, which is totally ridiculous. I like that you are so open and honest."

Makenna dropped her eyes, unable to meet his gaze. "Yeah, well, one look at me tells you that I definitely like to eat. No sense pretending otherwise."

"No sense in pretending at all." He brushed a kiss along her jaw, working his way toward her mouth. "And for the record, I think you're totally hot."

She let him kiss her, until guilt crowded its way between them. "We'd better get a move on," she reminded him.

"What do you think I was trying to do?" he grumbled, but he released her with a teasing grin and opened the car door.

Before reaching Sabbaday Falls, they found another waterfall just down the road, this one with picnic facilities near the water's edge. After taking a dozen photos, Makenna joined him at the picnic table to see what was left in the basket. "Half a club on wheat," he reported, pulling back the deli wrapper. "Plenty of crackers and cheese."

"Any of that vegetable dip and carrot sticks left?" Makenna asked hopefully.

"Mm, no carrots, but celery. And a full slice of chocolate cake and half a bottle of wine."

"Looks like we're in business," she grinned, assembling the collapsible wine flutes. "That was a very well-stocked picnic basket."

"It should be, for the price I paid," he grumbled.

As they ate, Makenna casually browsed through some of the many pictures she had taken on Kenzie's fancy digital camera. "I never knew New Hampshire was so beautiful," she confessed. "I just thought it was about political posturing, what with the primary and all. But it's so natural and raw up here, so rugged. I never knew."

"A buddy of mine is from here originally. That's how I know what to check out."

"I've taken some amazing shots, if I do say so myself!"

"Nothing like a little modesty," he teased.

"It's more what's in front of the camera, than the person behind it," Makenna murmured, but her tone was distracted. She chewed on her lower lip as she scrolled back through a few pictures, an uneasy feeling settling in her stomach.

Hardin picked up on her caprice instantly. He paused in the act of pouring their wine. "What's wrong?"

"Uhm, this guy. He's in a lot of our pictures." She turned the camera so he could see the screen. "I don't even remember seeing him. Most of the places we stopped, we were the only ones there. But when there were other people around, so was this guy. Every time. Don't you think that's a little odd?"

Hardin shrugged his well sculptured shoulders. "Maybe he's using the same guide map we're using. It could happen."

Makenna zoomed in on the face in the viewfinder, trying to make out his features. The overall shape of his bald head looked vaguely familiar, but she honestly couldn't say she had noticed him among the other tourists. "It's funny I didn't notice him at any of those places. Even in the pictures, it's almost like he's hiding in the background. He's always standing on the fringes."

"Well, you weren't focusing on him, after all."

"I don't mean fringes of the shot, I mean fringes of the scenery. How can he even see the waterfall, standing way over there?"

"I remember seeing him get out of his car when we were at one of the Cascades, the one with the snow still around the edges. I noticed the sun glinted off his car door and, just for a second, caused a really cool green prism. I was going to point it out to you, but it was gone as soon as he shut the door."

Something caught in Makenna's throat; she thought it was probably her heart. "Did – Did you say he was driving a green car?" she whispered.

"Yeah, a dark green Malibu. Hey, what's wrong? You're as pale as a ghost."

"I-I ..." She stopped to gather her thoughts, her breath coming in fast, short spurts. "I didn't tell you about what happened on my way up here, did I?"

"Since I have no idea what you're talking about, I guess not."

After she relayed the story of the green sedan trying to run her off the road, Hardin cursed angrily beneath his breath. She saw something dark and fierce blaze through his eyes, something almost frightening in its intensity. It occurred to her that Hardin Kaczmarek was not a man to be crossed; and this, the man she had lied to repeatedly about her own identity.

"Why didn't you tell me about this before?" he demanded. "Like when we were being run off the road by the gray car! Did you go to the police?"

"And what would I tell the police?" *That I wasn't who I claimed to be?* "I didn't get the license plate number or the make of the car. All I know, it was green and I think maybe a Chevy. And I didn't mention it to you because it was over and done with."

"Or maybe not," he muttered, gazing out toward the highway. "That might explain what happened this morning."

"I don't see how. I can't imagine the connection. I have no idea why the green car developed road rage, but obviously we were going too slow to suit the gray car. I guess drivers in New England are less tolerant than in Texas."

"But the green car, showing up here today, going to the same places we're going?"

"If it was even the same green car," she pointed out. "Look, you said yourself that the odds of meeting up with the same people were greater because of the small area and the whole tourist thing. Just like the Lewises, being on our flight and staying in the same town. Just like you and me, for that matter." She was trying to convince herself as much as trying to convince him; she badly needed the reassurance.

Hardin hesitated for a moment longer, still obviously on edge. He finally blew out a breath and relaxed. "Yeah, you're right. I'm sure it's just coincidence. It's probably not even the same green car. And it's not like he approached you or anything. Let's just put it behind us for now, and enjoy the rest of the afternoon."

Chapter 9

Half an hour later, they were trekking the dirt path running alongside another stream. The warmth of the afternoon sun was partially blocked beneath the canopy of trees, and the air was cooler so near the water. The further into the woods they went, the more the light and the temperature faded.

"Oh, wow, look at this. This is gorgeous!" Makenna called over the roar of rushing water as they approached Sabbaday Falls. The stream itself was a masterpiece, with boulders and huge rocks creating multiple mini-falls for the tumbling water as it rushed down the mountainside.

"Come on, let's get closer." He held her hand to keep her steady as they stepped onto one of the huge slabs of granite close to the water.

"I'm not sure we're supposed to be down here," Makenna murmured as she carefully maneuvered the rock, slick with water and occasional patches of ice. "The path goes that way."

"Haven't you ever heard to take the path less traveled?" he challenged with a wicked grin.

"Not sure they were referring to frozen rocks in the middle of a waterfall," she muttered, almost losing her footing.

"Steady, there. And remember, this is a three-tier waterfall. This is only the lower level. The main attraction is up there still. We're just getting a closer view of the bottom."

Makenna forgot all about forbidden paths as she found a solid foothold and stopped to examine her surroundings. "Look!" Makenna cried excitedly, pointing to the wall of rock on the far side of the stream. "Is that ice? It is! The water froze in place, falling over the ledge!"

"Pretty cool, huh?"

"Pretty cold, you mean!" she quipped, snapping away on her camera. "It's amazing that it's late April, and water is still frozen as it flows."

"From one Texan to another, I totally agree. Nothing we ever see back home, huh?"

After several minutes, they made their way across the rocks and backtracked toward the intended path which climbed alongside the water's edge. A log rail edged the rocky drop-off and designated steps were carved into the slabs of stone, providing safer viewing.

Taking the lead, Hardin led the climb toward the first bridge overlook. "Watch your step. There's lots of ice here."

"That's probably why there's orange caution netting," Makenna pointed out. "To keep us from going any further."

"Probably so," he agreed, stepping over the tape and ice and proceeding on.

Makenna eagerly followed, but held on to the rail for safety. They were at the second fall, where the water surged from the side of the rock wall, white and foamy and loud. She wasn't about to turn back now.

"You've got to see this!" Hardin called over his shoulder excitedly. The stream took a sharp left and water cascaded from ledges above, swirled into a rocky pool, then fell 40 feet in a riot of sound and spray and pure exhilaration. Once she caught her breath, Makenna snapped into action, taking a dozen pictures of the magnificent sight. She wished she could capture the sound of the water crashing against the rocks and the feel of the air, all frosty and tipped with shards of splashing water.

"Absolutely gorgeous," Makenna breathed.

They stood on the railed bridge, gazing into the rocky gorge and marveling at the force of nature that, through the years, had eaten its way through layers of solid stone and found its path to freedom. From their vantage point, they could see not only the three tiers of the waterfall, but for a good distance downstream. Fascinated, they watched as the water fell hard and straight, swirled, then tumbled and tossed, churning white and foamy, before settling into a smoother flow as it made its way down downstream.

"There's a bench up there, if you'd like to sit for a while." Hardin pointed out the bench nestled beneath the trees, farther up where the terrain was smoother. "It's farther away from the water, so you won't get wet. Should be warmer there, too."

Wiping away the fine sheen of water from her cheeks, Makenna grinned. "It sure has a far reach, doesn't it?" She started to turn away when something downstream caught her eye, a quick flash of sunlight glinting off metal. She couldn't see anyone, but she knew someone was coming up the trail. She felt a sudden unease creep across her skin.

"Hardin," she said. Her voice was too low for him to hear over the roar of tumbling water. She tugged on his arm. "Hardin!"

He turned around, immediately seeing the alarm on her face. "What is it?" he asked, bringing his head down close to hers.

"I-I'm not sure." She tugged on his arm, pulling him further away from the rail, and further into the shadows of overhead trees. "Someone's coming."

"So? It's a public trail," he reminded her.

"I have this funny feeling..." She raised her camera and adjusted the zoom so that she could get a better view of the tree-studded path below. She saw a bird, and a million pine needles, and patches of dirt trail. And then, just for a second, another flash through the trees. She zeroed in on the area and tried to detect movement. A few seconds later, she was rewarded with a clear view of a now-familiar bald head.

"It's him, Hardin. It's the man who's been following us, the one in the green car!"

"Calm down," he said smoothly, but she could feel the tension in his body. Even without taking her eyes off the trail, she knew Hardin was scanning the area around them, looking for their best escape route. "It could be perfectly innocent."

"Then why is he looking through a pair of binoculars?" she squeaked, realizing it was the lens that was reflecting the sunlight, not metal.

"Do you think he spotted us?"

"Not yet. So far he's looking below us."

"Crouch down, behind this railing," he directed. He was suddenly all business, his voice brusque. "Inch your way over and behind that boulder."

"What do we do? He knows we're here."

"But we're not alone. I saw another car and a couple of bikes in the parking area. There's a hiking trail that runs further back into the woods, so apparently there are more people around somewhere."

"But they might be a mile from here! How's that going to help us?"

"For all we know, the binoculars are for bird watching." Even to his own ears, the words didn't sound very convincing. "Do you still see him?"

"No. Yes, but I won't be able to for long. He's nearing a bend and I'll lose sight of him when he makes the next curve."

"Good. If we can't see him, then he can't see us. We're going up toward the bench. But instead of catching the trail back down, we're going past it, into that tree line. Remember how the trail leads alongside a high embankment?"

She nodded, keeping the camera focused on the man coming closer toward them. "Yes, I kept looking up into the woods, wondering if we'd see another moose."

"We'll make our way back across the higher ground, instead of the trail."

"What if it's private land?" she worried.

He didn't bother with a comment. "Tell me when he gets to the bend. That's when we'll make our move."

"He should be about there. No, wait, there he is." She zoomed in again and gasped. "Oh my god, Hardin, that's not binoculars, it's a scope! He has a gun!"

Hardin cursed. "We've got to get out of here. Keep low as you can, but get over to that bench and crouch behind it. The hiking trail leads right past the bench, so we've got to make sure he takes the path up here, and not the trail. I'll be right behind you. Go!"

With her heart thudding in her chest, Makenna bent low and did as Hardin instructed. The camera swung wildly from around her neck, until she finally held it against her chest as she made her way deeper into nature, opposite the direction of their car. It was difficult to climb uphill while crouched over, and her calves were screaming in protest by the time she was able to stop behind the bench and rest.

Just before reaching the bench, Hardin slipped away, keeping behind the cover of trees until he could see the hiking trail. When he saw no sign of the bald man, he motioned for Makenna to move further to her left, into the deeper cover of the forest. Using hand signals, he told her to stay low and motioned for her to take off her bright green jacket. She made fast work of stripping it off, turning it inside out to reveal the reversible black underside, then slipping it back on, all while moving forward in a stealthy duck walk. He gave her a thumbs up before turning his attention back toward the trail. When he was satisfied that the man had taken the steps alongside the water's edge, Hardin hurried across the opening and into the woods behind Makenna.

He caught up with her in no time. "So far, so good," he reported in a loud whisper.

"I can't keep crouched over like this too much longer. I've got to stretch."

"Go a little further before you do. And deeper into the woods. Left around that big root."

"But what if we get lost?"

"As long as we can hear the water, we won't get lost," he continued in a low voice. "But I can still see the trail below, so he could still see us."

Makenna moved left, deeper into the woods. She straightened a little with every step, until finally she was in a full upright position. "My back and legs are killing me," she whispered, flexing her back muscles but moving ahead.

"Sorry, but we don't want to be seen. You keep walking, try to stay down when you can, and try not to make any more noise than possible."

"Where are you going? You can't leave me here!" She said in a panicked voice, forgetting to whisper.

"Shh! I'm going to ease over to the edge, see if I can see anything. Keep walking, keep low, and keep quiet." He sounded more like a drill sergeant than her charming companion, but his no-nonsense attitude was strangely reassuring.

Makenna kept moving through the woods, careful not to step on fallen branches or snapping vines. She tried to move parallel with the edge of the drop-off overlooking the trail, always keeping it within sight on her right, but at one point she was forced to veer left around a cluster of trees. As she moved left, the trail below made a deep right curve, and she found herself momentarily lost. She backtracked and hunched low as she went around the trees, this time to the right. After that, she paused occasionally to make sure that was the sound of water she heard, and not just the blood rushing through her veins.

At last, Hardin caught up with her. He came through the woods at a quick pace, almost a sprint.

"We're nearly back to the road. When we get close, don't worry about being quiet," he told her, his breathing already a bit labored.

"When I say, just start running. Run as fast as you can to the car. You ready?"

She wasn't, but she had little choice, so she merely nodded. He crowded near her, encouraging her to quicken her pace as the terrain sloped back down. When the sound of passing vehicles could be heard, he said, "Okay, now! Run!"

Tree branches and saplings slapped and scraped against their arms as they ran through the edge of the woods. Makenna stepped on a brier and felt it snag her pants leg, threatening to tumble her to the ground. She snatched it away with her hand, ripping her palm in the process. "Go, go, go!" Hardin encouraged her, sensing her struggle.

There was one last drop, this one rather steep, and they would be at the roadside. Afraid she might stumble, Makenna chose to slide down on her bottom. She hit the ground running when her feet touched level ground.

They came out of the woods several yards from where they parked. "Is that the green car?" Hardin confirmed, as they ran toward the parking area.

"Yes!"

"Get behind the wheel!" Hardin said, tossing her the keys. She bobbled them once, twice, before securing them in her grasp. "Back out and be headed toward town."

"Where are you going?" He ran past the convertible, to the green sedan parked on the other side.

"Just start the car and be pulling out. Keep the doors unlocked for me."

She wanted to protest, but there wasn't time. Her hands shook as she unlocked the door and jumped behind the wheel. She was thankful they had put the top up to secure their belongings; it made her feel marginally safer as she started the motor and put it in reverse.

She backed the car out and idled near the side of the road, waiting there for Hardin as he asked. She could see him in the rearview mirror, stabbing all four tires of the green sedan with the long blade of a knife. She briefly wondered how he had gotten the knife on the plane, but when she got a glimpse of the bald headed man, she forgot all about the knife. He was running up the trail, almost out of the forest and back to the parking area.

"Hurry, Hardin!" she screamed through the window. She didn't know if he heard her, but he stabbed the back tire a final time, jerked his knife from the deflating rubber, and ran her direction. Even as he opened the door, he was urging her, "Go, go, go! Drive!"

She floored the gas pedal and Hardin was jerked inside at an awkward angle. "Go, go!" he insisted, pulling his foot in and slamming the door, even as they sped onto the highway. Makenna pulled out in front of an oncoming car, eliciting a long lay on the horn and some crude sign language. The back-end of the sports car threatened to switch ends with the front, but Makenna held it steady as she stomped once again on the gas pedal.

"Oh my god! What- What is going on? Why are these people chasing me?" Makenna finally found her voice. It came out high pitched and breathless.

Hardin didn't answer. He was turned around in the seat, watching as the bald man discovered his destroyed tires. The angry man kicked at the useless rubber, slapped his hand on the car's roof, then turned to glare at the retreating sports car as he raised a menacing fist and shook it. At least he didn't pull out his gun. "I bought us some time with the tires," Hardin said, turning back around. "All the same, get us the hell out of here."

Makenna concentrated on driving. Her legs were weak, her side was cramping, her hands were shaking. The combination of physical exertion, running, and fear for her very life left her breathing ragged and her nerves raw. She kept a tight grip on the steering wheel as her foot remained heavy on the gas pedal. They sailed past more amazing scenery, both oblivious to the roadside beauty as they compulsively watched the road behind them; even knowing the green car was disabled for now didn't stop either of them from watching for its reappearance.

After a long stretch of road traveled in tense silence, Makenna glanced over at Hardin. She had never seen a jaw so tightly clamped. His handsome face was more the mask of a stranger, hard and staunch and filled with tightly reined anger. He looked so fierce, so nearly dangerous, that her heart lurked just a bit in fright. He was not a man to have as an enemy, she realized.

"What-What now?" She forced the words out around the lump in her throat.

"We've got to ditch this car," he said, eyes steadily scanning the rearview mirror. He tensed when a pick-up truck came into view behind them.

"But it's a rental!" she protested.

"It's an easy target," he said bluntly. "Might as well take out an advertisement on which hotel you're staying at. Hard to miss a sweet little number like this."

"I suppose you're right," she murmured fretfully. They went another mile or so, with the pick-up still traveling behind them at a steady pace. It wasn't until the truck turned off onto a wooded lane that Makenna released the muscles she hadn't realized she clinched.

Beside her, Hardin obviously relaxed. Though several minutes had lapsed during their conversation, he picked up on the thread. "The police station is right beside our hotel. You could park it there. We'll go in and make a report, ask if you can leave the car in their parking lot."

"No!"

Hardin looked at her sharply. "Why not?"

"I-I don't want to bring the police into this." When he still looked dubious, she went on quickly, "I just want to go back to my hotel room and soak in a long, hot bath. My calves are screaming, from all that climbing uphill while crouched down so low, and my back is starting to really hurt. Not to mention my hand." She waved her ripped and bloodied palm his way. "I need a bath and a glass of wine. Not the police."

"We need to report this, Kenzie," he said sternly.

"And tell them what?" she asked. *That I'm not who I claim to be? That I've been lying to you this whole time and that I've committed fraud against Homeland Security?* "That a gray car was in a hurry to get around us and nearly ran us off the road, but that we didn't get the license plate number or even the make of the car?"

"Honda Civic, dark gray, probably a 2013 model. Massachusetts plates, red lettering, last numbers 27."

She refused to be impressed, continuing as if he hadn't spoken. "Or that some man shows up in several of my photographs, but never approaches me, never speaks to me, never threatens me? They'll say he was just a tourist, just like us."

"What about the gun?"

Makenna squirmed. "Maybe I didn't see a gun after all. Maybe it really was just a pair of binoculars. I don't think he could have hidden a rifle under his jacket, and I didn't see a long barrel sticking out when he came down the trail."

"You can put a scope on a Colt 357 or a 45 revolver."

Still she protested. "Maybe he's a hunter. Maybe it's squirrel season or rabbit season or something. I don't know and I don't care. I just want to go back to the hotel and soak in my tub and call it a day."

His jaw remained clinched as he studied her with his piercing blue eyes. After a long moment, she saw his curt nod out of her peripheral vision. "Fine. You take your bubble bath, I'll drop the car off at the police station."

"Then how am I supposed to get around? I have a job to do, you know. I promised K-" She caught herself just in time. "-ate, my editor, that I would do this."

"We'll call the rental agency, tell them there's something wrong with the car." He opened the glove compartment and found the pamphlet with the rental agreement. "Says here they have a branch a couple of towns over. I'm sure they'll be willing to swap out cars, especially if you'll settle for a lesser car than you paid for."

"In other words, not another flashy sports car."

"Here, we'll call them right now. Tell them you were stranded on the side of the road and had someone pull you to the police station. Tell them you have the mechanic here with you and hand me the phone."

"I-I'm not sure I can sound convincing."

"Sure you can."

Did his words have an edge to them, or was it just her nerves? He dialed the number, waited for the call to connect, then handed the phone to her.

"Yes sir, my name is Kenzie Reese. I was driving a car I rented from your company at the Manchester Airport, and all of sudden, it just died on me." She let her voice tremble just a bit, and injected just enough simpering Southern charm to sound vulnerable. "I don't know what to do! A nice gentleman came along and offered to tow me back to town, but now the car's just sitting in front of the police station and won't start. What on earth am I going to do? … Yes, sir. In fact, the mechanic is here with me now. Would you like to talk to him?"

She gladly handed the phone to Hardin, eager to get both hands back on the wheel. They were taking the winding road faster than she felt comfortable with, but getting back to the hotel was her main concern just now. She only half-listened as Hardin spouted off technical terms that she assumed had something to do with an engine, his voice taking on the nasal twang of a native New Englander. Again, she couldn't help but be impressed with his attention to detail.

When he finished his portion of the conversation, he handed the phone back to her. They were coming into the edge of town when she finally hung up and announced, "They'll swap me a four door sedan for the convertible, no later than day after tomorrow."

"And in the meantime, the convertible says parked at the police station." His tone brooked no argument, so Makenna merely nodded. "Pull up at the hotel and go on it," he continued, somewhat gentler. "I'll take care of the car. I'll come to your room when I'm done."

Again, she merely nodded. She was officially exhausted, and even talking seemed to be more effort than it was worth. She pulled into the circular drive at the front door and retrieved the picnic basket and her borrowed camera.

"Don't worry about anything else. I'll get it all out before I lock up. I don't want this car parked here any longer than necessary," Hardin told her, his eyes scanning the roadway as he slid behind the wheel.

"Okay, thanks," she murmured. She trudged into the front lobby, her mind already on the hot bath she was headed for.

Chapter 10

Makenna didn't see the woman sitting in the lobby waiting for her, but she definitely heard her. "Yoo-hoo! Kenzie! Hi, there!"

"L-Lisa." She was absolutely the last person Makenna wanted to see just now. Willing herself not to cringe, she attempted a smile. "What-What are you doing here? I thought we were meeting at the restaurant."

"We are, we are. I was just hoping to have a little chat with you, girl to girl. Got a minute? Where's that handsome hunk of a man you're usually with?" Her round eyes looked about eagerly for a glimpse of Hardin.

"He's, ah, taking care of the car," she said vaguely. She wavered where she was, before reluctantly going forward to join Lisa in the seating area. Better to talk here than in her room. "I'm headed up for a hot bath, but I've got a couple of minutes."

Lisa eyed the basket in her hand. "Ooh, romantic picnic in the mountains?"

"Something like that," Makenna murmured.

Lisa looked at her more pointedly, taking in her pale face and her bloodied palm. "Are you all right? You don't look so good."

"We were hiking in the woods and I took a tumble." For the most part, that much was true. "I'm pretty sore. In fact, I doubt I'll make dinner tonight. I think I'll just stay in."

"Oh, of course, of course. We understand. It's a good thing I dropped by this afternoon, then." She bobbed her head, setting off the motion of her full cheeks. Scooting to the edge of her seat, she touched Makenna's jean clad knee. "Sweetie, there's something I wanted to talk to you about, without Hardin around."

"Oh?"

Lisa glanced at the door to make certain the man in question had not returned. "I'm not sure how to say this, so please don't take offense. But I think there's more to your friend than meets the eye."

"I find that's the case with most people," Makenna replied slowly. She was tired, her palm hurt, her muscles ached, and her patience was wearing thin. If she had to listen to Lisa much longer, her ears would be in agony, as well.

"I hope you don't think I'm interfering," Lisa continued, not giving her a chance to reply, "but I knew his name sounded familiar. I have a friend who lives in New Braunfels, so I called her. Sure enough, she knows Hardin quite well. And she didn't have much nice to say about him."

"Honestly, Lisa, I appreciate your concern, but –"

"No, no, please hear me out. Oh, I know he seems charming enough, and Lord knows he's nice to look at, but there's something about Hardin Kaczmarek that you need to know." She lowered her voice conspiratorially and leaned in even closer. "He's had several run-ins with the law, particularly for domestic battery."

"Hardin?" Makenna couldn't keep the surprise from her voice. The man in question had been nothing but a gentleman, even chivalrous.

"I know, I know, but it's true," Lisa insisted in her nasally whine. "My friend, Cara Sims, was in a relationship with him. She said in the beginning he was charming and romantic. Then he became jealous and possessive and quite volatile. Abusive. She had to call the law several times."

"Hardin?" Makenna repeated in utter disbelief.

"She even described him, to make certain we were talking about the right man. Just under six feet, a hundred and seventy pounds of pure muscle, killer abs, great butt, amazing blue eyes, sexy smile."

"That definitely describes him."

"Apparently he has a terrible temper."

Makenna's mind flashed to glimpses she had seen of that temper. More than once today, she had thought he was not a man she would want to make angry. But that hardly made him abusive.... Did it?

"He's been arrested for disturbing the peace, destruction of public property, and several times for domestic abuse and battery. And not with just Cara. It appears to be a pattern with him," Lisa continued. Her husband wasn't there to elbow for emphasis, so she tapped Makenna on the knee smartly. She saw the younger woman's look of disbelief and hurried on to say, "Apparently his family has money and has kept his name out of the news and him out of jail. But Cara swears to me that he's the man who put her in the hospital with broken ribs and a concussion. I don't want to hurt you, I just wanted you to know what kind of man you were dealing with, honey. When you meet someone on vacation, you're meeting them out of context. You really know nothing about them, other than what they want you to know."

"Yes, that's true," Makenna murmured, thinking of her own situation.

"We girls have to stick together, you know. After all, if we don't look out for one another, who will? I just want you to be cautious, dear." The older woman patted her on the knee and gave her a sympathetic smile.

"I-I appreciate your concern, Lisa. I'll definitely keep it in mind."

Lisa rummaged through her purse and pulled out a small piece of paper. "Here. This has my cell phone number and the resort where we're staying. If you need anything at all, don't hesitate to call me. Even if it's just to talk, or if you need a new place to stay." Seeing her frown again, Lisa shrugged her rounded shoulders. "You never know, dear. If you give him the cold shoulder, he may become angry. He may stalk you after that. I also jotted down Cara's number, if you have any questions you'd like to ask her."

"Oh. Okay, thanks."

Much to Makenna's relief, Lisa stood up, signaling her visit was over. "You go on up and take that hot bath, dear. Wrap up that hand and get a good night's rest. Will you still join us for dinner tomorrow night?"

"Well, I -."

"With or without Hardin, dear. We'd be delighted to see you, either way."

Makenna felt a stab of guilt. Lisa's concern was heartfelt, yet Makenna had been quick to judge her based on her unfortunate voice. Vowing to give the woman a second chance, Makenna nodded. "I'll do my best to make it tomorrow night. And thanks again for the information, Lisa. I appreciate your concern."

"Of course, dear. Of course." After giving her an impulsive hug, picnic basket and all, Lisa scuttled out the door, leaving a very weary Makenna with too much to think about.

Ten minutes later, Makenna was immersed up to her neck in a bubble bath. She was surrounded by the essentials: soothing music, dimmed lights, hot water, and a glass of chilled wine. She didn't want to think about drivers with road rage or men with guns or handsome strangers with violent tempers. Blanking her mind, she methodically recalled all the beautiful scenery of the day – the mountains, waterfalls, covered bridges, and breathtaking vistas that were the White Mountains. A smile came to her face as she thought only of the beauty.

Her phone buzzed, alerting her to a text message. Hardin's name flashed on the screen, along with the words,

Can I come up?

Flinging suds from her fingers, Makenna dried them on a towel before texting back.

Asleep in tub right now.

TTY soon.

She took a sip of her wine and leaned back in the tub. Lisa's words kept swirling in her mind. Could it be true, was Hardin truly a man of violence? Domestic violence? Her heart screamed that it couldn't be so; he was so charming, so attentive, so easy to talk to. But her mind argued that he fit the MO so well; most abusers were charming in the beginning, until they lured their victims into their net. And she knew for certain Hardin had a dark side. She had seen his tightly coiled anger, his intensity, his hard mask of determination.

Still, she had trouble believing the worst of him. Her instincts about people were rarely wrong, and her instinct was telling her that Hardin Kaczmarek was one of the good guys. The Lewises, on the other hand.... Despite her earlier resolve to give them another chance, something about them still felt off.

With a sigh, Makenna took another sip of wine. If she got any more relaxed, she might really fall asleep in the tub.

When Hardin arrived, he was bearing gifts. He had a pizza in one hand, a bag of tortilla chips and salsa in the other.

Makenna breathed in the glorious aroma of a supreme pizza with something akin to reverence. "How did you know?"

"After a day like today, nothing else would ever do."

"See, this is why we get along so well," Makenna grinned, closing the door behind him. Surely she could trust a man who brought pizza and salsa! "Take it on over to the coffee table, we'll devour it there."

"How's the hand?" he asked, stepping into the sitting area.

"Sore, but fine. Just like the rest of me."

"At least you look refreshed." He let his eyes roam over her, not bothering to hide the appreciation in them. Her hair was still slightly damp, curling around her face and shoulders in dark rivulets. When wet, her locks appeared more chocolate than chestnut. She was wearing a pair of leopard print lounge pants, a simple white tank top, and a ridiculous pair of fuzzy green and pink slippers, all compliments of her friend.

"A hot bath does wonders for the soul," she quipped, ignoring the heat in his eyes. He, too, had showered and changed. He now wore navy wind pants and a light blue t- shirt that set off his abs and eyes.

"You're telling me. I feel like a new man." He plopped down on the sofa, smack in the middle of the cushions.

"What would you like to drink?"

Lifting a hip off the couch, he reached into his pants pocket and produced a bottle of beer. "I know you prefer wine," he said, "so I just brought the one."

"Looks like you thought of everything." She grabbed the rest of the wine from the refrigerator and a stack of napkins before joining him on the sofa.

They ate pizza straight from the box and poured salsa from the jar onto individual chips. It was casual and cozy and just what Makenna needed. She pushed thoughts of Lisa's accusations and car chases aside, concentrating on the easy conversation and good food and her oh, so charming companion.

"One last chip, and I'm done," Makenna proclaimed.

"You said that five chips ago," he teased.

"But this time I mean it. And stop counting." To prove she was done, she made a show of wiping her hands and brushing away all traces of crumbs from her face and her clothes. She sat back against the couch cushions, propping her slippered feet up on the coffee table in casual bad manners.

"Good thing I was done eating, Miss Stinky Feet."

"My feet do not stink!" she protested. "And what were you going to eat, cardboard? We wolfed down that entire pizza."

Nudging the empty box aside with his own shoe, he propped his feet up against hers. "Good point."

They sat in silence for a moment, until Makenna finally had to ask. "The car?"

"Safe and sound next door at the police station."

"What-What did you tell them?"

He looked at her for a long second before answering with a shrug. "Pretty much what you told the rental company. It seemed easier that way."

She blew out a relieved breath. She hadn't wanted to call any undue attention to herself from the police. "Now I just have to figure out how I'm going to get around tomorrow, until my replacement arrives."

"I'll take you where you need to go."

"That's not necessary." She answered so quickly, she wondered if Lisa's warning had anything to do with it. "I-I know you need to practice."

"I can still get in a few miles. Where do you need to go?"

"I was going to go further north, where the main power lines are slated to come through."

"Tell me again why Lisa Lewis thought the mob was involved?"

"Something about the Zaffino family. Apparently, they're an Italian mafia family with ties to renewable energy sources. The governments, both here and abroad, offer generous grants and subsidies to power companies who use green energy. That's just the kind of thing the mafia likes to exploit. It happened in Italy, but from everything I've been able to read, our government is keeping a close handle on things here." Makenna shrugged. "I think she was just being dramatic."

"I think I've heard that name before," he said thoughtfully.

"It sounds familiar to me, too, but I couldn't find much about them on the internet. There was one company in Chicago with a Zaffino on their board of directors, and another mention of that name in Houston. That was about it."

"So where does NorthWind come in?"

"They're the power company putting in the wind farms and the lines. From what I can see, they're perfectly legit."

"And what exactly is your assignment?"

"I'm covering the sociological and environmental effects of a major power company coming through the area. What it means for the land-owner, the average citizen, that sort of thing."

"Then you're not here to cover NorthWind or the Zaffinos or the mob connection," he clarified.

"Nope. To be honest, I didn't know there was a connection, or an alleged connection, until I heard about it from Lisa."

"So she actually told you something you didn't know? Scary thought."

With a mischievous grin, Makenna jabbed him in the arm with her elbow.

"Whoa, there, you really are learning a thing or two from her!" he protested, grabbing her elbow. "Poor Bob. That man must have a permanent bruise."

The mention of bruising brought back to mind Lisa's allegations. Makenna shifted on the couch and casually tucked her legs up under her, resettling into a position further away from him. If he suspected the move was deliberate, he never let on.

"How's your friend?" he asked suddenly.

"Who?"

"Your friend. The one in the hospital."

"Oh, yes, she's doing fine." At least, she hoped she was; she hadn't talked to Kenzie today.

"Who did you say it was again?" He was still munching on chips, and bit down into one as he spoke.

"We live in the same apartment building," she answered vaguely. Trying to sound casual, she toyed with the ties on her pajama pants. "Actually, you'll never believe what a small world it is. My friend's hospital roommate is from New Braunsfel."

"Oh, yeah?"

She looked up so that she could watch his reaction. "Yes, and she says she knows you. Her name is Cara Sims."

Hardin frowned thoughtfully. "Hmm, the name doesn't ring a bell."

"Are you sure? She seemed to know you pretty well. Described you to a tee."

"Cara Sims," he repeated, trying the name out. "No, I don't think I know her. Maybe she works in one of the stores around there. They all seem to know me quite well down at the lumberyard. Hey, yeah, I think I do know her. We did a remodel… No, wait, that was a Karen Simpson." He shrugged, looking completely sincere in his denial. "Whoever she is, I hope it's not serious."

Makenna's heart was thudding loudly as she tested the waters. "I think it was a case of domestic violence. Her- Her boyfriend beat her up."

"Scumbag!" he muttered in disgust. "I don't know how a man could ever do that to a woman, especially someone he supposedly cares about. Not that a real man ever would."

His adamant response left Makenna more confused than ever. Why would Lisa tell her such a thing, if it weren't true? And why would

Hardin pretend such disdain, if he were guilty of the same lifestyle? She put her hand to her suddenly pounding head and rubbed.

"Headache?" he asked.

"Little bit."

"Maybe we should call it a night. I don't know about you, but I'm beat."

"I am, too."

"Well, that's my cue." He was off the couch and on his feet before Makenna could untangle her own legs from beneath her. His abrupt departure took her by surprise.

"Lock the door behind me," he said needlessly as she followed him that way.

"You don't – You don't think-"

Seeing the stricken look upon her face and knowing exactly what she meant, he put a finger to her lips. "Shh. No, I don't think so. But it never hurts to use a little extra precaution."

"Okay, good," she breathed in relief.

"Is ten o'clock too late to get started tomorrow?"

"Considering I plan to sleep 'til 9:30, it sounds perfect."

"Good, then I'll make a few laps in the morning before we leave." He paused at the door to pull her into an embrace. He didn't try to kiss her, simply to hold her close. Despite herself, Makenna clung to him, needing the assurance of his strong, warm arms.

"Get some sleep," he said, dropping a chaste kiss upon her lips. "Goodnight."

"'Night."

That night, Makenna slept fitfully, dreaming of shrieking tires and flashing headlights and guns glistening in the sunlight.

But the most disturbing dream of all involved a pair of startling blue eyes and the cold, long blade of a knife.

Chapter 11

Denver, Colorado
September, 1993

"Charlie? Do you have your bags all packed?"

The little girl tugged at the overflowing duffle bag, dragging it off the bed. It hit the floor with a thud.

"What on earth do you have in there?" her mother frowned.

"I'm bringing some of my favorite rocks with me, so I can remember this place. I like it here." The little girl said with sullen defiance.

"You'll forget all about this place as soon as you see our new home. You're going to like it there, Charlie. Here in Colorado, you can't see very far because of all the mountains. But in Wyoming, you can see for miles and miles at a time."

"But I like mountains!" she whined.

"Wyoming has mountains, just not in the town where we'll live. But we'll visit them sometimes, so that you can climb on them and collect your rocks. Now, let's get you changed. We're through playing this game where we pretend you're a boy. You're going to be a little girl again."

"I liked being a boy! They get to play way cooler games than girls!"

"Yes, but it was just make-believe. You know that. This new game is better. You get to be a little girl named Amy, and you get to have your very own kitten."

"A kitten?" She brightened immediately. She had begged and begged her parents for a pet, but they always said no.

"I have some pretty new clothes for you," her mother said, pulling out a purple sweater and a pair of purple corduroy pants. "But you have to wear them and call yourself Amy if you want to keep your kitten."

The little girl looked into the mirror. Her mother hadn't cut her hair lately, and it was just beginning to touch the collar of her shirt. For a boy, it was a little long; for a girl, it was a little short, but being a girl again might not be so hard.

The boy game had been fun and allowed her to do fun things she couldn't do as a girl, like play with bugs and pop firecrackers and shoot BB guns and learn to burp the alphabet with her friend Joey. But she always had to remember they couldn't go into the bathroom together and she couldn't change clothes in front of him. She didn't like to use the men's restroom in public, because they were always smelly and dirty and had strange words and drawings all over the walls. And Joey's older brother sometimes showed them pictures of naked girls and told jokes that she didn't understand. Maybe it was time she stopped pretending to be a boy and started being a girl again. And she really did like kittens.

Still, she would miss Charlie. He had been a lot of fun.

Just before her mother stripped the dinosaur tee shirt off her, the little girl touched the reflection in the mirror one last time.

"I'll never forget you," she promised the image in her mirror.

Chapter 12

Further north of the resort towns, the rugged beauty of New Hampshire was on full display. There was less tourism here, and more of a rural flavor. Makenna had no problem finding the intended path of NorthWind's power lines; protest signs and banners were the only distractions marring the natural beauty of the area. Obviously the landowners and residents were against the power giant coming through their backyard.

They ate lunch at a small diner in one of the little towns, where the noonday discussion was all about the power company. Among the discord was a lone defendant of progress, a young college professor who tried to argue with his older comrades about the merits of the project; local jobs, modernization, green energy efforts, higher energy capacity. He made some excellent points, and Makenna asked to interview him after the debate waned. Kenzie's assignment was for the visual story, but Makenna wanted to tell her own version of the story with words. She was already gathering the information to aide in the photography assignment, so why not compile it and submit a freelance article to *Now* or some other magazine? It couldn't hurt, she told herself. And anything would help her dwindling bank account and her slim employment prospects.

By early afternoon, they were heading back toward their hotel. They stopped at a country store known for its selection of cheese and locally canned jams and jellies, selecting several varieties for souvenirs and sampling. They started a pile at the counter as they moved through the narrow aisles.

As they lingered over a display of maple candies and tried the array of samples offered, Hardin leaned in to steal a kiss. When her response lacked the enthusiasm of the day before, he straightened immediately and frowned. "Bad breath?" he queried. "Bad technique?"

Makenna sighed, shaking her head. "Bad night." She downplayed her response to his kiss. "I hardly slept a wink, what with all the cars racing through my dreams. Guess I'm more tired than I thought."

He touched her cheek with a gentle finger. "I understand. I was a little restless, myself."

"At least there's no sign of either car today." She offered the thought with a smile.

"That is something to smile about," he agreed. He stood there for a moment longer, his intense blue eyes studying her. "You sure you're all right?"

"Just tired," she said. "And I've got a lot on my mind right now, thinking about that little meeting at the diner and everything Simon Hanks had to say."

"He was a knowledgeable young man," Hardin nodded. "Hey, I saw some locally bottled sodas in the back cooler. I'm going to go check them out."

"Okay, pick one out for me, too."

"What flavor?"

"Surprise me."

Makenna popped another candy sample into her mouth and moved on along the display, looking for the corresponding selections in full-size. She sensed someone behind her but didn't bother to turn. "Find any good flavors?" she asked as she perused a label.

Instead of Hardin's pleasant tenor, she heard a low, raspy voice with a definite Northern brogue. "I've got a message for your father."

Makenna whirled around, knocking three packages of candy from the shelf with the sudden movement. One of the packages came open, noisily spilling little hard maple candies all over the wooden floor. A short man with swarthy skin and a dark ponytail stood directly behind her, blocking her path. His right hand was poised in his jacket pocket, and Makenna's first thought was that he held a gun. She immediately forgot about the candy scattered on the floor.

"I-I beg your p-p..." she finally managed to sputter. Then, with the sharp bark of total surprise, "What?"

"Tell your old man we're looking for him."

"My-? I'm afraid you me confused with someone else." When she started to turn back around, the man grabbed her arm with his left hand and jerked her hard in his direction.

"I know exactly who you are, Miss *Reese*," he said in a dark, threatening tone. He sneered her last name. "Tell Joseph Mandarino we're looking for him."

Makenna stared at him in total confusion. Who was Joseph Mandarino? What did that have to do with Kenzie's father? And how was she supposed to know where the man was? Even Kenzie didn't keep track of him.

"Tell him we have unfinished business," the man continued.

"I-I have no idea what- what you're talking about," Makenna stammered. "Or who you're talking about."

"I'm talking about your old man!" he snarled.

"So who's Joseph Mandarino?" By now she was more confused than frightened.

The man glared at her through narrowed eyes. He stood with his feet planted a foot apart, his shoulders squared, his mouth set in a grim line. It was a practiced pose that made grown men cower, but Makenna only frowned, totally baffled.

"Just give him the message," he growled. He whirled and was gone, leaving Makenna to stare after him.

Hardin found her that way, standing among the scattered candy, one bag still hanging limply in her hand as she stared toward the door.

"How does Orange Cream sound? Or Old Time Sassafras?" He was reading from the bottles in his hand and didn't glance up until he reached her. Seeing her pale face, he was immediately concerned. "Kenzie? Kenzie, what's wrong? You look like you've seen a ghost."

"No, he-he was flesh and blood," she murmured.

"What are you talking about?"

"There-There was a man. He came up and said he- he had a message for my father."

"Your father?" he asked sharply.

"Yes. It-it still doesn't make -"

He cut in without apology. "What did he look like? Where did he go?"

"Short, dark, with a ponytail." She gestured toward the door. "He left."

"Here, take this." He shoved the bottles into her hand and took off toward the door. Snapping out of her stupor, she stepped over the candies and hurried after him, watching through the window as he ran toward the road, searching for signs of the mysterious man.

"Ma'am, did you want that soda?" The salesclerk called from behind the counter. "You can put it up here with the rest of your things."

"Oh, yes, sorry." She looked down, almost surprised to see the cold bottles of soda in her hands. "I'm ready to check out now."

It took forever for the woman to ring up their selections. Hardin came to the door twice, impatiently checking on her progress. By the time she came out, two bags in tow, he was behind the wheel with the motor running. Makenna barely shut the truck's door before he peeled out.

"Did you get a look at what he was driving?" he asked.

She shook her head. "No."

"Tell me again what happened."

Makenna replayed the scene in detail. Hardin interrupted a few times with questions, then asked another when she was finished. "And you aren't familiar with the name Joseph Mandarino?"

"Never heard of it. I have no idea what the man was talking about. If he hadn't called me by name, I'd think he had me totally confused with someone else." *Actually*, she thought, *he does. So do you.*

Hardin banged a fist against the steering wheel, muttering a few choice words. Makenna frowned, wondering where the show of anger came from. She chose to remain silent, settling back into the seat and resting her head. Confusion was giving way to another headache.

They traveled in silence on their way back to the hotel. Despite the delightful scenery, they took little notice of their surroundings. Makenna's mind was whirling in a thousand directions, while Hardin's attention was devoted to the road.

A few miles from town, Hardin's savage oath jerked Makenna from her wanderings. "Oh, hell, no!"

She followed his gaze into the rear view mirror. Sure enough, a familiar gray car appeared behind them. It was several paces back, but when Hardin suddenly sped up, so did it.

"What is going on?" Makenna wailed miserably. "I don't understand why all this is happening!" Seeing Hardin's hand move beneath the seat and pull something out, she gasped. "What are you doing? What is that? Is that a gun?!"

"Damn right it's a gun," he said, laying the Glock in the seat beside him. "I'm tired of this game, but they want to play, we'll play."

"Play?" she squeaked. "That's a real gun! There's nothing play about that!"

He made no comment as he watched the gray car in the mirror. It followed at a safe distance behind, making no attempt to close the gap between them. Even when another vehicle pushed between them, the gray car kept its steady pace in the distance.

"What, do they think we don't see them?" Makenna asked in irritation. Being tailed at a conservative distance was almost as maddening as being followed at close range.

"They want us to know they're there," Hardin said with certainty. "But we're about to lose them. On the off chance they don't know where we're staying, I'm not leading them straight to our door. If they wanna find us, we'll make 'em work for it."

Another half mile down the road, Hardin found his opportunity. A vehicle still separated them from the gray car, and a string of oncoming traffic was coming from town as they neared the outskirts of the village. Without warning, Hardin took a sharp left across the other lane, onto a side street. By the time the gray car could follow, the truck was speeding down a twisting series of streets and lanes.

"Do you know where we even are?" Makenna finally had to ask, holding on to the grab bar above her head as they took a sharp curve.

"'Course," he said, flashing her a grin. To her amazement, he actually seemed to be enjoying the dizzy trail he led them down.

"I've never seen these streets," she said. They were in a semi-residential area alongside the mountain, far removed from the flashy facade of the resort town's front roads.

"I rode my bike here this morning. Our hotel is just up ahead," he assured her. Another turn, and they were on a bumpy access road lined with trees and mountain.

Sure enough, in just a few minutes he pulled into the backside of their hotel's parking lot. "Your hotel key will unlock that back entrance," he told her.

"Where will you park the truck?" she asked.

"Off site," was all he said. "If you can take one of the bags, I'll get the other."

Makenna eyed the gun still lying out in the open. "You know we need to talk," she told him.

"Every thing's going to be all right, Kenzie," he assured her. He caught her by the back of the neck and pulled her in for a gentle kiss.

She leaned her forehead against his. "What is going on? Why is this happening?"

"I don't know, but I'm going to find out. I'll be back in a couple of hours."

"Where are you going?" she asked in alarm.

"I'm just going to look around, see what I can see."

"But -"

"Shh, I'll be fine," he assured her, offering another quick kiss. "And I'll be back in plenty of time for our dinner date with the Lewises. Wouldn't want to miss that, after all," he grinned, feigning enthusiasm.

"If you're sure…."

"I am. Now scoot, so I can get this over with and find a place to hide the truck."

"Be careful." She glanced dubiously at the gun before gathering her paraphernalia and easing out the door.

"I'll call you in a little while," he promised.

He waited for her to get safely inside the hotel before gunning the motor and pulling out the back entrance.

Makenna deposited her things and immediately called Kenzie.

"What is going on here?" she demanded the moment her friend answered. "What have you gotten me into this time?"

"And hello to you, too, my friend. Yes, I'm fine, thanks for asking."

"You don't have to be sarcastic," Makenna grumbled. "I'm sorry I didn't ask first. How are you?"

"Fine. Black and blue and yellow around the edges, sore as all get out, but basically fine. I take it you're not?"

"Hardly. Who is Joseph Mandarino?"

"Wasn't he our Political Science professor second semester?"

"That was Medeiros."

"Oh, okay, then never heard of him. Why?"

"What about Tamara Mandarino?" She wasn't sure why, but that name suddenly popped into her mind.

"Hmm, nope. Why, who is she? Is she the woman with the irritating voice? Are they the couple from Texas?"

"No. But this afternoon some man gave me a message for your father."

"My father?" Kenzie squeaked, then grew quiet.

"Kenzie, what is going on? I'm being run off the road and stalked and approached by total strangers with messages for your father! What did you get me into?"

"What-What kind of messages?" Her friend's voice was little more than a whisper.

"Some cryptic message to tell him someone is looking for him."

"Wh-Who? This Mandarino person?"

"No, I'm supposed to tell him the same thing. I think." Makenna frowned, trying to recall the exact wording. "None of it made any sense. Maybe the man even thought your father's name was Joseph Mandarino, I'm not sure. I thought he had me mixed up with someone else, but he called me by name. Your name, that is." When her friend did not reply, Makenna repeated, "What is going on, Kenzie?"

"I-I don't know. Honestly."

"But you have your suspicions." She could tell by the hesitancy in her roommate's voice.

"Yes, I have my suspicions." Her sigh carried over the telephone. "I have serious suspicions about my father. I-I think maybe…"

"Maybe what?"

"I think he might have been involved in something he shouldn't have been involved in," Kenzie said quietly.

"Like what?"

"I don't know. Honestly. I just know we moved around a lot when I was a kid."

"That's hardly proof of doing something wrong, Kenzie. A lot of people move around a lot."

"We never stayed anywhere more than a couple of years, tops. I was never allowed to join any groups at school, never allowed to invite any friends over. Half the time I was home-schooled."

"I know, Ken, and I'm sorry you had such a lonesome childhood," Makenna said softly. She could hear the pain in her friend's voice, could feel it in her own heart.

"I was never allowed to have my picture taken with the class. I only have a handful of pictures to show for my entire childhood." There was a catch in her voice at the admission.

"Was it a religious thing?"

She laughed, the sound void of humor. "We never went to church. We never went anywhere, Makenna. We never made friends, we never socialized, we never had any fun."

"That doesn't mean your father was involved in anything wrong. It means he was a lousy father."

She could hear someone speaking to Kenzie in the background. "Look, the physical therapist just came in and I've got to go."

"Okay, but we're not done here. We have some serious talking to do," Makenna warned.

"You be careful, Makenna. I couldn't stand it if anything happened to you, especially because of me."

"I'm fine," Makenna said, hoping it was true. "Call me when you're done."

"Okay. Bye."

Makenna rubbed her hands over her face wearily. What a day! And she still had one more phone call to make….

She hesitated only a moment before she dialed the number Lisa Lewis had given her. She almost hoped the other woman didn't answer, but after three rings, she heard a soft Southern voice on the other end of the line. "Hello?"

"Is this Cara Sims?"

"Yes. Who is this?"

"My name is M –" she caught herself just in time, "McKenzie Reese. I got your number from Lisa Lewis. I had a few questions I wanted to ask you about a man named Hardin Kaczmarek."

"Lordy, that was a name I was hoping to never hear again!" the other woman said bitterly. "What did he do this time?"

"N-Nothing. I met him a couple of days ago, here in New Hampshire."

"New Hampshire? I didn't think he'd ever leave Texas, but good riddance, I'd say!"

"He's vacationing here."

The woman snorted. "Probably running from the law. I hear he's mixed up in all sorts of crap these days. You haven't fallen for his lies, have you?"

"I-I have no idea what are lies, and what are not," Makenna hedged.

"If words are comin' from his mouth, they're lies," the woman assured her. "Granted, it's a hot mouth capable of doing some amazing things, but tellin' the truth ain't one of them."

"Do you mind if I ask how you know Hardin?"

"Do you mean how did we meet, or how do I *know* him?"

"I-I suppose both."

"We met at a barbeque given by mutual friends. The man swept me off my feet. He was the best lookin' man I'd ever seen, and, Lord! What a fine body! He took me home that night, called me the next day, sent me flowers, did all the things no man had ever done for me before. He was the most charming, flattering, *nicest* man I'd ever met."

Able to visualize every word, Makenna nodded in total understanding. "What- What happened?"

"We moved in together. And all of sudden it all changed. He became obsessive and jealous and suspicious of everything I did. I wasn't allowed to have friends or use the phone or wear makeup or do anything that didn't involve him. And if I did, I paid for it. The first time it was just a busted lip. The last time I ended up in the hospital with a couple of busted ribs, a concussion, and a restraining order against him. They threw him in jail, overnight this time, and I high-tailed it out of there before he could come home and beat me again. I hope to God I never see him again as long as I live."

By the time Cara Sims finished with her story, tears were streaming down Makenna's face. She felt like the ground had shifted beneath her feet. She was alone in an unfamiliar state, caught up in some crazy scheme where people were chasing her and giving her cryptic messages for a man she didn't even know, and the one person she thought she could trust was a violent monster. Despite his charm and his wit and his tantalizing kisses, Hardin Kaczmarek was apparently guilty of domestic abuse, and it was hardly an isolated incident.

"You didn't give him this number, did you?" the other woman asked suddenly. "If he tracks me down, I'm afraid he might kill me this time!"

"No, n-no, of course not," Makenna assured her hastily. "I would never do that. And I'm sorry to have bothered you, but I needed to know if what Lisa told me was the truth."

"If she told you Hardin Kaczmarek was a low-down, lying, mean, rotten coward who beats on women, then, yes, she was telling you the truth. If she warned you to stay away for your own good, she was telling the truth. Believe me. Do yourself a favor and get as far away from the man as you can."

"Thank you for your time," was all she could manage before she punched the 'end' button and threw her cell phone on the couch, then curled herself into a ball and cried.

Until that moment, she hadn't realized just how much she really and truly *liked* Hardin Kaczmarek. It went far beyond the physical, even though there was a great chemistry between them; he was so easy to talk to, so seemingly sincere, so charming and witty. He was interested in *her*, and what she had to say, what she thought, how she felt. Makenna felt like she had known him for years, rather than a few days. Hardin made her laugh, made her feel special, made her feel alive. Best of all, he made her feel safe. Despite the crazy situation she found herself in, she thought she had an ally in him, a safe harbor in the storm. She had even found herself thinking there might be a future for them, once they got back to Texas. It was crazy, but she thought she might actually be falling in love with the man, even though she barely knew him.

It just went to show that people weren't always what they seemed. Apparently an evil and abusive man hid behind the engaging facade that was Hardin Kaczmarek. And he was armed with a gun.

Ignoring the fact that she, too, hid a secret, Makenna allowed herself five more minutes to wallow in self-pity. Then she wiped the tears away, resolved to end her relationship with the handsome stranger, hardened her heart to love, and deliberately reached for her camera. She still had a job to do, and the days here were quickly slipping away.

Chapter 13

Engrossed in her work, Makenna jerked when she heard the knock on her door. She glanced at the time as she went to answer, surprised to see that over two hours had elapsed. Peering through the peephole and seeing Hardin on the other side, she felt an unfamiliar wave of fear wash over her. Yesterday, her heart leapt with excitement when he was near; today she couldn't forget the terrible stories Cara Sims had told her.

She knew it was important not to make him angry. She needed to extricate herself from their budding relationship gently, without making him suspicious of her reasons. Praying she had the skills to pull it off, Makenna took a deep breath and unlocked the door.

"Hey," he said. Ever the gentleman, or so he pretended, he asked, "Can I come in?"

"Of course." She forced herself to open the door wide and pretend nothing was wrong. "Did you find out anything?"

Hardin ran his hand over the back of his head, ruffling his short hair. "Not a thing." When she hovered near the door, he sank onto a nearby barstool. She thankfully put the bar between them, stepping to the other side and casually leaning onto it.

"You didn't see the gray car anymore?"

"I got a glimpse of it cruising down the main road. I tried to keep up, following a couple of streets over, but I lost it. I even made myself visible and headed out of town three different times, giving them the chance to follow, but they didn't take the bait."

"What about the green Malibu?"

"Haven't seen it since yesterday."

"Was that only yesterday?" she asked, amazed that so much had happened in that time.

"Hard to believe, but yeah." He let out a weary sigh, running his hand over his hair again in a gesture of frustration. They both fell silent, lost in thought, before he straightened on the stool and changed the subject. "So, what time do you want to meet the Lewises? I say we get this over with as soon as possible and call it an early night. Say you have a lot of work to do or something."

Seeing the perfect opportunity, Makenna jumped on it. She hoped the wild pounding of her heart wouldn't drown out her words. She tried for a normal tone as she said, "Actually, that's no exaggeration. In fact, I think I'm going to have to cancel on dinner."

Hardin looked at her sharply. She saw the way his shoulders stiffened, even though he gave no other indication of displeasure. "Oh?"

"Honesty, I have a ton of work to do." She motioned to the coffee table, where her laptop sat amid scattered papers and notebooks and her camera equipment. "I've been working on it since we got back, and I'm nowhere near done. I only have a couple of more days here, and I need to see what I'm lacking, what I still need to shoot, who I still need to interview, that sort of thing. Talking to those people today gave me a lot more to think about. So I think it's best if I just stay in tonight, and work on the project."

Hardin was slow in responding. When he looked up, his blue eyes were clearly troubled, and Makenna felt her heart tumble and dive. The last thing she wanted to do was hurt him, even if what Cara Sims said was true. For four days, he had been her friend. In spite of everything she now knew about him, she was going to miss him, and the thought of what might have been.

"I understand," he said. He reached out and took her hand, forcing her to hold hands with him. "Really, I do. But I get the feeling there's more going on here. Or maybe I should say, 'not' going on."

"I-I don't know what you mean," she hedged, avoiding his eyes.

He ran his thumb over her fingers, causing shivers to dance up her arm. There was no denying these were shivers of delight, not fear. "I'm getting the distinct feeling that something has changed. For you, anyway. I had a great time yesterday." His tone was almost accusatory.

"I did, too!" The moment the words were out, she regretted them. She was supposed to be wiggling out of their relationship, not encouraging it. If she admitted how very much yesterday had meant to her, in spite of the car chase and the man with the gun, he would assume she was still interested. She was sending mixed messages, even to herself.

Makenna heaved a sigh and shuffled her way between honesty and excuses. "I did have fun yesterday. It was all fantastic… the mountains, the picnic, the waterfalls, the scenery-"

"The bridges," he broke in softly.

She glanced at his eyes, noting the twinkle in their blue depths. Darn, but the man was so downright *likable*! Being honest, she couldn't help but smile. "Yes, and the bridges. Everything was wonderful. Except for, of course, nearly being ran off the mountain by a speeding car and having a man follow us through the woods with a gun. I definitely could have done without either of those!"

"I'm not making light of all that, or of what happened today. But I'm not talking about that, Kenzie," he said reproachfully. "I'm talking about us. Something has changed between us, and I don't think I like it very much. I know I don't."

Makenna pulled her hand from his and straightened. "Look, I-I had an amazing time yesterday, in spite of everything. But…"

"There's always a but," he sighed. When she said nothing, silently nibbling on her bottom lip without looking him in the eye, he asked, "Was it something I said? Something I did?"

Makenna hesitated, not sure how to answer. What she finally said was absolutely the truth, even if not all of it. "This whole thing has been happening awfully fast, Hardin. I feel like I've known you forever, but the truth is, five days ago we were total strangers."

"I know," he admitted. "But I just felt this instant connection with you."

"I felt it, too. You're so easy to talk to." For an instant, she stumbled into his clear blue eyes. With a mental shake, she pulled herself out and continued, "But I came here on assignment, and I can't let my personal feelings come between me and the job I was sent to do. It's very important that I do a good job here, for a lot of reasons." *If you only knew!* "Please understand, I-I can't put a four day friendship before a life-long dream."

If she didn't know better, she would think that was admiration shining in his eyes. He nodded, but his brow wrinkled in consternation. "I do understand," he insisted. "And I can fully appreciate your dedication and your professionalism. It's just that… it felt like it was more than just a friendship. Whatever it is, I was hoping we could continue this –" he waved his hand back and forth between them, "once we got home. We don't live that far away from one another."

"I-I can't make any promises," she countered. "I have to concentrate on this assignment right now. That has to be my focus. That, and finding out what on earth is going on with these crazy car chases."

"So that's what we'll do. We'll keep things casual, *for now*," he emphasized with a glint in his eyes, "and we'll concentrate on finding out who drives these cars and why they're after you."

"I can't ask you to do that. You have to practice, and I've already taken up so much of your time. I'll be fine. I'm only here for two more days."

"Kenzie," he said, his voice suddenly sounding stern. "I may be willing to back off on pursuing a relationship with you, but there's no way in hell that I'm leaving you to fend for yourself against these unknown men. What kind of man do you think I am?"

His amazing blue eyes were filled with concern and something more. Hurt? Disappointment? Betrayal? She tried telling herself not to be moved by the azure depths, but he was making it difficult. Before she had to answer, she was saved by the ringing of her telephone.

"Sorry, let me get this," she murmured, racing around the bar to retrieve her phone off the couch. She didn't recognize the number, so her voice was a bit cautious as she answered, "Hello?"

"Yes, hello, Kenzie. This is Simon Hanks. We met this afternoon at the diner."

"Oh, yes, Simon, hello." She glanced at Hardin, who tried to hide the frown that flashed briefly across his handsome face.

"I enjoyed the talk we had today. You have a very inquisitive mind."

"And you were very helpful. You gave me some very good information and a lot to think about." Partly for Hardin's benefit, she expounded on the topic. "In fact, that's what I've been doing this afternoon, researching some of the points you made. It's created some very intense digging on my part."

"I'd be happy to share my notes, save you from all that work."

"Now you tell me!"

"I was thinking we might be able to have dinner tonight. I could give you my notes then."

He was hitting on her? Makenna tried to keep the surprise off her face as she stole another glimpse at Hardin. "Uhm… I really have a lot of work I need to do," she said, biting on her lip.

"You can bring your boyfriend along, if you want."

"He's not my boyfriend," she corrected him quickly. She refused to look at Hardin's reaction.

"What you asked me today, about the mob being involved.... I didn't want to discuss it there, but I may have some information you'd find interesting."

"What kind of information?"

"I'd rather not discuss it over the phone, but I think I have a file you would like to see."

"I think you might be right," Makenna agreed, fully intrigued.

"You'll have dinner with me then?"

"Yes, I'd love to. Except, I don't have a car. My rental broke down."

"I can pick you up."

"I'd appreciate it. What time?"

"I could be there in about an hour."

"That sounds fine." She gave him directions and agreed to meet him in the lobby in an hour. When she turned around, Hardin was no longer trying to hide his scowl. His face was set in hard lines, his frown obvious.

"That was Simon Hanks, the man from earlier today," she explained needlessly.

"So I gathered."

His cold tone and dark countenance reminded her of Cara Sims' accusations. A tiny prickle of apprehension worked its way up her spine. The last thing she wanted to do was provoke him.

"He-He has some information he wants to give me. He even offered his notes on all his research."

"Sounds like that will be helpful." Even though his words were conversational, his expression was still hard.

"I wish I had known that two hours ago, before I spent all that time doing my own research," she said wistfully. For some reason, she hesitated in telling Hardin about the mob connection. It was something Cara had said, although she couldn't recall exactly what it had been. Some inner voice cautioned her to keep this latest tidbit to herself for now.

"Then you should definitely go."

In spite of everything she now knew about him, her heart was sending mixed signals to her brain again. She was feeling guilty for breaking her dinner date with him, only to go out with another man and making the plans in front of him, no less. She could see the hurt in his blue eyes, the bitter slap of rejection upon his handsome face. He was being so understanding about it, so supportive. Could she have been wrong? What if Cara wasn't telling her the truth?

Stop it! Her mind hissed. She had covered enough stories on domestic violence to know that most perpetrators came across as charming and sincere in the beginning. Even after the abuse, these men could often elicit sympathy from their own victims with their act of remorse and sincerity. Men like Hardin were excellent actors. She could not afford to forget that.

"If his information is as good as he hinted, this could be the angle I was looking for, the one thing that will blow this project out of the water." Makenna chattered nervously as she walked toward the door, signaling that it was time for him to leave. "It could also save me a ton work on research. Really, I can't afford *not* to meet with him tonight."

At the door, Hardin turned around to face her. "I get it, Kenzie. And I understand. I may not like it, but I understand." He started to reach out to her, thought better of it, and dropped his hand. "Have a good time tonight. And be careful. Keep your eyes out for anything suspicious."

"I'm sure I'll be fine."

"I just want you to be safe, Kenzie. That's the important thing."

She felt the sting of tears behind her eyes. Why did he have to be so nice? She almost wished he would be mean, yell at her, accuse her of leading him on and dumping him for another guy. Anything to keep her from feeling so sad right now, from making her feel like such a heel; anything to keep her from caring about him.

"Thank you, Hardin," she said softly. Sincerely. "For everything."

He looked as if he wanted to say something more, to reach out for her again, but he held himself in check.

As she blinked away a tear, he was gone.

Makenna took a quick shower and changed into jeans and one of the blouses from her own closet, a simple plaid shirt layered over a tee. She waited in the lobby until she saw the professor pull up in a blue car, then met him outside before he had a chance to come in.

"Where do you suggest we eat?" he asked as he slid in behind the wheel.

"I hear there's a nice seafood restaurant just down the street," she offered. Anywhere but the restaurant where she and Hardin were supposed to be dining with the Lewises. She wondered if Hardin would brave the couple solo, or if he would beg off for the evening. *Stop thinking about him,* she scolded herself. *You put an end to it, and that's that. You had no choice. Now get over it.* Still, to think of the look in his gorgeous blue eyes....

"Are you cold?" Simon asked in concern, seeing her shiver.

"No, I like the chill in the air. It's a lot different from what I'm used to."

They chatted about the weather and their hometowns and colleges as they drove to the restaurant, settled at a table, and ordered their meal. It wasn't until the waitress was gone and they were nibbling on warm biscuits that they broached the topic that brought them together.

"So you really piqued my interest on the telephone," Makenna told him, tucking a curl of auburn hair behind her ear. "What was the information you wanted to share?"

"You asked me if I knew anything about the mob being involved in this project. Do you mind if I ask where you got your information?" he asked curiously.

"Honestly, I came across it totally by accident."

Simon Hanks nodded. In his late twenties, the Dartmouth College instructor had neatly trimmed blond hair and nice blue eyes, although they lacked the vibrancy of Hardin's. "That doesn't surprise me. As far as I know, not many people are even aware of the connection between organized crime and NorthWind Energy."

"So what is the connection?"

"Back in the late 80's, the government was trying to generate more interest in renewable energy and encourage power companies to pursue efforts in that direction. Because of the astronomical cost, the U.S. government and the IEPA were offering some very lucrative grants and incentives to American companies."

"IEPA?"

"International Energy & Power Alliance. Even though first generation technology like hydroelectric plants have been in practice here for over a hundred years, the government was pushing for companies to develop and practice second generation technology such as solar heating and cooling, wind power, solar photovoltaics, that sort of thing. In 1990, a new conglomerate came into existence, an energy company named Modern Power who promised to aggressively pursue and provide its energy through renewable resources. They were particularly focused on wind power."

Makenna frowned. "So where does the mafia come into play?"

"All over the field," Simon said with a dry laugh. "To begin with, half of the companies that made up Modern Power were either empty shell corporations or were legitimate companies owned, for the most part, by organized crime. The Zaffino family was the key player."

Makenna nodded. There was that name again.

"From what I gather, Modern Power used government funds to literally build one of the companies supposedly already under its umbrella. NorthWind existed only on paper until grants paid for it to be built. Early on, NorthWind was awarded several government contracts to build wind farms. The government practically paid them to build the farms, which they then sold to other power companies and, in one case, even back to the government, enabling huge profits."

As the waitress delivered their salads and left, Makenna nodded. "I know that emissions trading and energy credits can make for very lucrative business deals. It's an invisible commodity with an inaccurate scale of measurement, leaving the field wide-open for fraud and tax evasion. I don't know a lot about carbon credits or green tags, but even I can see how the system can be abused. And why organized crime would be attracted to the whole scheme." She cocked her head sideways, thinking. "But in the early '90's? Had the United States even started emissions trading back then?"

"The Clean Air Act of 1990 established the first cap and trade system in the U.S. as part of the Acid Rain Program. Modern Power was a very forward-thinking company. They could see the potential for future money making schemes, although I believe their main focus, at the time, was in obtaining free money from the government through grants and credits and subsidies. Many of those early grants were for research, but half the time no actual research was being done. Again, dummy corporations and non-existent research teams."

"How did they get away with it?"

Simon shrugged. "It was a new market with little accountability. Plus, there were fewer overseeing governing agencies back then. All they had to do was look good on paper, which they did."

"But NorthWind is a legitimate company."

"Now it is, but it was built on fraud."

"And you know this, how?"

He offered a sheepish smile. "Like you, I more or less stumbled upon it, quite by accident," he admitted. "When I was a kid, my uncle had a buddy who was an accountant for a big corporation. One day the guy came by my uncle's while we were all there for a family dinner. I was outside playing, building a house with blocks and dirt and sticks and anything else I could find. The buddy stayed outside and struck up a conversation with me while he waited for my uncle, even helped me put the roof on my house. He said he liked building things, too, but when I asked what he built, he laughed. He had this far-off look in his eyes. He told me he was building a future fortune for his boss.

"You know how people do, sometimes they say things to a kid because they know the kid doesn't really understand. Sometimes a kid is a safe sounding board. So that day, this guy starts telling me all about something called green energy, and how he was building make-believe companies so that one day his boss would get credit for them. I thought we were talking about green grass. While he sat there and told me all about false numbers and energy credits and using money from Uncle Sam and a bunch of other stuff I didn't understand, I was picturing smoke stacks built out of grass, and wondering what would keep them from catching on fire.

"When my uncle came out, he and the buddy went out to his car and had a heated discussion. About a week later, this guy's picture was on the news. He and his whole family had disappeared, and the police were asking for information on them. I couldn't understand how a guy and his wife and two kids could just vanish into thin air. I heard my family talking about it, and my uncle said he heard the mob was involved. Being a little kid, I was fascinated by the mob and gangsters and anything that reminded me of Dick Tracy. The movie had just come out, and my brother and I had all the action figures. Anyway, I heard my uncle saying he thought his buddy was involved in some sort of scam. Not only had he done something illegal, he then double-crossed the mob. My uncle thought he probably disappeared before the mob could get to him and kill him."

"How do you know they didn't just kill his entire family?"

"Because the mob was still looking for him. They even approached my uncle and scared the shit out of him, and that was a couple of months later."

Makenna chewed on her lower lip. "So you're telling me that one of the biggest power companies in the northeast was built on fraud and has ties to the Italian mafia. Apparently very few people know about the connection, yet you're offering me access to your files. Why?" she asked bluntly. A story like this could be huge, but she imagined it came with strings. "What do you want me to do with this information?"

"Nothing."

"Nothing? You do realize I'm a reporter?"

"I know who you are, Kenzie Reese." His blue eyes met hers without wavering. "And I believe you are a caring, responsible journalist who will take all accounts into consideration before pursuing this story."

"I-I don't understand. You tell me this incredible story but yet, you want me to keep it quiet? You want me to sit on a huge story that could have international implications of major fraud and wrong-doing?"

"Basically, yes."

"Why would you even ask that?" she asked, incredulous.

"Because I truly believe pursuing this story would do more harm than good."

"If what you have been telling me is true, NorthWind deliberately set out to deceive the government. They provided false information to obtain grants and subsidies, used public funds to make enormous profits for personal gain, and set up a massive scheme of deception that is still reaping benefits today. I'm sure the guy was talking about Emission Reduction Credits; report current high levels of pollution – on a non-existent power company, no less – so that once they built the company with government funds, they could be 'rewarded' for lowering their emissions. I'm not sure how they knew to do that way back then, but it was a brilliant scheme. And I think the public deserves to know about it."

"And what purpose would it serve? Modern Power may have used false information and ill-gotten monies to build their business, but NorthWind is now a globally responsible company who is both environmentally friendly and economically oriented. If you were to expose this story, thousands of jobs would be lost. This entire project would be scrapped, the firm's assets would be frozen, the economy would suffer, and no real purpose would be served."

"But what they did was illegal."

"There's no proof."

"You told me you had a file, you had research."

"I did do research. You did, too. Did you find any of this in the records?"

"No," Makenna admitted. "But you made the connection. How did you know NorthWind was the same company that man told you about when you were a kid?"

Again, Simon shrugged. "I was always haunted by that story… the look in the guy's eyes when he talked, the connection to the mob, the thought of an entire family disappearing … I was just a little kid when it happened, but I never forgot it. When this whole project with NorthWind came up and generated so much opposition, I wanted to know more about the company behind it. I started researching, and the whole time, I kept thinking about that guy and what he told me about building make-believe companies. I never found any blatant signs of wrongdoing, but I found a lot of loose ends, mostly those shell companies I told you about. Most of them had gone out of business, or changed names, or sold to legitimate corporations. Even the conglomerate itself is no longer in existence, having broken up several years ago. I did find one old story that hinted at suspected fraud, but nothing could be proven so no charges were ever made. But I somehow just knew this was the company that guy was talking about."

"What about the connection to the Zaffino family?"

"Nothing current. They may have initiated Modern Power, and I'm sure they were the ones who profited from the original grants, but there is no direct link between NorthWind and the Zaffino family."

Frustration mounted within Makenna. "I don't understand. If there's nothing to tie them together, how did you make the connection?"

"Through my uncle," the professor said on a sigh. "A few months ago, I brought the subject up. I asked him if his buddy was ever heard from again, and he said no. Then I asked if he had been connected to NorthWind Energy, and my uncle went white as a ghost. He asked me what I knew, why I would even think that, where I had gotten my information. He was so defensive, I knew I was on the right track. Then he started yelling at me to mind my own business and asked if I had any idea how powerful the Zaffino family was. Up until then, I had never heard that name. As soon as I got home, I researched them, discovered they are part of the Italian mafia. So I started looking at Modern Power and NorthWind from a different angle, trying to find a link to them and the Zaffinos. If I hadn't known what I was looking for, I would have missed it completely. But I finally found one name that told me I was right about everything."

"Your uncle's friend, the accountant?" Makenna guessed.

Simon's eyes twinkled. "Very astute, Miss Reese. Once I started looking for Joey Mandarino, I found the link I was looking for, although there's still no proof of any wrong-doing."

Makenna's throat went dry. "What-What name did you say?"

The waitress appeared with their main course. She presented the plates with a flourish, offered freshly cracked pepper, then fussed over them for what seemed to be another five minutes. Makenna was sitting on pins and needles, waiting for her to leave so she could hear the answer to the question she repeated.

"Who did you say… what was your uncle's friend's name?"

"Mandarino. Joe Mandarino. Why, have you heard of him?"

"I-I recently heard the name," she said in just above a whisper.

"Then you probably know the mafia is looking for him."

"The- The mafia?" Had the man who approached her been a member of the mob? Makenna's hand trembled at the very thought as she clutched her water glass.

Her companion seemed not to notice her sudden pallor. "Back in the beginning, while Joey Mandarino was setting out to scam the government, he was also scamming the organization he worked for. He got away with a cool million or so when he disappeared back in '91. But here's the interesting part. There was a special dividend to be paid upon completion of the project. If these new power lines really do go up, NorthWind stands to make literally millions in bonus dividends. The contract was signed and sealed years ago."

"And I'm sure the funds are set up to go to some offshore Swiss bank account," she guessed.

"I'm sure," Simon agreed. "The man has remained hidden all these years, but there's a chance he'll come out of hiding to claim his millions."

"Not if he's smart," Makenna murmured.

"He's brilliant. He set all this in motion over twenty years ago. He's managed to cover all his tracks, make everything look legal, and he's managed to stay one step ahead of the mob all this time. Still, we're talking about millions of dollars."

"How do you… how do you know the mafia is looking for him?"

"Because they contacted my uncle." This time, Simon Hanks' face was set in hard frown lines. "And apparently I wasn't as clever as I thought, doing my undercover research. Somehow they found out I was looking into old records, and they paid me a visit, as well." He looked directly at her, his blue eyes beseeching. "Believe me when I say this. You need to leave well enough alone. Don't ask any more questions about the mafia being involved. Don't draw any attention to yourself. Forgot you ever heard about a connection between the Zaffino family and NorthWind Energy."

Makenna stared at him, unable to comprehend everything he had just told her. But one thing was clear; attention had already been drawn to her. Evidently, the mafia thought she was investigating them. Why else would they be trying to run her off the road and be giving her cryptic messages to deliver?

"I asked you here today to tell you my story and to convince you not to take this any further. I'll give you all my notes, all the information you need about geological studies and environmental issues and the sociological impact of this project. I'll give you facts and figures, examples of economic benefits. I'll even provide you with the negative aspects of putting up these power lines. What I won't give you is any proof that the mafia is currently, or has ever been, involved with NorthWind. If asked, even by the authorities, I will deny it." There was no mistaking the sincerity in Simon Hanks' solemn voice. "For the sake of the economy, for the sake of progress, for the sake of my uncle and myself and for the sake of your own safety, forget we ever had this conversation. Forget the story you think you need to tell. Whatever fleeting fame that comes to your career won't be worth the aftermath. Take my advice. Drop this, before you or someone else gets hurts."

Chapter 14

Makenna slept fitfully, stirring and churning all night and waking from vivid nightmares that left her drenched in sweat. When the ringing of the telephone roused her just before seven o'clock, she was thankful for the intrusion.

Pushing curls out of her eyes, she peered at the number on her cell phone. With a frown, she recognized it as one she had recently called. "Hello?" she asked groggily.

"What did you do? Who did you tell?" Cara Sims screamed into the phone.

"What-What are you talking about?"

"I'm talking about the man who showed up on my doorstep at the break of dawn! How did they find me? You had to have told them!" the other woman snarled.

"I have no idea what you're talking about."

"You gave them this number!"

Makenna sat up fully in bed, dragging covers with her that she had tangled in the night. "Miss Sims, I didn't give anyone this number. What-what happened? Did Hardin call you?"

"Not Hardin. They're looking for Hardin! They came here, trying to find the scumbag. I told you he was bad news, I told you he was in over his head!" the woman said hysterically. "Now they're after me, threatening me if he doesn't give back the money he owes. How the hell am I supposed to come up with fifty thousand dollars?"

"Wh-Who-"

"You tell him to leave me the hell out of this! You tell Hardin Kaczmarek I never want to see his lying, cheating, scum ball face again, and for him to pay his own damn bills! Tell him these Zinno people better not come back here, or I'll save them the trouble and kill him myself!" With those angrily flung words, Cara Sims slammed down the receiver.

Makenna could only stare down at the phone in her trembling hands. She sat there for a long moment, blinking rapidly as she absorbed the other woman's words. 'Zinno'.... Zaffino. If they were one and the same, it meant Hardin was not only an abusive man, he was also connected to the mafia. Which would explain why he had a gun. And a long blade knife. It might explain a lot of things.

Was it Hardin they were after, and not her? Her sluggish brain tried to think.

Hardin had been with her on the mountain roadside and at the waterfall. But she had been alone that first night, and she had been alone when the swarthy man approached her at the store. He had called her by name, told her to give a message to her father; meaning, of course, Kenzie's father. Obviously, Hardin wasn't the only one they were after.

The phone buzzed in her hands, alerting her to a text message. She saw Hardin's name come up on the screen.

Need to talk to you, ASAP.

Makenna impulsively threw the phone across the bed, as if stung by the very message. Her heart thundered in her chest. What should she do? How could she ever face him now, knowing everything she knew? She didn't think she could bear to look at him again.

The phone sounded again, this time with an incoming call. Without touching it, she timidly checked the screen. It showed the number she had programmed in as the car rental agency. Her hands were still trembling as she answered the phone and arranged to meet the driver in an hour, in front of the police station. It occurred to her if she managed to make the switch without being seen, perhaps no one, including Hardin, would know what she was driving. The thought brought her a small amount of comfort as she gathered her things and went into the shower.

Her phone buzzed again, with another text message from Hardin.

While she was showering, the phone rang. She knew it was Hardin, even before she listened to his urgent words. "Kenzie, I've got to talk to you. Call me the minute you get this message."

There was no way he could know of her latest conversation with Cara Sims, or her suspicions that he was mixed up with the mafia. The barrage of messages most likely stemmed from his abusive personality. In his obsessive mind, he probably classified her dinner with Simon Hanks as a date and viewed it as an affront to his masculinity. He was starting the telltale signs of obsession; the proprietary possessiveness, the misplaced suspicions, the need for constant contact, the relentless harassment.

As Makenna got dressed, her phone buzzed again and again, with more messages from Hardin. When she heard the angry pounding on her door, her heart froze in her chest.

"Kenzie! Kenzie, are you in there? I've got to talk to you!" Even though he couldn't see in, Makenna flattened herself against the wall, making herself an inconspicuous as possible. She saw the door handle twist, saw the door itself give as he pushed on it from the other side, waited for him to burst inside at any moment. Instead, he remained in the hallway and bellowed, "Kenzie, open up! This is important!"

She heard him swear, felt the reverberation as he punched the door in frustration. When she heard him turn away and his angry footsteps retreat down the hall, she let out the breath she had been holding. It sputtered and huffed as it wheezed its way out.

He sent one last text message.

Gone to get truck.

CALL ME.

Urgent.

Waiting a full two minutes, Makenna grabbed her purse and headed out the door. She looked both ways before stepping into the back stairwell, thinking it might be a trick to lure her out. With the coast clear, she slipped out a side door downstairs and eased around the building. She scanned the area for any signs of Hardin. As an afterthought, she looked for the gray and green cars. Seeing nothing, she hurried across the parking lot and behind the police station, easing around its far side where there was modest cover from landscaped shrubs and trees. She waited there until she saw a blue car pull up and a man get out, wearing the rental company's uniform.

The transaction was done and Makenna thought she had made it without a hitch, when she saw Hardin's truck circle behind the hotel. Instead of getting in the car and risk being seen, she turned and slipped inside the police station. There, she pretended to be lost and looking for directions. When she stole a glance outside, she saw Hardin's truck again, this time in front of the station. She knew he couldn't miss seeing her little red sports car being loaded onto a flatbed trailer.

Makenna hesitated only a moment before she dialed the number Lisa had given her two days ago. She heard the squeaky voice answer on the second ring. "Hello?"

"Lisa, this is Kenzie. I need your help."

"What can I do for you? You sound distressed. Are you all right?"

"It's Hardin. You-You were right about him. I need to put a little space between us. Do you- do you think you could come pick me up?"

"Of course, dear. I'm on my way."

"Thank you, Lisa. You don't know how much I appreciate it. Oh, wait! I'm not at my hotel."

"Where are you?"

"The police station."

"The police station?" the other woman asked in alarm.

"It's right in front of my hotel, you can't miss it. I'll be out front when I see you pull up."

"Okay, I'm on my way."

Less than ten minutes later, Makenna was tucked into Lisa's Ford Edge and they were pulling out onto the highway. Makenna had watched Hardin pass several times, even make a round through the police station parking lot. She told the officers she was waiting on her ride and thanked them for their help. She considered talking to one of them about the situation she found herself in, but she was afraid she would have to show identification and her ruse would be discovered. She was reconsidering her decision when Lisa arrived.

"I'm so glad you called me, dear," Lisa said, maneuvering into the light traffic. "I'll do whatever I can to help. If you don't mind me asking, what happened?"

"I called your friend. She told me what happened between them, and how the real Hardin Kaczmarek is totally different from the charming man I met on this trip." Makenna blew out a weary sigh, lost in reflection. "You hear about this sort of thing, you see movies about the charming new guy turning into an obsessive maniac, but you never believe it can happen to you." Her voice turned sorrowful. "He seemed so nice." That was the hardest thing of all to accept. Hardin had seemed so genuinely nice.

"They always do, dear, they always do."

Makenna's phone buzzed and she looked down to see another message from Hardin. As if to prove her point, his message even had the hallmarks of a nice, caring man.

I'm getting really worried here.

Where are you?

Are you all right?

CALL ME!

"Him, again?" Lisa asked.

"Yes. It's like the tenth message this morning. He's called, even came up to the room. I just couldn't face him after I heard what all your friend had to say."

"What exactly did she tell you?"

Makenna relayed yesterday's conversation to the older woman. For some reason, she held back on telling Lisa about this morning's exchange, the one that frightened her the most. She didn't want to drag the other couple into a potentially dangerous situation. And, if truth be told, there was still something about the Lewises that troubled her. Even though she was putting her trust in them to keep her safe from Hardin, she wasn't ready to fully confide in them.

Makenna's unease mounted when they pulled into the resort where the Lewises were staying. They turned to a unit on the right, but her eyes fell upon a familiar gray Honda parked across the parking lot. She told herself it was a coincidence, that there were hundreds of cars like that on the roads, but the sight settled heavily upon nerves already stretched taut.

"Let's get you inside and settled. Have you eaten breakfast yet?"

She had to think about it for a moment. Food had been the last thing on her mind. "Uhm, no."

Lisa chatted about her favorite breakfast choices as she led the way up the walk and to a second floor unit.

"Bob, we're back!" she said in sing-song as she unlocked the door. To Makenna she said, "You go right on in, dear, and have a seat on the couch. I'll bring you a glass of water and then we'll see about some breakfast for us."

"I don't want to be any bother."

"No bother, no bother. There's a wonderful little bakery just down the street. They make bear claws that are out of this world. How does that sound?"

"I'm-I'm really not hungry. Honestly, I don't want to be a bother. I just needed to get away for a little while, have a few minutes to think." In hindsight, she realized that might be impossible with Lisa chattering non-stop.

"Have a seat, take a load off," Lisa insisted, going into the kitchen of the large open room. The over-sized accommodations made Makenna's room look tiny by comparison. "You can put your purse there on the coffee table. Just make yourself at home."

Makenna left her purse hanging cross-body, but took a seat on the plush sofa. Running a hand over the soft pile, she murmured, "I love this couch. And this condo is amazing. Did you book it through the travel agency you work for?"

"Yes, isn't it great?" Lisa beamed. She carried a glass of water, sloshing the contents as her rounded body waddled across the room. "Here, have some water. I'll go ask Bob if he'll make a donut run."

"I'm fine, honestly."

"Donuts make everything better," she said with a giggle. "Drink up and I'll be right back."

Makenna accepted the glass but sat it on the side table as she continued to look around the room. It was an awfully large condo for just two people. A glimpse down the hallway revealed several doors, indicating two or more bedrooms. Perhaps Lisa had deliberately chosen the over-large suite for her review. It was then that it occurred to her that Lisa was a free-lance reviewer, not a travel agent, and that the older woman hadn't corrected her mistake. Not that it really mattered; the room was still gorgeous, and it was still large enough for eight or more, rather than the two that currently occupied it.

Makenna rested her head back on the cushion of the couch, thinking how tired she was after a restless night and very little sleep. Maybe she could catch a quick power nap while Lisa was gone. She could hear the low sound of voices coming from the bedroom, the sharp bite of Bob's tone to Lisa's trilling whine, but she couldn't make out the words. Apparently they were having a disagreement and she bit her lip, hoping her presence wasn't causing any problems for the couple. They barely knew her, after all, and here she was barging in on their vacation.

Now too worried to sleep, Makenna sat up and reached for her water glass. Just as she brought it to her lips, her eyes fell on a set of keys on the coffee table. She immediately recognized the Honda logo on the key fob. She rolled her shoulders uneasily, lowering the glass without taking a sip. Why would a married couple get two rental cars on vacation? Who could *afford* two rentals cars?

Maybe someone who could afford to stay in a plush resort like this one, an inner voice argued. Even as she tried to rationalize it, the image of the gray Honda parked outside flashed through her mind. She drew in an unsteady breath and glanced at the papers that lay beneath the keys. There was an assortment of maps and tourist brochures, several of which Makenna had identical ones to, a few receipts, and the folder for a rental car agreement. Makenna glanced over her shoulder, still hearing the murmur of voices coming from the nearest bedroom. Bob's voice sounded odd now, and not as sharp. Maybe they were making up.

Reaching for the maps, Makenna scooped up the rental agreement and tucked it among the papers. Knowing she was overstepping the bounds of propriety, curiosity won over etiquette as she flipped open the folder. She scanned the details hastily... four-door 2013 Honda Civic... Robert Lewis .... Chicago, Illinois...

A gray Honda, she thought uneasily. *And Chicago?* She frowned. *I thought they were from Seguin.* She bit on her lip, vaguely noticing a tingle there. As she nibbled on her lower lip in distraction, Makenna saw one other item of definite concern. Except for the area code, the number on the agreement and the number for Cara Sims were exactly the same.

"What is going on?" she whispered aloud, but the words were hard to form. Alarmed, she realized her lips not only tingled, they were now almost numb. She glanced at the water glass on the table and a terrible suspicion started to form. Hastily replacing the brochures, she picked up the glass and sniffed its contents. Nothing. She dipped her finger into the water, allowing a drop to fall on the back of her hand before very carefully touching the tip of her tongue to her finger. There was no taste, no indication that the liquid had been tampered with.

Maybe it's my imagination, she thought, even as her hand began to itch. She stared at her offending skin, realizing she was in real trouble. From the very beginning, something about the Lewises had troubled her, something had felt 'off'. Now something was definitely wrong.

Lisa's whiny voice called out through the still-closed door. "We're calling in our order, Kenzie! You still okay out there?"

Makenna swallowed hard and forced her voice out, hoping it sounded normal. "I'm good! Take your time." *Please, take plenty of time. I've got to figure out what I'm going to do.*

First of all, she had to get rid of the water. Refusing to think about how much the beautiful couch must have cost, Makenna pulled the cushion away from the arm and dribbled water down along the seam. With any luck, she would be long gone by the time the water stain soaked through. Afraid to over-saturate the cushions, she looked for another place to pour the contaminated water. She leaned down and whipped the glass sideways, slinging a little onto the floor beneath the couch. That still left a quarter inch in the glass, and Lisa might be out any minute to insist she finish her drink.

There was an elaborate arrangement of artificial flowers in an urn beside the fireplace. Makenna zipped over to them, emptied her glass, and hurried back to the couch. She heard the bedroom door opening as she dove onto the sofa, so she pretended to be settling further into the cushions. She forced herself to look comfortable, casually throwing one leg up on the cushion beside her. She balanced her empty water glass on her knee and nestled her head against the sofa's richly upholstered back.

"I'm sorry to run out on you like that, dear," Lisa said in her nasal whine. Makenna noticed that her eyes flicked briefly to the empty glass. "We couldn't decide on bear claws, jelly filled donuts, or apple fritters. So we ordered them all."

Makenna gave a drowsy yawn. "Sounds delicious," she murmured. She pretended to be having trouble rousing. "Sorry, I think I may have drifted off. I didn't sleep well last night."

"Go right on back to sleep, dear. I'll wake you up when Bob gets back with the pastries."

"I don't mean to be rude…"

"Not at all, not at all. I need to work on a report, so I'll just sit here quietly while you nap." She vaulted her short body onto one of the barstools and reached for an electronic notebook.

There goes my exit through the front door, Makenna inwardly groaned. Praying she wasn't making a mistake, she got slowly to her feet. Her legs were wobbly with fear, but hopefully Lisa would mistake it for grogginess. "If you don't mind, I'm going to get more water."

"I'll get it for you," Lisa offered.

"No, no, you stay there," Makenna insisted. She bypassed Lisa and the bar on her way to the sink, where she quickly rinsed out the glass and refilled it halfway. As she turned back around, she scanned the room for escape routes and faked a wide yawn.

"I don't know why I'm so sleepy all of a sudden," she said, allowing her words to slur. Another hefty yawn, half hidden behind her hand. "Goodness, I am so tired." She tried to look embarrassed. As she retraced her steps toward the couch, she staggered just a bit, making a grab for the granite bar. "I-I don't feel so well," she told her hostess, abandoning her water glass. "I think- I think I should lie down. Do you have a bedroom?"

If she hadn't been looking, she would have missed the smug look of satisfaction that crossed the rounded sphere of Lisa Lewis's face. "Of course, dear. Right this way." She jumped down from the barstool and rolled past Makenna, leading her down the hall and to the second door on the left, at the back of the unit. Makenna was careful to move slowly, letting her body sway and her legs to give slightly as she moved through the bedroom doorway. Lisa was prattling on about taking a good, long nap; she could even stay the night if she would like, they had plenty of room.

When Makenna got to the general vicinity of the bed, she took a nosedive onto the covers, making certain she landed with her purse beneath her. The last thing she wanted was for them to take her cell phone while they thought she was sleeping. She forced herself to stay where she landed, sprawled unceremoniously upon the bed in an uncomfortable position. She made no response when Lisa called her name. She remained perfectly still when the other woman poked her leg. With her face buried in the covers, she allowed herself a tiny smile when Lisa laughed triumphantly and left the room, shutting the door firmly behind her.

Makenna stayed in the same position for another long moment, making certain the other woman was truly gone. Only when she felt it was safe to do so did she move to a more comfortable angle, but she remained on the bed as she attuned her ears to the noises around her. Soon she could pick out the voices coming from the adjoining bedroom, and bits and pieces of the conversation.

"… better not get in our way…" came from Bob.

"….enough to knock-out a full grown horse…" from Lisa, with a laugh. "Should have seen…"

"Buys us a few hours. Now get on the phone and …"

Very quietly, Makenna eased off the bed. The light was off in the bedroom, but plenty of morning sun streamed through the curtains.

She peeked out the window, noting the wooded area behind the resort; she also paid attention to the straight drop-off down to the ground, a full story below. Drawing a shaky breath, she tiptoed to the wall separating the two bedrooms and put her ear against it. Willing her heart to settle and quieten, she listened for what was being said in the next room.

"We have the girl in confinement," she heard Lisa say. At least she thought it was Lisa; the voice didn't sound quite as nasal as usual, not quite so irritating. "No trouble. She should be out for several hours.... Are you ready?... Don't worry, we're professionals. We can handle things on this end. I've taken care of Kaczmarek for now, but we'll need to find a more permanent solution." Makenna heard her laugh, and then listened in astonishment as Lisa's whiny voice said, "Don't you worry, dear," then suddenly morphed into the soft tones of Cara Sims as she continued, "I've created a monster out of our pesky friend. She fell for it hook, line, and sinker, as those ignorant Texans like to say. She won't be turning to him for help any time soon." The petulant whine returned as she finished, "That's what she's got her new best friend, Lisa Lewis, for.... Call me when you're ready for her."

Makenna heard her own gasp as it resounded in the room. Both hands flew to her mouth as her eyes rounded. She hurried back to the bed, afraid they had heard her. She got back into position, all the while her mind whirling in a thousand directions.

They had duped her. None of those things about Hardin had been real; Cara Sims hadn't even been real. Her heart soared at the realization. For a split second, she chided herself for not trusting her own instincts, but now was not the time for regrets. Now was the time to devise a plan of action.

For all intent and purposes, she had been kidnapped. She may have come here willingly, but she could not leave the same way. They had tried to drug her and thought they had succeeded. They thought she would be out for several hours, which definitely gave her a window of opportunity.

Later, she would think about whom they had called and why they were kidnapping her and what they would do to her "when you're ready". For now, she just had to concentrate on escaping.

She heard the door open and sensed someone come into the room. Her face was buried in the covers so she could not see, particularly with her eyes squeezed tightly shut as she concentrated on taking slow, even breaths. Judging from the lack of floral perfume, she assumed Bob had stepped inside to check on her. She felt him approach the bed, jostle it with his knee, then wait for a response. She pushed her tongue into the roof of her mouth and pulled a breath up through the diminished nasal cavity, making it sound like a light snore, but she lay still as stone. After a long moment, he turned and retraced his steps, closing the door quietly behind him.

For a few moments, Makenna was too weak to even try to move. Relief flooded through her, followed immediately by a new surge of fear. Even though they expected her to sleep for hours, they would probably check on her periodically throughout the morning. She would have to escape between those times.

No time like the present. She turned her head slightly to make certain he had left the room. She heard them talking again, something about food, and listened as their voices trailed away toward the living room. Taking her cue to act, she slipped off the bed and went to the window. It was a long way to the ground, but it was her only choice, and her only means of escape.

As silently as possible, Makenna released the latches on top of the window. She bit into her lip when one of them made a distinct click. She was thankful her mouth was still half-deadened. When both locks were free, she began the arduous task of raising the window, making as little noise as possible. She had to tug to get the movement started, and her heart lodged halfway up her throat when the window suddenly heaved open a noisy first inch. After that, it eased upward smoothly, silently, until it was fully extended.

Makenna leaned out the window and judged the distance down. At least twelve feet, but it couldn't be helped. She tested the windowsill and found the metal cold and sharp, particularly on a soft belly. She would need something to soften the pinch.

As she grabbed a pillow from the bed, she noticed the adjoining bathroom for the first time. On a whim, she locked the door from the inside and silently pulled it shut. With any luck, they would check the bathroom before they checked outside, perhaps offering her a few more minutes of head start. With that thought in mind, she re-made the bed so that the missing pillow was not obvious.

Taking the time to switch her phone to mute, she placed the pillow on the window ledge, then carefully pulled herself up into position. She teetered for a moment, not certain how to proceed, before she decided to go out feet first. She managed to get one leg up and out the window, but even through the down of the pillow, the metal windowsill bit into her flesh as she balanced herself in limbo.

Had the situation not been so serious, Makenna might have laughed at the sight she must make. For a single moment of pure panic, she thought she was stuck in the window, half her body in, the other half twisted as she attempted to push her other leg through the suddenly too-narrow opening.

She heard a loud rip and then her leg was free, plunging out the other side of the window. With both feet now dangling in thin air, the full weight of her body was pressed into the metal sill. She supported herself on her elbows, trying to inhale fully when her body felt sliced in two. She pulled down on the windowpane above her, trying to hide evidence of her escape. She tugged at the curtains, pulling them closed in front of her face, hoping they would not be the first thing her captors noticed when they stepped into the room.

It was becoming increasingly difficult to breathe. Her lungs and diaphragm felt crushed, her arms ached from holding the suspended weight of her body from the window ledge, and her legs were trashing about, trying to find purchase on the side of the house. She gave one last tug of the window, pulling it as close to her head as possible without decapitation, then eased her head out of the room, to be suspended with the rest of her. With a futile glance down at the ground below, Makenna said a quick prayer, took a deep breath, and pulled the pillow with her as she curled her body into a ball, mid-air, and rushed down to meet the earth.

She hadn't expected the fall to hurt as badly as it did. She landed with a bone-jarring thud, rattling the teeth in her head and compressing every joint in her body. The force of the sudden stop knocked the breath from her lungs, as tears pricked her eyes.

For a long moment, she simply lay there, wondering if she had just killed herself. When she reasoned that she was in too much pain to be dead, she gingerly tried to move. One leg screamed in protest, but both moved when she shuffled them. She had landed on her side, the pillow crunched up in front of her. So much for softening the blow. Makenna moved her neck and rolled her head, hearing joints crackle and pop all down her spine. With her breath now restored, she couldn't stop the low moan of pain that escaped. Every part of her body ached, including her lips; nothing like a second floor fall to awaken even deadened nerves.

She allowed herself the luxury of another twenty seconds, then she pulled herself up on raw palms and scraped knees. Keeping hunched over to make herself as low to the ground as possible, she glanced up at the window and was relieved to see no sign of movement behind the almost-closed glass pane.

She stepped a few feet away from the window and promptly tumbled down a steep incline.

This time, the pillow offered a modicum of protection as she buried her face into it and rolled clumsily down the side of the hill. She thrashed her way through damp, stale leaves and the painful pricks of a thousand twigs. Vines and briers tugged and ripped at her clothes. She rolled over rocks and let out a painful "woof" as a particularly sharp stone gouged into her side. She was rolling freestyle, at times head over heels, at times sideways, and at one point skidding on her back.

After the longest and most painful seven seconds of her life, she lost her momentum and began to decelerate. Slow motion was so much worse than the mind-numbing flash of her rapid descent. She heard herself whimper in fright as she rolled to a stop, just inches from a tree.

Again, she lay still as she assessed the damage to her body. Makenna lifted bloodied palms that stung like the devil. As she picked out a small stick embedded in one palm, she noticed more blood trickling down her arm from the other direction. Her shirt was ripped near the elbow, revealing a gash in her battered skin. She checked her head for major lumps and bumps, finding only a few small cuts but an abundance of leaves and twigs tangled in her auburn curls. Her left leg protested movement and somewhere along the way, she had lost a shoe. Instinctively she reached for the purse worn across her body and panicked when she only felt a leather strap. Had it broken loose? She tugged, until finally the strap reversed itself and her purse slid back in place, tucked against her chest once more. Tears of relief stung her eyes when she felt her cell phone, safe and sound in its zippered pouch.

A glance up at the condo told her there was still no movement. Feeling momentarily safe beneath the trees at the bottom of the ravine, Makenna lay there on her back for a few more moments and gathered her wits. Then she held the phone above her and dialed Hardin's number with bloodied, bruised, and trembling fingers.

"Kenzie!" he barked into the phone. Hearing the mixture of relief and worry and anger in his voice was her undoing. Tears streamed down her face as he demanded, "Where the hell have you been? I've been trying to reach you all morning! Are you all right?"

"N-N-No," she managed to wail. "Hardin, you've got to help me!"

"Where are you? I'll come pick you up, just tell me where you are." His first instinct was to fix the problem, whatever it was. Almost as an afterthought, he asked, "What's wrong?"

"Every-Everything. I'm sorry I doubted you, Hardin, I'm sorry I didn't believe in you. But she said all those bad things about you, and you had a gun." She knew she was blabbering, but she couldn't help the tears that tumbled down her cheeks and pooled in the tangled mess that was her hair. Her heart sank all the way to her backbone as she realized how foolish she had been to doubt the strength and goodness of the man. He had offered help and security, and she had believed the worst of him.

"I don't really know what you're talking about, but that's not important right now. Just tell me where you are and I'll come get you." She could hear him up and moving, already in action.

"I-I'm at the Lewises. Or I was. I escaped."

"Escaped!"

Rolling onto her side, Makenna knew the longer she stayed there, the more danger she was in. Holding on to the tree trunk for support, she managed to pull herself up with only one small cry of pain.

"Kenzie! Are you all right?" he demanded, hearing the yelp through the phone.

"Yes. No. I-I'm not sure. Listen, I'm in the woods behind their hotel, near the creek, the one that runs all the way to our hotel. I'll come to you. It's not safe to stay here." She was already limping her way toward the access road.

"I don't know what's going on, but stay low, like we did at the Falls," he instructed. "Keep along the creek, under the cover of trees when you can. I'll be there as quick as I can."

"Go by my room. Get my camera. And bring me some shoes." She winced as she stepped on a rock. She looked down at her friend's pants, now ripped and stained and ruined. "And pants."

"Damn, girl, what happened?"

"Long- ouch!- long story." A stick jabbed through the thin protection of her sock and ripped the sole of her foot. "Just hurry."

"I'm on my way."

Chapter 15

She kept low, limping her way from one stand of trees to the next. Movement was slow and painful, but Makenna dared not stop, for fear they would catch her. She felt marginally better when the Lewis' resort was out of eyesight, but she still had a long way to go to reach Hardin, and she would soon be out of cover. Just ahead, the trees thinned out around a bridge and a large expanse of rocky terrain. There would be no chance of staying hidden once she reached the open space.

Makenna pulled her phone out again and dialed Hardin's number.

"I'm almost there," he said by way of greeting.

"I-I've got to stop," she panted. "I'll wait here by the bridge. Honk when you come up."

"See you in less than two minutes."

A fallen log provided a much-needed place to rest. If only for a minute and a half, the meager break was long overdue. Makenna winced as she lowered herself onto her bruised bottom. She ached all over, but her left leg was screaming in pain. She rested in the shadow of the concrete bridge until she heard two short beeps of a car horn. Relief flooded through her when she saw the black pickup slam to a stop. She struggled back to her feet, almost stumbling when she put weight on her left leg.

Hardin's handsome face was already creased in a scowl at the sight of her disheveled appearance. Sticks and stems and dried leaves poked from all directions of her unruly locks. Her pants were muddy and torn, revealing one skinned knee and part of the other thigh. She wore a purple oxford shirt that was torn on one arm and missing a few buttons. Now was not the time to notice the pink bra with its black lace trim. Mud and blood were smeared across her face, arms, and hands. One foot sported a shoe, the other a toe-less sock.

"Damn, sweetheart, what happened? You look terrible!" he said, jumping from the truck.

"Is that your best pick-up line?" she asked weakly.

As she flung herself into his arms, he caught her and gathered her close. His voice was rough with relief as he teased, "It worked, didn't it?" He squeezed her tightly, until she yelped in protest. Releasing her immediately, he assessed her condition. "You need medical attention."

"I need to get out of here."

"Come on, I'll carry you." He bent to put his arms under her knees, but she swatted them away.

"No! No, I'm too heavy for you to carry. Just let me lean on you, I can make it."

He held her by the waist as she hobbled her way around the front of the truck. "Taking a nap along the way?" he asked, nodding to the pillow she still clutched to her.

"Thought it would soften the fall."

Judging from the grimace on her face when she tried to step up into the pickup, Hardin guessed it hadn't worked. He took matters into his own hands and bodily lifted her inside the vehicle. Too weak to protest, Makenna allowed him to deposit her in the seat. He shut her door and was back behind the wheel before she could draw a deep and painful breath.

She glanced into the back seat and saw Kenzie's camera and most of her luggage, as well as two pieces of his own. Seeing her line of vision, he apologized. "I got what I could, but I had to leave some of it. I only had time for one trip."

She nodded in understanding. “Where will we go?”

“The mountains.”

Makenna frowned. “We’re in the mountains.”

“We’re on the side of the mountain. We’re going *in*,” he said, pointing to the dense mass of trees that cloaked the hillsides. “Do you think they’ve noticed you’re gone yet?”

“I-I don’t know. I hope not.”

“If we can make it to the cut-off road without them seeing us, we’re good.” He didn’t bother saying what would happen if they didn’t. He looked over at her again, wincing at all the scrapes and cuts and blood he saw. “There’s a bottle of water and some napkins in the console. You can clean up some of those cuts while you tell me what happened.”

She reached for the bottle, smearing it with blood.

“Cup your hands and hold them out in front of your legs,” he said, taking the bottle and opening it with one hand. He somehow managed to watch the road, the rear view mirror, and her, all at the same time. “It’s going to sting, but it’s the fastest way. Don’t worry about the floorboard.” He dribbled water into her cupped hands with more finesse than expected, given they were traveling at a high rate of speed.

Makenna tried not to cry out when the cold water splashed into the many nicks and cuts that covered her raw palms. She rubbed her hands together gently, letting the red tinted water fall onto the floorboard. They repeated the process once more before she signaled it was enough.

“Our turn is right up here,” he said, handing the bottle over into her cleaned hands. Fresh blood seeped from a few of the deeper scratches, but the worst of it had washed away. They were nearing the resort she had escaped from, but several hundred feet before the entrance on the right, Hardin took a road that led off to the left. Makenna watched behind them, making certain they weren’t followed. So far, so good.

“I never noticed this road before,” she admitted. If it had a road sign, she had missed it. She finally turned back around in the seat and surveyed the simple mountain road they traveled down. "How do you know where to go?"

"That buddy of mine I told you about who used to live here? He still has a cabin in the woods. I called him this morning, and he said we could use it." Watching the road with one eye, Hardin fiddled with his phone. "He sent me directions."

Pouring water onto a folded napkin and dabbing it onto her cheek, Makenna used the visor mirror to clean her face. Her cheek was already beginning to swell above an angry red scratch that grazed the bottom of her jawline. Bags under one eye looked puffy and dark, and the other eye sported red where it should have been white. More scratches clawed their way down her throat and disappeared into the pink of her bra, which she belatedly noticed was on display. Tugging her button-less shirt together, she was reminded of the gash near her elbow. The sleeve of her shirt was soaked with blood and she soaked another two napkins before the flow finally stopped. But of all her aches and scrapes, her leg hurt the worst.

"Tell me what happened," Hardin said impatiently, setting the phone on the seat where he could glance at it occasionally.

She knew she owed him an apology, front and center. "I'm sorry, Hardin. It's my fault for believing Lisa. I-I should have trusted you. And I should have trusted my instincts. All along, I thought you were so nice, so likable. And something about them just felt off. I should have listened to my own heart."

"What are you talking about?"

"That night we got back from the mountains, Lisa was waiting for me at the hotel. She-She told me some things about you. I found them hard to believe, but she gave me the woman's number. And when I called her, she sounded so sincere, so convincing…"

"What woman?"

"Cara Sims. She said- she said the two of you had been living together, she said you started off all sweet and charming and kind, but that you changed. Got possessive. Abusive." Makenna watched his face for signs of anger. Instead, she saw sadness. She quickly defended herself. "I'm sorry, Hardin. I shouldn't have listened to her, I shouldn't have believed her. But she described you so well, and she sounded so truly frightened. I-I trusted the wrong people. You've been nothing but kind to me, and I believed the worst."

"At least that explains the cold shoulder I got," he murmured. "I was beginning to think it was my kissing technique."

He was being kind again, infusing humor into a tense situation to make her feel better. "You're an excellent kisser, and you know it," she told him honestly. "And I'm sorry I doubted you. Deep down, I knew you weren't that kind of man, I knew you were honorable and decent, but I – I guess I just got scared."

Hardin reached over and took her hand, which she latched on to greedily. "For the record," he said, seeking out her eyes, "I've never lived with a woman."

"Good to know," she murmured, filing the information away for future use.

"And I would never – ever – hurt a woman physically. Any man who beats on a woman is no man at all. But I can understand how you would believe what she had to say. It's good that you're cautious. These days, a woman has to be. But that still doesn't explain what happened."

"This morning, Cara Sims called me."

"That's the name you asked me about before. I swear, I've never heard of the woman."

Makenna waved away his frown. "I know. Anyway, first thing this morning she called me, all hysterical. Said some men came to her house, looking for you. She said you owed them a lot of money, hinted you were involved with the mob. About that time, you started calling me, and texting me. And yes, I was inside when you came to the door," she admitted sheepishly. She could see the displeasure on his face, but mostly she saw the hurt. She squeezed his hand, trying to make him understand. "I know, I know. I was an idiot. But I was scared. You were calling every five seconds, and it fit in so well with an abusive, possessive personality. I didn't know what to do, so I called Lisa." She blew out a breath, blanching when the action hurt. "Huge mistake," she muttered derisively.

They came to a simple intersection without stop signs or street names. Hardin extricated his hand from hers and turned the truck to the right. The altitude was already beginning to rise and this road was narrower, and obviously less traveled. Here and there a driveway hinted at a dwelling nearby, and occasionally a road jutted off into the woods, leading further into the wilderness. The pickup truck traveled steadily on, following the thin ribbon of asphalt up the mountainside.

"The first hint of something wrong was the gray Honda parked at their resort." Makenna continued with her story as she cleaned her scraped knee. "Ouch. The second hint was the rental agreement I found on their coffee table for said gray Honda. Bob is from Chicago, by the way, not Texas. The poison they slipped into my water didn't bode well, either."

"Poison?" he asked sharply.

Makenna discovered that it hurt to shrug. "Poison, sleeping pills, something. It was enough to make my lips go numb, and enough to knock me out for several hours, if I drank it like they thought. I poured it out, pretended to be suddenly very drowsy, and asked to lie down."

"Smart girl," he said with approval, his blue eyes twinkling.

"I could overhear them talking. I-I'm not sure, but there may have been another man in the other room." She frowned, just realizing that fact. "Bob's voice sounded funny a couple of times, so maybe it was a third person. And would you believe that irritating voice isn't Lisa's real voice? Or maybe it was real, and the other voices were the fake ones. She sounded different when she made a telephone call to someone and told them she had me 'in confinement'. She said she had taken care of you for the moment, but it wasn't a permanent solution. Then she started talking in Cara Sims' voice, and I knew it had been her all along." She pushed her fingers through her hair, which immediately snagged in the jumbled curls. As she worked on untangling the ends and freeing them of sticks and leaves, Makenna finished her story of escape. "She told the person on the other end to let her know when they were ready for me. I didn't know what she was talking about, but I wasn't hanging around to find out. Bob came in once more to make sure I was truly asleep, and then I opened the window and sneaked out."

"Ground floor?"

"No such luck. I think my ankle joints are now location in my shoulders, and all my teeth have rattled loose. I landed a lot harder than I thought I would. Just when I realized I hadn't died in the fall, I stepped off a huge incline and tumbled all the way down to the creek. For a few minutes there, I thought death might have hurt less." She rolled her neck and shoulders, and even Hardin could hear them crackle.

"You're lucky you didn't break something."

"The jury's still out on that one," she murmured, gingerly moving her left leg so she could see it better. She had a fairly decent view of the swelling beneath the ripped denim.

"Maybe we should get you to a doctor." His foot faltered on the gas pedal as he peered at her sharply.

"No, I don't think anything is actually broken. Bumped and bruised and sprained and swollen, but not broken. I hope."

"Kenzie, if you're hurt that bad, we're going back down," he said firmly.

"If we go back down, we'll both be hurt bad. As long as this cabin we're going to has hot water, I'll survive. Let me soak for three or four hours and I'll be good as new."

The truck hit a deep rut in the pavement and lurched sideways. Makenna discovered new bruises on her backside, and when she grabbed for the dash, the sudden movement re-opened the gash at her elbow. Fresh blood trickled down her arm, but it was the throbbing in her leg that caused her breath to catch in her chest.

"Sorry 'bout that," Hardin apologized. "You okay?"

"Uh-huh." A nod was the best she could manage until the worst of the pain subsided. She stuffed the pillow beneath her leg to offer a small amount of elevation and protection.

Hardin looked over at her and grinned unexpectedly. "Pretty exciting vacation, huh?"

Makenna rolled her eyes. Only a high-octane male would declare these recent events as exciting. Her version ran along the lines of terrifying. Horrific. She told him as much.

"At least it's not dull," he offered.

"Hardin, what is going on? What is all this about?" Makenna groaned aloud as she rested her weary head against the seat and discovered another lump on her skull.

He didn't answer as he maneuvered a large pothole in the road. He managed to miss the worst of it, but there were plenty more to follow. The condition of the road was getting progressively worse, making it obvious that it received little traffic and therefore even less attention.

"Why don't you try to rest?" he suggested. "We still have a little ways to go, and I need to pay attention to the road. We take a fork up here somewhere." When he looked down at directions on his phone, the front wheel of the truck found yet another pit in the road. Makenna grunted and he apologized. "See what I mean?"

As the narrow blacktop road wound and climbed its way higher onto the mountain, the trees became denser. Hardin found the fork he was looking for, which was really more like a trail into the woods. Asphalt gave way to gravel. Trees and underbrush crowded near the roadway, making two-way traffic questionable at best.

"We're looking for the third lane to the right," Hardin said as they bounced along the graveled path. Lanes and pathways leading off the remote mountain road had been few and far between. Makenna had gotten a glimpse of one rooftop amid the trees, but no other signs of habitation were evident. Hardin peered through the truck's window, squinting into the late morning sun. "We passed one a while back, and I think that classifies as the second."

"You might could get a four-wheeler down it," she agreed dubiously.

They hit another bump, jostling her leg. "Not much further, sweetheart, and we can get you comfortable," he promised. "Look for a huge fallen tree with a driveway just past it. That's where we're headed."

Two dozen bumps later, Hardin turned the truck onto the small lane to the right. Scattered leaves and small limbs littered the path that cut through the woods. No one had been down the road in quite some time. At one point, Hardin had to get out and move a larger limb in order to pass. As an afterthought, he stopped and replaced the log across the road. "You never know," he said with a wry shrug, reminding Makenna of the danger they were still in. Just because no one seemed to be following them didn't mean they were safe.

The lane ended in a large clearing. A small log cabin was nestled amid the trees, a picturesque setting that brought an odd ache to Makenna's chest.

"What's wrong?" Hardin asked, noting the sudden pallor to her already pale skin. He pulled up close to the house and stopped near the porch.

"I-I don't know. I have the oddest feeling..."

"Your leg?" he asked in concern.

"No, no, not physical. I feel like.... I don't know. I feel like I've been here before, but I know it's impossible."

Makenna stared at the cozy scene before her. She couldn't shake the sensation that she had seen this cabin before. She had a sudden sense of crisp fall air, scented with pine needles and baked apples and the odd whiff of moose dander. She could almost hear the crunch of colorful leaves beneath her feet.

Hardin looked at her sharply, but he said nothing as she sat up straighter and unfastened her seatbelt. She drank in the sight before her, trying to justify this overwhelming sense of deja vu.

"I'll go get the key," he said, getting out of the truck. She continued to stare at the cabin as he disappeared around one side. Moments later he returned, grinning as he held up a key.

Makenna already had her door opened and was struggling to get out.

"Hold on, hold on," he said, unlocking the cabin door and swinging it open. He jumped down off the porch and reached her side with a long stride. "I'll help you, if you'll give me a minute."

"I want to see inside," she murmured. "I already see it in my mind. A hall and bedrooms on the right, a kitchen in the back. A big blue couch."

"Here, put your arm around my neck. I'll carry you."

"No, I'm –"

"Not too heavy," he finished for her, lifting her into his arms. It was true, she was heavy, but he was in excellent shape and found the challenge manageable. At the doorway, he paused, turning her so she got the full view of the cabin.

It was a one-room cabin, cozy without being crowded. Makenna's eyes flew to the kitchen at the back, traveling forward to the bed on the left side of the room, the seating area on the left. Not a thread of blue was in sight.

She burst out laughing. "So much for deja vu!" she giggled. "Guess it reminded me of something I saw in a movie." Hardin re-shifted her in his arms, causing her to protest. "You can put me down now, before I break your back."

"Yeah, one cripple is enough," he teased, but he made no move to put her down.

Makenna had to admit, she enjoyed being in his arms. His chest was hard and solid, his arms corded with muscle. He was delightfully warm and he smelled completely male. It was a heady combination.

He carried her toward the couch. "Do you think you can stand for a second, while I check the cushions for mice?"

"Mice?" she squeaked, tightening her grip on his neck.

"Yeah, mice, those tiny little critters smaller than my big toe. Don't tell me you're afraid of them?"

"I'm not afraid of them," she corrected. "I'm petrified of them."

He merely chuckled, carefully depositing her so she could lean against the arm of the couch. He lifted up the brown and tan plaid cushions, beat them once or twice to create a billow of dust, patted down the sides and back, and declared it mice-free.

Makenna leaned on his arm and hobbled her way to the front of the sofa, where she sank gingerly onto the cushions, mindful of her bruised backside.

"Here, swing your legs up and rest, while I open some windows and unload the truck." He placed a green throw pillow beneath her leg as he examined the injury. "It's pretty swollen. We need to get some ice on it."

"Do we have any ice?" she asked doubtfully.

"In the truck," he nodded. "Just lay back and rest."

Instead, Makenna examined her surroundings. Along with the couch, a faux leather arm chair and a rustic Adirondack with plaid cushions clustered around a large stone fireplace. Windows bordered either side and were now wide open, their simple green curtains billowing as fresh breezes stirred the stale air in the room. At the back of the cabin, the kitchen consisted of a small set of rough pine lower cabinets with open shelves above, and compact vintage appliances. A scrubbed pine table with benches defined the dining area of the cabin. To the left of the small refrigerator she could see a bathroom, again with vintage fixtures. Her greedy eyes zeroed in on the old claw-foot tub.

She turned her head to look behind her, to the bedroom portion of the cabin. One chest of drawers, one nightstand, and one bed. The mattress seemed to sag just a bit the middle, but the red, green and tan tartan plaid bedding looked fluffy and inviting. Later, she would worry about the fact that there was only one bed; she had no intentions of moving off this couch any time soon.

Hardin made several trips in, carrying luggage and shopping bags she recognized from their visit to the little country store. Had that really only been yesterday? In amazement, she watched as he carried in two Styrofoam ice chests and, even more surprisingly, two picnic baskets like the one they shared on the mountain.

"Hardin, where did all this come from? When did you have time to get it?" She twisted on the couch to follow his movements into the kitchen, where he deposited his load. "*Why* did you get it?"

"Let me move the truck and I'll explain everything."

"Why are you moving the truck?"

He shrugged nonchalantly, but she wasn't fooled. "It might be best for it not to be out in the wide open."

"Wide open? We're far enough back we might have to pump in sunshine," she reminded him. "No one's going to just happen upon us back here. If they make it this far back, it's because they know we're here."

He continued out the door as if she hadn't spoken. He backed the vehicle against the far side of the house, where it was hidden from immediate view of the lane. It was facing forward, ready for action. *Or escape*, she realized. He caught the end of her weary sigh as he came in a back door off the kitchen.

"I didn't know there was a back door," she said without opening her eyes. They were suddenly too weary to keep open.

"And a porch. You should see the view from back here. Gorgeous."

He began unloading, banging his way through the cabinets and refrigerator and squeaky Styrofoam coolers. Thinking she would simply rest her eyes for a few more minutes, Makenna drifted off to sleep. She didn't rouse until she felt the cushions sag at her side, jostling her leg and causing new discomfort.

"Sorry," he murmured, "but we need to tend to your leg and some of your cuts." Very carefully, he placed a dishtowel on her battered leg, then topped it with a plastic bag filled with ice. The pressure and the cold immediately hurt, but she knew it would help in the long run. He had found a bottle of alcohol and some antibiotic cream and clean rags to apply it all with.

"If you're going to torture me, the least you can do is take my mind off it by telling me what the heck is going on," Makenna said testily. He had started his administrations on her feet and planned to work his way up. Her left foot, the one minus the shoe, was badly battered and bruised. Blisters were already forming and there was at least one fairly deep cut, along with the gouge left by the stick. He was using bottled water to wash away the blood and mud and filth, and even though he was trying his best to be gentle, it still hurt. Everything on her body hurt.

As he cleaned her foot, slathered it with ointment and then slipped one of his own clean white socks onto it, he started to talk. "Last night, I kept our date with the Lewises. You owe me big time for that, by the way. Anyway, I noticed there were a lot of inconsistencies with their stories, a lot of things that didn't make sense. I called it an early evening, then did a little surveillance. When I noticed the gray Honda parked at their resort, I wanted to see who was driving it. This morning, Bob went for an early donut run."

"You stayed up all night?"

"That's why I was trying to get a hold of you so early this morning. I was trying to warn you about the Lewises."

"I'm sorry I didn't call you back. I'm sorry I didn't trust you."

He set her doctored foot down and looked her directly in the eye. "You can, you know. You can trust me."

She was alone in a secluded cabin with him, in the middle of the New Hampshire White Mountains. She had only a vague idea of how to get back to town, which was miles away. She had only known him for five days, and for the past twenty-four hours she had believed him to be abusive and cruel, then believed he was involved with the mob. She had no idea if her cell phone worked up here or where the nearest neighbors were. There was one bed, one vehicle which he held the keys to, one route of escape. And she wasn't the least bit frightened; not of him, at least.

"I do trust you," she told him softly, her green eyes earnest.

"I'm glad." His fingers trailed up her ankle, sending shivers of delight dancing up her leg, injured though it was. He pushed the hem of her jeans up, revealing a half dozen scrapes and scratches. He cleaned them all with alcohol and smeared on more antibiotic salve. Moving along, he readjusted the ice pack and peeked at the assortment of cuts visible beneath the gaping denim of her torn pants. Skipping that leg for now, he moved to the right thigh, which was exposed by more ripped denim.

"You're definitely in style with the ripped jeans," he said, wiping alcohol across a cut on her thigh.

"Ouch, that burns! And these aren't even my jeans. Ken-" She caught herself just before she said the wrong name. "Makenna's going to kill me for ruining her jeans."

He didn't even notice the slip. His attention was on the creamy white flesh beneath his fingers. Slick with ointment, his fingertips slid easily over her skin, radiating out from the scrape, reaching beneath the flap of ripped fabric to trace along her hip. When his fingers touched lace, Makenna shifted her leg and pulled him from his wanderings.

"Sorry, I got sidetracked," he admitted. He took her right arm in his hands, examining the gash at her elbow. "That probably needed a stitch or two, but I guess a bandage will have to do. I'll see if I can find one. I'll get you some Tylenol, too."

"Could you bring me a cracker or something to go with it? I don't think I've eaten today, and it might upset my stomach."

"You don't *think* you've eaten?" he chastised. When she made a helpless gesture with her face, he just shook his head.

Makenna cleaned up several of the smaller cuts on her hands and arms while Hardin was gone. When he returned, he was sporting a newly discovered first aid kit. "Eat these crackers before you take the Tylenol. I'll bandage your elbow and hands, clean up the rest of your scratches, and then we'll have some lunch."

She hissed in pain when he cleaned the slash on her elbow and pulled the torn skin together best he could, securing it beneath a butterfly bandage. By the time he covered all the cuts and lacerations on her hands, one palm was completely wrapped in a thick white bandage, the other only slightly less bound. He swabbed the numerous nicks on her cheeks and neck, blew gently when the alcohol stung the deeper scrape on her jaw, tried valiantly to keep his eyes focused on the scratches *above* the pink bra. Her breath caught and hung when his fingers gently traced the red whelps that trailed over one ivory globe and disappeared beneath pink satin. It was one of Kenzie's bras, a thin and frilly concoction of pink satin and black lace. Makenna's skin was beginning to sizzle, and she worried the delicate lace might burst into flame under the heat of his fingers. The heat in his gaze alone was enough to cause spontaneous combustion.

Hardin's breath quickened, and his voice had a rough edge when he spoke. "That should hold you for now. Hungry?"

Captive to his piercing blue eyes, Makenna didn't trust herself to speak, so she merely nodded. He might have been asking if she wanted food. He might have been asking if she wanted him. The answer to either question was the same; yes.

His hand was slow in moving. His fingers trailed gently away from her skin, whispering a promise.

"Let's get a bite to eat," he suggested, standing and moving into the kitchen. While he gathered their lunch, Makenna pulled her shirt together and tried to do the same for her scattered thoughts.

"I picked up a few extra things, but it seemed easier to just buy a couple more of these," he said, bringing back one of the prepackaged picnic baskets.

"When did you buy all this?"

"This morning. When I couldn't reach you, I decided to have everything ready for when I did finally talk to you. I filled up with gas, bought ice and a few supplies. I'm not sure how long this will last us, but eat what you want. You need your strength after all you've been through today." He examined the over-stuffed sandwiches, sealed in plastic wrap. "Turkey on rye, ham on white, or club on wheat?"

"How about we split the club and one of the others?"

He winked at her. "A girl after my own heart. And there's more of that veggie dip you liked so much."

The bulky bandages made her of little use digging in the picnic basket. She finally gave up and let Hardin do all the work in assembling the lunch. She noted how he brought out the vegetables and dip, but only one package of crackers, and none of the fruit or cheese. He also left the wine and decadent cake slices, offering only the small assortment of cookies.

"How long will this need to last us, Hardin?" she asked solemnly, thinking of his earlier statement.

"As long as it takes."

"For what?"

"To keep you safe," he said simply.

Makenna had the urge to get up and pace, but her battered body kept her from doing so. Instead she flung herself back against the couch cushions, then regretted the hasty move when her bruised back collided with the upholstery. She growled in frustration. "We can't stay up here forever. Sooner or later, and I'm guessing sooner, we have to go back down this mountain."

"I'll figure something out." He sounded much more confident than Makenna felt. He pushed half a ham sandwich toward her. "Eat."

"I've lost my appetite."

"Eat, and I'll draw you up a hot bath. Then I'll pour you a glass of this wine," he bribed.

"Deal!" she grinned immediately, reaching for the sandwich.

"But eat slowly, it may take a while for the hot water to heat up," Hardin cautioned.

"I'm surprised this place has electricity, as remote as it is."

"The wonders of modern society. It's hard to find any place that's completely unspoiled anymore. People may complain about progress and how those ugly power lines destroy nature's beauty, but if you notice, most of them do their complaining from the comfort of their air-conditioned, well-lit homes, signing petitions on their smart phones or their computers, while sitting in front of flat screen televisions. They don't mind using electricity, they just don't want to be bothered with how it gets to them."

Makenna closed her eyes. "With all that happened today, I completely forgot about my dinner last night with Simon Hanks, and everything I learned about NorthWind."

"Yes, how was your date?" he asked wryly. He tried to hide it, but she saw a flash of hurt in his incredibly blue eyes at mention of the other man.

"It wasn't a date, Hardin." She finished her half of the ham sandwich and reached for the club, realizing how hungry she truly was. "That's what all this is about, you know. Electricity."

He didn't look surprised.

"Simon was very informative, both on and off the record. He told me an amazing story about the mafia and NorthWind Energy. I'm still trying to process it all." She paused with a frown. "He then told me to forget our entire conversation, and said he would deny everything if asked. He said it was for my own safety, and for his. The thing is, I'm hardly the first journalist to cover the story on these controversial power lines coming through, but something I've done has caught some unwanted attention. Apparently I've already made some people nervous."

"Obviously."

"But I still have absolutely no idea how Bob and Lisa Lewis play into this."

"My guess is, they're connected to the mob."

"The mob?"

Even as she squeaked the words, she knew it was so. Why else would they have drugged her? It was Lisa Lewis who had first mentioned the mafia's connection to NorthWind. Bob had been driving the car that tried to run her off the mountainside. Lisa had told someone on the phone, probably someone within the Zaffino organization, that Makenna was 'in confinement' until they were ready for her. It made sense they were working for the mob.

"I-I guess I can see that. But why were they on the plane from Austin? I hadn't started the assignment yet. How did they know I was reporting on NorthWind? Do you think they have contacts inside *Now Magazine*?"

"Organizations like the Zaffino's have contacts everywhere. It's amazing – disheartening, really – to know how far-reaching their influence truly is."

"You- You sound like you've done some research, too." She wasn't sure why, but a cold dread was seeping into her heart. There was something he wasn't telling her, something she wasn't certain she wanted to hear.

"You might say that." His voice was hesitant, his eyes on the drink in his hands. "I actually am quite familiar with the Zaffino Mafia and their organization here in the States. I know that they are absolutely ruthless in business. And for them, everything is business. They don't like to lose, and they do not tolerate insubordination or disloyalty. Anyone who dares to double-cross them winds up dead, or wishing they were."

Makenna swallowed hard. "How-How do you know this, Hardin?" she whispered in dread.

"Before I explain, I need to tell you something." He moved forward, kneeling down on his knees in front of her so his movements wouldn't jostle her leg. Very gently cupping her bruised face in his large hands, his amazing blue eyes settled on her green ones. There was honesty and sincerity in his gaze, and something that looked a little like regret. She tensed immediately. "What I said the other day about that instant connection… I've never felt that before, Kenzie. The minute we started talking, I felt something click in place. It was like…. I found a piece of myself I didn't even know I was looking for." He struggled to find the right words. "Yesterday, when you started pulling away… it wasn't good, Kenzie. It nearly killed me. I've known you less than a week, but somehow… I can't imagine not having you in my life." They were heady words, romantic and potent, spoken in a voice rough with emotion. "But I have to tell you something, Kenzie. I have to be honest with you."

I should do the same, she thought guiltily, staring into his wonderful blue eyes.

He pressed his lips to hers in a quick, urgent kiss. "You are an amazing woman. Beautiful. Funny. Sexy." Another hard kiss before continuing. "Intelligent. Inquisitive. So open and genuine it blows my mind." He kissed her a third time, as if to press the words into her soul. She fidgeted at his last words, overwhelmed with guilt, but he never noticed. "Did I mention sexy?" he murmured against her mouth.

Tears were already rimming her eyes, so Makenna just sniffed and nodded. She instinctively knew she would not like where this conversation was leading.

"But you deserve the truth, Kenzie. Everything I've told you has been true, everything I've felt for you has been real."

"B-But?" she asked cautiously, knowing there was definitely a 'but' coming. She bit into her lower lip as she waited.

"But…. I didn't get on that plane by accident. I deliberately followed you to New Hampshire."

Makenna remembered the thrill she had felt that day, when the handsome stranger had chosen to sit beside her on the flight. A piece of her heart crumbled, even as she struggled to make sense of it all. "Why?" she whispered.

"My family really does own a construction company, where I occasionally work. And I really do plan to ride in the Ride for the Hills charity event. But what I didn't tell you is what I actually do for a living."

With absolute dread, knowing he was about to break her heart and tell her he was part of the Zaffino organization after all, Makenna had to hear him say it. "Which is?" she whispered.

"I'm a Special Agent with the Texas Rangers," he informed her.

She was stunned by the words. They were polar opposite of what she had expected, and her heart soared. He really was one of the 'good guys', just as her instincts had told her.

But her relief was short lived when she heard his next words, spoken quietly but firmly. "And I know who you are."

Chapter 16

The blood drained from Makenna's face. *He's here to arrest me?* She wondered. *All because I impersonated my best friend? It's because I got on the airplane, using false identity. I knew I'd get caught! Kenzie's schemes always get me in trouble! But why did he wait so long? And how –*

She interrupted her own thoughts to sputter incoherently, "Who... Wha-What.. What are you talking about?"

"I know who you are, Kenzie." His voice was low, solemn. Official.

"I-I'm not sure..."

"More importantly," he continued, "I know who your father is."

"My father?" she asked in genuine surprise. *Then you still think I'm Kenzie Reese.*

"Yes. I know that your father is Joseph Mandarino."

Makenna stared at him, completely dumbfounded. Kenzie's father was involved with the mob? He was the one who set up the scam that later became NorthWind? Her best friend's father had cheated the government, then double-crossed the mafia?

Seeing the look on her face, Hardin frowned. He moved to the nearby chair, his eyes still on her shocked expression. "You really didn't know?"

Her mind flew back to her last conversation with Kenzie. When she asked Kenzie about the name Joseph Mandarino, her friend had answered without hesitation. When she asked her about her father, Kenzie's voice had been filled with doubt, with a sense of guilt even, but with absolute honesty. She was certain Kenzie didn't know the truth.

Shaking her head, Makenna's heart broke for her closest and dearest friend.

Hardin stared hard at her. "How could you not know?" he asked softly, with more curiosity in his voice than accusation.

Now's the time to tell him the truth, her conscience whispered. Yet something held her back. It was more than her own preservation – as a law officer, he would be bound by honor to arrest her for false impersonation, fraud, and a host of other indiscretions; she remained silent out of a sense of loyalty to her friend, perhaps even a sense of protection. Kenzie might be in a great deal of danger, and Makenna was not about to throw her to the wolves without knowing exactly what was going on.

"We-We moved around a lot," she finally answered, recalling the conversation with her friend. "We never stayed anywhere longer than two years at a time. I- I just thought my father was a drifter."

Hardin looked like he still had doubts, but one question was paramount to the rest. "Kenzie, it is imperative that we find your father before the Zaffinos do. Where is he, Kenzie?"

"I don't know."

"Sweetheart, this is no time to be worried about family loyalty or whether or not you're selling out your father. We're his only chance at making it out of this mess alive. If you know where he is, you have to tell me."

"I-I have no idea where he is!" Makenna said, able to look him full in the eye and speak with absolute certainty. "Honestly."

Hardin reached across and took her hand in his. "I believe you," he said, holding her gaze.

His touch, his tender look, brought back the knowledge that their relationship was based on lies. He had followed her on that plane and deliberately sat beside her. It hadn't been chance, hadn't been fate, hadn't been magic; it had been premeditated. Had anything about the past six days been real between them?

"Yes, Kenzie," he whispered as he read her mind. "It was real. This," he squeezed her hand, bandage and all, "is real."

So many lies. Yours. Mine. The thoughts circled in her head, cutting off her breath. *Maybe too many to get past.* She closed her eyes to the bright beauty of his blue gaze, but her fingers clung hopefully to his.

"So what now?" she asked. "I have no idea where... my father is," she stumbled over the words, "but they will never believe that. That's why Lisa kept questioning me about my family, that's why that man gave me that message, that's why the Lewises tried to drug me." It was all clear now. "They think I can lead them to Joseph Mandarino."

Another realization dawned. "That's what you thought, too."

"My assignment was to keep an eye on you, keep you safe."

As hastily as her bruised muscles would allow, she pulled her hand away from his. "Assignment." She intended to spit the word at him with disdain; instead, it came out sounding heartbroken.

"You're more than that to me, and you know it," he growled defensively. "Don't look at me like that. Don't hold my job against me."

"It's not the job I hold against you. It's the fact that *I* am the job." She pulled as far away as the narrow gap between them allowed. She would love to get up from the couch and put some real distance between them, but her injured leg made it impossible. "You pretended to be interested in me to-"

"No. Wait right there. There was nothing pretend about my interest in you."

"Of course not. I'm sure your paycheck and sense of duty is very real," she said, her voice cool. "But tell me, how did you know I would be on that plane?"

"I was called in at the last minute. One of our other Rangers, Travis Merka, was assigned to your case. He had been... keeping an eye on you–" he chose his words carefully, only to be interrupted by her outburst.

"Spying on me, you mean!"

"- for the past few weeks, since word came down that the mafia was looking for your father. When *Now Magazine* assigned you to this job, speculation was that you asked for it, knowing the connection between your father and NorthWind Energy. You would be returning to your home state, and-"

"Wait! What did you just say?"

"You would be returning to your home state. Your family was living in Conrad when you disappeared. Which, by the way, probably explains that sense of deja vu. You probably remembered something from your childhood."

Except, I'm not who you think I am.

"Anyway, Merka was set to follow you up here, make sure no one from the mafia was doing the same. A couple of hours before the flight, he was in a wreck. Blindsided while he was following you, actually. Ended up in a three-car pileup that sent him to the hospital. I was called in an hour before your plane took off."

A sick feeling settled in the pit of Makenna's stomach. Kenzie's accident had been no accident, after all. Someone had deliberately hurt her, as well as the Ranger assigned to protect her. The mafia had taken out both threats with one car wreck, only to have their efforts thwarted when she posed as her friend and boarded that plane.

Makenna rubbed her temples, frowning when she encountered a bruise on her temple. She couldn't even worry without it hurting! "So why were the Texas Rangers involved?"

"Homeland Security. Organized crime. Your father worked for one of the top crime syndicates in the world and is on the FBI Most

Wanted list. From what I understand, he just fell off the grid in '91. Disappeared into thin air."

Having heard the same thing from Simon Hanks, Makenna wasn't surprised by his statement. "So how was his daughter found, but not him?"

"You're asking the wrong person. I wasn't in on the paper chase. I do know that a few years ago, they thought they had a line on your father. He was going by Reese at the time, living in North Carolina. I'm guessing that was about the time you struck out on your own. I heard they eventually found you through your college grants and student loans, although that wasn't until about a year ago."

"They've been spying on me for a year?" She wondered if Kenzie had any idea.

"Not spying," he corrected. "Monitoring. Keeping an eye on you, as much for your own safety as for the sake of finding your father. A few months ago, word came down that the mafia was renewing their efforts to locate Mandarino. Until then, surveillance on you had been electronic, making certain you hadn't booked any international flights, that sort of thing. When your safety became an issue, Ranger Merka was assigned to your case. About a week ago, it became apparent the Zaffinos had their eye on you, as well."

"I-I didn't know," Makenna murmured. If someone had been watching Kenzie, they had more than likely been watching her, as well, since the two roommates did virtually everything together. She had never once suspected that either of them was being followed.

"If it makes you feel any better, they are professionals, after all. You weren't supposed to know they were there."

"Why didn't they approach me at home? Why follow me all the way up here?"

"I'm sure they were hoping you would lead them to your father."

"I guess they weren't expecting such a dysfunctional family," she murmured. Again, her heart ached for her friend, and she said a thankful prayer for her own closely-knit family. The next chance she got when Hardin wasn't around, she would call or text her mother.

"I'm sorry, but we still haven't been able to locate your sister. For your sake, I wish we could. But maybe she's safest if she remains hidden."

"My *what?*"

"Your sister." Hearing the utter shock in her voice, Hardin looked up sharply. She had visibly paled. "Kenzie," he said slowly. "You do know you have a sister… right?"

Makenna shook her head, her mind in a whirl. Kenzie would have told her. No way would Kenzie have kept something like this from her! How many times had she heard Kenzie say how lonesome she had been as a child, how miserable without anyone but her cold and distant parents? Her friend had been a lonely, only child. "There- There- There has to be some kind of mistake," she finally managed to say.

"When Joseph Mandarino disappeared in 1991, it was with his wife and twin daughters."

"*Twins?*" Makenna barely croaked the word.

"Whether it was to save the child or to save themselves, your parents evidently gave away one of their children. It made finding you that much more difficult; everyone was looking for a family of four, not three." Hardin stroked her hair with gentle fingers, recognizing the distraught look upon her face as one of shock and anguish. He hated being the one to break her heart. "You have a twin sister," he said gently. "How- how did you not know?"

Confused, worried, totally heartbroken for her friend, Makenna shook her head helplessly. "I-I don't know. I guess I was too young to – to remember."

"Ah, sweetie, come here," Hardin said, gathering her up in his arms. He held her close, trying to offer some sort of comfort.

Too shocked to do anything else, Makenna clung to him greedily, soaking up his warmth and strength. Her brain was too numb to make sense of it all, but her body was anything but numb. As the physical exertion of the day caught up with her and her body screamed in pain, she eased away from him.

Makenna blew out a deep and weary breath. "I could really use that hot bath now."

After starting her bathwater, Hardin helped Makenna hobble to the bathroom. She hated being dependent on him, even if he was being paid – *paid!*- to help her. The very thought stung her pride and bruised her heart.

It was a tiny little room, just large enough for the essentials, and the door couldn't swing all the way open because of the large claw-foot tub tucked along one wall. But the tub was filling with hot, steaming water, and that was the only thing Makenna was concerned with right now.

"Call me if you need me," Hardin said, leaving her at the door. "I put your bag and some towels in there for you."

"Thanks." She shut the door, noticing there was no lock, and shuffled her way inside. The borrowed clothes she peeled off were beyond repair. She blushed when she saw the huge rip in the thigh of the jeans, realizing she had given Hardin more than a glimpse of what lay beneath. Tossing the ruined garments aside, she took care of the essentials, then began the arduous task of easing her body into the tub.

She bit back a cry as torn and tender flesh made contact with the hot water. It was difficult maneuvering herself over the rim of the tub and into its midst, but after the initial pains subsided, the water felt heavenly. She scrubbed away dirt and dried blood and managed to submerge herself well enough to wash her hair. Discovering new cuts on the top of her crown, she couldn't bite back the moan that slipped out.

"You okay in there?" Hardin called out.

Finding her voice, she answered with a cautious, "Yes." She lay back in the tub, relaxing her sore and bruised muscles as the warm serum worked its magic. The warm water even lessened the ache in her heart, the one left there by the knowledge that to Hardin, she was only an assignment.

A few moments later, there was a soft knock on the door. "Delivery," Hardin called through the wood. "I promise not to look." Without waiting for her protest, he pushed the door open against the tub. Through the mirror above the sink, she could see he had one hand over his eyes as he stepped into the room, holding a glass of wine in the other. "Tell me when I'm close."

A little more of the pain in her heart faded, the bitterness dwindled. Did most Rangers go to such trouble for their 'assignments'? Taking the wine from his flailing hand, she took a sip and gave a moan of pure pleasure. "Ah, a hot bath and chilled wine. I take back whatever I may or may not have said about you. You, Hardin Kaczmarek, are a prince among men."

"Just a prince?" he teased. "I'm a king, and don't you forget it!" He chuckled as he backed out the door and shut it behind him.

Makenna stayed in the tub as long as she could, until the water turned tepid and her skin started to pucker. With regret, she finally pulled the plug and watched as the water seeped out. Her naked body was quickly chilled as she debated the best way to get out of the tub, given all her injuries. With cuts on her hands and a left leg that wouldn't support her, her only choice was to turn over onto her knees and ease out of the tub, much like she had eased out of the window that morning. This time naked and shivering, Makenna balanced her torso along the rim of the tub. She immediately found more bruises where the windowsill and at least one sharp stone had bitten into her flesh. By the time she swung her right leg over the rim and hauled the rest of her body out, her skin was covered by a fine sheen of sweat. The clumsy effort made her fledgling escape from the second story window this morning look like a choreographed ballet.

Just getting out of the tub stole away all her hard-earned energy. She had to rest before she dug through her bag, which was a messy combination of her own toiletries and personal items and those of her best friend's. At the top of the bag, items were jumbled and tossed, as if Hardin had taken his hand and swiped it across the counter of her hotel bathroom in haste. With enough digging, she found clean panties, a front-hooking bra of sheer black lace, and a mismatched set of pajamas.

The pajama bottoms belonged to her, the lower half of a modest dark gray set of jersey knit. The top belonged to Kenzie, a skimpy camisole top of red satin. It was shorter than Makenna preferred, revealing too much of her full hips and buttocks, and the red clashed with her auburn hair, but a quick glance into the mirror told her that her wardrobe was the least of her worries. One eye was still streaked red from a broken blood vessel, the other now officially a 'black eye'. Her cheek was puffy, and against her pale skin, the numerous scratches appeared angry and red. Sighing, she finished dressing, doctored what scrapes and scratches she could, brushed out her long curls, and cleansed the wounds that had re-opened to seep fresh blood.

Another twenty minutes later, she opened the bathroom door, tired and spent.

"I was about to send in a search party," Hardin said, appearing at her side to help her back to the couch.

"Sorry. Every time I got cleaned up, something new started to leak." She held her bleeding palm up in example.

"We'll get you fresh bandages and try to keep the rest of your blood inside you, where it belongs."

Hardin re-wrapped her hands and put a fresh butterfly bandage on the deep gash at her elbow. He patched the stick wound on her abdomen and wrapped her left foot, securing it with another of his socks. Fresh tears stung her eyes as Hardin doctored the newly discovered cuts on her scalp. He finally finished by propping her leg on the pillow, adding a fresh ice pack, and instructing her to rest. Her eyes drooped immediately.

She roused when he came back a few minutes later. "One last dose of medicine to make you feel better, and I'll let you take a nap."

He sat down beside her with a huge slice of chocolate cake and another glass of wine. When she made a helpless gesture with her heavily bandaged hands, he chuckled. "Allow me." He fed her a big bite of the decadent cake, his eyes twinkling with merriment as it smeared messily against her lips. To her every two bites, he took one for himself. He even held the wine to her lips, so that her injured hands could rest.

He was so charming, so handsome, so all-around *likable*. Lovable. Sighing with pleasure, Makenna felt another shard of her anger and hurt slip away. Chocolate was so much more satisfying than pride.

As the wine and the chocolate and the man worked their special magic, Makenna felt her eyes grow heavy. Licking her lips after the final bite of cake, she snuggled down further into the cushions of the couch. "You were right," Makenna murmured, thinking of his earlier declaration. "You are a king!"

Chapter 17

Pine Bluff, Arkansas
December, 1998

"But I don't want to move again!" She stroked the purple fur of her favorite Furby, finding comfort in the toy animal's soft down. Its huge eyes were as sad as her own were when her mother delivered the dreaded news.

"Your father has a new job, Lisa. We're moving to the sunny state of Florida."

"Florida? That's too far away!" the eleven-year-old girl wailed. She had finally made a friend, the first real friend she had had since Joey, all those years ago.

"You'll love Florida," her mother insisted. "Sandy beaches, lots of sunshine, Disney World."

"As if you'd ever take me there," the preteen muttered beneath her breath. She stared at her reflection in the mirror, finally accustomed to being a blond after more than a year. It was the first time her mom had suggested changing her actual hair color. Style, yes; each new name came with a new hairstyle. But changing the color, along with the style, was a new twist to a game grown old and weary.

"I want to pick my own name this time," the girl said.

"You're going to be Madeline. Maddy for short, if you like."

"No."

The single word of defiance stopped her mother in her tracks. "I beg your pardon?"

"I said no." She tried to sound brave, she tried to sound determined, but her mother had that gleam in her eye, the one that said there was no sense in arguing. Still, the girl stuck out her chin and stood her ground. "In the last five years, I've been Amy and Jessica and Tara and now Lisa. For one weekend, I was even Bobby." She shuddered as she recalled having to play the part of a boy again, this time at age ten. "We've lived in Wyoming and Utah and Illinois and two places here in Arkansas. If I have to move again, I get to pick my own name this time."

Her mother stared at her for a long moment. She seemed to be weighing her options. Something flickered in her stare before she sighed and said stiffly, "Very well. And what name do you pick?"

She considered for a moment. With a big smile, she thought about her favorite television show. "Felicity," she announced triumphantly.

"Felicity? What kind of name is that?"

"Mine," she said smugly. "It's my new name."

"Fine. But we're changing your hair color."

"Can I be a red-head this time?"

"Absolutely not. A nice light brown should do nicely," her mother said briskly.

With a sigh, the girl turned back to the blond in her mirror. Lisa had been fun to play, and she had enjoyed having a friend for a change. But truth be told, having to keep so many secrets from her friend had been exhausting.

By now, the girl knew it was not normal to move every few months and to change an entire family's identity. Sometimes, she pretended her parents were celebrities, and they moved so often to avoid the paparazzi. Other times, she imagined they were spies for the government, carrying out top-secret missions of bravery and skill. But more often than not, she worried they were criminals, trying to outrun the law. She thought it might be best not to know the real reason, so she never asked. Until today, she never offered any resistance; she simply packed up her meager belongings and went where they took her, no questions asked.

Touching the image in the mirror, she wanted to remember how good it felt, just once, to be a typical kid with a best friend; she might not get that luxury with her next identity.

"I'll never forget you," she promised the blond girl in her mirror, pressing their palms together. "I'll never forget."

Chapter 18

Cold air whipped into the cabin the next morning, reminding the two Texans they were far north of the Guadalupe River. They had left a window cracked for fresh air during the night, neither realizing that the temperature in late April would fall so far below freezing on the mountainside. Now they were scrambling for cover, layering socks and quilts in an effort to get warm.

"As soon as my toes thaw out, I'll make us some coffee," Hardin promised.

"As-As soon as my l-lips thaw out, I'll dr-drink it." Makenna's teeth were chattering so badly it was difficult to talk. "I-I can't believe it's so- so cold."

"I can't believe we both slept through the night and didn't *know* it was this cold!"

They had decided the logical thing to do was to share the bed. Makenna found some prescription pain pills in the bottom of her overnight bag and took one to ease the pain and stiffness that was taking over her weary body. Hardin helped her prop her leg on a pillow and get adjusted in bed, waited for her to fall asleep, then crawled in beside her. He thought having her warm, soft body next to his would be too seductive for sleep, too stimulating, but he underestimated his own exhaustion. There was something comforting about the sound of her even breathing next to him, something so completely right about sharing her bed, even without sex, that he soon followed her into a dreamless sleep. They both slept the whole night through, awakening this morning to find themselves huddled together for warmth in the frosty cabin. Hardin had ventured out from the covers just long enough to bring them both back socks and all the extra blankets and quilts he could find.

Half an hour later, Hardin had a toasty fire blazing in the fireplace and a pot of coffee on to brew. Makenna took one sip, declared it awful, then nursed the remainder of the cup from her new position in front of the fire. They ate a breakfast of crackers, cheese, and fruit, and tried to drink the hot liquid Hardin called coffee. They ended up throwing out the first pot and brewing a second, but rationed the remainder of the grounds for later use.

As expected, Makenna's bruising was worse, ranging from an angry red to the darker stages of purple and black. Her numerous cuts had finally sealed over and there was no fresh blood loss, but the stiffness and aches in her body had grown twofold.

"But your leg is better, you think?" Hardin confirmed, bringing another cup of coffee to her station on the couch.

"I think so. With all the cuts and blisters on my foot, I can't really stand on that leg anyway, but I think the pain is more manageable this morning."

"Good. Because I think I've come up with a plan on how to get out of here."

Makenna perked up, eager to hear the details as he settled in the chair near the couch and shared his idea. "There will be a full moon tonight. There should be enough moonlight for me to take the bike down the mountain. Last night you said you left your new rental car in the parking lot at the police station, so I'll jump in it, come back and pick you up, and we'll be out of here before full daylight."

"Where will we go? You know they'll be watching the airport."

"That's why we won't fly out of Manchester. We'll go to Boston and fly out of Logan International. I've already been in contact with officials there."

Makenna drew a deep breath, thinking of a dozen things that could go wrong with his plan. "What-What about me? Where will I be while you're gone?"

"Safe and snug up here in the cabin."

She shook her head. "No. I'll wait in the truck, somewhere down the mountain."

"Kenzie-"

"If you leave me here, I'll be totally vulnerable," she cut him off. "If they somehow find their way up here, there's only one way out, and they won't leave that as an option. If we take the truck halfway down, you'll be that much closer into town, and we'll be that much closer to getting out of here before daylight. And if for some reason they do find me, I would at least have the possibility of escape."

"I'd have to find a good place to hide the truck, somewhere it couldn't be seen from the road." Hardin thought aloud as he considered her suggestion. "I guess I could make a run this morning, find a spot somewhere you'd be safe."

The thought of him getting caught was more frightening than the thought of being left alone in the cabin. "You'll be careful?"

"Of course. And on the very remote chance that they somehow tracked us up here, I'll have the advantage, because I'll be on a bike. I don't have to stick to the road. I can slip in and out of the woods, even by foot if necessary. I would be able to hear and see them, long before they'd see me."

"I guess," she said uncertainly.

"I won't be gone all that long. And you had a good idea about the truck." He lifted his coffee mug in salute.

An hour later, Hardin assembled a handful of things within easy reach of the sofa; a glass of water, her phone, a small snack, keys to the truck "just in case", and the Glock. She protested, but he gave her a stern look that brooked no argument. The morning was warming up nicely, so he banked the fire to keep it from overheating the cabin, brought an ice pack for her leg, and promised to be back as soon as possible.

The moment he was gone, Makenna grabbed her cell phone. Thank goodness she had a signal! Giving Hardin time to get his bike and ride out of the clearing, she dialed Kenzie's number.

"Makenna!" her friend cried when she saw who was calling. "Where have you been? I've been trying to call you for two days! Are you all right?"

"Not really."

"Is it the assignment? Are you having trouble with getting photos?"

"No, it's much bigger than just the assignment. We're in a mess, girlfriend. Tell me you're all right."

"I am. I'm getting better every day. I'll probably be released tomorrow, in fact, so we'll both be home about the same time. But something else is wrong, I can hear it in your voice. What is it?"

"Everything! And it's way too much to explain over the phone. I have to ask you some questions, and you have to be absolutely honest with me."

"Okay," her friend agreed slowly, sensing the seriousness of the situation.

"What is your father's name, Kenzie?"

"My father? Why do you keep asking me about my father?"

"Please, Kenzie, just let me ask the questions. Please trust me on this. I'll explain it all later. What is your father's name?"

"Leon Reese."

"Has he ever gone by any other names?"

There was a long silence on the other end of the line. When she finally spoke, Kenzie's voice was strained. "Richard Adams." Her voice fell an octave. "Eddie O'Connell." Almost in a whisper, she continued. "Murray Bickerman. Somebody Black." Her voice was defeated as she whimpered what names she could recall, in no particular order, no designation of given names or surnames. "Ronald. Stanley. McWhorter. Ross. Jefferson."

Makenna's heart ached for her friend, but she pushed on. "Did he ever go by the name Joseph Mandarino?"

"That's- That's the name you asked me about a couple of days ago."

"That's right. Are you familiar with it?"

There was a long hesitation. "I want to say no, but there's something oddly familiar about it. I don't remember it, but yet... Why are you asking all this, Makenna? What does my father have to do with this?"

"Do you know where he is, Kenzie? Do you know where your father is?"

"No. I haven't heard from him in months."

Makenna frowned. "I thought it had been more like years."

"I haven't talked to my mother in years," her friend clarified. "My father actually called me about six months ago. He said he was passing through Texas, thought he'd give me a call. As if he has to be in the same state with me to give any thought to his only child," Kenzie said derisively.

Makenna noticed the words 'only child'; her friend definitely did not know about her twin. Forcing herself to focus, she asked, "What was he doing in Texas, Kenzie? And where does he live now?"

"As always, he was evasive. He was in the Dallas area, scouting out a job. He said my mother had stayed home, and later in the conversation he said something about the weather in Nashville, so I assume they are living in Tennessee. Honestly, that's all I know," she huffed. "Now are you going to tell me what's going on?"

Makenna did not answer immediately. She believed her friend. Perhaps it was best not to tell Kenzie what she had learned. It wasn't merely to spare Kenzie's feelings, it was for her safety; the less she knew about the truth, the less use she was to the mafia. "When I get home," she finally said. "Until then, don't talk to anyone you don't know or who doesn't have a direct reason to talk to you. When you get home, be sure and lock the doors. Don't let anyone in."

"I'm not a little kid, Makenna. I know not to talk to strangers," she said testily. "What is all this about? Do I really have to wait until you get home tomorrow to find out?"

"I-I may stay over a couple more days."

"Why?"

"I told you, I'll explain later. Please, Kenzie, promise me you'll be careful."

"You're starting to scare me."

"And if you should hear from your father, or from anyone asking about your father, let me know. It's extremely important."

"Now you're definitely scaring me."

"I'm just trying to keep you safe."

"From who?" Kenzie asked in bewilderment.

"Please, Ken. Just trust me. And be careful."

"It sounds like you're the one who needs to be careful!"

"I'll be fine, Kenzie." Even as she made the promise, Makenna knew it might not be true. "I'll try to call you tomorrow. Take care of yourself."

"You, too, girlfriend. You too."

Chapter 19

"I think I found a good spot to hide the truck," Hardin reported when he returned. "Good cover, easy in, easy out. Other than being cold, I think you should be fine to wait there."

"I'll wear plenty of layers," Makenna promised. To be honest, she hadn't thought about how cold it would be, sitting in a vehicle during the dark, cold hours of night. But it would be better than waiting up here, miles away, with no chance of escape.

"Let me take a quick shower and find us something to eat, then we can work out our strategy. After that we should take a nap. I figure if we leave around 10:30 tonight, it will put me reaching town before one. With any luck, we should get to Logan by four. There's a 5:50 flight into Austin I plan to be on."

The fire had all but burned out, but Makenna sat staring at the fireplace, lost in thought. Tiny curls of smoke escaped from the ashes, racing upward to the chimney. Would their escape be like that? A race to get away? Fear clutched her stomach as new worries assailed her. Dozens of 'what ifs' entered her mind.

But the moment Hardin stepped from the bathroom, dressed in his wind pants and a clean white t-shirt that clung to him like a second skin, all her worries – every thought in her head! – vanished faster than the smoke tendrils. The man definitely knew how to fill out a t-shirt. Makenna couldn't fault the fabric for clinging to his sculpted abs, hugging his chiseled chest, circling around his bulging biceps. Her eyes did the same. With so much masculinity stuffed into one simple shirt, the entire room suddenly felt smaller. She knew she was staring, she knew she should look away, but her eyes and her brain were not communicating. Her mind, in fact, was completely muddled.

Makenna tried to shift her focus to something else. Her eyes trailed up to his face, so handsome and captivating in its own right. Tiny droplets of water clung to the trim beard that cornered his jaw, and his hair appeared a few shades darker when wet. By the time her eyes finally met his, the extraordinary blue depths twinkled with smug mischief. He was fully aware of his effect on her.

"What they say about hot water is true," he proclaimed. "It does wonders for a body and soul." He padded over to his suitcase on the bed, offering a nice view from the rear. Even the man's bare feet were sexy.

Makenna reminded herself to breathe normally. So she was alone in a secluded mountain cabin with the sexiest man she had ever seen. So what? She had slept beside him in the same bed last night. True, pain and exhaustion had overruled hormones, but she had survived the night without making an idiot of herself. Why ruin it now? Just because she was feeling better and her hormones were making themselves known was no reason to come undone at the mere sight of his powerful body on display.

Deciding the fall had shaken something loose in her head and regions much further south, Makenna chided herself for noticing details like the obvious strength in his feet, the taut stretch of muscle down his thigh, the firm rise of his buttocks, the sharp blade of his honed shoulders. *Assignment.* She reminded herself. *I'm just his assignment.*

"Why don't I rustle us up a meal and we'll eat outside on the back deck?" he asked. "It really is an amazing view."

She was enjoying the view just fine, thank you, but she suddenly needed the space offered by the outdoors.

Using the very muscles she had ogled, Hardin helped Makenna hobble outside. The back porch extended onto a small deck that overhung a steep rocky slope. The view beyond was magnificent, even with its barren trees and dormant grasses. Makenna stood against the rail, careful to keep the weight off her foot while she enjoyed a few moments in an upright position. She imagined what the view must be like in a few more months, when everything was green and lush.

And when she thought about the same view in the fall, the breath quickened in her chest. She could imagine all the vibrant colors, the oranges and golds and reds. Like yesterday, an odd ache stabbed in her heart, and the image in her mind felt more like a memory than a figment of her imagination. Struck again by an overwhelming sensation of deja vu, Makenna contemplated its meaning until Hardin returned with their meal.

"The other picnic basket has fried chicken and potato salad, but I figured we could save that for tonight," he told her as he unloaded the assortment in his arms. "This isn't exactly a conventional meal, but it should be filling."

Makenna surveyed the offering of crackers, two kinds of chips and dips, pimento cheese, chocolate chip cookies, and the locally bottled sodas from the country store they visited. "Looks delicious," she grinned. "And I've always believed in a balanced diet — a cookie in each hand."

"See?" Hardin grinned back. "That's why I fell for you in the first place!"

He went about the task of opening containers and arranging them on the table, oblivious to the wild hammering of her heart. The heavy thud was almost painful, and Makenna idly wondered if she had damaged her heart in the fall. No doubt it was bruised, if only by the knowledge of what could never be. His playful words were simply a reminder that their would-be relationship had been doomed from the beginning; neither of them were who they first professed to be.

After eating, Hardin brought out the first-aid kit and tended to her wounds. Most of them were healing well enough to be left unbandaged. He put another patch on her abdomen, wrapped her foot once again, taped up the gash still puckered near her elbow, and put another ice pack on her leg, even though the swelling was down and the pain was more manageable.

"At least this is the same hand I hurt at Sabbaday Falls." She was trying to look on the bright side as Hardin fussed over her hand. The older cuts, the ones left by briers when she stumbled at the Falls, were puffy and red with infection. She hissed when he insisted on cleaning them out and smearing them with a thick layer of antibiotic salve. He also put generous amounts on two of her fingers where tiny strips of skin were missing, and on a third where a cut sliced over her knuckle. Her entire palm was a mess, crisscrossed with old and new scrapes and lacerations, and the hole left by the stick. Wrapping it with thick bandages seemed the only solution.

"If I haven't said it before, I'm really sorry you were hurt yesterday," he told her solemnly. "If I could have stopped it, you know I would have."

Makenna struggled to follow the thread of the conversation. *What is wrong with me? I'm acting like a teenager!* He was hunched over her hand, muscles flexing and rippling as he wrapped her palm with exquisite care. His fingers were warm where they touched her, his touch strong but gentle. He was close enough she could detect the lingering scent of soap on his tanned skin, and it was having the strangest effect on her senses. *It's that stupid t-shirt he's wearing. Who can think straight with so much testosterone staring you in the face?*

"It was my fault, really," she murmured. "I should have answered your calls, I should have heard you out. I should have trusted you."

"I understand. You didn't know who to trust yesterday. But now?" She could hear the quiet desperation in his voice, the fear. When he looked up to catch her gaze, she saw the intensity in his amazing blue eyes.

Did she trust him? It was a two-fold question.

With her life? Yes.

With her heart? She wasn't sure.

"I pegged you as one of the good guys all along," she answered.

"Yet you believed the worst of me." His voice held more hurt than accusation.

"It's that suspicious nature you accused me of the other night at dinner."

When he didn't look convinced, she squirmed and averted her gaze. "Look, I don't have the best track record with men," she admitted. "It was easier to believe you were evil, than to think I might really have a chance at finding the right guy this time."

A pleased smile hovered around his well-formed mouth. "The right guy, huh? I like the sound of that."

"I should have known you were too good to be true," she muttered. She was aggravated that she still found him so charming, so downright irresistible, even with his smug little grin.

"What's that supposed to mean?"

"You didn't just happen on that flight," she reminded him. "You didn't just happen to sit beside me. We didn't just happen to have some magical connection. It wasn't true. It was all an illusion."

"No," he said flatly. "That's where you're wrong. I could have sat behind you, you know. I could have sat across the aisle. My assignment was to make contact, nothing more. Establish a rapport. Keep a watchful eye on the situation and anyone who might approach you. I could have done that as a casual acquaintance. But one look in your eyes, and I was a goner." He reached out to touch her hair. The curls twined around his fingers greedily, trapping his touch in a silken snare.

"I found myself plopping down right beside you. The more I talked to you, the more I wanted to know about you. Not because of the assignment, but because you were the most interesting and intriguing woman I had met in a very long time." His voice was now low and thrilling as his fingers played in her hair. "I didn't have to kiss you. I didn't intend to kiss you," he admitted. "The Captain will have my hide for getting personally involved, but I couldn't help it. There's just something about you…" He gently pulled her in for a kiss. It was long and lingering, and not nearly enough.

"How can you say there's no magic?" he whispered against her lips. "How else do you describe this crazy feeling? You feel it, too, I know you do." He pulled just far enough away so that his blue eyes could challenge her to deny it.

He already knew her well enough to detect a lie, so she didn't bother with one. "Of course I feel it," she whispered. She rested her forehead – bruises, cuts and all – against his and forced herself to think beyond her heart. "But right now we need a different kind of magic. The kind that can get us off this mountain without being seen."

Hardin was slow in turning loose. "You're right. But when we get out of this mess…." His husky promise sent a delicious shiver of anticipation down her spine as he held her face close a moment longer. Drawing a deep and unsteady breath, he finally set her away and turned his mind to business. "Okay, so let's find a solution."

They discussed their plans for the night, what would happen in different scenarios, what bags to grab if time was of the essence when they switched vehicles, and, most importantly, what escape route she should take if someone found her before Hardin returned.

After an hour of strategy, Hardin stood up and stretched. Makenna couldn't help but watch, fascinated, as his muscles flexed and bowed. "I think we should lie down and try to take a nap. It's going to be a long night."

"I suppose you're right," she sighed. She struggled to her feet, gasping when his strong arms swooped beneath her and he hefted her into the air.

"Hardin, put me down!" she cried, swatting at his arm.

"These muscles aren't just for looks, you know," he teased. He hadn't missed her hungry gaze moments before.

"But-"

"But nothing." Ignoring her protests, he carried her through the door and deposited her at the entrance to the bathroom. "I'll give you a few minutes while I bring in the food."

Makenna took a few extra minutes to study her sad reflection in the mirror. The red was gone from her one eye, but the other was still ringed with a darkening bruise. Her cheek was still a little puffy where the scratch ran along her jawline, but most of the scrapes and scratches looked better today. Makeup would cover most of them; unfortunately, she wasn't wearing any right now. Staring at her image, Makenna was reminded of the little game she had played as a child. Back then, she had murmured compliments to the girl in the mirror, noting how pretty she looked, or how she liked her hair, or commenting on what she was wearing. There would be none of those compliments today!

Hardin knocked lightly on the bathroom door. "Coming," she said, splashing water onto her face in hopes of giving her pale skin some color. He pushed the door open in time to see her forlorn gaze in the mirror.

Then her eyes tangled with Hardin's, and the sudden flame of desire she saw there took her breath away. In one long stride he was at her side, scooping her up into his arms. This time she didn't even protest as he carried her to the bed and eased her down with utmost care, his mouth covering hers.

Mindful of her hurt leg and her many scrapes and bruises, Hardin held himself above her, supporting his weight on his knees and one elbow. The other hand wove a magical path over her skin. His fingers slid down the length of her arm, climbed back up on the tender underside. When his knuckles brushed against the side of her breast, she gave a little whimper. Waiting for permission, his fingers hovered over the soft mound. A deep, unsteady breath pushed the tender flesh up, into his palm. As his fingers curled and gently squeezed, Makenna bit back a tiny groan of pleasure.

Dipping between the buttons of her borrowed shirt and the lacy edge of her bra, Hardin's long fingers dug gently down, until he found the rosy tip he sought. This time Makenna's breath caught in her throat, strangling there with a moan of utter need.

Hardin's nimble fingers released buttons and found the front release of the borrowed bra. Ignoring the bandages on her hand and on her arm, refusing to listen to the voice in her head and the warning in her heart, Makenna reached up to pull him close. She didn't care that she had a wound on her torso and scratches across her chest. She needed to feel the weight of his body pressed against hers, she welcomed the heavy pressure of his muscles, so hot and hard and taut, burning into her soft flesh.

"Your cuts…" he murmured, trying to avoid as many of them as possible.

She was having none of it. "Kiss them and make them better."

He started with the scratch along her jaw, offering tiny little kisses of healing. Down the column of her throat, over the creamy expanse of her collarbone and upper chest, his hot, moist mouth rained curing kisses of pleasure and need. The winding red whelp led his healing tongue down to the fullness of one breast, where he continued his therapeutic methods.

Cradling his head in her hands, bandages and all, Makenna squirmed beneath him. When he pushed her shirt aside and bent to kiss the white patch of gauze on her abdomen, her stomach muscles quivered and her very center turned to molten lava.

"Hardin." She half-breathed, half-begged his name.

His fingers trailed along the waistband of her pants, inching the stretchy fabric down a whisper at a time. His hot mouth worked its way back up the trail of her ribs, licking and kissing and nipping along the path. By the time his tongue found the hard nub of her nipple, his fingers had worked their way down to the moist heat he craved.

"We-We can't do this," she panted, but she held his head to her breast, wanting more.

"I'm pretty sure we can," he teased, turning his attention to her other creamy mound.

"It's not… it's not right."

"It feels right."

It feels wonderful. He twirled his tongue around her nipple, coaxing it and teasing it, until it puckered into a pinpoint of sheer need. At the seam of her very soul, his fingers were prodding and poking, stroking, stirring up sensations of urgency and overwhelming desire.

But you don't even know me by my real name! Before she completely lost control, she reminded herself of that fact. She had to stop things now, before she went over the edge.

"Hardin."

"Please, baby. Please let me make love to you." He pressed his hard body against hers, his desire obvious. His mouth moved to hers, claiming it in a mind-blowing kiss that curled her toes and made her forget all her qualms about being less than honest with him. Another deft move of his fingers, and she was on the verge of coming all to pieces. Another stroke and she would be lost. "Please, Kenzie. I want you so much."

Hearing her friend's name, uttered in the throes of passion by the man making love to *her*, was enough to bring her down from her climb to the stars. Shifting her legs, Makenna struggled against his hand.

Hardin immediately stilled. "Did I hurt you?" he asked in concern.

Because it was easier to let him believe that than to reveal the truth, and because she secretly feared she was a coward, Makenna managed a slight nod.

"Oh, baby, why didn't you tell me?" He rolled off her, careful of her side. "Why didn't you say something? Why didn't you stop me? Damn, I'm such an idiot. I'm sorry, sweetheart, I didn't mean to hurt you."

He was so sincere, so contrite, that tears sprang to her eyes. Seeing the watery drops, he misinterpreted and went into another barrage of self-loathing, which made her cry even more.

"I'm-I'm fine. Really," she insisted. When he still looked doubtful, still looked disgusted with himself, she reached out a hand and ran it over his chest, thrilling at the feel. "Just hold me, please."

Hardin did so gladly, careful to gather her close without disturbing her injuries. Makenna snuggled against him, loving the feel of lying in his arms, yet all the while feeling guilty for letting him think he had physically hurt her. She wanted to tell him the truth, wanted to tell him everything, but there was still too many questions in her mind, and she wanted to protect her best friend. So she lay there, tucked against his side, and ran her hand along the planes of his chiseled chest, down the contours of his rippling ribs, across the rub board of his abs. Beneath her hand, his skin was hot and firm, a true work of art fashioned from flesh and heat.

"Kenzie," he growled in warning, as her hand wandered dangerously low.

"Oh!" She jerked away, startled by the wanderings of her own eager hands.

"I'm trying to be a gentleman here and keep my hands to myself," he told her tightly. "Maybe you should do the same."

Secretly thrilled at the power she held over his amazing body, she tucked her hand beneath her leg and actually giggled. "Maybe I should," she agreed.

"I'm glad one of us thinks this is funny," he mumbled in a thick voice. "Maybe you should try to go to sleep now."

"Maybe you're right."

"Or maybe we should both take a cold shower."

"Maybe so."

"Maybe you should stop giggling and close your eyes." It was becoming a game now.

"Maybe I should."

"Maybe you should do it right now."

"Maybe you should, too."

"Maybe I will."

"Maybe I will, too."

"Maybe this time next week you'll be better, and we won't have to stop."

"Maybe- Maybe so."

"Maybe I should just kiss you right now, and shut you up."

"Maybe so."

"No maybe about it," he said gruffly, turning to kiss her.

"None at all," she whispered, welcoming his lips.

Snuggling down beside him once more, Makenna smiled. "Sleep tight."

A smile hovered around his mouth as he settled his head against his pillow. "Maybe."

Snuggled together on the bed, they slept for a couple of hours. Evening shadows darkened the cabin when they awoke, alerting them of the evening yet to come. As Makenna sat on the edge of the bed and packed their bags, Hardin pulled together their last meal at the cabin. He found a Thermos in the cabinets and filled it with hot water so it could preheat, thinking a pot of hot coffee would help to keep her warm while she waited along the mountainside.

After they ate, Hardin repacked their remaining food into a picnic basket and made certain the coals were no longer glowing in the fireplace. Makenna tidied the cabin best she could, and soon it was ten thirty, and time to leave.

They drove down the mountainside mostly in silence, both lost in their own thoughts. Hardin went over the directions with her again, making certain she knew which way to go if she had to make a quick escape. They devised a signal for when he approached, and a code word he would use if, for some reason, something went terribly wrong and he was not alone when he returned. Half way down the mountain, Hardin pulled off the road, maneuvering behind a dense copse of tangled vines and small trees with thick undergrowth. Killing the engine, he got out of the truck, walked back to the lane, and shone his flashlight into the brush from different heights and angles. Satisfied that the truck would not reflect any oncoming headlights, he then popped the hood and dismantled the truck's own lighting panel.

"This way you can start the truck every hour or so and run the heater, without the headlights or interior lights coming on," he explained as he helped her from the passenger side, into the driver's seat. He tucked a borrowed blanket around her and made certain she had the Thermos of coffee, a flashlight, and a few snacks within easy reach. "Don't go crazy with the heater, but don't freeze yourself, either.

If you have to make a getaway, remember that you can pull out of here either way, whichever path is clear. I'll call when I get to the car. It should take me about thirty to forty minutes to get back up here after that. I'll let you know when I'm close."

"Are you sure you'll be safe?" New doubts and worries attacked her. She clutched at his arm, afraid to let him go.

"I'll be fine," he assured her gently. "I can slip in and out of town before anyone even sees me."

"But it's so dangerous. And so cold! Are you sure you have on enough clothes?"

"Probably too many, once I get started," he chuckled. The air was so cold his words came out in puffs of steam, but he knew the ride would be strenuous enough to work up a sweat. He tugged off a glove and cupped her face with his bare hand. He wanted to feel the softness of her cheek against his palm. "I'm more worried about you. I'm letting in cold air, standing here in the door, and it's going to get plenty cold while you just sit here. As soon as I leave, turn the truck back on and get the heat up to a comfortable level, then wait as long as you can to turn it back on. We need to conserve fuel, but we can't have you getting frostbite, either."

"I'll be fine. I have on three pairs of socks, two layers of clothes, a jacket, and a blanket. There's another blanket if I need it, and the Thermos of coffee. And I'll turn on the heated seats while the motor's running. I'll be as snug as a bug in a rug."

"Maybe this will help, too," he murmured, moving in for a kiss.

"Mm." Warmed by the heat of his mouth on hers, she didn't need the extra layers of clothing. In fact, she preferred no clothing at all.

"I need to go," he finally whispered, his face still pressed against hers. She could hear the reluctance in his voice.

"Be safe." She tried to keep the fear out of her voice.

"I'll be back for you as soon as I can." One more quick kiss, and he shut the door behind him. In the moonlight, Makenna watched as he unloaded the bike, tinkered with a few adjustments, then swung onto it with that smooth, lithe grace he possessed. He waved as he peddled away from the truck and disappeared into the night.

Makenna stared into the shadows long after he was gone. She tried to shake off the sense of despair threatening to engulf her. It was going to be a long, cold night, with only her over-active imagination to keep her company.

So many things could go wrong tonight. What if Bob and Lisa were watching the car? What would they do to Hardin if they caught him sneaking into town? What would they do to her if they followed him back here, or if they found her before he returned? Possibilities swirled in her head, fueled by her fears. She spent the next half hour imagining different scenarios, none of which brought any comfort. As the cold set in and she began to shiver, she started the pick-up and let the heater run. Soon the cab was filled with the blessed warmth, but she knew the chill of fear running down her spine wouldn't ease until Hardin had returned.

With her backside toasty from the heated seat and her toes sufficiently thawed, Makenna killed the motor and settled in for another hour. She stared out into the night, knowing she would find the mountain setting delightful under different circumstances. Beneath the full moon, the asphalt road was a glowing dark ribbon woven between shadowed lace. The moon was bright enough to see into the edge of the woods, where individual trees and branches could be deciphered, giving the shadows a lacy effect. She tried to concentrate on the beauty, admiring the willowy limbs and spindly trunks, but the solitude of the night was nearly overwhelming.

When she saw movement in the trees, her breath froze in her chest. Finally her breath sputtered out, jagged and painful, as she kept her eyes trained on the woods. The shifting shadows played tricks on her vision, morphing into demons, teasing her with glimpses of movement. She saw a possible arm, the fangs of a wolf, a shuffling shadow that could have been a man's head. Inside the silence of the truck, her heart hammered out a crazy tempo of fear, and even she could hear her own coarse breathing.

After at least fifteen minutes of scrutinizing the shadows, Makenna convinced herself it was only her imagination playing tricks on her. She forced herself to close her strained eyes. Opening them again, she saw a shaggy leg stepping from the shadows. As her heart tripped over a double beat and began to race, she saw the rest of a body appear. Tall and lanky, the shaggy moose stepped cautiously into the moonlight, followed by its calf. Makenna was laughing and crying, both at the same time, as relief flooded through her.

Deciding not to stare into the shadows after that, Makenna tried concentrating on something pleasant. She would think of Hardin. Hardin, with his hard, taut body, and his mind tingling kisses. Hardin, with his funny sense of humor and his amazing blue eyes. Hardin, with his whispered words of magic and his hints of a future together. Makenna closed her eyes and smiled. Hardin.

An hour later, she was staring into the shadows once more, swearing she saw something move. No moose stepped forth this time. It was time to start the motor again but she was afraid to, knowing the sound would give away her hidden location. Her fingers and toes were so cold they were numb, and her backside not far from it. The cold had seeped into her bones and her many cuts and bruises, making them ache worse than ever. She was cold and stiff and hurting, but as bad as her discomfort was, her fear was even worse. She held out until her teeth began to chatter and the noise began to grate on her nerves. Only then did she turn the key and allow the warmth to flood the vehicle.

The clock slowly ticked off the minutes, dragging their way into hours. It gave her entirely too much time to think, too much time to piece together the puzzle rattling around in her head. When her phone rang, the sound was loud and jarring in the empty cab, even though she had the volume turned low. Her fingers were clumsy as she nervously brought the devise to her ear and whispered a hoarse, "Hello?"

"Kenzie."

Hardin's voice was music to her ears. She closed her eyes, savoring the sweet sound. "Did you make it? Are you okay?"

"I'm fine. I made it here to the car without any problems. I can't say for sure without a detector, but the car doesn't appear to have a tracking device on it."

"Are you sure we shouldn't get the police in on this?"

"I told you, I didn't get a good vibe when I talked to them about the gray car. And I saw an officer talking to Bob the other morning. Could have been innocent, but the way he kept looking over his shoulder, I don't think so. I'm not willing to risk it."

"You're the expert. I trust your judgment," she told him.

"How you holding up?"

Did she have to divulge all her secrets? Should she confess to being afraid of the shadows? "I'll be fine when you get here."

"On my way, babe. See you in just over a half hour."

"Please be careful."

"Always, sweetheart. Always."

Thirty-eight minutes later, Hardin called again, saying he was close. Another minute and a half ticked away before Makenna saw headlights. She slid down behind the dash in fear, until the lights blinked twice, a third time, and she was certain it was him behind the wheel. He pulled up close to the truck and left the motor running as he came to get her.

"Hardin!" She fairly launched herself into his arms, relief making her weak.

"Kenzie, are you all right?" He peered down at her, worried by the tears that streaked her face.

"Just-Just so relieved you're back!" She hugged him hard, then pulled away to gather her things from the truck.

They made quick work of transferring their belongings from the truck into the car. Hardin helped her hobble to the passenger seat of the car, tucked her inside, and then hurried to get behind the wheel. He pulled out of their hide-away, less than five minutes after he arrived.

"You might as well get some sleep," he told her.

As they hit one of the many potholes littering their path, Makenna grimaced. "Not likely, at least until we get on a smoother road."

"Sorry. I know it's rough, but I don't want to waste any time. We need to make that 5:50 flight."

"What then, Hardin? Obviously the mafia knows I live in Austin."

"I already talked to the FBI. They were putting out a BOLO for Bob and Lisa and both the gray and green sedans. Hopefully they already have the Lewises in custody and the Zaffinos know we're onto them."

"But if they still think I can lead them to Joseph Mandarino…"

"We'll just have to convince them you can't."

Chapter 20

Fayetteville, North Carolina
May, 2006

"Where do you think you're going?" her mother asked tersely. She came into the bedroom and saw the suitcase lying across the bed, already crammed full with clothes.

"I'm leaving," the girl answered.

"Don't be ridiculous. You can't just walk out the door."

The girl turned to look at her mother, the woman who, for the past eighteen years, had fed her body but starved her soul. Until now, she hadn't realized how much her mother had aged, how she looked a decade older than her forty years. Her once lovely face was lined and haggard, her eyes dull and tired. But her body was rigid, like always. Rigid and cold.

Squaring her shoulders, the girl lifted her chin and said saucily, "Then maybe you should tell me how it's done. You have plenty of experience at just picking up and walking away. Tell me, Mother, how does one walk out of one's old life? What's the proper way?"

"Don't get smart with me, young lady. Your father and I have provided for you the best we could."

There was no sass in the girl's reply, just sadness. "Your best wasn't good enough."

Her mother flinched and took a step backwards, as if the girl had physically hit her, but her shoulders remained square and stiff. "Where will you go?"

"I've been accepted to a college in Texas."

"Texas?" A light flickered in the older woman's dull eyes.

"Don't worry, it's not going to cost you a dime. I've gotten a scholarship and applied for financial aid."

"How? When did you do all this?" her mother asked sharply.

"I've been working on it for months, not that you noticed. The school counselor helped me." The girl returned to her packing. Sadly enough, her entire world fit into two mis-matched suitcases, one cardboard box, and a worn duffle bag.

"When will you leave?"

"I called for a cab to take me to the bus station. It should be here in an hour."

"You weren't going to tell us good-bye?" The only indication of emotion was the high-pitched trill in her mother's voice.

"I was never allowed to say good-bye in the past," the girl reminded her bitterly. "I didn't see any need in starting it now."

Her mother made no comment, gave no facial response. She simply watched the girl pack. The girl wasn't even surprised when her mother slipped quietly out the door.

She was surprised, however, when her mother returned.

"I have something for you," she said, holding out a manila envelope.

"What-What is it?" the girl asked warily.

"Money. There's five thousand dollars in there. It should help you make a fresh start."

The girl stared at the envelope, clearly in shock. Her mother had never offered her more than twenty dollars at a time. "I-I don't understand."

She gave a nonchalant shrug. "We were planning to leave next month anyway. You take this. We can wait another month or two." Her demeanor changed abruptly as she handed the girl another envelope, this one larger and heavier. The words 'Warranties, etc.,' were scrawled across its crumbled face. "Do not open this," she said emphatically. "Keep this somewhere safe. Never lose this. But never open it."

"What-What is it?" The girl took the envelope hesitantly, as if touching it might be dangerous. The look on her mother's face told her that it was.

"It's life insurance."

"I don't understand..."

"You aren't supposed to. For your own safety, listen to what I am telling you." Her mother's voice was urgent. "Keep this envelope safe, never let anyone know you have it, and never open it."

"But why-"

Her mother cut off her questions. "You'll know when the time comes." She stepped back, and for the first time a look of uncertainty, a look of vulnerability, crossed her lined face. "I always did what I thought was best for my family. Try to remember that."

"I don't understand," the girl repeated, her whisper thick with threatening tears.

Squaring her shoulders once again, the older woman's face slipped back into its mask of indifference. "It would be best if you were gone when your father returns." She moved stiffly to the door. "Take care of yourself. Make a good life."

The girl watched as her mother walked stoically out of her life. No goodbyes, no hugs, no sentiment whatsoever.

It had been that way her entire life.

Wiping away her tears, the girl quickly finished packing, adding the two new envelopes to her purse. When she was done, she looked around the sparsely furnished room she had slept in for the past twenty months, feeling little emotion.

She stepped to the mirror, examining her reflection. Eighteen, but she felt – she acted - a decade older. She touched her palm to the cool glass and vowed this would be the final time. No more nomadic lifestyle for her. This time when she left, she was leaving with the same look, the same name. This time, she was leaving on her own terms. And where she settled, she would stay.

"I'll never forget you," she told the girl in her mirror. "I'll never forget you, so that I'll never be like you. My new life starts now."

Chapter 21

They made the airport with time to spare. Even after buying tickets and eating an early breakfast, they had to wait for their flight. Hardin kept a careful watch on their surroundings, alert for signs of danger. Seeing the opportunity to make a private phone call, Makenna accepted his help as she limped her way to the ladies' room.

After taking care of necessities, she pulled up her jeans and settled, fully dressed, on the commode to make a phone call. The line connected on the third ring.

"Mom?" When she heard her mother's voice, even though it was a groggily spoken hello, a lump formed in her throat.

"Makenna? Makenna, honey, is something wrong?"

"I-I need to talk to you, Mom. I'm sorry to wake you. I know it's early." She glanced at the time on her cell phone, realizing it wasn't even four-thirty yet in Texas.

She heard her mother murmur something, then her father's sleepy response. Even muffled, their voices were a welcomed and heartwarming sound. "Don't worry about the time. Is something wrong?"

"I need to ask you something, Mom."

"Anything. Do you need something? Money? I'll give you my credit card number right now. Let me get my purse-"

"No, Mom, I don't need money. I just need to ask you a few questions."

She heard her mother stifle a yawn. "Yes, yes. What would you like to know?"

Makenna squeezed her eyes shut and started the conversation she had never before broached. "When- When you and Daddy adopted me, was it a sealed adoption?"

Madeline Reagan was silent for a moment before answering. Makenna could swear she heard her mother's heart breaking, even over thousands of miles and cellular airways. "Why do you ask, Makenna? You've never shown any interest in knowing about your… your real parents."

"You and Daddy are my real parents," she was quick to say. "The only parents I've ever wanted, the only parents I'll ever need. Please believe that." Makenna sniffed away a tear. "And I'm not asking because I want to find them. Not for myself, anyway. But-But something happened while I was up here. Mom, I think I remember living here as a child."

"I-I don't know, honey. Honestly I don't. I'm afraid I don't know much about your first three years."

"What do you know? How did you and Daddy get me?"

She heard her mother sigh. "You know the church in San Antonio where Tracey and Peter got married last year? Your Aunt Patsy used to be secretary there. One morning when she got to work, there was a precious little girl curled up on the back pew. I happened to be in town, meeting her for breakfast at her office. I took one look at the little girl with her big green eyes and long reddish brown curls, and my heart absolutely melted. We were already in the system from having adopted your brother Seth. With the help of our lawyer and our friend who was a social worker, we were able to take you home with us. When no one came forward to claim you, we were able to legally adopt you within a few years." She could hear the tears in her mother's voice. "But you were our daughter, long before the courts said so. We loved you from the very first moment we saw you."

"As far as I'm concerned, you and Daddy are the only parents I've ever had. Please understand, that's not what this is about. I just need to know if you have any clue to my real identity."

Madeline Reagan was slow in answering. "You had a little satchel with you. It had a change of clothes, a children's book, a little doll, and a blanket." Her voice was sad as she recalled the meager possessions. "I'm sorry, Makenna. I kept them for you, of course. But that's all I know about your first three years."

"Did I tell you my name? Was it by chance Tamara?" The name Tamara Mandarino once again popped into her mind.

"You didn't talk much. What little you did say was often gibberish. We named you Makenna, after ourselves. Part Madeline, part Kenneth."

News of speaking gibberish cemented her suspicions. "Mom, I-I think I have a twin sister," Makenna said hesitantly.

The statement did not surprise her mother. She could almost hear her nodding through the phone. "I've often wondered," she said softly.

"You knew?" Makenna gasped. "How did you know? Why didn't you say anything?"

"The two of you are so much alike, yet polar opposites in many ways, like two halves of a whole. You have the same mannerisms, the same tilt of the chin when you're angry, the same laugh. But Kenzie never speaks of her parents. She never hinted at having a sister. We never said anything, because we weren't sure she knew."

"She doesn't. She doesn't know I'm her twin sister," Makenna said sadly. "Oh, Mom, it's not fair! It's not fair that they gave me away and I had such a happy childhood, when they kept her and made her so miserable. Poor Kenzie never had the home I had. She never had real parents, like you and Daddy."

She heard a sniff on the other end of the line. "That's the sweetest thing you've ever said to me," her mother said in a voice thick with tears.

"Thank you, Mom. Thank you and Daddy for making me your daughter," Makenna whispered.

"We love you, sweetheart. And we love Kenzie, as if she were own daughter, too. In all the ways that matter, she is."

"I-I have to go now, Mom. But is Daddy awake? Can I speak to him for a minute?"

She could hear the phone being handed off, then her father's sleep roughened voice. "Makenna? How's my girl?"

"I think I'll be okay, Daddy. I just wanted to hear your voice. And I wanted to tell you I love you."

"I love you too, baby girl."

"I've gotta go now. Give everyone a kiss for me."

"Will do. Be safe and hurry home."

Wiping away her tears, Makenna dropped the phone back into the zippered pouch of her purse. She had always known she was adopted, but had never felt the need to know about her birth parents. They had chosen to give her away, after all.

Makenna hobbled her way up to the row of sinks, where she washed her hands and blotted her face with cold water. She still looked pathetic, what with her black eye and assorted cuts and scrapes, and now the added dark smudges of a sleepless night. New worry lines creased her forehead, compliments of a man named Joseph Mandarino, a man whose blood ran through her veins. She puffed out a sigh, realizing her life had just become very complicated.

From behind her, she heard a woman speak. Her blood ran cold at the sound of the nasal whine, minus the Southern drawl. "Well, well, well, look what the cat drug up."

Makenna's eyes flew up, meeting Lisa Lewis's cold gaze in the mirror.

There was another woman at the sinks, and it was for her benefit that Lisa cooed her next words. "You poor dear. I warned you about that man. Looks like he beat you again."

Makenna darted her gaze to the other woman, hoping for help, but she saw her shocked expression as she shirked away, a small gasp escaping her lips.

"It's not what you think," she tried to assure the woman, who was already turning to leave. "Please, don't go! I need your help."

"I'm here to help you, dear," Lisa sneered. "If only you had listened to me the first time, none of this would have happened."

"Hardin didn't do this to me, and you know it!" Makenna hissed. "This happened when I was trying to escape from *you* and whatever drug you put in my drink!"

"Don't be silly, dear, why on earth would I have drugged you?" Lisa was still speaking in her cheerfully piercing voice as if nothing was wrong, but her cold, flat eyes told a different story. She stepped up close to Makenna, trapping the younger woman between the sink and her round belly. She dropped her voice so that anyone else in the restroom would not be able to hear her next words. "Drugging you will be the least of your worries, little lady. You're coming with me."

"No I'm not!" Makenna tried to move away, but her injured leg made her efforts slow and jerky.

"Don't make a scene," Lisa warned lowly. "You're going to walk out that door and down the corridor with your good friends the Lewises and no one will ever be the wiser."

"Hardin would never allow that."

"Pretty boy has no say so in the matter."

"What do you want with me?" Makenna cried, wrenching her arm free of Lisa's grasp. She wondered if the other woman knew who she really was, or if she still thought she was Kenzie?

"Your father. We want your father."

"I have no idea where Joseph Mandarino is." With a sudden surge of bravado, Makenna lifted her chin defiantly. "And even if I did, why would I tell you?"

Lisa looked at her with calculating eyes. "Because if you don't, people are going to get hurt. Starting with your boyfriend out there. Then maybe I'll send someone to your apartment, to visit your roommate. Wouldn't it be sad if your apartment developed a gas leak, and the whole building went up? With all your friends still inside?"

Obviously she still thought she was talking to Kenzie Reese.

And obviously she had no conscience whatsoever.

"I'm telling you, I have no idea where Joseph Mandarino is."

"Take a guess."

"Possibly Nashville."

"We'll check it out. Now come on."

"Why do I need to come with you? Where are we going?"

"Years ago, your father got a little too greedy. He arranged for several millions of dollars to go into his own private bank account as soon as this NorthWind project goes on-line. The Zaffinos want to make a simple trade. His daughter for their money."

"You're- You're holding me for ransom?"

Lisa shrugged her rounded shoulders. "Call it what you like. It's really just a business transaction."

As another woman stepped into the restroom, Lisa's voice turned syrupy with concern. "You poor dear, look what he did to you! Don't you worry, I won't let him touch you again!"

"Wait! What are you – My leg! I can't walk!" Makenna gasped in pain as Lisa tried to drag her from the restroom.

"He broke your leg, too? That brute! We'll have him arrested this minute!"

Makenna shook her head, trying to force words through the pain. She reached out a hand to the woman Lisa was dragging her past, but she could only manage a faintly whispered, "Help me."

"I'm helping you, dear," Lisa cooed, shooing the other woman away. To an onlooker, it looked as if she was supporting Makenna's weight, rather than forcing her to move. "And I promise to protect you. That man can no longer hurt you."

The moment they stepped into the corridor, Makenna's eyes searched for Hardin. She saw him at the water fountain across the way, his back to her. When she would have called to him, Lisa jerked her arm and threatened, "Don't even think about it. If you want him to leave this airport alive, keep your mouth shut."

Makenna watched as the bald man from Sabbaday Falls stepped up beside Hardin. His hand was in his jacket pocket, suggesting a weapon. Before Makenna could see what would happen, a motorized cart zipped up beside her, blocking her view of Hardin. Bob was in the driver's seat, wearing an ill-fitting airport uniform on his long, lanky frame and a cap that concealed much of his face.

The moment the cart stopped, Lisa was pushing Makenna into it, where she fell ungracefully inside. Unable to use her left leg as an anchor to sit up and scoot over, Makenna was sprawled over the entire seat, leaving Lisa still outside the vehicle.

Seeing her opportunity, Makenna acted fast. Already half-lying on the seat, she reached down and used her hand to press firmly on the accelerator. The cart lurched forward, knocking an unsuspecting Lisa to the ground. As the back wheel drove over her leg, the wounded woman shrieked in pain, her grating voice loud and piercing. More concerned with the assignment than his wife, Bob stomped his foot on the petal and sped away, leaving her to writhe there on the ground.

Makenna snatched her hand from beneath his shoe and struggled to an upright position, yelling and waving her arm to catch Hardin's attention. Bob reached out to grab her, struggling to maneuver the motorized cart among the crowd with just one hand.

Borrowing one of Lisa's moves, Makenna jabbed her elbow into his bony side with all her might. He jerked, causing the cart to whip to the right. Makenna pulled on the steering wheel as hard as she could, using both hands as she battled him for control of the wheel. The cart made another sharp right and curled into a spin. Pedestrians in the corridor shrieked and ran. The tail of the cart caught a newsstand and sent papers and magazines flying in all directions, just before the rack came down with a resounding crash. Bob stomped his foot on the brake and the cart made a crazy zigzag as it skidded down the corridor, scraping and bouncing along the far left wall. They finally came to a stop, lodged amid the front counter of a coffee shop.

Bob was pinned behind the steering wheel, coffee beans raining down onto his head. Makenna managed to free herself from the mess and hop a few feet away, well out of his reach. She looked back and saw a security officer running toward them, followed closely by Hardin, who was literally dragging the bald man along with him. Lisa was still squirming on the floor, surrounded by a small crowd and at least one person in uniform. As another officer joined the sprint toward them, Hardin thrust the bald man into his path.

"Texas Ranger," he barked. "Hold this man in custody."

Without the baggage of the hefty bald man, Hardin easily outran the first officer and reached the wrecked cart well before the others. Sweeping Makenna into his arms and pulling her trembling body close, he tucked her against his right side. He presented on the left, his voice harsh as he spoke to the man behind the wheel.

"Bob Lewis, you are under arrest for kidnapping!"

Watching Hardin in motion left Makenna in awe. She was filled with warring emotions of pride and fear.

There was no doubt Hardin Kaczmarek was a highly trained professional. After making certain she was not injured, he settled her into the nearest seat and went about the business of securing Bob Lewis until the proper authorities arrived. With all three would-be kidnappers detained and handcuffed, Hardin calmly and systematically helped the officers understand the injustices involved. Makenna was fascinated with his stoic facial expressions and body language; despite his casual attire, there was no denying the hard edge of his professionalism and his no-nonsense approach to the law. Even though he was not the officer in charge and was clearly out of his jurisdiction, he possessed an air of command that garnered the respect of his fellow lawmen.

Knowing that such a vibrant, masculine male was attracted to her – more than attracted, if she dared to believe- brought a peel of pleasure to her heart, a glow of pride to her cheeks. Knowing that she lied to and deceived such an honest, dedicated man of the law sent a ripple of fear down her spine, a stab of cold dread to her soul. How would he react to the news she had been misleading him all this time? Could he ever forgive her?

When paramedics arrived with two stretchers, one for Lisa and one for her, Makenna protested. Lisa was still wailing in pain, between adamant denials of any wrongdoing on her part and accusations aimed at Makenna's reckless driving. Makenna – with her injured leg, black eye, re-opened and now bleeding elbow wound, bandaged foot and hand, and all her various cuts and bruises – suffered in silence. She resisted when the paramedics tried to treat her, until Hardin extricated himself from the circle of lawmen and appeared at her side.

"Sweetheart, you need to have your leg seen. You need stitches in your arm and maybe on your foot and hand. Go with the medics." His tone was gentle but firm as he squatted in front of her.

"I'll be fine," she denied.

"You can't walk," he reminded her. He touched her face gently, his amazing blue eyes filled with concern. "Do this for me. Please?"

Makenna knew that once she was admitted to the hospital, her true identity would be revealed. She had to be the one to tell Hardin, if there was any hope of him ever forgiving her. "Hardin, I-I have to tell you something."

He brushed his thumb over her cheek, careful of the scratch running along its edge. "We have many things to talk about, babe. There are so many things I want to say to you, tell you. But all of that can wait. I need you well." His voice dropped an octave, so that only she could hear. "We have unfinished business, after all." There was enough heat in his gaze to steal her breath and hold it hostage.

When it released with a sputter, she tried to make him understand the urgency of her request. "B-But-But I need –"

"I need *you*." He silenced her protests with his softly spoken words. His eyes glowed with promise. "I need you healthy and well. Please, sweetheart, go with the paramedics. I'll be right there beside you, all the way." The kiss he dropped on her lips was brief and chaste.

"I-I guess," she agreed reluctantly.

"Ranger Kaczmarek?" A policeman called him, so Hardin gave her a last smile of encouragement and left her with the medics as he stepped away.

An hour and a half later, Makenna was dressed in a less-than-fashionable hospital gown, propped up on pillows in the ER exam room. She had been poked, probed and prodded, and they hadn't even touched her leg, except for x-rays. Makenna knew that when the doctors and nurses were through with her, law enforcement would take over. They would have endless questions for her, she was sure.

When the curtain parted and she saw Hardin step inside with a big smile and a small bouquet of flowers, her heart melted.

"How's our patient?" he asked. He leaned over the bed rail and kissed her gently.

"I hurt more now than I did when I came in," Makenna complained. "They insisted on scraping off most of my skin and pouring pure acid into every one of my scrapes and cuts."

Hardin chuckled. "I doubt it was quite that bad."

"Easy for you to say. You aren't sporting thirteen new stitches."

"Ouch. Thirteen?"

"Five in my arm, two on my side, four on my foot, two on my palm."

"My poor baby," he crooned, kissing her again. This time his lips lingered.

"Hardin," she whispered, moved by the tenderness and the touch of desperation in his kiss. "I have to tell you something."

"I have to tell you something, too." He rested his forehead against hers, his warm breath fanning her face. "When I saw you with them, being taken away from me… God, woman, I was never so scared in my life. I was so afraid of what they might do to you." His whisper was gentle on her lips. "I was afraid of losing you."

A tear trickled down her cheek. He caught the salty drop with his tongue. She could taste it when he kissed her again. "You already mean so much to me," he whispered. "The thought of losing you…" His kiss deepened, flavored by more of her tears and his own sense of anguish. "Kenzie, I think I'm falling in love with you."

His hoarsely whispered admission caused her tears to fall harder. She pulled away, unable to meet his gaze.

He straightened, but not fully. "Too soon?" he asked ruefully. "That was one of the things I was going to tell you about myself. I tend to be a little … intense." He searched for the right word. "I've been called extreme, avid, even over-zealous at times. I prefer to call myself passionate. When there's something I want, something I believe in, I don't hold back. I don't believe in halfway." He took a tendril of her dark copper hair and twirled it around his finger. "I understand if this is too much, too soon. But I believe in us. I believe what we have is real. And when it's something as important as you and me, I can be a patient man."

Makenna managed to shake her head, biting on her lip to keep it from trembling. "It's not that," she whispered. "I know we've only known each other a few days, but – but I feel the same. But there are things you don't know about me. Major things."

"I'm willing to dedicate the next sixty or so years to learning every single thing about you, big and small."

"You-You may not feel that way when you hear what I have to say." She took a deep breath of courage. "Hardin –"

Before she could continue, the doctor chose that moment to step into the cubicle. "Hello there, Miss Reagan. I'm the Orthopedic, Dr. Moran. How are you doing this fine morning?"

"I've-I've been better," Makenna said, darting a glance at Hardin. He had a slight frown of confusion on his handsome face as he stepped back and made room for the doctor.

"I can imagine. It appears you took a pretty bad tumble. Luckily, most of your wounds are superficial, except for this leg. I have some good news and some bad news on that front."

"And that would be…?"

"The bad news is, you do, indeed, have a hairline fracture in your left fibula. The good news is, it won't require surgery. I think if you keep it elevated with plenty of ice to reduce swelling, you should be fine with an air cast. It will give you the support you need to keep from doing further damage. Stay off it for a few days as much as you can, then you should be good to go. Check with your own doctor in about two weeks so he can evaluate your progress. Any questions? Is this Mr. Reagan? Will he be the one taking care of you?"

"Hardin Kaczmarek," Hardin supplied, extending his hand. "And, yes, I plan to keep a close eye on Miss Reese."

The doctor frowned, glancing down at the chart in his hands. "I'm a little confused. This says your name is Makenna Reagan. Am I in the wrong room?" The doctor glanced around, clearly not understanding the situation.

"No," Makenna murmured softly. She avoided Hardin's eyes as she said spoke louder. "No, Doctor, you're in the right room. And yes, my name is Makenna Reagan."

Chapter 22

Makenna could feel the anger rolling off Hardin. It came in waves.

If the doctor noticed the tension in the room, he chose to ignore it. He gave her a few more instructions, told her someone would be in to move her to the casting room, and then was gone. Only then did Makenna dare to steal a glance at Hardin.

He was wearing his stoic officer face. No emotion showed, not even in his eyes. That was what frightened Makenna the most.

"Hardin, I can explain," she whispered.

"Which part can you explain, *Miss Reagan?*" He emphasized the name. "The part where you lied to me, and have been lying for the entire week? The part where you lied to the police, told them your name was Kenzie Reese? Why would you do that, anyway? Especially given all the trouble your friend is in? Do you realize you were almost drugged, almost *kidnapped*, because you were pretending to be someone you aren't?"

"You don't understand. Kenzie is my best friend. I would do anything for her. So when she was in a car wreck – the wreck where your Ranger friend was injured – right before her plane left, she asked me to take her place. This assignment was very important to her career, and – oh, my gosh! Where's her camera?" Makenna interrupted herself to look around frantically for her friend's fancy camera.

"I have it. It's safely locked in the car."

"Good. Oh, and what about our luggage? I guess it made the flight, even though we didn't."

"Taken care of." He was obviously irritated at her wandering thoughts. "You were trying to make me understand why you've been lying to me all week?"

Makenna laid her head back on the pillow, staring up at the white ceiling tiles. She was so tired, so weary and exhausted, not to mention in significant pain. But she had to make Hardin understand. He was too important to her. The entire story came gushing out of her, mingling with her fears and tears.

"Against my better judgment, I agreed to take her place on this trip and pretended to be her. But I felt so guilty about it. That's why I was so nervous on the plane. I just knew they were going to catch me any minute, pretending to be someone I wasn't. Do you think they'll press charges against me? Not that I don't deserve it. I know what I did was wrong. Especially lying to you. I'm so sorry, Hardin. I-I felt so horrible about not telling you the truth. Everything I told you was true, everything about the Reagan and Reese families was true, I just … switched perspectives. I told it from Kenzie's point of view. And then when all this crazy stuff about Joseph Mandarino started to happen, I didn't tell the truth because I wanted to protect Kenzie. If everyone followed me to New Hampshire, thinking I was her, at least she was safe. How could she defend herself, laid up in a hospital room with a broken leg? And she truly has no idea who her father really is. I couldn't just throw her to the wolves."

"You could have trusted me." Finally, there was some emotion in his voice; pain and betrayal.

"I should have," Makenna admitted on a whisper, rambling on. "But I foolishly listened to Lisa, and believed the worst of you. And then I found out you were a Ranger, and I knew you would be duty bound to uphold the law. I not only used her plane ticket, I pretended to be her when I rented the car. I'm sure that's some sort of insurance fraud or something. And then when we were about to make love, and you called me the wrong name... it nearly killed me. I'm sorry, I let you think you had hurt my leg, but it was my heart that was hurting, and my conscience." Tears streamed down her face as she talked. "And then... and then you told me about the other daughter, the twin, and I was so confused. How could I tell you who I was, when I wasn't even sure myself?"

"I don't think I follow," Hardin said with a frown. She was talking so fast, it was hard to keep up.

"I've always known I was adopted. But I never wanted to find my birth parents, because Madeline and Kenneth Reagan are the absolute best parents in the world and I am so lucky to be a part of their family. It never mattered to me, or to them, that we didn't have a blood connection. Somewhere in the back of my mind I was afraid something like this would happen, that if I ever looked for my parents they might be terrible people, so maybe it was best to just never know. But the cabin and the feeling of deja vu and the game I used to play in the mirror..."

She stopped to take a deep breath, exhausted after her endless line of chatter. She would have continued, but Hardin broke in, the light of understanding dawning in his eyes.

"You said you were like the same person, split in two," he murmured, recalling something she had told him. "You said you were so much alike. You looked alike, sounded alike." With a sense of certainty, he nodded and said, "You're the other twin."

Makenna closed her eyes, still trying to absorb the truth. "I never knew. Never even guessed. Seriously, Kenzie and I can finish the other one's sentence. We know exactly what the other is thinking. People mistake us for sisters all the time. From the very beginning, we were so close, and I knew I was adopted, yet it never occurred to me that we might actually be sisters."

"Of course not, if she thought she was an only child," he reasoned.

"But shouldn't I have known? I feel like I'm a terrible person, because I didn't recognize my own twin."

"A twin you never knew existed. Besides, deep down you did recognize her. You've told me more than once that she is just like a sister to you."

Despite his own anger and disappointment, Hardin was trying to make her feel better. Makenna's heart melted. He was such a good man. No wonder she had fallen for him so quickly. She hoped his compassionate words meant they still had a chance, but right now her thoughts were focused on her best friend. Her sister. "I can't wait to call Kenzie. To tell her!"

Before she could savor the anticipation of that conversation, a nurse came in, followed by an aide. "Ready for a ride? We need to take another x-ray, then get you fitted for a cast." The pretty, young nurse let her eyes trail over Hardin. "You can wait in the family waiting room. She should be done before long."

Hardin didn't seem to notice the nurse's interest. He leaned over the bed, pressing the forgotten flowers into Makenna's hand, even as he pressed a hard kiss onto her lips. "This conversation isn't over," he told her. "Makenna."

Her name sounded wonderful upon his lips, even if it was said in a tight voice. "Hardin?" she whispered. "Please tell me you don't hate me."

He sighed, resting his forehead against hers. "I don't hate you, Makenna Reagan."

They weren't the words of love from fifteen minutes ago, but they were hope. She was smiling as she was rolled from the room, bed and all. She buried her face in her bouquet, touched by his thoughtfulness.

Hardin Kaczmarek was an amazing man.

It was early afternoon by the time they arrived at Makenna's apartment. Even though a police officer accompanied her, Hardin insisted on driving her home and helping her inside. He carried her luggage, held the elevator for her, helped her manage with the bulky crutches and air cast. He was the perfect gentleman, but he was careful not to touch her more than necessary. Makenna noticed, and the fact broke her heart.

"Kenzie! Ken, I'm home!" she called as she unlocked the door.

"On the sofa!" her friend called from within the apartment.

Makenna turned to Hardin, uncertain if he planned to come in or not. Without waiting for an invitation, he pushed the door opened and carried her bags in.

"It's about time you got home, girlfriend!" Kenzie complained. "I've been going out of my mind, wondering – oh my gosh! What happened to you? Why are you on crutches?" she cried when she saw Makenna come awkwardly into the living room.

"I fell down a steep incline. Long story."

"Is it broken?"

"Hairline fracture, nothing as bad as yours. How are you doing? Can I get you anything?"

"How?" Kenzie hooted. "Neither one of us can walk and carry something at the same time! This should be hilarious!" As she noticed the man standing behind her friend, his muscled arms easily sporting a suitcase, camera bag and computer bag, her green eyes lit with appreciation. "If he's the cab driver, I won't bother replacing my car!"

Makenna laughed. "Kenzie, this is Hardin Kaczmarek. Hardin, my roommate, Kenzie Reese."

Hardin deposited the bags and extended his hand to the dark haired woman propped among pillows on the sofa. "Nice to finally meet you, Kenzie. I've heard a lot about you." His eyes darted to Makenna for the briefest of moments, reminding her of all they still had to work through.

"And I haven't heard *enough* about you," Kenzie cooed, squeezing his hand. She, too, glanced at Makenna. "So he knows?"

With a sigh, Makenna nodded.

"Wow," Hardin said, looking from one woman to the other. "You two really do look a lot alike." Kenzie's eyes had as much hazel in them as green, and her black hair had none of the copper tints hidden within Makenna's tumbling curls. But their pretty faces had the same heart shape, their noses had the same tipped end. Even their smiles were alike, although Kenzie's was more flirtatious.

"That's what everyone says, but just wait till they see us now! We're twins!" Kenzie grinned, pointing at both of their broken left legs.

"I think that's my cue to leave," Hardin murmured, low enough that only Makenna could hear. "Where would you like me to put your things?"

"Don't worry about them, I can get them."

"Really?" he asked, eying her crutches.

"Okay, maybe I need help with the suitcase. My room's the one on the right." She nodded to the hallway off the far wall. "On second thought, it's mostly Kenzie's stuff, so take it to the one on the left. Either way, it doesn't really matter."

"The other luggage arrived earlier," Kenzie informed her. "I still can't believe you missed your flight."

It had seemed the easiest explanation at the time. As Hardin carried the small case to the bedroom, Makenna maneuvered to the opposite end of the couch and eased herself down. She propped her foot on the coffee table, alongside her roommate's.

"Aren't we a pathetic pair?"

"I told Linda she could stop playing nurse as soon as you got home, but looks like I was wrong. Now she'll have two patients!" Kenzie laughed. Lowering her voice, she leaned toward her friend. "Oh my gosh, Kenna, he is totally hot! You scored big time with him, girlfriend."

A look of uncertainty came across Makenna's face. Kenzie wanted to question her about it, but the man of topic stepped out of the bedroom. Even across the room, his sculpted chest was easily visible beneath his t-shirt.

Shaking his head with a reluctant grin, Hardin came forward. "You two look pathetic. How are you going to function here by yourself?"

"I'll call my mom. She'll be more than happy to baby us for as long as needed," Makenna said.

"Ooh, maybe she'll make us some of her homemade chicken noodle soup. And some brownies." With a twinkle in her eyes, Kenzie all but drooled. "Maybe this whole broken leg thing will be totally worth it."

Hardin laughed. "I think I'm going to like you, Kenzie Reese," he declared. His gaze slid to Makenna and he winked, as if they shared a secret. She was more concerned about sharing a future with him than a secret, but maybe this was the first step. "So until Wonder Mom gets here, what can I get for you two lovely ladies? Something to eat, drink?"

Kenzie motioned to the array of snacks that already littered the coffee table. "Our neighbor checks in on me every couple of hours and keeps me fed. I'm good, but Kenna might need something."

She needed a hug, but Makenna wasn't going to beg. "Water might be nice."

"If you don't mind me roaming around in your kitchen, I'll get you some."

"Glasses are in the cabinet between the sink and fridge."

The moment he was gone, Kenzie turned to her roommate. "Okay, what's going on? I can see there's definitely something between you two, but you're acting all weird. What's up?"

Makenna sighed. "He's having trouble with the fact that I lied to him from the very beginning about who I really was. He's all about truth and honor. By the way, did I mention he's a Texas Ranger?"

Her eyes widened. "Baseball or law enforcement?" Either was impressive.

"Law enforcement. So you can see where he might have a problem with me impersonating someone else, especially since I broke several laws doing it. Not to mention…"

"What? Not to mention what?" When she stopped mid-sentence, Kenzie pressed her to continue.

"Before I told him the truth, he told me he thought he was falling in love with me." Tears glistened in her eyes as she admitted the rest. "Since then, the closest he's said is that he doesn't hate me."

"Aw, sweetie," Kenzie said, reaching out for her best friend's hand. "What about you? How do you feel about him?"

"He's amazing, Kenzie. He's such a genuinely good guy. He's funny and sexy and brave and strong. I could go on and on."

"You've got it bad," her friend said softly, reading the lovesick expression on her face.

"And I've probably ruined it by agreeing to this entire farce in the first place," Makenna whispered miserably.

"I'm sorry. I should have never asked you to do it. Me and my schemes. They always get us in trouble."

"It wasn't your fault. I knew better, and still I went along with it. And even after that, I could have told him the truth. I should have, the very first time he kissed me."

"Good kisser?" Kenzie asked with a grin.

"Amazing." She said the word through the side of her mouth as Hardin rounded the corner from the kitchen. As he came forward, she eyed the items he carried on a tray. "That looks like more than water."

"Just a few things I know you like," he shrugged. "Carrots with ranch dressing. It's not quite the same as that dip in the picnic basket, but maybe it will do. And I found some chocolate to feed your addiction."

"Oh, girl, this man is definitely a keeper!" Kenzie proclaimed, her smile wide and approving. "And he knows you so well."

Hardin unloaded the tray within easy reach, added a pillow beneath Makenna's foot, and brought her laptop and camera to rest against the end table by her side. "Anything else I can get you before I go?" he asked, crouching down in front of her at eye level.

"I-I think that about does it."

"I see you have your phones and the remote within reach, and both sets of crutches." He shook his head again, still astounded by their unique predicament.

"We're good, Hardin," Makenna assured him, even though the warble in her voice said something different.

"Then I guess I should go." His blue eyes sought hers and held. She could see uncertainty in their depths, mingling with regret and sadness and more than a touch of desperate desire. Her own green eyes misted, and she nibbled on her lower lip.

Seeing Hardin's hungry gaze follow the movement, Kenzie tried to be gallant. "Give me five minutes to get moving, and I can give you two some privacy." She started to push up from the couch, but Hardin motioned for her to stay.

"No need to uproot yourself." He spoke to Kenzie without taking his eyes off Makenna. He reached out a hand and touched her cheek, fingering the fading scar. "Don't let her forget to doctor her cuts and scrapes. She has thirteen stitches. She needs to clean them and change her bandages daily."

"Girlfriend, what did you do?" Kenzie asked, eying her suspiciously. "I was in a car wreck and didn't get as banged up as you!"

"She'll tell you all about it," Hardin assured the other woman, his eyes still roaming over Makenna. His gaze was hungry, thorough, as if he were trying to memorize what she looked like. Fear clutched in

Makenna's chest and made breathing impossible. "She has a lot of things to tell you."

Kenzie tried to be polite and look away, but she was fascinated with the scene playing out before her. The man was obviously reluctant to say goodbye, but there was a wariness in his amazing blue eyes. He was staring at her best friend as if he wanted to devour her, but he made no effort to do anything other than touch her face. Tears were now streaming down her roommate's face, a sight Kenzie seldom saw.

Hardin leaned in, resting his forehead against Makenna's for a long moment. They were both struggling to get their emotions under control. Kenzie forced herself to look away, to give them a modicum of privacy as they whispered to one another.

"You'll be all right here till your mom comes?"

"We'll be fine."

"You have a lot to talk about."

"Yes."

"So do we."

"Yes."

"Makenna-" Hesitantly.

"Hardin." Desperately.

Instead of saying more, he pressed his mouth to hers. "I've got to go," he whispered.

"Okay."

"I'll call you this evening."

She nodded slightly, the movement bumping their faces together. His mouth grazed hers again, open and hungry for the slightest contact.

"Hardin, please –"

"It's going to be all right, sweetheart." He finally offered her the reassurance she craved. He rested his forehead against hers again, his fingers tangling in her curls out of habit. "There's a lot we have to hash through right now, a lot of it to do with the case. We've got to make sure you two are safe, before you and I sit down for a talk. But it's going to be okay, babe, I promise."

"I trust you," she said without hesitation.

He touched his mouth to hers again. She thought she tasted a promise in his kiss this time.

"I'll call you," he repeated. He got to his feet, his fingers – and his eyes – trailing slowly away from her face. To Kenzie, he said, "It's been a pleasure meeting the infamous Kenzie Reese." A teasing light came to his eyes and gave Makenna even further hope.

"Likewise, I can assure you."

He looked back at Makenna, suddenly uncertain again. "You're sure you're okay? I feel like a heel, leaving you two like this."

"Like you said, Kenzie and I have a lot to talk about." There was a trace of hopefulness, excitement, even, as she glanced at her sister.

"Okay, so I'll go." He was obviously having trouble with his own decision. "I'll lock the door on my way out. There will be an officer on watch at all times, but I want you to let me know if anything happens, if anyone tries to contact you, if something doesn't feel right. Call me if you need *anything*."

"Officer?" Kenzie butted in, alarmed. Drawing their sharp attention, she made an innocent face and held up her hands in surrender. "Okay, okay, I'm sorry. I know I shouldn't be listening, but an *officer*? What is going on?"

"Call me," Hardin repeated sternly, ignoring the outburst. "No matter what time it is. Promise you'll call."

"I promise."

He leaned down for one more quick kiss. "Take care. Later, babe."

"Later." She watched him walk to the door, her heart heavy. Just as he reached for the door, she called his name and he turned around. "Thank you for everything. Be careful."

He winked at her. "Always, sweetheart. Always."

Hardin was barely out the door when Kenzie turned to her friend and demanded answers. "What is going on? Why is there an officer outside? What happened this week?" She took a deep breath and asked in dread, "It has to do with my father, doesn't it? All those questions you were asking… what has he done?"

"I've got a story to tell you, Kenzie," Makenna said slowly. "Remember how you said I needed to go on this trip to get out of my rut, add a little excitement to my life? Well, I did that, all right. You can't imagine all that has happened this week. It's going to sound a little far-fetched, but believe me, it's true. So here goes…."

Chapter 23

An hour later, Kenzie was still shaking her head, trying to organize the information into a conceivable thought.

"I have no idea what to say," she murmured for the dozenth time. "I just can't believe this."

"I know, sweetie. It's a lot to comprehend."

"And someone tried to kidnap you? They tried to hurt you, because they thought you were me, and they thought you – or, I – could lead them to my father? *Our* father? Oh, God, I can't believe we're sisters!" Her thoughts were going round in circles, but for all the sorrow on her face, the joy of having a sister, a twin, brightened her eyes.

"My mom really wasn't that surprised, you know," Makenna said softly, as the sisters sat with their heads touching, coal against copper. "She said she had always wondered."

"You know, I think Mom, your mom, has hugged me more times than our birth mother ever did." Long ago, Kenzie had taken to calling Makenna's parents Mom and Dad.

"I'm so sorry, Ken. I'm sorry I was the lucky one who was given away, and that you had to stay behind, with them," Makenna whispered.

"I wonder which child they thought they were helping the most... the one they gave away, or the one they kept."

"I wonder if they thought of either of us, or just themselves."

The sisters sat in silence, contemplating their parents' motives and the lives altered forever by their actions.

"I remember, you know," Kenzie finally whispered. "I thought it was my imagination, the warmth I remembered feeling when our palms met. I convinced myself it was just the game I played with the girl from my mirror, that the palm I touched was my own. But I remember the warmth of your touch. It was real. You were real."

The sisters hugged, their tears mingling.

After a while, they went back to their musings, trying to make sense of it all. They were interrupted when their neighbor Linda came to check on them and when Makenna called her parents to tell them she was home. Without waiting to be asked, Madeline Reagan said she would be there within the hour. And then it was back to the wonder of it all, rehashing the topic again and again.

"Another thing I don't understand," Kenzie said at random. "If these Zaffino people have been watching me for a couple of weeks, not to mention the Rangers, how did they not see the resemblance between us and figure out before now that we were twins?"

Makenna shrugged. "Hardin and I discussed that on the plane. It was a charter by the way, did I tell you that? Anyway, I guess the chance of twins, separated at such a young age, with one of them being adopted out, then somehow finding one another again years later, totally at random, was such a long shot that no one even considered it." She smiled as she remembered a conversation from earlier in the week. "When I first told Hardin that my best friend and I looked so much alike, I could see the gears turning in his head. Now I know he was putting the pieces of the puzzle together, but he decided they didn't fit, simply because it seemed too improbable."

"It is pretty incredible, you know. Of all the universities out there, we somehow chose the very same one, and even wound up in the same classes."

"You know what they say," Makenna grinned, "Two great minds think alike!"

"And this great mind is thinking what a hottie Hardin Kaczmarek is. Do not let that man get away, sister dear."

"I'll try not. But you heard him. We have a lot to hash through. And right now, as much as my heart says differently, my brain knows that the top priority is to focus on our safety. These Zaffino people are no one to take lightly, Kenzie. I know it sounds like something out of a movie, but they're the real deal."

"But neither one of us has any idea where our father is."

"But until the Zaffinos get wind of that fact and are convinced it's true, we still may be in a lot of danger. I guess it's a good thing we'll both be laid up for the next couple of weeks. As long as we can't go anywhere and the police are here to keep an eye on us, we should be relatively safe."

"If not, we could always call your handsome Texas Ranger to watch over us!" Kenzie suggested with a cheeky grin.

Two days later, Hardin appeared at their door. The twins were in the living room, sorting through pictures Makenna had taken, putting together a presentation for *Now Magazine*. When Makenna heard his pleasant voice at the door, her heart did a triple somersault and her nerves went on high alert. She was thankful she had just taken a shower and was wearing something other than pajamas.

Yesterday, the sisters had indulged in a totally lazy day by not even getting dressed. Today, however, Makenna was sporting a pair of jean capris and a new aqua t-shirt from the White Mountains.

She heard her mother's delighted laugh and knew Hardin Kaczmarek had already charmed another female in her family. So far he was three for three.

"Girls, you have visitors. Handsome Texas Rangers, no less. You gentleman have a seat, and I'll bring in coffee."

"We don't want to be a bother, ma'am." Hardin smiled at her mother and Makenna could have sworn she saw the woman blush.

"Oh, no bother at all. I'll just be a jiffy. Please, have a seat." With only a half effort to hide her actions, Madeline Reagan sent her daughter a wink and a thumbs-up sign of approval.

Makenna would have rolled her eyes at her mother's theatrics, but her eyes were suddenly glued to Hardin. It was the first time Makenna had seen him in a button-up dress shirt. The mere sight of him in his uniform – starched white western shirt, pressed khakis, navy blue tie, white straw hat, cowboy boots, shiny silver badge - was enough to make her mouth water. She was so busy staring at him, she almost didn't notice the man beside him.

"Makenna." Her name on his lips was like a caress. Makenna felt her world shift before slowly settling into place, centering around the handsome man with a badge.

They stared at each other for a long, hungry moment, their eyes drinking in the sight of the other. They had spoken on the phone twice, texted several times, but this was the first time they had seen each other since coming home. They might have continued to simply stare at one another, but the man with him quietly cleared his throat.

Hardin snapped out of his trance, but his eyes still lingered. "Ladies, let me introduce Ranger Travis Merka. Merka, these two beauties are Makenna Reagan and twin sister Kenzie Reese."

Travis Merka was several inches taller than Hardin, with long legs and a lean physique. Where Hardin's muscles were well defined and larger than life, Travis's were less obvious at first glance. Blond and clean-shaven, the handsome but somber Ranger had surprisingly dark eyes beneath his straw hat.

"Nice to meet you," Makenna murmured, trying unsuccessfully to pull her eyes from Hardin's. She had missed him like crazy, not realizing the half of it until this moment.

"So," Kenzie said saucily, "you're the one who's been watching me for the last couple of weeks." Her tone was almost accusatory as she eyed the tall Ranger.

"That's right, ma'am. Just doing my job." His tone was cool and detached.

"Guess you didn't see the car that plowed into me," she smirked.

"Actually, ma'am, that was my car that hit yours. The perpetrator ran into me, causing a chain reaction."

Taken aback by his honesty, Kenzie had no ready reply. Instead, she turned her focus to his partner. "Hey, Hardin, how's it going?"

"Good. And you?" Out of politeness, he forced his gaze to the woman sitting on the couch beside Makenna.

"Learning to walk with these sticks." She gestured to the ever-present crutches. "I don't graduate to a walking cast for another couple of weeks still."

"All in good time," he assured her, seating himself in one of the chairs flanking the sofa. Travis Merka took the other. "I'm glad to see you two looking so well and healing." Once again, his hungry gaze roamed over Makenna, noting the fading bruises and a mere trace of the scratch along her jawline. With great discipline, he kept his eyes from following the known path of that scratch.

"Getting better every day," Kenzie declared. Makenna remained silent.

"Good. That's good." Hardin paused for a moment, before leaning forward. "As much as I wanted to see that for myself, we're here today in an official capacity. Ranger Merka and I have been assigned to security for you two ladies."

Makenna's heart did another acrobatic feat. Her first thought was of joy. *I'll get to see him every day!* Reality set in almost immediately. *We're still in danger.* "For-For how long?" she managed to ask.

Travis Merka spoke up. "For as long as it takes, ma'am, to keep you and your sister safe."

"But I thought you had that woman with the terrible voice locked up! Her husband, too, and the bald man," Kenzie said.

"We do," Hardin assured her. "And it turns out Lisa's real name is Irene Goldberg, and she's not even married to Bob. They were simply on assignment. But until we can convince the mafia that neither of you have any idea to your father's where-abouts, either Ranger Merka or I will be with you at all times."

"How do you convince them of that?" Makenna asked quietly, her face pale.

"We're putting word out among our informants and the lines of chatter. It may take a few days, but they'll get the word."

"And in the meantime?" Kenzie asked.

"As Ranger Kaczmarek said, one of us will be with you. You'll have round-the-clock protection from the Ranger service. If there's somewhere you have to go, we'll take you. If someone comes to visit you, they have to be cleared by us first."

"So basically we're being held prisoner in our own home."

"You're being protected, ma'am." His tone was calm, but his dark eyes flashed with irritation at Kenzie's smug retort.

"Why the sudden change? We've been fine these past two days, with the police officers stationed in the lobby." Makenna suspected there was something they weren't telling them.

Hardin's eyes lit with appreciation of her sharp mind. "Intel got word that Ray Foto boarded a flight to Texas. He's the man believed to have approached you in the general store. Bob and Lisa – or Irene – were contract hires, probably by Foto himself. He's a major player in the Zaffino organization."

Madeline came into the living room, carrying a tray of coffee and freshly made brownies. Hardin further charmed her with his appreciation of her culinary talents, and after just one bite, even Travis Merka presented her with a smile that brightened his solemn eyes. Makenna noted that the power of his smile was not lost upon her sister, even though she tried not to show it.

"Tell me, Mrs. Reagan," Hardin said as he reached for his second brownie. "Does your daughter share your talents in the kitchen?"

Madeline gracefully arched her brow. "She has her specialties," she said diplomatically.

"Doesn't matter," Hardin said, wiping crumbs from his mouth. He shot Makenna a look that warmed her blood and caused her heart to hammer wildly in her chest. "I'm an excellent cook, if I do say so, myself."

The encouraging words were all Makenna had to sustain her for the next week and a half. Although she saw Hardin almost daily, he kept a polite distance and was nothing if not professional.

As promised, he or Travis stayed close for the next several days. Some days, one of the men would be stationed in the lobby, where their presence made all the tenants in the building feel safe and protected. The apartment dwellers were told they were part of a pilot program, a new task force aimed at random protection for residents of the city. On other days, the Rangers watched the apartment complex while parked on the street in unmarked cars, or occasionally sat in a chair outside the women's door, where only the few people along their hall were privy to the fact. At night, the men took turns sleeping on the sofa in the living room, and one time each, they stayed inside the apartment for the duration of the day.

Yet other than polite conversation and the occasional lingering gaze, Hardin made no attempt to communicate with Makenna on a personal level. The stress of seeing him, day in and day out, yet being held an arm's length away, was wearing on Makenna's nerves. When her doctor's appointment finally arrived, she was more than happy to get out of the apartment and spend it in the company of Ranger Merka, while Hardin stayed at the apartment with her sister.

"Good news, Makenna," the doctor reported. "Your x-rays look fine. I wouldn't do any running or jumping for a couple of weeks, but I think you will be able to go without your air cast. Just take it easy, continue to elevate your leg while you're sitting, and call me if you have significant pain. Anything requiring more than Tylenol to ease the discomfort should be of concern. Make a follow up appointment for next month, but I think you'll be fine."

"That's wonderful!" she said with a smile of true appreciation.

As she left the doctor's office with only a slight limp, she made a suggestion to her companion. "Let's celebrate with a Starbucks run. I've been craving one of their scones and a Skinny Vanilla Latte."

"What kind of scone?"

"Orange cranberry."

"I might could be persuaded," Travis decided, a small smile hovering around his tight mouth.

Ten minutes later, they were sitting in the back of the trendy coffee shop, sipping their coffee and enjoying their crumbling treats.

"Mm. You don't appreciate the little things in life, until you have to go without for a while," Makenna said, savoring the taste of the delectable scone. "I was going stir-crazy in that apartment."

"I'm sorry, Miss Reagan, but it's for your safety."

"Seriously? You're still calling me Miss Reagan? You sleep on my couch every-other-night. Call me Makenna."

"Makenna, then," he said. His unexpected smile would have flipped her heart, had it not already belonged to another.

"I suppose the timing has been pretty good," Makenna had to admit. "Neither one of us has felt much like getting out, what with our crutches and all. And Kenzie says she doesn't have a thing to wear that matches her cast."

The slightest of expressions crossed Travis' handsome face, but Makenna saw it. Biting back a smile, already knowing the answer to her question, she said, "You and my sister don't seem to get along all that well. Why is that?"

"My job isn't to get along or not get along with my clients. My job is to protect them." He made the statement with a stoic look set upon his face.

She was aware of the spark between her sister and Travis Merka, but she was even more aware of the danger she and Kenzie were in. Sobering, she asked, "So how much longer do you think we'll need protecting?"

"Hard to say. We have reason to believe that our message has been received, but so far there's no indication that Foto has left Texas."

"Do we know he's in Austin?"

"Last known whereabouts was San Antonio, eight days ago. There have been reported sightings of him here in the Capitol, but nothing conclusive."

"And so we wait…" Makenna spoke softly, but her heavy sigh said it all.

Chapter 24

With Makenna back on her feet and both women feeling better each day, Madeline returned to her own home for a few days. Before leaving, she stocked their refrigerator with soups and casseroles and pre-made salads, and made enough brownies and cookies to treat half the apartment building. Yet when the girls saw a commercial for their favorite pizza establishment, they begged the Rangers for a supreme pizza from The Pie Shack.

Much to their surprise, it was Ranger Merka who swayed the vote in their favor. He, too, had a weakness for the traditional styled pizza fired in a wood oven, and he was the one to call in the order, then wait in the hallway to clear the delivery boy's credentials.

While they waited for its arrival, Makenna and Hardin set the table, working in quiet unison. It was the first meal the four of them would be sharing together, without Madeline, and Makenna still wanted it to be nice. They had all gotten spoiled to her mother's little touches of a correctly set table, matching glasses, dessert with every meal, and an occasional simple centerpiece. Tonight might only be take-out, but Makenna wanted them to eat on ceramic plates and drink from real glasses.

"I think I've got this right," Hardin said, placing the napkin on the left side of the plate.

"Mom would be so proud," she teased.

"Just wait till you meet my mom. All the silverware has to match, as well." His blue eyes were twinkling as he offered a rare glimpse of hope for the future.

Kenzie was slowly making her way into the dining area, but travel on the crutches was still slow and painful. "Sounds like the pizza is here," she said, swinging toward the door when she heard the knock. She knew it was safe to open, because Travis was on the other side. He might not be the friendliest of men, but he was definitely a professional.

She opened the door, allowing the delivery boy to enter with two hot and steaming pizza boxes. "Mmm, smells great," she breathed, balancing herself on one foot as she held the door open. She glanced briefly at the man, thinking he was older than most of the college-aged men who worked for the restaurant, but she admired him for at least working, and not living off welfare. He was dressed in their typical summer uniform of baggy cargo shorts and tee with a slip-on apron vest, both emblazoned with The Pie Shack logo.

When Travis didn't immediately follow the man inside, she poked her head out the door. "Travis?" she called, frowning into the empty hall.

"He stepped away for a few minutes," the deliveryman offered.

Around the corner, Makenna froze. She knew that voice. Her eyes flew to Hardin, who was frowning the moment he heard the words. Before he could move forward, she grabbed his arm. Eyes wide, Makenna mouthed a silent message. "That's the man from the store. Foto."

Hardin immediately put himself between her and the dangerous man. With hand signals, he motioned for her to stay where she was.

When he made a cautious step forward, so did Makenna. He turned to glare at her, but she gave an imperial lift of her chin, the defiance clear in her eyes. In a very brief battle of wills, waged solely by the daggers in their eyes, Hardin fought for control, but Makenna wielded her might; that was her sister in there, after all. Hardin's silent glare warned her to stay behind him and follow his lead.

In the foyer, Kenzie was closing the door in confusion, locking it out of habit, and turning back to the short man holding the pizzas. She was perplexed by the sinister smile on his face as he leered at her.

"You couldn't follow my instructions, could you, little lady? You couldn't just give the message to your father."

"What? What are talking about? That wasn't my father who ordered -" Her words wavered as it suddenly dawned upon her who the man was. Behind him, she saw Hardin approaching stealthily, signaling for her to keep talking. "- the pizza," she finished lamely. Trying to sound normal, she forced herself not to look at Hardin. "That was my boyfriend who ordered," she continued, her strained voice gaining strength. "Did you get the order wrong? He'll be really mad if you put anchovies on his pizza. Let me see if you got it right."

"Cut the act. You know exactly what I'm talking about. I told you back in New Hampshire, tell your old man we're looking for him."

"I have no idea where my father is. I haven't seen him in years." She didn't bother explaining he had her confused with her sister. Another step, and Hardin would be within arm's reach of the man. "And if I remember right, he doesn't even like pizza!"

With a swift upward jerk of her crutch, Kenzie knocked the pizzas from his hands as Hardin rushed forward. He grabbed the man from behind, but the flimsy material of the apron promptly tore free under Hardin's grasp. As the man staggered forward, he grabbed Kenzie's crutch and she pitched sideways, right into his chest. He quickly used her body as a shield, jerking her roughly against him as he demanded Hardin move out where he could see him.

"Ouch, you're hurting me!" Kenzie yelled angrily. "Give me back my crutch!"

"Turn her loose, Foto," Hardin growled.

"Or what? You don't have a gun on you, and you don't have backup. I took care of the Ranger in the hall, by the way." Foto's smile was as cold and lifeless as his eyes. He took a step back, keeping Kenzie tight against him.

"You heard the lady. She has no idea where her old man is." Hardin tried to keep the man talking while his mind raced for a solution. Foto was right; his gun was in his holster, back in the living room. Thank God Makenna had followed his instructions and remained in the dining area. If he could keep Foto moving, he might could slip in front, reach around the open doorway into the small galley kitchen, and grab a knife from the knife block. He knew it sat on the edge of the counter. "Joseph Mandarino was a lousy father. She left home the moment she turned eighteen and hasn't seen him since."

A look of uncertainty flashed in the Italian man's eyes, but was gone in an instant. "I've got to find Mandarino. You might say it's a life or death situation." From seemingly nowhere, he produced a knife and held it to Kenzie's throat. With her solidly in front of him, he started backing away, dragging her with him until his hip brushed against the dining room table.

Hardin darted a glance into the room, wondering where Makenna had disappeared to. Not that it mattered. As long as she was out of sight, she was safe, at least for the moment.

"Exactly what do you plan to do, Foto?" He continued to speak in a calm, rational voice, even as he crept forward at a snail's pace. "What's next?"

"You're going to back up, and let me out of here."

"Fine." Pretending to be agreeable, Hardin leaned casually against the kitchen doorway, his hand groping inside. "But leave the lady here."

"No way. She goes with me. Even if she can't lead me to Mandarino, she's my ticket out of here." He held the knife closer, the cold edge of steel touching against her neck.

"You know I can't let you take her out of here." He groped blindly for the knives, his straining fingers finally brushing the edge of the wooden storage block.

"And how are you going to stop me?" the other man leered. "And get your hand out here where I can see it."

Beneath the table, Makenna gathered her courage. She had never stabbed a person before. She stared at the backs of the short man's legs, wondering where would be the most painful and damaging spot of entry. She tested the weight of the forks in her hand, judging the right amount of force to use. She might have only one chance, so she had to make it count.

"There are surveillance cameras in the hall. They're directly fed into Ranger Headquarters," Hardin lied. "Right now, at least two dozen highly trained professionals are on their way here, including two or more expert sniper rifleman. You don't have a chance of escape."

"For the lady's sake, you'd better hope that's not so. She'll never live to see- Ouch! Son of a bitch! What the - Awwrgg!" He screamed in pain, lurching to the side, as Makenna drove the tines of three forks into the fleshy soft spot beside his right ankle.

Blood spurted in her face, but she refused to acknowledge the horror. After burying the shiny tips in his flesh as far as she could, she left the forks hanging, dangling there from the tissue and tendons they stabbed. From her hiding spot, she could see Kenzie's legs shuffle away, and Hardin's feet rush forward. Makenna immediately picked up the butter knife and remaining fork, and jabbed them into the calf of Foto's left leg. As the man howled in anguish and started to fall, she twisted the utensils with all her might.

Kenzie fell away to the side, half hopping, half dragging her plastered foot until she was clear of the scene playing out in the dining room. She collapsed against the front door as Hardin and the swarthy man wrestled on the floor just feet away, both fighting for control of the knife. It was a fierce battle of raw strength that had first one man on top, then the other. With a loud grunt and the unmistakable snap of bone, the knife flew from the gangster's hand, but he continued to fight. As the men exchanged blows, the sounds of flesh hitting flesh echoed in the apartment. With an almost primal cry, Hardin flung his body on top of the Italian one last time, trapping Foto under him.

Confident Hardin had the upper hand, Makenna crawled past the fighting men. When her hand brushed against the discarded knife, she slung it out of the way and kept crawling. She continued on her quest to her sister, who was now sobbing at the foot of the door.

As Hardin straddled Foto's compact body and pummeled his face with his fists, the door began to tremble under the fierce pounding of Travis Merka's angry hand. "Open up!" he demanded. "Open this door before I break it down!"

"Oh my gosh, Kenzie, I was so afraid for you! Are you all right?" Makenna demanded, even as she slid her sister's trembling body away from the door. Calling through the door, she told Travis to give them one minute to move out of the way. "Come on, honey, we've got to move. You don't have to get up. Just slide."

Once clear of the door, she reached up and unlocked it. Travis burst through immediately, blood dripping from his forehead and seeping from the white expanse of his shirt, but his gun was drawn and already trained on the man beneath Hardin.

"Kaczmarek!" he barked. "Lay off, man. I've got him."

Out of breath, Hardin sat back on his heels, resting heavily upon the other man's stomach. He glanced at his own bloodied knuckles, then at the corresponding blood and bruises on the twitching man's swollen and battered face.

"Can't-Can't breathe," the man gasped.

"Having trouble, myself," Hardin replied, his breath heavy and labored. He rested for another long moment, until Foto's face began to turn purple and his breath came in short and strangled gasps. Hardin finally moved away, taking no care in where his knees or feet might hit in the process. He heard multiple grunts and groans as he rolled away, some of them his own.

Laid out flat on the floor, Hardin gulped in deep breaths of air and gathered his wits. "Makenna!" he bellowed.

"I'm here. I'm here!" Scrambling onto her knees, Makenna hugged her sister one more time, then crawled to Hardin. "I'm fine. Kenzie's fine. We're both fine. Are you- are you all right?"

"Will be," he huffed out the words. "Soon as I'm holding you."

Makenna flung herself onto his sprawled body, knocking even more wind from his lungs. But his arms came up to encircle her and his mouth met hers in a crushing, claiming kiss. As Makenna whimpered and returned his kiss with salty tears, her hands roamed his shoulders, his face, his hair. She frantically touched him, making certain he was in one piece.

Behind them, Travis swayed just a little as he kept his pistol trained on the writhing form of Ray Foto. "Raymond Foto, you are under arrest." After reading the criminal his rights, Travis kicked at Hardin's foot. He was still kissing Makenna and holding her as if his life depended on it.

"Are you going to help me here, or do I have to do this all myself?" he complained. "I'm the one who's bleeding, after all."

Makenna slowly moved off Hardin, reluctant to turn loose. As she struggled to get to her feet, Travis offered her a hand. Unsteady on his feet, he nearly toppled them both to the floor.

"Are you all right?" she asked sharply, noting his pasty skin and the red that continued to spread across his chest.

"Back-up is on the way. And as soon as you quit kissing my partner, I might let him take over so I can have a seat." But instead of waiting for Hardin to get to his feet, Travis leaned into the wall and sank slowly to the floor.

"Kenzie!" Makenna called over her shoulder to her sister. "I think he's really hurt."

Kenzie quickly scooted her way across the floor, her frantic gaze on the Ranger's sallow face. As his head lolled back against the wall, Kenzie took his face in her hands and tried to rouse him. "What is it? Where are you hurt?" She saw a gash on his head and blood trickling down his forehead, but the cut didn't appear to be deep. His chest, however, was oozing blood. Without thinking, she ripped open his shirt, gasping when she saw the huge slash across his chest. Foto's knife had sliced through the muscled tapestry, marring the perfection of his chest.

"So much blood," she murmured, feeling light headed herself. "Makenna, call someone! Call 9-1-1. He's lost so much blood!" She put her hands to his chest, trying to stop the flow from seeping between her fingers. She cried out helplessly when it kept coming, squirting out with each pump of his heart.

"Don't die!" she begged. "Please don't die! I-I need you to take care of me! I thought we could- I wanted to - please, don't die on me!" She sobbed as she sagged into his chest, blood and all. She pressed a kiss onto his lips, even though he was unaware of her efforts to save him.

In the distance they could hear sirens. With Makenna's help, the two sisters dragged Travis away from the wall, until he was lying on his back. Together they pressed their hands against his chest, trying to slow the blood flow. The moment Hardin had Foto immobilized and handcuffed to a chair, he wheeled around and assisted the women, frantically begging his partner to hold on, even as the police and the paramedics burst through the door.

Within minutes they had Travis on the gurney, pumping fluids into his prone form, and then they were whisking him off to the hospital, with his friends in close pursuit.

Chapter 25

They had been in the private waiting room for over an hour. Kenzie alternated between pacing clumsily around the room and sitting with her foot propped up on the small coffee table. She hadn't complained, but her leg was hurting terribly now, after being forced to bear weight when Foto dragged her across the room. She needed a painkiller, but she wanted to be awake and fully alert when they got news about Travis.

He was already in surgery when they arrived, and they were still working on him. No vital organs had been damaged, but he had lost a lot of blood and the cut was deep, requiring extensive repair.

Hardin and Makenna sat huddled together on the sofa, awaiting word on his friend. A few fellow Rangers and police officers drifted in and out, some there in an official capacity, others there simply out of concern. Ray Foto was also in the emergency room, being treated for a broken wrist, torn Achilles and a punctured lung. He was under heavy police guard and had no chance of escape. That fact, at least, gave some comfort to the twin sisters and all who cared about them.

Makenna's parents came as soon as they heard the news, and now Madeline Reagan was serving coffee and a tin of homemade cookies to the worried group in the waiting room.

"Hey, Kaczmarek," one of the other Rangers called from across the room. He was helping himself to a cookie, wearing a big grin. "I think

Mrs. Reagan's going to give your mom a run for her money on who gets to be Den Mom," he joked.

"There's always room for another," Hardin smiled, winking at Makenna's mom. He pulled Makenna closer to him, savoring the feel of her against his side. When he looked down at her, he spoke so that only she could hear. "You know, in about ten minutes my family is going to burst through that door, and things are going to get a little crazy."

"How so?"

"No telling who all is coming. My parents for sure, probably my sister Meagan. Definitely my little sister Anna. She's had a not-so-secret crush on Merka for a couple of years, even though she has a steady boyfriend. Merka doesn't have a lot of family of his own, so mine has sort of adopted him."

"Like my family did Kenzie?" she asked, looking over at where her father was helping Kenzie get comfortable in a corner chair.

"Exactly. So with the stress of worrying about Merka, and the added excitement of getting to finally meet you, things will probably be a little loud and boisterous. I told you that my family can be pretty overwhelming and in-your-face. Just giving you a heads up." He brushed his lips against her hair as he spoke.

"They know about me?" she asked with a pleased smile, pulling slightly away so she could see him better.

"Of course. My mom's already trying to figure out how to get all the letters on the family quilt."

Makenna frowned, completely baffled. "What are you talking about?"

"Whenever someone new comes into the family, either by birth or marriage, my mom embroideries their name on a square of this big huge family quilt she made. You're going to present quite a challenge with all those letters. She's been worrying over it for days."

He spoke nonchalantly, almost comically, but Makenna saw the glimmer in his blue eyes. It looked a little like nerves. Tucked so closely beside him, she could feel the sudden tension in his body, could detect the breath that hitched in his chest. Her own heart began to hammer as the implication of his words sank in. She stared into his face, watching it melt with tenderness as he gazed down at her.

"What are you saying?" she whispered, clutching his hand she held. "Wh-What letters?"

"I'm saying I love you." He scooped her cheek into the palm of his hand and whispered the words that only she could hear. "I don't care if you call yourself Kenzie or Makenna or Lula Belle. But my mom's having a heck of a time trying to get all sixteen letters of 'Makenna Kaczmarek' to fit onto one square." His blue eyes twinkled as he couldn't help but tease, "Don't be surprised if she doesn't ask you to shorten your name to Mac so that it fits better."

"Ma-Makenna K-Kaczmarek?" she squeaked. It already sounded perfect together.

"Don't tell me you're one of these modern women who expects me to change *my* name after we get married, are you?" His lips grazed her temple. "My mom would have to re-stitch my square to say 'Hardin Reagan', and that just doesn't sound right."

"Married?" The word came out breathless. Hopeful. Full of awe.

He pretended to fret. "Too soon?" he sighed, repeating his words of two weeks ago. "I told you, I don't believe in half-way. I want marriage, children, the whole forever thing. And even though he's concerned that we haven't known each other very long, your father has already given me permission to propose."

As Hardin moved his face alongside hers, not quite touching, teasing her with his nearness, Makenna's gaze flew to her father. He caught her eye across the room, glanced at the man nuzzling her side, and gave a slight nod of approval. Makenna sent him a wavering smile before she closed her eyes, losing herself to the words Hardin continued to whisper in her ear.

"So that's what I'm doing," he said, grazing her cheek with his trim beard. It tickled, but the shiver running through her was one of anticipation. Sheer delight quivered along her skin. He nestled closer, kissing her jaw. "I was planning a nice romantic dinner, candlelight, a ring," he admitted, nibbling on her ear lobe. "I didn't plan on doing it in a crowded hospital while I waited for word on my best friend's recovery. But in about five minutes, maybe less now, my family's going to burst in here, and all hell's gonna break loose." His mouth moved along her cheek, edging closer to her mouth. "And I really need to know. Makenna Reagan, will you marry me?"

"Yes." She breathed the word into him, pushing it into his soul, as he finally claimed her mouth with his. They were oblivious to the people around them as they deepened the kiss, lost in the wonders of love and joy and a future together.

Kenzie's voice finally penetrated the fog of euphoria that shrouded them. "Knock it off, you two. Here comes the doctor, and he's smiling." She was already up and balanced on her crutches, eager to hear what the doctor had to say.

"He's smiling," Hardin said, his mouth still against Makenna's. "That means it's good news. Everything's going to work out."

Too overwhelmed to speak, Makenna could only nod.

"Everything is right in the kingdom." As he kissed her once more, she could feel the smile upon his lips. "Foto has been caught, Merka's going to recover, and I'm going to spend the rest of my life with you. I feel like a king."

She finally found her voice. "A king among men," she murmured with a smile.

They got to their feet, joining the circle gathering round the doctor. As they pressed close to hear the report, Makenna slipped her hand into Hardin's and leaned in to whisper in his ear.

"In case I forgot to say it earlier, I love you, Hardin Kaczmarek. And I can't wait to be your queen."

Alight with pleasure, his blue eyes sparkled royalty.

Note from Author

I hope you enjoyed reading "The Girl from Her Mirror". Did you know the waterfall on the cover is my personal photo of Sabbaday Falls?

I would love to hear your opinion of this book, and welcome your comments and suggestions. Contact me personally at beckiwillis.ccp@gmail.com, www.facebook.com/beckiwillis.ccp or http://www.beckiwillis.com .

If you could also take a moment to leave a brief review on Amazon and/or Goodreads, it helps other readers know if this story is right for them.

Thank you for allowing me to entertain you through the pages of my imagination. Happy reading!

Coming Soon!
Mirror, Mirror on Her Wall
(Book Two of Mirrors Don't Lie)

Chapter 1

Kenzie Reese stared into the mirror. She saw worry lines around her eyes, too many for someone only twenty-six years old. *Probably one for each of the lives I was forced to lead,* she thought derisively.

She leaned in for closer inspection. *No*, she corrected herself, *not quite that many wrinkles. Yet.*

Just twenty-six, but long ago she lost count of the many towns where she lived, forgotten some of her aliases; had never known her real name, in fact. As the child of rambling parents, Kenzie changed identities like most children changed heroes. Change, for her, was merely a way of life.

And there were more changes coming, she could feel it in her soul. Changes always made her cranky, made her jittery. Kenzie hated the unsettled feeling that crept into her body, tightening her nerves and playing havoc with her head, both physically and mentally. The pounding headaches could be soothed with pills and sleep; there was no such cure for the anxiety plaguing her mind. It taunted her, baiting her with the possibility of her worst fear coming true: she would have to move. Again.

Forcing the horrible thought from her mind, Kenzie concentrated on surveying her image. If she ignored the worry lines and the bulky blue and white air cast circling her left leg, she could pass for elegant. The royal blue silk hugged her upper body, accentuating generous breasts before gathering in flattering folds around her curvy hips. The sweetheart neckline offered a tantalizing but demure glimpse of cleavage, highlighted by the twinkle of tiny diamonds and sapphires strung along a simple white gold chain. Matching earrings dangled from her earlobes, peeking out from the dark curls piled atop her head. Without the cast, the waltz length dress would complement her legs and show off her strappy silver heels; with the cast, the overall look of sophisticated grace and elegance was spoiled. Kenzie sighed, knowing it could not be helped. At least the cast explained her uneven gait, made worse by the difference in heel heights. There would be no sexy high heels tonight, just a single black pump with a low profile. It was the best she could do under the circumstances.

With another sigh of resignation, Kenzie started to pivot away from the mirror, but an old habit stopped her mid-turn. As a child, she played a game with her mirror, talking to the girl from the other side. Far too often, the image had been her only friend.

Placing her palm to the cool glass, touching the reflected image of another palm, Kenzie remembered well the game she played. Each time her parents made her move, she would stand in front of her mirror and study the girl she was leaving behind. She would say her goodbyes in front of her mirror, tucking away the memory of yet another city, another name, another step removed from reality, and she would promise never to forget that particular girl, that particular piece of her soul.

Usually when she stood in front of her mirror, touching her reflection, it was with a solemn face and a heavy heart. But today a smile stole across her face, bringing a sparkle to her green eyes and a glow to her cheeks. A delighted giggle flavored her words as she said aloud, "Mirror, mirror, on her wall. She has a sister, after all!"

As if on cue, Makenna Reagan stepped into the room. "Is someone talking about me again?" Her eyes met Kenzie's in the mirror, holding the same merry green twinkle. She came further into the bedroom, her gaze sweeping over Kenzie's reflection. "Oh, Ken, you look gorgeous!"

Makenna stepped up behind her sister and smiled at their double reflection. There were a handful of differences, yet the images were very similar. Makenna stood an inch taller and a few pounds heavier, but the curvy shape was the same. Dark auburn hair hung loose around her shoulders, whereas Kenzie's black locks dangled from a fashionably messy up-sweep. The natural curls were alike, framing the heart shape of their faces. One wore silk, the other denim, but the clothes were inner-changeable; in fact, Kenzie borrowed Makenna's dress for the evening. Both women had green eyes and charming smiles.

Those smiles stretched wide now, as they shared the same silly grin through the mirror.

"Remember that day we first saw each other?" Kenzie asked. "I walked up to the mirror in the bathroom, and there I stood, wearing the wrong hair and the wrong clothes!" On the first day of college in Texas, she met her true and forever friend over the row of sinks, a kindred spirit named Makenna Reagan. Their connection had been immediate, their friendship permanent.

"I bet the expressions on our faces were priceless to anyone watching," Makenna mused. "But I think the funniest part is that we both immediately put our palms up to touch, just like you were doing when I walked in. It was like a living mirror."

Kenzie's grin turned rueful. "Too bad it took us eight years to figure out we were actually sisters. Twins, at that!"

Makenna squeezed her shoulders, careful not to muss her hair. "The important thing is, we know now. In our hearts, we were always sisters, even when we didn't know there was a blood connection."

"But how did we miss it? On some level, deep down, shouldn't we have known we were sisters? We know exactly what the other is thinking, for heaven's sake. We can finish the other one's sentence, answer a question that was never asked."

"How could we have known? My parents adopted an abandoned three year old; your parents never told you that you had a sister."

"All this time, I just assumed we were mind readers, both naturally brilliant and uncommonly in-tune to those nearest us," Kenzie grinned.

"And don't forget endearingly modest."

Identical grins beamed through the mirror.

"So what am I thinking right now?" Makenna challenged her sister.

"Well, on some level you're thinking about Hardin, because he's all you ever think about these days." A guilty flush confirmed Kenzie's theory. "Which I don't blame you for," she said quickly. "The guy is smokin' hot and crazy about you. You're going to have gorgeous babies together and I get to be the doting aunt. But aside from Hardin, you have a little bit of free brain space available, and it's zoned in on this dress. Which I swear I will not ruin tonight. I'll drink wine white, not red, and I'll avoid all tomato products."

"Smart choices. See that it comes back stain-free." Makenna sternly poked the dress in question to drive her point home. Then, with a soft smile, she said, "All joking aside, and even that cast aside, you look absolutely beautiful tonight."

"Thank you, sister dear. It's not exactly the way I planned to make my debut back into the public, but at least with it being a hospital event, the cast sort of goes with the theme of the evening."

After nearly a month and a half of confinement, Kenzie was going out for the first time since her car accident. Along with a broken leg and cracked ribs, she had suffered a bruised spleen, surgery, and a huge hospital bill; sadly, her car had not survived. Her date tonight was with the cute intern she met while in the hospital and they were attending a fundraiser for a new orthopedic wing.

"Who knows, you might even start a new trend, theme-dressing for an event!" Makenna quipped. "Oh, there's the doorbell. Guess your date is anxious to get the night started."

"Would you mind answering? I still need to put on lipstick."

As Kenzie applied a glaze of red to her lips, she took a deep breath to steady her nerves. Her car wreck had been the catalyst for an unimaginable string of events to unfurl, and the changes of the past few weeks still had her reeling.

On the day of her accident, Kenzie was set to leave on a photography assignment in New Hampshire. Just before going in for surgery, Kenzie managed to con her best friend into impersonating her on the trip. Until then, Kenzie had no idea the mafia was watching her, hoping to access her father through her. While she was laid up in an Austin hospital, the mob followed the wrong woman to New England and chased her through the White Mountains, attempting to kidnap her. When Makenna returned six days later, Kenzie learned a shocking truth about her past; her father was a criminal and she had a sister.

Between recuperating from surgery and hiding from the mafia, Kenzie hardly left their apartment for almost five weeks. Normally the life of any party, she had to admit her social skills were now feeling a bit rusty. Even though the Texas Rangers assured her she was safe now, it was disconcerting to know the Italian mafia – and the Rangers - had been following her for months without her even knowing it.

With a final glance into the mirror, Kenzie tucked a stray curl back into place and practiced a smooth gait as she made her way to the door. If she moved slowly and held her head high, the cast did not look too awkward. Or so she convinced herself.

Kenzie rounded the bedroom door, expecting to see the doctor. She did not expect to see the Texas Ranger, but there he was, all six feet, four inches of the man. He was talking to Makenna and a rare smile lifted the corners of his full mouth. Kenzie's breath suddenly tangled in her lungs and had trouble squeezing its out way.

It was the first time she had seen him out of uniform, yet there was little variance in his casual clothes from his work wardrobe. Instead of khaki, his long legs spanned an impressive length of starched dark denim. The tie was absent and rather than standard white, his pressed western shirt was cream colored. Yet even without the iconic silver star pinned to his chest, he had the sharp, commanding look of a lawman.

The familiar cowboy hat and boots were in place, pulling Kenzie's eye the full length of him. Her eyes raced over him greedily and a strange pain invaded her heart. It felt a lot like longing, a little like panic. It was not the first time she had experienced the feeling; two weeks ago, in this very room, she felt the same overwhelming sensation, followed by raw fear.

Before she could contemplate the meaning of the odd sensation, the lawman looked up.

The smile on his handsome face slowly wilted. Complete surprise stole over his features and his jaw actually dropped. For one heart-warming, spectacular moment, Travis Merka was rendered completely awestruck, something Kenzie instinctively knew rarely happened. His dark gaze swept over her, brushing her with a caress.

Kenzie had scant seconds to enjoy the look of wonderment on his face. The fleeting expression was gone almost immediately, replaced by the familiar cool mask of professionalism. Had it not been for the faint glow still smoldering in his brown eyes and the lingering heat along her skin, she would think she had imagined the entire thing.

"Miss Reese." The officer greeted her formally, but his low voice floated along her senses, stirring up ripples of awareness.

"Ranger." She hated the breathlessness that accompanied her response.

Busy staring at one other, neither saw the smile Makenna tried to hide. "If you'll excuse me…," she murmured. They never noticed when she and her fading words slipped from the room.

After a long moment of silence, Kenzie and Travis both spoke at once, asking the same question. "How are you?"

"Ladies first," Travis insisted.

"I'm fine," Kenzie assured him. She looked down at her leg, wiggling bare toes from within the bindings of the cast. "At least I'm free of the crutches. Another week or so, I can ditch the cast and be good as new." She swung her eyes up and probed the expanse of his chest, looking for any signs of lingering injury. Her mind flashed back, once again seeing the blood that dripped from his forehead and poured from the deep slash across his muscled chest.

Travis did not miss the tremor of horror that shivered through her. He reached out a long finger and lifted her chin, forcing her to look up at him. "I'm good. Honestly." His voice was gentler than before, but firm enough to be convincing. "Takes more than a knife across the chest to put me down."

"There was also a bottle across the head," Kenzie reminded him. Two weeks ago, mobster Raymond Foto had impersonated a pizza delivery boy and come to this very apartment, intent on kidnapping Kenzie. He had surprised the Ranger stationed outside in the hallway, cracking a bottle over his head and slashing his chest before leaving him for dead.

"That part still stings." He made the admission stiffly, dropping his hand.

How could he take his life so casually? Irritation made her voice sardonic. "Spoken like a typical male," Kenzie scoffed. "Your ego is more fragile than your life."

His dark eyes glittered at her remark and his mouth turned down in a frown. "I see your smart mouth survived the ordeal."

Somehow, the man always managed to rile her. She met him four weeks ago, when Ranger Hardin Kaczmarek brought him to the apartment and announced that the two of them would be protecting her and her sister. She knew it was not Travis's fault that, months before, he had been assigned to her case, but it irked knowing he had been spying on her for weeks without her knowledge. In fact, he had been following her the day of her accident; it was his car that plowed into hers, landing her in the hospital. The mafia had been tailing them both and found a way to take out both threats with one well-timed chain reaction.

Yet it was not the job or the accident that annoyed Kenzie so; it was the man himself. During their brief acquaintance, they mostly argued and were at odds with one another, but even Kenzie knew the real reason he irritated her so much. There could be no fire without a spark, and Ranger Merka set off all sorts of sparks within her. Without a doubt, he was the best looking, sexiest man she had ever known, but her instant attraction to him rankled her. One look into his dark soulful eyes and she was feeling all sorts of strange and complicated feelings. She immediately put up her guard, protecting her heart with sharp words and stinging wit.

Sparks or no sparks, Kenzie bristled at his comment. "I'm sure you were hoping Foto's knife would slip and cut my vocal chords."

His body stiffened and his words came out sharp and menacing. "If that SOB hurt you..."

She did not expect him to react so strongly to her mouthy retort, but his quick burst of anger was for the mobster, not her. "He didn't," she was quick to assure him.

To her surprise, his mood changed abruptly. His next words came out slow and warm. "Heard I have you to thank for not bleeding to death."

She might would have blushed at being heralded a hero, but the horror of the event was still fresh on her mind. There had been so much blood. Travis had staggered into the apartment, held the gun on Raymond Foto after Hardin engaged him in a fistfight, took charge until the other Ranger could regain his breath and put the man in handcuffs, and only then had Travis crumpled against the wall, sliding down to the floor in a steady stream of blood. Kenzie crawled to him, ripping open his shirt to see where the flow stemmed from. In her mind's eye, she could still see the deep gash marring the perfection of his chest. With each pump of his heart, blood gurgled and spurted forth, soaking everything in red.

Kenzie closed her eyes and shuddered as she recalled those awful moments and the ones that followed. Up until she saw the blood smeared all over him, she would have sworn she disliked the tall Texas Ranger assigned to keep tabs on her. But in those awful seconds, she realized her feelings for him were very complicated, and she momentarily panicked. For a few defeated moments, she had given up hope. She fell against his chest, blood and all, and begged him not to die. There were things she had to tell him, things she wanted to ask him, things she thought there would be time for later. She pressed a kiss onto his lips, begging him to hold on, whispering her hopes for a future with him. And in that brief moment of weakness, when she let her guard down and allowed herself to be vulnerable, Travis Merka slipped into her heart.

"Kenzie? Are you alright?"

Forcing the bloody images from her mind, she nodded and opened her eyes. He was watching her in concern, his handsome face set with a frown.

It was the first time she talked to Travis about the incident, the first time she had even seen him. She had gone to the hospital that night, waited there with the others while he was in surgery, but she never went back to see him. She did not feel she had the right. Their paths had not crossed since.

"Too much blood makes me woozy." She hoped her explanation sounded plausible. "And there was so much blood."

"Paramedics said if it wasn't for you, I might have bled out."

Once she snapped out of her panic that day, Kenzie had gone into action. With Makenna's help, they drug him flat out on the floor and used their hands to apply pressure to his chest, somewhat staunching the flow of blood. After handcuffing Foto to a dining room chair, Hardin aided the women in saving his best friend's life until the ambulance arrived.

Kenzie credited them now. "I wasn't the only one. Makenna and Hardin helped me."

"But they didn't kiss me."

Kenzie gasped, her eyes flying to his face when she heard the lowly spoken words. Behind his cool mask, his dark eyes were liquid pools of warmth.

"You- You were conscious?"

"You didn't really think I'd sleep through our first kiss, did you?"

"Not sleep, exactly. Did you… Could you hear what I was saying?"

He shrugged a broad shoulder. "I knew you were there, telling me to hang on. I could hear your voice. You and Hardin, both yelling at me to hang on."

"I'm glad you listened." She intended for the words to come out sassy, but they barely slipped by on a whisper.

"You gave me good reason to."

She had never heard this low, sensual tone in his voice, never seen this light in his dark eyes. Anticipation shimmied its way along her nerve endings and she tingled all over. Breathing was difficult. "Which- Which was?"

For a big man, he moved gracefully. One step, and he was sidled up against her. "To see if the next kiss is even better," he murmured. His large hands slipped around her waist as he pulled her close to his long, lean body. "Kiss me, Kenzie," he instructed lowly. "Kiss me like you did that day."

"That day, I was so scared," she admitted on a whisper. Her fingers slipped between them to gingerly trace where the savage cut had been. "There was so much blood. You were so pale." She couldn't help but shiver.

"I'm fine now, Kenzie," he assured her in a voice that was strong yet gentle.

Kenzie's eyes floated shut as she leaned in to kiss him. There was such strength in his embrace, such warmth. Such security. That was her biggest weakness of all. She threaded her fingers into the short blond hair at his nape and fitted her mouth against his, eager for another taste of him. He allowed her to control the kiss, as her tongue traced the seam of his lips before venturing inside to explore the warm cavern of his mouth. Travis submitted to her wanderings, enabling her to set the pace and the intensity of the kiss. But when her tongue pushed deeper into his mouth, his control snapped. With a growl of impatience, he took possession of the moment and swept her along in a maelstrom of heat. Kenzie forgot she was waiting on her date to arrive, forgot that Travis most often made her angry, forgot to breathe.

The doorbell buzzed once, twice, before it penetrated into their private world. Travis was slow in releasing his hold on her as Kenzie pulled away to stare up at him. Her arms fell away from his shoulders as a sharp rap on the door finally brought her to her senses.

She stepped toward the door, making the mistake of putting her full weight on her left leg. A sharp gasp escaped her lips and Travis moved to catch her by the waist, but Kenzie shook him away. She refused to meet his eyes as she took a brief moment to collect herself, then pulled the door open.

"I was beginning to think I had the wrong apartment!" the man on the other side of the door said with a smile. He stepped forward, his gaze skimming over her with pleasure. "You look gorgeous." A teasing tone came into his voice as he said, "I've never seen you in clothes before."

Behind her, Kenzie heard Travis's sharp intake of breath. She ignored the tall lawman as the intern dipped his head to kiss her in greeting. At the last second, she turned her face, offering him her cheek.

This time, it was the doctor's frown she ignored as she moved a step back to invite him inside. The tuxedo-clad doctor faltered when he saw the other man standing just feet away, wearing an expression like thunder. The air was thick with tension as Kenzie hastily made introductions.

"Robert, this is Ranger Travis Merka. Travis, Doctor Robert Bradford. He was one of my doctors while I was in the hospital." She turned a sunny smile to the physician, trying to drum up the enthusiasm to go through with tonight's date. Even though they had hit it off at the hospital and spoken several times on the phone since then, seeing him again in person did not thrill her the way she thought it would. With a slight sense of panic, she hurriedly recalled his great personality and his sense of humor, reminding herself that he was not all staid and disapproving, like someone else in the room.

If the situation had not been so embarrassing, it would have been humorous. The two men sized each other up as if they were taking measurements for a customized coffin. When it took longer than necessary to shake hands, Kenzie babbled nervously to fill the uncomfortable silence. "What Robert meant is that he's never seen me dressed. I've always been in bed. In the hospital bed, I mean. I was never wearing clothes. Street clothes, that is." Could this situation get any more awkward?

Apparently so. As Travis extended his hand to the doctor, his eyes drifted past the man to Kenzie. His dark gaze went to the telltale signs of her smudged lipstick. Lifting a thumb to his own mouth, he swiped it beneath his lip to clear away any corresponding smears on his own face.

Not only was the gesture obvious, but it carried a sensual weight that settled deep in Kenzie's belly and caused her face to burn even hotter than it already did.

To his credit, the doctor handled the situation gracefully. There was no denying the sexual tension between his date and the lawman. "Kenzie, if tonight doesn't work for you..."

"No, no, don't be silly! I've been looking forward to this all week!" Kenzie deliberately turned away from Travis, so that she could not see that tiny smudge of red lipstick, still lingering there is the corner of his mouth. She was sorely tempted to reach up and wipe it away, so she busied her hands by clasping them around Robert's arm. "In fact, I'm ready if you are."

The doctor glanced at Travis. "You're staying?" he asked uncertainly, his tone a bit wary.

Travis was slow in answering. No doubt it was a method of intimidation, as if a reply was inconsequential. Kenzie released a shaky breath of relief when he finally offered a response. "I have something I wanted to discuss with Kenzie's sister."

"Oh. Oh, I see." The doctor sounded relived, then surprised. "Sister?" He gave Kenzie a quizzical look. "I thought you said you were an only child?"

"Long story. Come on, I'll tell you about it on the way." Kenzie pulled him toward the door, eager to escape the disastrous situation. She grabbed the silver handbag from the entry table and practically pushed Robert ahead of her and out the door. Just before stepping over the threshold, she paused long enough to glance back at Travis. Her step faltered, right along with her heart.

When she could think of nothing to say, he came to her rescue. "I just came over to say thank you. So, thank you."

"It was-" She stopped short of saying 'nothing'. Of course it was something. She had helped save his life. It was everything. Her voice was soft as she said instead, "- my pleasure." She stared at him across the room, wondering if he could hear the thundering of her heart from there.

When Robert gently cleared his throat in the hallway, Kenzie knew it was time to go. "Goodbye, Travis," she whispered, pulling the door firmly shut behind her.

About the Author...

Becki Willis has been writing since grade school, although her early works are best left unpublished. She majored in Journalism at Texas A&M University, but soon got sidetracked with life... marriage to her high school sweetheart, raising two wonderful children, launching careers she loved but that had little to do with writing. In 2013, Becki resolved to pursue her lifeling dream of becoming an author. She published her first book in November, sold her successful gift shop/ restaurant in December, and dedicated herself to her new career.

An avid history buff, Becki likes to go antiquing and visiting historical sites. Other addictions include reading, writing, unraveling a good mystery, and coffee. She loves to travel, but believes coming home to her Texas ranch is the best part of any trip.

Becki loves to hear from her readers and encourages them to contact her at beckiwillis.ccp@gmail.com or on Facebook.

Made in the USA
Charleston, SC
01 April 2016

Deja de PREOCUPARTE

Estrategias comprobadas para padres de familia

Ron Ball

Deja de preocuparte

Estratégias comprobadas para padres de familia

por Ron Ball

Traducción del original: Worry No More!

ISBN: 978-1-942991-17-5

Publicado por
Editorial RENUEVO
www.EditorialRenuevo.com
info@EditorialRenuevo.com

Dedicatoria

Dedico este libro a seis personas que han dado sentido y dirección a mi vida—mis padres, Print and Christine Ball; los padres de Amy, Dave and Ann Sague, y nuestros hijos fantásticos, Allison y Jonathan. Papá les ama.

CONTENIDO

RECONOCIMIENTOS

Muchas gracias a la persona clave en el desarrollo de esta información—mi esposa Amy. Yo no puedo imaginar a una madre más abnegada. Mi deuda de gratitud también al personal de Editorial Tyndale House por su paciencia y la gran ayuda que me brindaron. Y, como siempre, mi agradecimiento a Dexter Yager—el mentor que ha cambiado mi vida.

Ron Ball

INTRODUCCIÓN

¿Sentiste eso? Es el viento soplando—el viento que te mueve a ti y a tus niños en su propia dirección. Es el viento de los tiempos. En el idioma alemán lo llaman *Zeitgeist,* el «espíritu de las edades». Es el viento que puede destruir tu hogar y dispersar tus hijos en su propia egocéntrica dirección.

Este viento empuja a tus hijos hacia una vida egoísta sin Dios y crea perdición. El viento es propulsado por lo que los eruditos llaman una visión del mundo—una manera de ver el mundo y la manera que funciona. Esto es lo que esa visión del mundo promueve:

- La rebeldía como expresión de independencia
- El desprecio por los padres como parte del crecimiento
- Experimentación sexual como algo que se espera de la adolescencia
- Uso de drogas y alcohol como señal de la edad adulta

El viento sopla a través de un sistema de los medios de entretenimiento que refuerza su influencia con el apoyo de películas, TV, revistas, libros, juegos y «estrellas», que por voluntad propia fluyen con la corriente.

¿Por qué crees que ahora es fácil divorciarse, tener niños fuera del matrimonio, olvidarse de ir a la iglesia, y la rebeldía en contra de la autoridad de los padres? En parte porque el viento se está moviendo fuertemente hacia esa dirección.

Durante mi niñez, en los años 1950s y a principios de los años 60s, el viento todavía soplaba en apoyo de la seguridad de las familias y bases morales bíblicas. El viento soplaba a favor de las creencias conservadoras judeo-cristianas. No todos iban en la misma dirección del viento, pero ciertamente el viento ayudaba a mucha gente a moverse en una dirección estable y espiritualmente positiva.

En realidad era más fácil hacer lo correcto porque lo correcto era apoyado por los medios de comunicación, por la comunidad académica, por la iglesia y virtualmente por casi por todos a los que les importaba. Sin embargo, el viento dio un giro drástico a mediados de los años 60s. Comenzó a soplar en contra del honor, los buenos modales, la pureza sexual e incluso el matrimonio. Ese viento aún sigue soplando hoy en día.

¿Qué haces, entonces? Te conviertes en alguien grosero y descortés porque el viento está soplando en una dirección incivilizada? ¿Abandonas a tu familia porque el viento está soplando en esa dirección? ¿Le faltas el respeto a tus padres porque el viento está llevando a tus amigos lejos de sus padres? o ¿cavas y construyes una barrera para el viento? ¿Peleas en contra? ¿Te resistes hasta que suficiente resistencia hace que el viento cambie? ¿Le dices al viento: «¡Ya fue suficiente! Nosotros vamos en el camino de Dios, no en tu camino?»

Josué 24.15 declara: «Pero yo y mi casa serviremos al Señor» (LBLA). Josué tomó una postura cuando la mayoría de sus seguidores querían moverse con el viento de otros dioses. Él estaba en una minoría distinta y aun así dijo NO. ¡El resultado fue maravilloso! Una nación completa resistió el viento nuevo y renovó su compromiso con el Dios Todopoderoso. ¡Qué maravilla, el viento cambió! Esto es lo que tú puedes hacer con tu familia y por otras familias en todas partes.

Cada sociedad es solamente una generación a un paso del desastre. Las culturas avanzadas reconocen esto y trabajan fuerte para educar a cada nueva generación con los valores y creencias de la anterior, ya que se considera que una generación es generalmente de veinte años, nosotros siempre estamos solamente a veinte años de la victoria o el fracaso, de la luz o la oscuridad, del cristianismo o el paganismo.

Decide ahora recuperar esta generación—por Jesucristo, por la moral, por la familia, por los matrimonios buenos—tú puedes ayudar a cambiar el viento antes que se convierta en un huracán salvaje y fuera de control que amenaza con aniquilarte a ti y a quienes amas.

¿En qué dirección está el viento soplando en tu casa?

¿Estás listo para hacer algo al respecto?

CAPÍTULO 1

Un vistazo a la cultura de hoy

En la suite de un hotel en Orlando reinaba la ansiedad, líderes de negocios emocionados y sus cónyuges. La gente estaba aglomerada en cada espacio disponible. Nosotros habíamos invitado a estas parejas para una noche de discusión y descubrimiento. Nuestro objetivo inmediato era explorar nuevas tendencias de negocio.

El flujo de la conversación era dinámico—estábamos pasando un bueno momento—cuando de repente todo cambió. Un dueño de negocios llamado Josh cambió el tema de los ingresos y economía y comenzó a hacer preguntas de sus hijos. Él tenía un matrimonio exitoso y una compañía que estaba en crecimiento. Su compromiso con Jesucristo era vibrante y real, pero sus preguntas revelaron incertidumbre acerca de la crianza de hijos cristianos positivos. Su amor por su familia era fuerte y de apoyo, pero él deseaba tener más conocimiento en cómo desarrollar técnicas efectivas para ayudar a que sus hijos tuvieran éxito en la vida.

Sus preguntas crearon una avalancha de respuestas. De repente, los líderes de negocios se convirtieron en madres y padres. Una pareja tras otra preguntaron acerca de la música pop, las drogas y los problemas sexuales. Ellos necesitaban destreza para analizar y entender el mundo en general y la cultura que rodeaba a sus hijos. El resto de la noche pasaron examinando la sociedad, la cultura y los estándares bíblicos, así como planeando estrategias para tener hijos cristianos, seguros y exitosos.

Ven conmigo ahora a una jornada similar. Esta es tu oportunidad de profundizar en una cultura dominante, para obtener conocimiento profundo de las muchas influencias que atraen a tus hijos.

Si te preguntaran ahora: ¿Qué está pasando por la mente de tus hijos? ¿Cómo dirigen su vida hoy? ¿Cómo crees que van a dirigir su vida en el futuro? ¿Qué dirías?

Bueno, todos tenemos que saber más del mundo en el que viven nuestros hijos. ¿Qué están aprendiendo acerca del carácter, negocios, dinero, éxito y sexo? ¿Cuál es su punto de vista en cuanto al matrimonio y los padres (los de ellos y los de sus amigos)? ¿Les gusta leer y pensar? ¿Están equipados para tomar buenas decisiones de con quién van a salir y escoger buenas relaciones? ¿Están espiritualmente vivos y creciendo?

¿Qué tan bien conoces su mundo? ¿Entiendes de qué manera les afecta la sociedad secular dominante? ¿Entiendes bien tu papel como padre y como esposo o esposa? ¿Sabes lo vital que es el éxito en tu matrimonio para el éxito en la vida de tus hijos?

Este libro va a contestar muchas de tus preguntas. La intención no es tanto que sea una lista de ideas para la crianza de los hijos, sino más bien que sea un mapa que te ayude a través del campo minado de la confusión de la familia moderna.

¿Estás listo? Veamos lo que está pasando en el mundo de tus hijos y lo que puedes hacer al respecto.

Nuestro mundo cambiante

Actualmente en los Estados Unidos hay seis generaciones con vida. Primero, está la que algunos demógrafos e investigadores llaman «la generación perdida». Nacida entre 1883 y 1900, estos individuos son muy pocos y distantes entre sí—mayormente porque tendrían que tener, en el año 2000, más de cien años. En seguida está la «Generación GI», nacidos entre 1901 y 1924. Luego está la «Generación silenciosa», nacida entre 1925 y 1942. Enseguida está la famosa «Baby Boom» (explosión de natalidad después de la Segunda Guerra Mundial) nacida entre 1943 y 1960. Y finalmente, dos generaciones han entrado recientemente a la gran mezcla cultural, la «Generación trece» (también conocida como generación X) nacidos entre 1961 y 1981 y la «Generación del milenio», nacidos entre 1982 hasta el Siglo 21.

Aunque estas generaciones varían en cuanto a antecedentes, experiencia y edad biológica, todos ellos han sido afectados por los siguientes tres cambios:

Cambio #1: Cambio económico

En épocas anteriores, la gente solía soñar en grande—buenos trabajos, casas grandes, carros grandes. Sin embargo, hoy en día, según la revista *American Demographics,* los cinco campos de trabajo de más rápido crecimiento son: 1) oficinistas y cajeros; 2) personal para cuidado de personas; 3) conserjes y trabajadoras domésticas; 4) meseros y meseras; 5) conductores de camiones. Ninguna de estas profesiones son oportunidades para soñar en grande o tener gran ingreso. Las buena noticia es que las grandes oportunidades abundad para ti y para tus hijos. Hay disponibles para ti maneras diferentes de producir ingresos. El mercado de multinivel y la Internet son solamente dos áreas de potencial asombroso en las cuales tú puedes construir aún un mejor futuro.

Cambio #2: Cambio social

Existe una preocupación creciente de nuestro mundo que está comenzado a provocar un regreso a la moral y los valores. Por ejemplo, el libro *What Americans Believe,* publicado en 1990 por Barna Research Organization en California, es el resultado de esta pregunta hecha en una encuesta nacional en los Estados Unidos a la gente. La pregunta fue la siguiente: ¿Si pudiera cambiar algún aspecto de su vida, cuál sería? Las respuestas fueron sorprendentes.

Aquí están las trece más importantes:

1.- **Buena salud** - El 93% de los encuestados mencionaron que ésta era su preocupación principal. Ellos deseaban sentirse bien y estar en buena salud.
2.- **Integridad** - El 76% nombraron la confiabilidad y la honestidad como algo muy importante. Ellos deseaban sentirse bien con lo que hacían. No querían hacer nada que fuera en contra de sus principios.
3.- **Relaciones personales estrechas** - El 73% anhelaban esta clase de relaciones. Esa es la razón por la cual los negocios de redes han crecido a pasos agigantados —porque quienes están involucrados, no solamente pueden tener un buen ingreso y mantener a su familia, sino también puede formar lazos de amistad.
4.- **Una relación cercana con Dios** - Muchos estaban sorprendidos por esta respuesta del 72% de la gente —especialmente porque los encuestados no fueron motivados para dar esta información.
5.- **Vivir más cerca de la familia extendida** - Un 67% quería estar más involucrado con la familia.
6.- **Vivir cómodamente sin temor financiero** - El 59% de los encuestados dijeron que les gustaría vivir sin tener que enfrentar estrés monetario diariamente.
7.- **Vivir una larga vida** - Un 51% no solamente deseaba sentirse bien y disfrutar, sino también vivir mucho tiempo.
8.- **Ser parte de una buena iglesia local** - Nuevamente, aunque a los encuestados no se les pidió que dieran respuestas religiosas, eso es lo que el 50% deseaba.
9.- **Poder influenciar a otros** - 40% querían tener influencia positiva y productiva en esos que les rodeaban. Deseaban hacer una diferencia en el mundo.
10.- **Tener un trabajo bien remunerado** - 36% pensaba en términos para producir más ingresos.
11.- **Dejar de ser empleado** - 35% quería tener dinero suficiente algún día, y de esa manera no tendrían que levantarse e ir al trabajo ya fuera que les gustara o no.

12.- **Tener una casa más grande** - El 23% deseaba tener un lugar más amplio para vivir.

13.- **Fama y reconocimiento** - Aunque solamente el 10% dijeron que querían fama, yo realmente creo que el número es mayor. ¿Por qué? Porque si le preguntas directamente a los individuos cómo se sienten acerca de la fama, ella se siente incómodos y reacios a admitir que ellos desean tener dicha experiencia. Ellos no quieren que tú pienses que son ególatras. Pero si tú le das a la gente algún reconocimiento, retírate y mira cómo responden. Tú vas a ver su sonrisa en su rostro y brillo en sus ojos.

Recuerda esto: si mucha gente desea que el mundo vuelva a tener morales y valores, existe una gran posibilidad de hacerlo realidad para tus hijos. ¡Qué emocionante!

Cambio #3: Cambio político

Durante cada intervalo de dos años entre elecciones nacionales, los valores cambian como resultado de una nueva generación uniéndose a la población de votantes.

Por ejemplo, cada dos años, 8 millones de nuevos miembros de la «generación del milenio» van a unirse al electorado nacional, y 6 millones de individuos de GI y Silent Generation (Generación silenciosa) van a desaparecer. Eso significa que la política de nuestra nación va a cambiar siempre y cuando las ideas de las generaciones cambien.

Con cada elección, es importante que recordemos que los principios judeo-cristianos que formaron las bases de las ideas americanas y la cultura social y política, siguen siendo esenciales para que podamos seguir prosperando como nación. Si las abandonamos, estamos perdidos.

El Sueño Americano

Yo he viajado lo suficiente para saber que cada siglo tiene algo especial para contribuir al mundo. Cada uno tiene una cultura en particular, una historia, una herencia que puede contribuir a nuestro entendimiento y conocimiento de la vida humana. Yo disfruto Europa Occidental. Yo estoy fascinado con el Lejano Oriente y Australia.

Pero mientras viajo alrededor del mundo, yo me sorprendo de la cantidad de personas que siguen cautivadas de lo que piensan del sueño americano. El hambre de noticias del país que ha inspirado al mundo por doscientos años.

Nunca hemos tenido una nación que haya nacido de la manera que nació América, y eso la hace única. Verdaderamente es de «experimento americano», como lo dicen algunos expertos. Es un tocino en cuanto a los principios de libertad, justicia, y libre empresa para el mundo entero. No por gusto los Estados Unidos ha escogido el águila como su símbolo nacional—feroz, autosuficiente, valiente, fuerte, poderosa y gloriosa.

Sin embargo, en el presente la gloriosa águila está herida. Existen cinco razones por las cuales la cultura americana es una cultura en declive y estas razones son una amenaza para el bienestar de nuestros hijos.

Amenaza #1: La modificación de la historia americana en las escuelas

Quizás estés o no familiarizado con el término «desconstruccionismo», pero es básicamente la filosofía de que la historia como lo sabemos ha sido corrompida por prejuicios ideológicos y filosóficos y debe romperse y ser hecha políticamente correcta. Para poder hacer esto, las escuelas están dispuestas a hacer desaparecer nuestra historia, para destruir nuestra herencia.

Mujeres y hombres jóvenes de hoy saben tan poco acerca de la herencia espiritual. Ellos no saben que el Congreso Continental estaba lleno de hombres que leían la Biblia mientras escribían las Constitución. Ellos no saben que Patrick Henry, quien es conocido por su famoso clamor, «Give me freedom or give me death» (Déjame libre o mátame) le dijo a su hermana, «Lo más importante en la vida es que un día nos juntemos en el cielo por medio de Jesucristo, nuestro Señor y Salvador». Benjamín Franklin dijo, «Esta república no puede ser construida a menos que sea construida bajo el Dios Todopoderoso». Estos hombres realmente reconocían la importancia de la dirección de Dios.

Este reconocimiento de la prioridad de la dirección de Dios tuvo un impacto en América. Por ejemplo, aquí está una lista pequeña de lo que requerían enseñar los profesores de la Universidad Harvard:

- ***piedad*** - vida piadosa, justa que respete la autoridad de Dios
- ***justicia*** - ser ecuánime, no engañar
- ***respeto sagrado por la verdad*** - de la única fuenta, la Biblia
- ***amor por la patria*** - la tierra comprada por la sangre de sus patriotas
- ***amor por la humanidad*** - cuidado y compasión arraigada en las creencias judeo-cristianas que todos fuimos creados iguales
- ***benevolencia universal*** - un gran compromiso a dar tiempo, ingreso y servicio para el bien de otros
- ***industria*** - trabajar fuerte para generar ingresos
- ***frugalidad*** - la ciencia del manejo de dinero: cómo ganarlo, cuidarlo y hacerlo crecer
- ***castidad*** - una vida sexual pura que reconoce que el sexo fue creado solamente para el matrimonio
- ***moderación*** - balance y disciplina en todas las áreas de la vida
- ***templanza*** - tener balance personal en el uso de alcohol y el placer

Las mismas doce cualidades estaban enumeradas en la Legislatura del Estado de Massachusetts cuando fue votada como ley en 1789. ¿Por qué? Porque Harvard no existía para dañar sino que para ayudar. No para destruir sino que para construir y fortalecer la República Americana.

En contraste con hoy en día, los niños en las escuelas de primaria y los jóvenes en las escuelas secundarias y universidades no tienen la menor idea de las bases bíblicas de nuestro país. Escucha esta cita: «¿Se puede considerar que las libertades de una nación son seguras cuando hemos removido la única base segura—una convicción en la mentes de las personas de que esas libertades son un regalo de Dios?» ¿Quién crees que escribió esto? ¿Un pastor? ¿Un maestro cristiano? ¿Un evangelista? No. Lo escribió Thomas Jefferson.

Thomas Jefferson es también el mismo hombre a quien se le culpa, en algunos círculos, por redactar en la Constitución esa frase ambigua y controversial, «separación de la iglesia y el estado». Pero esa frase no aparece ni en la Constitución de Estados Unidos, ni en la Declaración de Derechos, (Bill of Rights).

Fue escrita en 1801 como respuesta a una petición de un grupo de ministros bautistas de Danbury, Connecticut. Ellos escucharon un rumor de que a cierta denominación se le iba a dar la autoridad para ser iglesia estado de Estados Unidos, así como la Iglesia de Inglaterra es la iglesia oficial del Reino Unido. Y ellos estaban alarmados. ¿Podría ser esto posible? De haber sido así, esto le hubiera robado a América la libertad por la cual habían peleado tan fuerte para ganar. La respuesta de Jefferson fue que no se preocuparan—había una muralla de separación entre la iglesia y el estado. Así que el gobierno estaba destinado a ser protector de la religión, no enemigo de ésta. Era para protegerse en contra de gobiernos o dictadores.

Ya sea que seas cristiano o no, tú no puedes entender la historia de América sin tomar en cuenta sus raíces judeo-cristianas.

Amenaza #2: La epidemia de niños egoístas

Robert Bellah, en su libro *Habits of the Heart* (Hábitos del corazón) examina las actitudes americanas. Su conclusión fue que la mayoría de nosotros somos tan egoístas que no hacemos nada sin antes determinar qué beneficio personal podemos sacar. Él dice que ya no somos una nación de donantes y colaboradores; nos hemos convertido en personas que se enfocan en sí mismas en lugar de ser personas honorables que hacen lo que es correcto simplemente porque es correcto. Somos personas interesadas que hacemos lo correcto solamente si nos beneficia. Enseña a tu hijo a ser dador y vas a cambiar su vida para mejor y también el futuro de su país.

Amenaza #3: La redefinición de la verdad

Todas las redes importantes traen rutinariamente expertos que nos dicen que el matrimonio está obsoleto, que las actitudes sexuales son personales y no tienen impacto en la sociedad y que cada persona puede hacer lo que él o ella desee. Sin embargo, mucha de su información es contradictoria y con frecuencia en clara violación de la Biblia.

Cuando estaba en la escuela de posgrado, me quedé atónito en una de mis clases cuando el profesor entró, encendió una pipa y se burló de Estados Unidos de América por los siguientes cuarenta y cinco minutos. No era una broma, él estaba hablando muy en serio. Se burló del capitalismo, nuestro sistema de gobierno y de todo lo que nos representa. Luego él se burló de Jesucristo. Se carcajeó de los cristianos conservadores, ofendió a esos que creen que la Biblia es la Palabra de Dios, pero lo que este brillante y amargado doctor en filosofía no dijo, es que su salario era pagado por el poder adquisitivo americano, el cual provenía de muchas de las cosas de las cuales él se estaba mofando.

Permíteme darte otro ejemplo. Muchos «expertos» políticos dicen que la presidencia de Reagan fue un fracaso miserable, pero aun así, aquí está lo que el Primer Ministro de Inglaterra, Margarte Thatcher dijo acerca de él, el 8 de marzo de 1991: «En la década de los 80s, los valores occidentales fueron puestos en el crisol y salieron de ahí con mayor pureza y fuerza. Gran parte del crédito va al Presidente Ronald Reagan, y me entristece que algunos se rehúsan a reconocer sus logros, porque el cambio fue mundial bajo su presidencia.»

La presidencia de Reagan sentó las bases para muchos logros extraordinarios, algunos de los cuales se llevaron a cabo durante administraciones sucesoras. Aquí están solamente unas pocas cosas que él ayudó a lograr: La Guerra Fría (Cold War) fue ganada sin hacer ni un disparo. Europa Oriental recuperó su libertad. El Muro de Berlín fue derribado y Alemania fue reunificada dentro de NATO. Alemania y Japón, las naciones vencidas en la Segunda Guerra Mundial prosperaron tremendamente, e irónicamente, se convirtieron en los acreedores en el nuevo mundo de paz. Una Unión Soviética debilitada se vio obligada por la competencia militar y económica del Occidente a reformarse a sí misma. Sin embargo, a pesar de estos logros estupendos, Reagan es difamado por la prensa liberal—incluso cuando sus reducciones de impuestos estabilizaron los impuestos federales en un poco más del 19% del producto doméstico bruto.

Lo que esto significa es que debes enseñar a tus hijos a probar a los expertos. Observa sus credenciales y examina sus orígenes. No aceptes simplemente lo que dicen sin investigar los hechos por ti mismo. Además, pregúntate por qué están ellos diciendo lo que están diciendo. ¿Tienen ellos una agenda escondida? ¿Están tratando de empujar un concepto que es de naturaleza diferente contra Dios y sus valores?

Mientras abordas esta pregunta, vas a descubrir que muchas de estas personas no solamente tienen una agenda escondida, ellos son dirigidos por el ego—comprometidos con su propia necesidad de celebridad.

Amenaza #4: Educación sexual no bíblica

Nuestra columna vertebral moral—nuestra posición moral y entendimiento—está siendo destruida y nuestra moral en sí está siendo reformada y moldeada por los medios liberales.

Por ejemplo, en California, la educación sexual en

el currículo es llamada «elección inteligente de estilo de vida sexual». Se presenta a los niños del séptimo grado. Su propósito es permitir que los niños establezcan su «estándar meramente personal de conducta sexual». Dicha educación es también promovida en las películas, videos musicales MTV e Internet y crea confusión sexual. Están preparando a tus hijos para una vida de destrucción, con sentimiento de culpabilidad e infelices porque ellos no esperan para tener sexo dentro del matrimonio, en lugar de decirles que se abstengan de tener sexo hasta el matrimonio. Por lo tanto, en lugar de evitarse ellos mismos una vida llena de dolores de cabeza, nuestra sociedad les entrega condones e información de anticonceptivos.

Tus hijos tienen que saber que Dios no pone reglamentos para hacernos miserables. Él no crea reglas porque está enojado con nosotros, porque quiere entorpecer tu estilo, o porque Él está tratando de robarnos la libertad o placer. En lugar de eso, Él está tratando de darnos un plano para que podamos tener una vida más plena. Porque Él nos creó y sabe lo mejor. Sus principios nos protegen y éstos nos ayudan a proteger nuestra nación si los seguimos. Si no los seguimos, agotamos nuestra fuerza corriendo tras placeres hasta que ya no tenemos la disciplina y la fuerza para vivir la vida de forma efectiva. Nuestra sociedad pierde su base moral porque ya no creen en un Dios a quien todos deberíamos rendir cuentas. Esto deshace el tejido social, porque en este contexto todo lo que cualquier persona piensa hace, está bien. Si no existe un estándar externo para vivir, entonces ¿quién puede decir lo que es correcto e incorrecto?

Eso fue lo que sucedió en la Antigua Roma; también le puede suceder a América.

La Ley de Dios dice que hay un comportamiento correcto e incorrecto y que sí hay tal cosa como la inmoralidad. Sin la Ley de Dios, nuestro país va a permanecer en la oscuridad. Como lo escribió el gran orador griego Crisóstomo (Circa A.D 40-112) «Como un hombre con ojos adoloridos, la luz le parece dolorosa a la gente sin bases morales, mientras que la oscuridad, lo que les impide ver, se convierte en nada más que algo relajante y agradable». En otras palabras, un hombre en una cueva llega a estar tan cómodo con la oscuridad que rechaza la luz: le lastima. Las enseñanzas de Dios sobre la moral son un rayo de luz ardiente; ellos abren tu corazón y tu vida a la verdad. Aunque la confianza lastima, también te salva de ti mismo—si obedeces lo que dice esa verdad.

Incluso la parcialidad de los medios de comunicación de hoy en día están en contra de los principios cristianos. Por ejemplo, toma el término "homofóbica". Fóbica, significa tener un temor neurótico e irracional por algo y los medios de comunicación están tratando a quienes se oponen a la homosexualidad como homofóbicos. En otras palabras, presentan a estas personas como irracionales y neuróticas, solamente porque no apoyan un estilo de vida que es responsable de la devastación de millones de personas, pero la homosexualidad es un estilo de vida que nunca ha producido nada bueno. Solamente crea una angustia y agonía en la gente que se encuentra atrapada en su abrazo.

Otro ejemplo es llamar a un bebé, «tejido fetal», para que así pueda ser moralmente respetable deshacerse de dicho «tejido». Después de todo, tu cuerpo es tu propiedad, ¿verdad? ¿Por qué crees que el término pro-elección (o a favor del aborto) fue escogido por esos que están a favor del aborto? Porque suena noble. América—yo estoy a favor de tu elección, especialmente porque cualquiera que sea la elección que decidas hacer es la correcta para ti. Lo que quienes están a favor del aborto no toman en cuenta es que la elección de una persona es, en este caso, destruir la vida de otra—al bebé que no ha nacido no se le da el derecho a elegir. Así que ¿la elección de quién es más importante? ¿Estar a favor del aborto significa que tienes el derecho de elegir quitarle la vida a un niño que no ha nacido porque es una inconveniencia para ti, o porque quizá haya algún problema con el bebé?

«Descuidar al anciano, al incapacitado, o al que no ha nacido, significa que nuestra cultura está descuidada», Charles Colson escribe, «pero hay otras cosas más importantes que conseguir tus derechos. Es más importante hacer lo correcto.» Si solamente estás preocupado por obtener tus derechos, estás tratando el sexo como una función animal—no como un conector espiritual entre un hombre y una mujer que se aman el uno al otro para toda la vida y tienen un matrimonio estable. Para ti, el sexo es solamente placer y satisfacción.

Alexander Solzhenitsyn, un hombre que sufrió a causa de la falta de moral de su gobierno dijo esto: «Las fuerzas del mal han iniciado su ofensa decisiva. Tú puedes sentir su presión, pero aun así, tus gritos en las publicaciones en América están llenas de sonrisas pre-recetadas y copas levantadas. Pero yo pregunto, ¿Cuál de qué se trata tanta alegría? Cuando nuestras morales son hechas nuevamente, cuando éstas son re-dirigidas, nosotros no tenemos base, no tenemos núcleo.» Tú no puedes tener moral—un sentido de lo que es bueno y malo—sin Dios.

Amenaza #5: La aceptación de mal comportamiento

Los estilos de vida llenos de pecado ya no nos sorprenden; de hecho, se han vuelto comportamientos aceptados. Esto es lo que Dios dice acerca de esta moda: «Horribles y sorprendentes cosas han pasado en esta tierra—los profetas dan falsas profecías, y los sacerdotes gobiernan con mano de hierro. Y peor que eso, la vida de mi pueblo es así!...Desde el más pequeño hasta el más grande, engañan a otros para no conseguir lo que no les pertenece a ellos, sí, incluso mis profetas y mi sacerdotes son así!» (Jeremías 5.30-31; 6.13).

Para que América pueda cambiar, la gente se tiene que parar y convertirse en héroes que van a pelear. Nosotros no podemos esperar que alguien más haga el trabajo. Cada uno de nosotros tiene que involucrarse en la política y espiritualmente. Nosotros tenemos que trabajar activamente por un cambio. Nosotros no podemos dejar que el liberalismo y relativismo y el vacío moral se deslicen por más tiempo. Ya no podemos sentir éxtasis por la «celebridad», porque los héroes reales son gente como nosotros—madres y padres que están comprometidos a quedarse ahí con nuestros hijos, enseñarles valores cristianos y criarlos a la manera de Dios, adultos con morales.

Es debido a que gente como tú ha decidido defender lo que es correcto, ya están soplando vientos más frescos. Las iglesias conservadoras están prosperando, la tasa de natalidad en las adolescentes están bajando, el uso de drogas en adolescentes se está reduciendo y millones de americanos votaron recientemente para elegir a un presidente conservador con valores morales.

Nosotros ciertamente deberíamos de tomar estas amenazas más seriamente; la guerra todavía no se ha ganado. Nuestros niños siguen viviendo en este mundo lleno de estas amenazas, pero las marea está cambiando—Dios está trabajando y la renovación de América está aumentando. ¡Lo más importante que hay que recordar acerca del proceso de decadencia, es que puede revertirse!

Veinticinco puntos culturales sensibles, y cómo afectan éstos a nuestros niños

Nuestro mundo cambiante no es lo único que afecta a nuestros hijos socialmente. Existen veinticinco puntos a los cuales yo llamo «puntos culturales sensibles» que representan la manera en que muchas personas se sienten acerca de la vida. Debido a que nuestros hijos son parte del mundo, ellos no tienen otra opción más que se afectados por estos puntos de vista. A medida que aprendes cuáles son, puedes averiguar estrategias más efectivas para combatirlos en tu propia familia.

Punto #1: La mentalidad «no es justo»

Muchos adultos consideran que no están ganando tanto dinero como sus padres. ¡La economía se está degenerando, y eso no es justo! Por ejemplo, el año pasado después de la Navidad, CNN entrevistó a gente en centros comerciales y les preguntó porqué estaban regresando ciertos regalos.

Una joven, rodeada de sus amigas bien vestidas, llevaba un buen número de bolsas. Cuando le preguntaron porqué estaba devolviendo los regalos ella dijo, «Bueno, yo simplemente no los quiero». Cuando el reportero le preguntó qué regalo deseaba devolver primero, ella respondió, «El que no puedo. Alguien me dio un pésimo billete de veinte dólares, ¿puedes creer eso? Y ellos tuvieron al atrevimiento de pensar que me estaban dando un buen regalo.»

Mientras la chica se escurrió en el pasillo con sus amigas, yo me senté en mi silla frente a la televisión y pensé, qué pésima actitud—especialmente cuando a alguien le importaba lo suficiente para darle parte de sus ingresos.

Pero ese mismo incidente es una representación de la manera en que muchos miembros de la generación actual piensan: que ellos merecen una casa (una casa grande) que ellos son dueños de un trabajo con salario alto, y que no es justo si ellos no consiguen ambas cosas.

Tristemente muchas compañías están conscientes de esta impulso para poseer el sueño americano. Estas corporaciones contratan mujeres y hombres jóvenes que están terminando la universidad, les prometen posiciones de trabajo y avances, y comienzan dándoles cantidades de dinero que nunca antes han ganado. Pero lo que sucede es que estas corporaciones exigen gran lealtad y terminan por agotar a la gente. Los empleados renuncian o son despedidos porque ellos están agotados o no pueden con la presión. Su propia idea de injusticia en realidad contribuye a su caída.

Por lo tanto, enseña a tus hijos que la vida no siempre es justa y que tienen que trabajar duro. Su vida también tiene que ser un balance entre las obligaciones y el entretenimiento.

Punto #2: Desorden

Yo lo admito. Yo tiendo a ser un poco descuidado en mi área personal de trabajo. Aunque a mí no me gusta decirlo, mi estudio con frecuencia parece como si por ahí ha pasado un huracán bombardeando. Periódicos y mensajes telefónicos esparcidos por todas partes.

Algunas veces el ritmo de nuestra vida moderna es tan rápido que pasamos mucho tiempo simplemente jugando a ponernos al día y tratando de organizarnos. ¿Por qué? Porque dentro de cada uno de nosotros hay una necesidad sicológica y emocional por el orden.

Para que la vida tenga sentido, tu ambiente privado tiene que tener sentido. Cuando le enseñamos a nuestros hijos a que organicen sus vidas en un orden más sensato, ellos van a tener un incremento de productividad.

Punto #3: Cansancio crónico

¿Están tus hijos continuamente cansados? Si es así, quizás haya alguna explicación física o emocional de ese cansancio. Pero mucha gente está cansada debido al agotamiento emocional y estrés. A ellos no les gusta lo que hacen, ellos no disfrutan la vida, e incluso a ellos no les gusta quienes son. A esto yo le llamo, «privación de sueños».

Cuando yo era joven, estaba en el programa de postgrado que odiaba, pero yo no sentí que debería ir hacia otra dirección. Así que, después de obligarme a mí mismo a quedarme en el programa por varios meses, yo tenía dificultad para levantarme en la mañana—incluso cuando me había ido a la cama temprano la noche anterior. Con frecuencia dormía hasta la una de la tarde, salía de la cama y me arrastraba a mí mismo a la clase a última hora. También comía en exceso. Como resultado de mi «privación de sueño», yo comencé a experimentar cansancio crónico. Pero cuando terminó el programa, una oleada de energía comenzó a caer en mi vida. Yo quería levantarme todos los días en la mañana y comenzar a moverme. Yo estaba nuevamente emocionado de la vida.

Por eso creo firmemente que la mayor parte del cansancio crónico no es resultado de una vida demasiado ocupada y mal administrada. Es una deficiencia de dormir bien, cuando en la vida no tienes nada que te entusiasme. Enseña a tus hijos a buscar la verdadera razón detrás de su cansancio. ¿Será que es porque no tienen un sueño verdadero que perseguir?

PUNTO #4: LA INCERTIDUMBRE DE LA AUTORIDAD MORAL

Ha habido un crecimiento de alternativas filosóficas que le dan la última fuente de autoridad a las personas en lugar de a Dios. Por ejemplo, ya no nos preocupamos por la moral de nuestro presidente. No importa si es honesto, auténtico, comete inmoralidad sexual, o rompe sus votos sagrados del matrimonio, siempre y cuando él cumpla con sus deberes básicos como presidente.

Parece que a los americanos les importa menos y menos la moral de nuestros líderes, siempre y cuando ellos trabajen en programas que hacen feliz a algunas personas. Pero si la moral en las autoridades ya no es importante, pronto estaremos viviendo en una nación completamente sin alma, donde cualquier cosa mala será posible—e incluso legal.

¿Por qué hubo un Adolfo Hitler? Porque la sociedad alemana cambió su definición de moral y permitió que él se convirtiera en un monstruo moral. La nación puso la moral en segundo plano para traer de regreso la economía y el poder alemán.

América podría fácilmente estar en el mismo lugar. Y como el presidente, más allá de otros líderes en nuestra sociedad, es un símbolo público de lo que debería ser lo mejor de nosotros, no lo peor, él también tiene que ser una persona piadosa. Después de todo, él debería reflejar nuestras fortalezas como nación, no nuestras debilidades. Eso no significa que nosotros esperamos un presidente perfecto, sino una persona que refleje nuestras mayores inspiraciones y objetivos como nación. Más que nada, los Estados Unidos deben regresar a una estabilidad moral, haciendo nuevamente que los principios bíblicos sean el estándar de conducta.

Así que enseña a tus niños que Dios es la autoridad principal—y que Sus estándares son los que debemos de seguir.

Punto #5: Persuadir vs. Semonear

El estilo personal de tus hijos y la manera en que ellos se acercan a las personas tiene que llevar el sello de la cortesía. Las personas desconfían de las enseñanzas; quieren ser persuadidos.

Por ejemplo, aunque nos encanta hablar a otros de nuestra relación con Jesucristo, no tiene ningún beneficio para mí forzar la información en la vida de otros. En lugar de eso, mi obligación es ser amorosamente persuasivo y escuchar sus preguntas con todo respeto.

Cuando una persona que iba en la misma fila de asiento de avión que yo e iba expresando sus ideologías acerca de la reencarnación, una escritura se me vino a la mente: «Y así como está decretado que los hombres mueran una sola vez, y después de esto el juicio» (Hebreos 9.27).

Yo sé que la Biblia nos enseña que nosotros no nos autoreciclamos en vidas diferentes, así que me preguntaba cómo debería contestarle a ella. Si le decía, «Idiota, ¿cómo puedes ser tan estúpida para creer eso?» Ella me callaría inmediatamente. Si le decía: «Ah, por si acaso, yo creo que la Biblia dice...». Ella quizás me vería como uno de esos cristianos que se cree muy santo, tratando de forzar mis creencias en ella.

Por lo tanto, en lugar de hacer eso, le pregunté por qué creía eso. Viendo que yo era amigable, ella respondió de una manera positiva y me permitió compartir con ella lo que yo creía y mientras recogíamos nuestras pertenencias para salir del avión, oré para que nuestra corta conversación tuviera impacto eterno. Por lo tanto, enseña a tus hijos a que se acerquen a otros con cortesía y con persuasión amable, en lugar de hacerlo como si quisieran enseñar algo.

PUNTO #6: NIÑOS ASUSTADOS

Mucha gente tiene temor de lo que está pasando en la sociedad y anda en busca de contrarrestar sus influencias negativas.

Según los investigadores demográfico sociales Neil Howell y Bill Strauss, cada día:

- 2.500 niños americanos son testigos de un divorcio o separación de sus padres
- 90 niños son quitados de sus padres y puestos en hogares temporales
- 13 jóvenes entre 15 y 24 años cometen suicidio
- 16 jóvenes son asesinados
- un joven común de 14 años mira 3 horas de televisión y hace una hora de tarea escolar
- 2.200 niños abandonan la escuela
- 3.610 adolescentes son asaltados – 630 de ellos son víctimas de robo, y 80 son violados
- más de 100.000 estudiantes de escuela secundaria llevan armas de fuego a los escuelas
- 500 adolescentes comienzan a usar drogas
- 1.000 adolescentes comienzan abusar de alcohol
- 1.000 niñas se convierten en madres solteras

La cultura americana está en problemas. ¿Pero son fatales estos problemas? No necesariamente, si nos levantamos y hacemos algo para detenerlos. Como Howell y Strauss escribieron: «La gente ya ha tenido su pequeña borrachera, su poquito de droga, deuda, catástrofe de divorcio. Su pequeña fiesta donde consumieron demasiado de todo. Ahora es tiempo de hacer una limpieza en la historia…una generación que salió de la época del anhelo a sacó todo del clóset, nunca soñó que algún día levantaría una generación a quien no le importaría poner unas pocas cosas en su lugar.»

PUNTO #7: UN GUSTO POR LA BASURA

En un libro titulado The Carnival Culture (La Cultura del Carnaval), un profesor de la Universidad de Florida dijo:

«Existe una difusión en toda la sociedad por el gusto por la vulgaridad que ahora lo tenemos como común denominador más bajo desarrollándose en nuestro entretenimiento. La mayor cantidad de elementos básicos y vulgares están comenzando a dominar y esto no puede ser bueno para nuestra sociedad. Esto nos embrutece, nos roba refinamiento y nuestra sensibilidad para una vida y cosas mejores».

Yo creo que él está en lo correcto. Estamos en la coyuntura donde el gusto por la basura se está volviendo algo serio. Como escribió un investigador: «las personas están negociando los bienes y raíces y sus cónyuges diversificando y desmantelando a sus familias, destruyendo los límites del gusto musical, de la cultura, del cine, televisión y arte».

Comparemos esta moda con comer comida chatarra. No es malo si ocasionalmente como ciertas comidas que no son buenas para mí, pero si consumo esta comida chatarra, alta en calorías y grasa todo el tiempo, mi cuerpo va a colapsar. Eso es también una verdad en la cultura.

En los años de 50s, casi todos los programas de televisión y 90% de todas las películas producidas eran consideradas adecuadas para los niños. Éstas eran películas tan buenas que Nick y Nite todavía ponen estos programas antiguos hoy en día. ¿Por qué? Porque éstos representan la inocencia, la dulzura y la bondad. Además, son muy cómicos, muy entretenidos, sin un lenguaje crudo y vulgar como el de muchos programas y películas de hoy. ¿Te das cuenta de lo que sucede a los niños cuando les permitimos ver el entretenimiento que producen hoy en día? Ellos descienden a las alcantarillas de la basura de la cultura y empujan los límites del gusto por la cultura más hacia abajo. Como escribió un profesor de la Universidad de Florida: «Nosotros tenemos un carnaval de cultura cuando la vulgaridad gobierna y la basura domina». Eso quiere decir que están entrenando a la gente a no pensar, a no tener educación y a no responder con inteligencia a lo que están observando.

Nosotros tenemos que responder a este peligro de una manera positiva y útil.

Por lo tanto, enseña a tus hijos a ser lectores y espectadores que disciernen. A pensar las cosas y evaluar lo que miran para decidir si deben o no volver a ver ese material.

Punto #8: Verdad vs. Sentimiento

La cultura de hoy está entrenado a las personas a «estar en contacto con sus sentimientos». ¿Pero es eso tan útil como parece? Los sentimientos pueden cambiar de momento a momento.

Una de las grandes crisis de nuestro tiempo es que la gente no piensa; ellos simplemente se «tragan» lo que dice los políticos y los medios de comunicación. Un buen ejemplo es un programa reciente de ayuda para la salud. Cuando la revista *National Review,* junto con la organización Gallop, hizo una encuesta nacional sobre el programa, 70% de los que respondieron estaban a favor.

Sin embargo, cuando los mismos investigadores fueron de nuevo a esos mismos individuos y les leyeron párrafos del programa—incluyendo el hecho de que ellos no iban a poder escoger su propio doctor, y que todo el cuidado de la salud iba a estar controlado por el gobierno el 87% decidieron no estar de acuerdo con el programa. ¿Cuál es la diferencia? Los sentimientos de las personas hacia el programa cambiaron cuando ellos fueron confrontados con dichos hechos irrefutables.

Así que enseña a tus hijos la diferencia entre sus sentimientos y los hechos. Infórmales que los hechos permanecen; los sentimientos cambian.

Muchas personas hoy en día ni siquiera investigan los hechos. Ellos han elegido ser dependientes de lo que dicen los expertos en lugar de pensar por sí mismos. Pero hay muchos «expertos», y esos expertos pueden estar equivocados. Los niños tienen que ser entrenados a examinar lo que otros dicen. Así que muéstrales cómo investigar las fuentes y elaborar su propia información.

No solamente comuniques lo que escuchas que alguien más está diciendo. Asegúrate de que puedes confiar en el origen examinándote a ti mismo. Recuerda, no se trata de sentir o no sentir si el origen es correcto, se trata de que sepas o no qué es.

Así que enseña a tus hijos a pensar por sí solos en lugar de simplemente creer lo que los expertos les dicen. Además, infórmales si algún «experto» contradice la Biblia, ¡porque eso quiere decir que esta persona siempre está equivocada!

Punto #9: La mala trampa del dinero

Todavía existen grandes segmentos de nuestra sociedad que creen que es malo ganar dinero. Pero esta gente también quiere trabajos, de los cuales ganar dinero. Es una contradicción en lógica. De alguna manera esta gente ha sido convencida de que el avance material es malo porque es capitalismo, y el capitalismo es el origen de la crisis de nuestra cultura, pero eso no es verdad del todo.

Enséñales a tus hijos a pensar correctamente sobre el dinero—que es útil como herramienta, pero que no se debe abusar.

Punto #10: Confusión en cuanto a lo bueno y lo malo

Muchos niños han caído víctimas de esta filosofía predominante de nuestro tiempo: lo único que cuenta cuando tomas una decisión, es que sea práctica y útil. No importa si es moralmente correcta o equivocada, siempre y cuando la uses para lograr lo que quieres. Siempre estás pensado si hay algo de beneficio para ti y eso llega a ser tu única agenda.

Charles Colson decía que estamos produciendo una «generación sin consciencia»—una generación de niños a quienes no les importa lo que es correcto e incorrecto, que no se sienten culpables cuando cometen un crimen. Eso significa que van a tomar decisiones no éticas y no les va a molestar.

Neil Postman, un profesor de comunicaciones de

la Universidad de Nueva York dice, «Tenemos una generación moralmente vacía que toma decisiones por las razones prácticas más vacías».

Hemos escuchado a algunas personas decir: «Yo te voy a decir lo que es moral: lo bien que te sientes después de hacer algo. Inmoral es cuando te sientes mal después de hacer algo». Tristemente, esta filosofía es similar a la definición de la moral comunista en la antigua Unión Soviética: lo que era bueno para la causa comunista era automáticamente moral. En otras palabras, si le «volabas» la tapa de los sesos a alguien por el avance del comunismo, eso significaba haber hecho algo moralmente bueno. Si dormías con alguien con quien no estabas casado para conseguir secretos para tu gobierno, eso era moralmente bueno. Si constantemente mentías, engañabas o destruías gente, pero lo hacías para el avance del comunismo, eso era moralmente bueno.

¿Qué tienen que ver los Estados Unidos de América con esto? Debido a la falta de fibra moral, nuestra propia sociedad está volviéndose vulnerable a los mismos efectos que sufrieron los soviéticos.

Pero esa forma de vida es un error y moralmente vacía. No existe la verdadera moral sin un Dios santo, personal e impresionante a quien rendirle cuentas. Dios es el Creador de toda la moral y el origen de toda justicia moral. Sin su influencia en nuestros corazones, nuestra cultura de hoy se convertirá en algo aún con menos consciencia y cada vez más funcional.

Así que enseña a tus hijos que lo correcto es correcto y lo erróneo es erróneo.

Punto #11: La obsesión con el «dinero rápido»

¿Por qué existe tal epidemia por los juegos de azar en personas menores de treinta años y particularmente en las instalaciones universitarias? Porque la mayoría de las personas quieren ganar dinero rápido. Ellos se enfocan en el dinero como su manera para hacerse exitosos.

Investigadores como Strauss y Howell hablan acerca de este interés obsesivo en el dinero. «Cuando la generación del ayer era joven, les enseñaron a enfocarse en la aprobación adulta, a incrementar objetivos que no tenían nada que ver con dinero. Cosas como tener buenas calificaciones escolares, convertirse en Eagle Scout, conseguir insignias Scout y premios de distinción en concursos. Al alimentarlos y recompensarlos de esa manera, esos chicos se guiaban por un patrón de conducta que los llevaba a crecer en situaciones donde el dinero gravitaba hacia ellos.»

En tiempos pasados cuando los hombres y mujeres jóvenes no se enfocaban meramente en ganar dinero; se enfocaban en convertirse en buenas personas. Se esforzaban por tener disciplina y carácter. Trabajaban para desarrollar destrezas, buenos hábitos de trabajo y una actitud positiva para que cuando llegaran a ser adultos, serían personas tan buenas en todo el sentido de la palabra que el dinero fluiría hacia ellos.

Pero eso no significa que ganar dinero siempre va a ser fácil o que no implica tomar decisiones difíciles y hacer sacrificios. Enseña a tus hijos a esperar porque esperar por gratificación es algo bueno, porque puede llevarte a un mayor éxito a largo plazo.

Punto #12: «¡Estoy aburrido!»

Parece contradictorio que las personas puedan andar apresuradas y estar agotadas y aun así estar aburridas, pero es debido a que vivimos en una cultura de múltiples opciones, nosotros creemos que debería de haber siempre una opción de entretenimiento disponible. Cuando no la hay, nos sentimos aburridos, aunque quizá estemos muy ocupados.

Cuando raramente tenía un fin de semana libre y trataba de llevar a mi familia a cenar fuera, descubrí algo increíble. Los restaurantes estaban tan llenos que siempre teníamos que esperar por horas. También las tiendas estaban llenas con gente ocupada. ¿Por qué? La mayoría de las personas están peleando contra el aburrimiento. Tratan de colmar sus fines de semana con algo entretenido para así tener una cantidad de relajamiento para impulsarlos a su nueva semana de trabajo. Seguro que hay mejores maneras para que nuestra sociedad invierta su tiempo y energía.

Enseña a tus hijos a que no tienen que estar aburridos. Existen muchas oportunidades para que formen parte de ministerios maravillosos y actividades emocionantes. Si ellos se involucran con otras personas, el aburrimiento será lo último y lo de menos en sus problemas y desafíos.

Punto #13: Estrés en la niñez

La televisión y los medios de comunicación son maestros cuando se trata de crear crisis. Sin embargo, la mayoría del tiempo estas crisis están fuera de tu control. Ver mucha televisión y exponerse a los problemas del mundo le puede dar a los niños «crisis de cansancio». ¿Por qué? Porque están siendo bombardeados con problemas en los cuales ellos no puede hacer mucho. Despierta sus emociones, su mecanismo de intervención es activado a lo más alto, y luego se queda estancado. Eso produce frustración. Tus relaciones familiares se trivializan cuando las conversaciones comienzan a girar en torno a nuevas cosas.

Así que no permitas que la crisis de cansancio cree una atmósfera artificial de estrés. Eso puede ser un enemigo para el hogar—incluso sin que tú lo sepas. Eso enseña a tus hijos temor y preocupación en lugar de enseñarles plena confianza en Dios. Así que, ¿cómo puedes cambiar esto? Enseña a tus hijos a orar por las crisis que están sucediendo alrededor del mundo y confiar el resultado a Dios. Enséñales cómo llenar sus mentes con información útil y cómo enfocarse en áreas donde ellos puede hacer un impacto.

Punto #14: Multiculturalismo

¿Qué es multiculturalismo? ¿Qué representa? Según la definición académica actual: es la creencia que todas las culturas son diferentes, pero esencialmente iguales.

Esto no tiene sentido a partir de una base histórica.

Aunque algunas personas quizás hagan muecas cuando yo digo esto, históricamente es cierto que algunas culturas son superiores a otras, pero eso no significa que tú, como miembro de una cultura, eres automáticamente mejor o peor que otro individuo de otra cultura. Nosotros deberíamos tener mucho e igual respeto por todos los individuos, sin importar su trasfondo cultural. Lo único que significa es que ciertas culturas producen mayores beneficios que otras.

Por ejemplo, la civilización occidental, basada en sus principios positivos judeo-cristianos de empresa libre, trabajo duro y disciplina, ha producido beneficios impresionantes para nuestra sociedad. ¿Por qué más gente de todo el mundo está pidiendo a gritos venir a los Estados Unidos de América? Para ellos, Estados Unidos representa oportunidad económica y libertad personal. Debido a que estos rasgos han sido un éxito en Estados Unidos durante los últimos doscientos «y pico» de años, no debemos restar importancia a éstos o atrevernos a ofender a otras culturas. Podemos respetar otras culturas sin abandonar nuestras creencias en Dios y beneficios posteriores de la cultura a la cual pertenecemos.

Enseña a tus hijos a entender la sociedad moderna y multicultural, pero dentro de un marco cristiano.

Punto #15: «Mala intención»

Existen aquellos que creen que deberíamos de tolerar toda clase de comportamiento de nuestros hijos y no poner objeción a la rebeldía y egoísmo. Sin embargo, aunque debemos dar a nuestros hijos su espacio propio, no debemos aceptar actitudes y comportamientos que son destructivos e incorrectos.

Cuando estamos en contra del comportamiento incorrecto, algunas personas nos ven como personas malas: es extremista. Pero nosotros no debemos abandonar la moral y la verdad. Nuestra responsabilidad es compartir la verdad dentro de un contexto de una actitud respetuosa, incluso cuando otros no responden respetuosamente. Eso significa que tomamos dolores extra para ser sensibles a otros, especialmente cuando estamos lidiando con temas controversiales. De otra manera, es posible que no sean nuestras creencias las que sean rechazadas, sino la manera áspera y hostil en que nos acercamos a otros.

Los niños, especialmente, tienen desconfianza de la maldad. Eso quiere decir que nosotros no debemos dar la impresión—nunca—de crueldad. Siempre opera con la mayor cortesía y respeto hacia otros.

La clave para tratar bien a otros es la Regla de Oro de la Biblia: «Trata a otros como te gustaría que te trataran a ti». ¿Te gusta ser amenazado? ¿Intimidado? ¡Claro que no! Así que trata a tus hijos como a ti te gustarían que te trataran. De otra manera, ellos simplemente pensaran que eres malo y no van a escuchar lo que les dices.

Asegúrate de decirle a tus hijos todos los días lo mucho que te importan y lo mucho que los amas. Recuerda que una parte crucial de amarlos es ponerte firme—sin ser malo—en las áreas de la disciplina.

PUNTO #16: ¿LIBERTAD SEXUAL?

Desde los años 60 en adelante, los Estados Unidos ha sido absorbida por una búsqueda ilimitada de libertad sexual y personal. ¿Y qué ha pasado? Esta nación sufre de bancarrota sexual y moral debido a lo que le llaman «revolución sexual». Las familias son inestables y se están destruyendo.

La evidencia de la fallida revolución sexual está alrededor de todos nosotros. Nos confronta todos los días con las tasas de aumento de ilegitimidad, relaciones destruidas, enfermedades de transmisión sexual (incluyendo la epidemia de SIDA) y la epidemia de divorcios.

Un muchacho joven en sus veinte, afirma bien nuestra posición como país: «Hemos experimentado una traición fatal con nuestra generación del "baby boom". Ellos nos dijeron que el sexo era solamente para disfrutar, que no había necesidad de tener restricciones, que las limitaciones no eran importantes, y nosotros lo creímos. Nosotros nos "tragamos" la mentir, pero hemos sido traicionados. Porque ahora tenemos dificultados pare tener relaciones, para construir buenos matrimonios, y tener buenas familias.» Y este muchacho joven no está solo. Muchos jóvenes están aturdido y confusos—y están buscando dirección.

Así que enséñale a tus hijos acerca del sexo—los lineamientos de Dios y las consecuencias de no seguirlos. No esperes que alguien más les dé dirección.

Punto #17: Los niños y la culpabilidad

La culpabilidad se desarrolla en la sociedad de hoy. Los niños se sienten culpables de cualquier cantidad de situaciones reales o imaginarias. Ellos se siente culpables por sobresalir...y por tener éxito.

Algo de culpabilidad es buena. La culpabilidad nos puede recordad que tenemos que regresar a nuestra manera piadosa de vivir. Nos puede llevar a darnos cuenta que, debido a que fuimos hechos a imagen de un Dios maravilloso que nos ama, nosotros no podemos violar los Mandamientos de Dios acerca de la moral, sin pagar un precio interno. Aunque nos sentimos culpables cuando la culpabilidad nos infesta, esa culpabilidad es también un recordatorio más de lo valioso que somos para Dios. De hecho, la Biblia dice que no hay manera de medir lo precioso que somos para Él. Y en realidad Él construye en nosotros un mecanismo de culpabilidad para enseñarnos lo que es bueno y lo que es malo.

Pero algo de la culpa es socialmente inducida—y falsa. Aquí hay algunos ejemplos:

- **Culpabilidad ambiental** - (si no estoy haciendo algo para salvar la selva tropical del mundo, demuestro que no me importa el mundo a mi alrededor)
- **Culpabilidad personal** - (yo trabajo fuerte, pero no parece que avanzo tanto como mi compañero de trabajo, Jim. ¿Qué estoy haciendo mal?)
- **Culpabilidad de la imagen corporal** - (Yo tengo que lucir como las modelos de las portadas de revistas o nadie va a querer salir conmigo)

Dichas culpabilidades falsas le quitan productividad a la gente, y solamente se originan en un lugar: del rey del desaliento, Satanás.

Los niños deben tener pocas reglas, simples y fáciles de entender. Se debe tener la expectativa que las obedezcan —y deben de ser corregidos cuando no lo hacen. Pero así como Pablo dice en Efesios, no exasperéis a tus hijos. No los fuercen a sentirse impulsados por la culpabilidad, llenos de miedo, neuróticos, gente perfeccionistas que no puede vivir en paz. Corríjanlos y entrénenlos, sí, pero siempre háganlo con ternura y suavidad. Nunca corrijan sin una dosis generosa de amor y perdón. Recuerden Efesios 2.4, «Dios es rico en misericordia, y Él nos ama tanto». Ustedes también tienen que ser ricos en misericordia con sus niños. Le haces un bien a tus hijos cuando les enseñas la diferencia entre verdadera y falsa culpabilidad.

Punto #18: El temor al fracaso familiar

Con el rompimiento de la familia, muchos niños son dejados sin raíces. Según un estudio psicológico de niños de padres divorciados, «más de un tercio de hombres y mujeres jóvenes entre las edades de 19 a 21 años, tiene poca o ninguna ambición diez años después de que sus padres se ha divorciado. Ellos van derivando por la vida sin tener metas, con educación limitada, y un sentido de impotencia.

Esto no significa que todas las situaciones de divorcio van a causar desarraigo, particularmente si ambos padres trabajan juntos para proteger, ayudar, amar, alimentar, y guiar a sus hijos a través de esta situación difícil. Pero con cada ruptura de familia, exista una gran probabilidad de que los hijos van a batallar, no solamente en el presente, sino también en el futuro.

Quizás ellos se pregunten, «Bueno, si el matrimonio de mis padres no funcionó, ¿qué puede funcionar? ¿Qué hay de seguro en el mundo si mi familia no lo es? Es por eso que es tan importante que las familias permanezcan tan unidas como sea posible y disfruten el compañerismo y apoyo cariñoso. Nuestros hijos necesitan dirección constante de parte de los padres comprometidos.

Dicha necesidad es demostrada por una conversación que fue documentad por la Internet entre dos personas que estaban usando computadoras. Ellos estaban hablando del matrimonio y de la familia. Yo lo repito aquí, ya que es un verdadero relato de nuestro tiempo, y de la manera que se sienten nuestros hijos cuando las familias se desintegran.

Usuario 1: *Si en ese entonces hubiera sabido de los filósofos charlatanes que decían que estaba bien que nuestros padres se olvidaran de recogernos de la lección de piano, mi hermano y yo habríamos incendiado un par de librerías.*

Usuario 2: *Si me permites una pregunta indiscreta, ¿Siguen juntos tus padres?*

Usuario 1: *Claro que no. De hecho, de los diez que vivimos en esta casa, seis de nosotros tenemos padres diferentes.*

Usuario 2: *¿Cuándo pasó eso a tu familia?*

Usuario 1: *Cuando yo era estudiante de primer año de secundaria. En aquel tiempo no me importaba nada. Yo me sentía mal por mi hermano y hermana menor porque no estoy seguro que a ellos se les hayan enseñado alguna vez lo que es tener una pareja romántica estable. Mi padre me preguntó una vez, «¿Te hubiera gustado que me quedara, aunque hubiera sido miserable?» Claro, esto fue mucho después del hecho, y yo no tuve ganas de discutir con él, pero cada vez que pienso en mi hermana pequeña, de repente un coro de, «sí, sí, sí, yo quiero que te quedes», se me viene a la mente.*

Yo no menciono este tema para lastimar a aquellos que están atravesando, o han atravesado por el trauma de divorcio. Muchos tienen razones que van más allá de lo que yo pueda entender, incluyendo abuso. Pero lo que estoy tratando de mostrar es que América tiene una epidemia de divorcios fáciles y convenientes que podrían haberse arreglados si las dos partes involucradas hubieran tenido el deseo de hacerlo.

Según la organización Gallup, «cada año desde 1984, entre 72% y 79% de adolescentes piensan que las leyes de divorcio en este país son demasiado blandas». En 1977 solamente un 55% hicieron esa declaración. ¿Qué quieren decir eso? Yo creo que es simple. Más y más hombres y mujeres jóvenes que han experimentado el trauma de divorcio en sus familias, están diciendo, «Ya fue suficiente». Los niños merecen una familia unida que los apoye.

Así que enséñales a tus hijos la importancia de ser parte de una unidad—tu familia—y muéstrales con tus propias acciones que tienes gran respeto por el compromiso matrimonial que hiciste.

Punto #19: El temor al crimen violento

En los últimos dos años, cada organización de votación de Estados Unidos ha descubierto que el problema social número en la mente de la mayoría de gente en América, es el crimen. Crimen violento. La gente está preocupada acerca de la invasión del crimen en un ambiente que el los creyeron que era seguro y protegido. Y ese crimen es mayor cuando las familias no tienen para protegerse a sí mismas. Ellos no pueden pagar para instalar un sistema de alarma contra ladrones o mover a su familia a un mejor vecindario, donde el crimen es menos prevalente. Ellos no pueden escapara del sistema de crimen.

Así que monitorea el ambiente de tus hijos. Conoce sus amigos personalmente. Revisa su horario. Mantenlos en lugares seguros. Protégelos de cada película, televisión y programa de noticias que sea muy explicito. Dales la mayor sensación de seguridad que te sea posible. Recuérdales constantemente de la protección de Dios sobre ellos.

Punto #20: Ningún sentido de propósito

Cada día los hombres y mujeres de todo los Estados

Unidos van a trabajar sin ningún sentido de propósito. No tienen ninguna misión en la vida; viven sin orientación.

El gran líder de negocios Billy Florence cree que es la razón por la cual la gente decide construir su propio negocio. «El dinero es un gran motivador, pero aún más que eso, la gente necesita ser motivada por una misión. Ellos necesitan una razón para trabajar a altas horas de la noche y levantarse temprano en la mañana. Ellos necesitan una razón para acumular kilometraje en su coche; necesitan una razón invertir equidad de sudor en lo que están tratando de desarrollar; necesitan una razón para ser un dador; una razón de contribuir; una razón para trabajar; necesitan una misión. Es por eso que creo que ser dueño de tu propio negocio es parte de una misión de construir una América mejor, la construcción de una vida mejor para tu familia.»

Si te sientes como que no tienes una misión, mira a tu alrededor. ¿Qué es lo que realmente te apasiona? Si eres un padre, debe ser tu responsabilidad de ser buen padre. Y puedes demostrar tu compromiso a esa misión por la forma en que gastas tu tiempo y dinero.

Date cuenta de que tus hijos también necesitan una misión. Hazlo como parte de tu misión de ayudarles a encontrar su propio propósito único.

Punto #21: La gente en onda

Si estás preocupado acerca del prestigio, y tienes una necesidad profunda de mostrar tus creencias por medio de la manera en que actúas, te vistes, y gastas tu dinero, también tus hijos serán así. Si tú crees que estar en las aglomeraciones es el camino hacia el progreso, estás equivocado. La personas que son demasiado sensibles a tener un estatus, nunca llegan a ser productivas o exitosas.

Por ejemplo, los estudiantes que eran súper populares en la escuela secundaria, usualmente no hacen mucho después de salir de la secundaria. Ellos se han convertido en alguien tan absorto por ser populares que no aprendieron a dar; ellos solamente saben recibir. Y por lo tanto ellos no pudieron entrar en los principio de dar, servir, y trabajar en unidad, que es lo que hace que una familia se mantenga unida en contra de los pronósticos. Enseña a tus hijos que son grandiosos, tal y como son, que no necesitan competir por posiciones en la aglomeración.

PUNTO #22: LA MENTALIDAD DE «LO MEREZCO»

Cuando te han dicho que tienes tantos derechos, la palabra carece de sentido. Todo se convierte en un derecho, y nada es una responsabilidad. Por lo tanto, se convierte en un enigma gigante para encontrar la manera de conseguir tus derechos todo el tiempo. Y eso puede ser tremendamente agotador, particularmente en un entorno familiar, cuando todo el mundo empieza a competir por sus derechos.

Así que, enseña a tus hijos que todo ser humano tiene derechos, pero que no todo el mundo consigue lo que quiere todo el tiempo. Hay un toma y daca en cualquier relación humana.

Este sello de nuestra cultura—«yo merezco un montón de poco esfuerzo»—es muy oneroso. Significa cada vez menos niños dispuestos a trabajar a través de cualquier relación que les podría causar algo de dolor. Menos están dispuestos a prometer «para siempre» a un cónyuge. Es mucho más fácil sólo «probarlo» y vivir con esa persona.

Pero como dice el viejo refrán, «Nada bueno viene barato». Asegúrate de arraigar ese principio en la vida de tus hijos.

PUNTO #23: UNA VIDA DEMASIADO COMPLICADA

La vida y las elecciones que tenemos que hacer pueden ser abrumadoras. Como resultado, mucha gente está cansada, y están en busca de una vida más simple. Para poder hacer la vida menos complicada, ellos están comprando ropa de alta calidad, y menos piezas. Ellos están luchando para hacer sus períodos de descanso parte de su itinerario. Ellos están tratando de cambiar prioridades que han estado fuera de control.

Ellos quieren regresar a fundamentos del compromiso familiar, los fundamentos de estabilidad y seguridad, los fundamentos básicos de control de deudas. Y eso es exactamente los que los hijos quieren—conceptos de amor, tiempo y comunicación.

Con tu propio ejemplo, enseña a tus hijos a disfrutar de una vida simple y menos complicada.

Punto #24: Influencia de entretenimiento

Muchas personas se han convencido que el entretenimiento es uno de sus derechos, y nunca cuestionan qué está haciendo el entretenimiento para su beneficio espiritual, emocional y psicológico. Si acostumbras a ver violencia, puedes convertirte en alguien insensible a la vida humana.

No es fácil decir «no» a dichas películas. Yo mismo batallo con esto. A veces estoy cansado, yo he estado corriendo locamente, y yo quiero ir a ver una película buena y popular. Pero cuando salgo de ver dicha película, me siento espiritualmente decaído. Yo me siento hundido psicológicamente, como si hubiera sido agotado en lugar de ser energizado. Desde que me di cuenta de esto, yo he estado trabajando muy fuerte para mantenerme alejado de las películas y programas de televisión violentos. En lugar de eso, yo trato de pasar mi tiempo haciendo algo productivo.

Y la violencia no es lo único malo para las almas de los niños.

A lo que yo llamo «celebritismo» ha convencido a muchas muchachas jóvenes, así como también a mujeres con baja autoestima de que son feas y que no valen nada porque no lucen como las bellas actrices que ven en la pantalla.

¿Cuánto más seguros serían nuestros niños si las familias se quitaran de enfrente de la televisión y pasaran tiempo juntos haciendo actividades más productivas?

Por lo tanto, recuerda revisar las opciones de entretenimiento para tus hijos. Al hacer esto, también estás protegiendo sus corazones y sus mentes.

PUNTO #25: HAMBRUNA ESPIRITUAL

¿Te has sentido espiritualmente hambriento alguna vez? Si es así, tú no estás solo. Millones de personas se sienten de esa manera. Así como ellos anhelan la comida física, también anhelan por comida espiritual para llenar su alma. En el transcurso de mi vida, yo he descubierto la verdad liberadora acerca de la hambruna espiritual, hay solamente una cosa que puede saciarla. En realidad, esa cosa es una persona: Jesucristo, el hijo de Dios que murió en la cruz por nuestros pecados. Si aceptas esa verdad y Cristo llega a ser algo personal para ti, tu alma va a ser liberada. Tu alma hambrienta va a ser recibida por alguien que está contigo 24 horas al día, y quien espera por ti en el cielo.

Si decides no aceptar a Cristo, vas a pasar toda tu vida corriendo tras una felicidad escurridiza y buscando satisfacción para tu alma. Así que, asegúrate que tus hijos sepan que con Cristo ellos nunca van a cuestionar si su vida tiene significado. Al fin van a estar en paz con Dios quien los creó, que los conoce íntimamente, y que los ama mucho más que cualquier otra persona. Pero solamente cuando tú mismo experimentas y conoces el amor incondicional de Dios por ti, le puedes trasmitir eso a tus hijos.

CAPÍTULO 2

¿Qué clase de padre eres?

Yo nunca olvidaré la vez que Amy, nuestra hija Allison, y yo, nos mudamos a nuestra nueva casa. Esa noche, todos nosotros, incluyendo el perro, y los muñecos de peluche de Allison, tuvimos que dormir en la única cama que había disponible. Después de una noche de cansancio tratando de que todos estuvieran cómodos, yo hice una pausa por un momento solamente para mirar a Allison, y vi a esta dulce niña, una cara de casi siente años, ella se veía tan inocente y tan llena de promesa. Y yo me di cuenta del gran amor que sentía por ella—un amor que no se puede explicar en términos humanos. Ese amor hizo que yo deseara lo mejor para ella, e hizo que yo sintiera la necesidad de criarla de la manera correcta; que la animara a conocer a Jesucristo nuestro Salvador; y la ayudara a aprender todos los principios de cómo trabajar y llegar a tener éxito.

Una vez un pastor de Kentucky me contó acerca de dos funerales que tuvo consecutivamente. Ambos era de hombres jóvenes de la misma familia. Ambos tenían un padre en común, padre que era aplaudido por su tremendo éxito financiero y su carrera profesional. Sin embargo, sus hábitos personales de consumo de alcohol habían creado un «golfo» entre él y sus hijos, dañando su relación de manera irreparable. Con dos de sus hijos muertos, el padre tenía dificultad para mantener una relación con el hijo que le quedaba. Aunque él amaba mucho a sus hijos, su irresponsabilidad y falta de disciplina habían destruido no solamente su relación con ellos, sino también toda su vida. No es de extrañar que en las fotos que colgaban en las paredes de la oficina de él con sus tres hijos cuando era bebes, él parecía nostálgico. Los más probable es que a él le hubiera gustado empezar de nuevo.

En contraste con la historia de apertura. Aunque el segundo hombre amaba a sus hijos, amarlos no era suficiente. Aunque ames mucho a tus hijos, tú aún tienes seguir ciertos principios cuando los estás criando.

Los siete tipos de padres

¿Sabías que una de las claves para tener hijos exitosos eres tú? Si tú eres inmaduro, lo más probable es que produzcas hijos inmaduros. Si tienes problemas de drogas y alcohol, es más probable que produzcas ese mismo problema en tus hijos. Yo digo que es más probable porque no es una fórmula automática. Los niños no son meramente títeres. Algunas veces ellos eligen seguir malos caminos aunque tengan padres buenos; otras veces, hijos que no han tenido padres que hayan sido unos modelos de conducta, resultan ser un gran éxito debido a su determinación y decisiones sabias.

Pero eso no significa que tú, como padre, te sientes a observar que simplemente el desarrollo de tus hijos suceda. Un libro que leí recientemente dice: «Tú vas a criar los mejores hijos que seas capaz de criar.» A simple vista, quizás esto parezca un elogio. Sin embargo, lo que el autor está diciendo en realidad es que tú debes ser tan bueno con tus hijos como lo eres contigo mismo. Si eres haragán e irresponsable, también tus hijos serán así.

Por lo tanto ¿Qué clase de padre eres? Evalúate a ti mismo usando los siente modelos o tipos de padres que se describen a continuación. Quizás seas uno de ellos o una mezcla de varios.

#1: El padre severo

¿Eres exigente y siempre presionas a tus hijos? El pastor y orador Charles Swindoll cuenta la historia acerca de una plática que escuchó de sus hijos por casualidad. Ellos estaban comentando acerca del hecho de que su padre nunca se carcajeaba. Él siempre parecía serio en todo y nunca se divertía con ellos. Escuchar esas palabras afectó mucho a Swindoll. Él se lamentó, preguntándose qué estaría haciendo para causarse estrés a sí mismo (¿esperando que le diera un ataque al corazón en el futuro?) en su trabajo, su vida personal y la vida de su familia. Él no quería que sus hijos se reunieran en su ataúd, miraran hacia abajo y dijeran: «Bueno, por lo menos era serio, pero que pena que nunca nos carcajeamos con él».

Yo creo en la disciplina y las reglas. Yo no creo en la permisividad de dejar que los hijos hagan todo lo que quieran y se salgan con la suya, pero tampoco creo que honres a Dios con tus hijos siendo muy severo y les hagas la vida miserable. Tú no quieres que tus hijos crezcan llenos de culpa y pensando que nunca son los suficiente buenos.

¿Por qué son los padres excesivamente severos? Usualmente existen dos razones:

- Quizás ellos se sientan culpables por los errores que ellos cometieron. Ellos no quieren que su hijos cometan los mismos errores.
- Ellos se sienten inadecuados o inferiores en su propia vida. Padres severos quizás no sepan ser buenos padres. En lugar de admitir que ellos no tienen las respuestas y que necesitan ayuda, ellos exageran. Ellos se presentan como un jarro de agua fría proverbial, solamente para compensar por su inexperiencia y falta de conocimiento. Pero al hacer eso quizás ahogan emocionalmente la vida de sus hijos.

¿Cuál es la solución? Yo creo con todo mi corazón que el problema de culpa fue resuelto en la cruz de Jesucristo. Debido a que Jesús se sacrificó a sí mismo voluntariamente, tú puedes venir a Él para que te perdone. Puedes rechazar tu pecado y egoísmo y pedirle a Jesús que sea tu Salvador. Él te va a perdonar y hacerte totalmente limpio.

No uses tu culpabilidad interna para crear presión en tus hijos. En lugar de hacer eso, admite que tienes insuficiencias. Habla con tu cónyuge, un amigo en quien confíes o un consejero. Haz tu propia investigación a través del estudio de la Biblia y otros libros. Tú no quieres que tus hijos crezcan con una opinión de que su padre y su madre nunca se rieron con ellos, nunca se divirtieron. A pesar de que tus hijos tienen que tener cierto respeto saludable por ti, tú no tienes que ser un aguafiestas.

#2: El padre perfeccionista

Esta es la clase de madre y padre tipo sitcom que todo lo que hacen es perfecto. Ellos facilitan y alivian los problemas en solamente treinta minutos, pero lo que sucede en realidad es que están manipulando a sus hijos. Están tratando de poner perfección en ellos. Aquí hay una buena definición de una persona perfeccionista: «Alguien que realmente se esfuerza por hacer algo y luego hace que todos los demás paguen por ello».

¿Por qué los padres que quiere todo perfecto actúan de esta manera? Porque quieren que sus hijos sean una extensión de ellos mismos. Si te sentiste inadecuado en la escuela, quieres tomar a tus hijos, ponerlos frente de todo el mundo y mostrarles a todos los demás que no eras un imbécil, un nerd o un necio. Después de todo, tus hijos te salieron bien.

Pero los hijos no son trofeos que podemos colgar en la pared y los padres perfectos que tratan de hacer esto, ponen a sus hijos bajo estrés. El Dr. David Elkind, autor de *The Hurried Child* y *All Grown Up* y *No Place to Go,* declara que el estrés es el problema de salud número uno en los niños de hoy. Los niños están estresados porque los padres los están «perfeccionando».

¿Eres un padre perfeccionista? ¿Estás tratando de cumplir tus metas fallidas poniendo a tus hijos en exhibición? Si es así, recuerda que tú no eres dueño de tus hijos, Dios es el dueño y si pones mucha presión en ellos para que sean perfectos, van a crecer pensando: yo no soy perfecto, eso quiere decir que no valgo tanto la pena o soy un perdedor. Hoy en día muchos adultos están atrapados en este círculo sin fin como resultado de la manera perfecta en que fueron criados por sus padres.

#3: El padre descuidado

Los padres descuidados son demasiado flojos para disciplinar a sus hijos o pasar tiempo con ellos. Llegan a casa después del trabajo y ven televisión es mucho más importante para ellos. Los padres descuidados no se dan cuenta que el peor error que el padre descuidado puede cometer es ser egocéntrico—pensar en sí mismo primero en lugar de pensar en lo que sus hijos necesitan.

Sí, quizás trabajes duro, pero aquí está algo importante que tienes que recordar: Tú solamente estarás con tus hijos temporalmente y la clase de relación que tengas con ellos cuando sean adultos depende de lo que tú hagas ahora.

#4: El padre callado

Este tipo de padre evita cualquier relación emocional con sus hijos. Los hombres que crecieron con la idea equivocada de que no mostrar sus emociones es la manera correcta de ser hombre son particularmente vulnerables a este tipo de paternidad.

Si eres una madre o padre callado, estás creando un mar emocional entre tus hijos y tú que quizá no puedas cruzar cuando ellos sean adultos. Involúcrarte emocionalmente con ellos ahora hace que cumplas tu responsabilidad y vas a cosechar tremendas recompensas más adelante.

#5: El padre estúpido

Tú no tienes que ser altamente inteligente para ser buen padre, pero no debes elegir ser estúpido. Los padres estúpidos piensan, «Ah, yo crecí y llegue a ser adulto ¿Por qué no habrían de hacerlo mis hijos? Yo no tengo que saber todo acerca de la crianza de los hijos para ser buen padre.

Con frecuencia los padres «estúpidos» son aquellos que luchan internamente. Así que échate un vistazo a ti mismo. ¿Tienes problemas emocionales de alguna clase? ¿Sientes ocasionalmente que no eres amado? ¿Tienes problemas relacionándote con tu cónyuge? ¿Alguna vez has estado deprimido o has batallado con temor, insuficiencia o preocupación? ¿Eres adicto al trabajo? Bueno ¿Dónde crees que obtuviste esos sentimientos o tendencias? De tu niñez.

Nadie sabe todo lo que se necesita saber para criar hijos. Amy y yo tampoco. Es por eso que nosotros estudiamos acerca de cómo criar hijos. Nosotros estudiamos la Biblia—la mayor sabiduría escrita para la vida cotidiana y muchos otros recursos. Elige estar informado. Haz lo que tengas que hacer para aprender cómo criar hijos excelentes.

#6: El padre enfermo

El padre enfermo no es aquel que está enfermo físicamente; él o ella está emocional y/o mentalmente enfermo. Por ejemplo, el hombre que mencioné en la apertura de nuestro capítulo, que estaba esclavizado por el alcoholismo y virtualmente arruinó a sus hijos, era un padre enfermo. Otro ejemplo es la mujer excesivamente posesiva que no deja ir a sus hijos jóvenes adultos, incluso cuando ellos comienzan a revelarse en contra de ella y quieren irse de la casa.

Como resultado, ellos no quieren saber nada de ella cuando llegan a ser adultos.

Si eres un padre enfermo, tienes que buscar ayuda para ti mismo antes de ayudar a tus hijos. Primero busca la sanidad de Dios, porque Él te ama tremendamente. Quizás tú fuiste abusado—sexual, física o emocionalmente—cuando eras niño y todavía llevas esas cicatrices. Quizás creciste en una familia donde tus padres eran severos, perfeccionistas, descuidados, callados o estúpidos y tú estás enfermo a causa de eso. En lugar de sentir lástima por ti o considerarte a ti mismo una víctima, piensa en tus hijos. Usa el amor que tienes para ellos para darte a ti mismo el poder para cambiar. No descuides la ayuda profesional que te pueden dar algunos consejeros que confían en Jesucristo.

#7: El padre exitoso

La madre o padre exitoso tiene sabiduría y la mayor fuente de sabiduría es La Palabra de Dios, la Biblia. La palabra hebrea para sabiduría tiene el sentido de entender por qué y cómo funciona la vida y eso es diferente de simplemente tener conocimiento. Tú puedes saber mucho sin saber realmente cómo usar esa información.

Un buen ejemplo de sabiduría de crianza en la Biblia se encuentra en Deuteronomio 6.4-7:

> *Escucha, oh, Israel, el Señor es nuestro Dios, el Señor uno es. Amarás al Señor tu Dios con todo tu corazón, con toda tu alma y con toda tu fuerza. Y estas palabras que yo te mando hoy, estarán sobre tu corazón; y diligentemente las enseñarás a tus hijos, y hablarás de ellas cuando te sientes en tu casa, y cuando andes por el camino, cuando te acuestes y cuando te levantes.*

El elemento más poderoso de estos versículos es el elemento de estilo de vida. En realidad tú vives estas enseñanzas. Eso quiere decir que deliberadamente decides enseñarles a tus hijos esos principios de Dios. Tú, no simplemente esperas que de repente ellos los aprendan.

Habla con tus hijos acerca los principios de Dios para una vida exitosa cuando ellos se levanten, durante la comida, cuando vean películas juntos. Si haces esto, vas a ser un padre exitoso y también le vas a dar a tus hijos la mejor oportunidad de tener éxito y construir un ambiente maravilloso en el hogar.

Construyendo un ambiente maravilloso en el hogar

Cuando un entrevistador le preguntó a Sr. George Bush padre, cuál consideraba ser su mejor logro, él contestó: «De lo que estoy más orgulloso es del hecho que nuestros hijos todavía quieran venir a casa». Un padre exitoso produce un ambiente en el hogar que atrae a los hijos de regreso a casa por su propia voluntad, incluso cuando ya son adultos. Los hijos en realidad añoran tu compañía y eligen estar cerca de ti. Como dijo Gordon MacDonald en su libro *The Efective Father*: «El reto es saturar la rutina de la vida normal con el plan y la presencia de Dios. En resumen, asegúrate que la vida dentro de tu hogar sea tan positiva, tan atractiva y tan satisfactoria, que todo lo demás en el mundo exterior se vea pálido en contraste con lo que el niño recibe cuando está con su familia». ¿No es eso algo poderoso? Esa es la clase de hogar que necesitas. Esa es la clase de trasfondo familiar que tienes que producir.

¿Y cómo puedes crear ese ambiente? Trata estas once maneras y vas a revolucionar tu ambiente hogareño.

Manera #1: Recuerda el contrato no verbal

Los niños no son tontos. Ellos sienten que existe un contrato emocional implícito entre padres e hijos. Así es. Cuando los padres les dan a los hijos ciertas responsabilidades, esperan que los hijos cumplan con esas responsabilidades y si los hijos lo hacen, reciben ciertos privilegios.

En otras palabras, existe una actitud básica de justicia entre padre e hijo. Los hijos siempre son súper sensibles a la justicia, aunque ellos no siempre estén en lo correcto en cuanto a la percepción de lo que es justo y lo que no lo es. Tener conocimiento de eso es clave para tener una relación saludable con los hijos. Es por eso que es importante que te esfuerces y nunca faltes a tu palabra con tus hijos. Cuando se presenten circunstancias en la cuales necesitas hacer algo que no tenías planeado, explícaselo a tus hijos y ayúdalos a entender. De otra manera, vas a violar la confianza que tienen en ti.

Conforme los niños van creciendo, debes de darles responsabilidades mayores y con el cumplimiento de esas responsabilidades, privilegios mejores. Si les das responsabilidades sin privilegios, vas a violar nuevamente ese contrato implícito y cuando eso sucede en la niñez, especialmente en los años de adolescencia, te vas a enfrentar a una relación más complicada.

Algunos padres, por miedo a que sus hijos se rebelen, no les dan ningún poder para tomar decisiones, pero esa es una de las maneras para que ellos se rebelen porque estás creándoles resentimiento. Lo podrás ver en la mandíbula apretada de tu hijo, en la tensión de su lenguaje corporal, incluso si tu hijo es joven.

Amy y yo siempre hemos sido honestos con nuestros hijos. Les decimos la verdad y esperamos que ellos nos la digan también. Esta es una base para el contrato de justicia. Nadie juega con nadie. Nosotros trabajamos para ser honestos en toda circunstancia. Nuestros hijos lo merecen.

MANERA #2: DATE CUENTA DE LA DIFERENCIA ENTRE LOS PENSAMIENTOS Y EMOCIONES DE TU HIJO

Así como el Dr. David Elkind teoriza, «Un niño tiene sentimientos como los de un adulto, pero no piensa como un adulto». Por lo tanto, si esperas que tu hijo tenga una perspectiva adulta, siempre vas a estar decepcionado. De manera similar, simplemente porque tu hijo está en edad preescolar no significa que no pueda ser lastimado profundamente—o estar muy emocionado. Los niños sienten dolor, ira, sufrimiento, amor, decepción, anticipación, temor, aprensión, drama, y poder. Pero ellos no procesan esos sentimientos como lo hacen los adultos.

Yo recuerdo cuando mi hija, quien es normalmente agresiva, rehusó a caminar una cuadra a la casa de su abuela. Cuando yo la cuestioné, ella dijo de manera desafiante, «Yo no voy a ir» mientras yo seguí con mi cuestionamiento, yo descubrí que Allison tenía miedo. «¿De qué?» le pregunté. «El hombre» contestó ella. Yo investigué hasta que averigüé que varias semanas antes, un hombre había silbado y había llamado a mi madre cuando ella estaba caminando con Allison. Allison tenía miedo que ese hombre la agarrara. Ella no podía transmitir sus sentimientos de miedo de una manera lógica al pensamiento adulto de una situación que había pasado varias semanas atrás y el hombre probablemente ya no estaba por ahí.

Tus hijos no siempre van a responder lógicamente de la manera que tú quieres que ellos respondan. ¿Por qué? Porque quizás ellos estén reaccionando a una emoción que es muy real para ellos. Así que no juzgues sus pensamientos. Date cuenta que hay una diferencia entre sus pensamientos y sus emociones.

Manera #3: Trabaja duro en tu actitud, por encima del rendimiento

Digamos que estás tratando de ayudar a tus hijos a desarrollar una actitud saludable, un enfoque positivo de la vida. Estás usando la sabiduría de la Biblia y quieres reforzar su actitud. Quieres decirle a tu hijo: «¡Bien hecho!» cuando tiene un buen rendimiento, pero al mismo tiempo, quieres animarlo a tener la actitud correcta cuando haga una tarea. Los niños tal vez hagan cierta tarea porque tengan miedo de no hacerla, porque tienen miedo de meterse en problemas si no lo hacen o quizá hagan el trabajo porque quieren un dulce que les prometiste. En lugar de eso, enseña a tus hijos el valor de tener una actitud positiva hacia el trabajo. Dales recompensa por el rendimiento, pero trabaja más para reforzar una actitud positiva.

Manera #4: Usa los recuerdos de tu propia niñez para discernir

Aunque los niños de hoy en día están creciendo en una generación y ambiente diferentes al que tú creciste, aún así te puede ayudar a recordar cómo te sentías tú cuando eres niño.

Yo recuerdo cuando tenía nueve o diez años y mi familia se mudó para Huntington, West Virginia. Aunque no era muy lejos de la pequeña comunidad de Kentucky donde yo crecí—solamente como una hora de distancia—la mudanza fue algo traumático para mí. Solamente hice pocos amigos al inicio, pero a medida que pasaba el tiempo, me ajusté mejor. Cuando tenía pocos meses de vivir ahí, me metí en problemas. Me salí una hora de la escuela con un amigo mío que era rebelde, pero agradable, de una manera medio atrevida. Él dijo que tenía un permiso especial de la escuela para irse a casa y que su madre estaba ahí. Por lo tanto, caminamos seis cuadras hacia su casa, tomamos coca-colas, y comimos papas fritas. De pronto me di cuenta que su madre no estaba en casa. Cuando regresamos al campus de la escuela, una maestra nos descubrió y nos reportó a la oficina del director. Pues bien, mi nuevo «amigo» le dijo al director que yo lo había obligado a hacerlo, que era mi culpa. El director llamó a mi padre y a mi madre y les dijo que yo me había ido de pinta. Cuando mis padres me castigaron en casa, yo no podía creerlo. Después de todo, era inocente, estúpido, pero inocente. Por años, tuve un resentimiento oculto en mi corazón por ese incidente. Estaba enojado, no solamente con la escuela, la maestra, el director, sino también con mi padre, porque le creyó a ellos en lugar de creerme a mí. En la edad adulta, ya me di cuenta que mi padre me había castigado por irme de pinta y por estúpido. Pero cuando era niño, yo no pensaba de esa manera. Yo espero recordar cómo me sentí yo, cuando mis hijos hacen algo estúpido.

¿Recuerdas cómo te sentiste la primera vez que te hicieron *bullying* (acoso) en la escuela? ¿O cuando tu maestra te dio demasiada tarea que no pudiste respirar por días? ¿Cuándo tu madre te obligó a usar esa playera pasada de moda o algún pantalón y los chicos se rieron de ti? Usa esos recuerdos para analizar bien las cosas con tus propios hijos.

MANERA #5: BUSCAS PUERTAS DE OPORTUNIDAD

Mantente alerta a esos momentos de aprendizaje porque lo que le enseñes a tus hijos va a echar raíces en su corazón. Por ejemplo, cuando el perro de la familia murió, yo estaba tan triste como mi hija, pero me di cuenta que los momentos de dolor podrían ser un momento clave para enseñar a mi hija una verdad, así que le dije: «Allison: cuando pierdes algo, está bien que te pongas triste, pero no te concentres en lo que has perdido. Concéntrate en lo que todavía tienes. Piensa en todas la cosas buenas, los tiempos felices que tuviste con el perro». Cuando se presenten esos momentos de enseñanza, la puerta del corazón de tu niño está abierta y es probable que ella acepte lo que digas, pero si dejas pasar ese momento y la puerta se cierra en tu cara, entonces es como tratar de pasar un libro bajo una puerta cerrada. No dejes ir esos momentos. Son demasiados preciosos—a veces muy pocos y muy esporádicos.

MANERA #6: MUESTRA RESPETO

Debido a que nuestros hijos están siempre a nuestro alrededor, no es inusual sentirse abrumado por el cuidado constate (y molestia) pero incluso en momentos de frustración y agotamiento, es siempre importante mostrar respeto hacia tus hijos. ¿Cómo muestras respeto hacia tus hijos? De tres maneras:

- **ESCUCHANDO** - ¿Te has sentido alguna vez culpable por haberte sentado con la mirada perdida mirando hacia la nada, haciendo tu lista de planes, mientras tu hijo está tratando de explicarte algo? Estoy seguro que cada padre lo ha hecho. Pero muestra respeto escuchando a tu hijo—dándole a él o ella toda la atención. No solamente escuchando, sino realmente escuchando—tomando el tiempo de internalizar lo que tu hijo está diciendo.
- **ACERCÁNDOTE** - Por un momento, trata de imaginar tu comunicación con tu hija como si ella te estuvieran llamando a tu número de teléfono. ¿Va

a sonar siempre ocupado—beep, beep, beep—y nunca le va a entrar la llamada? ¿O va a escuchar un alegre y jovial «¿Hola?».

Tú haces citas con otros, entonces ¿por qué no las haces con tu hijo? Desafortunadamente, el tiempo con nuestros hijos es el tiempo que ignoramos y olvidamos fácilmente.

¿Por qué? Porque el niño no tiene un poder inmediato para hacer que cumplas con la cita. Pero tristemente, el niño retiene la memoria de citas que hemos olvidado y quizás nos pague esas citas con rebeldía cuando sea adolescente.

Así que desarrolla acercamiento con tus hijos. Déjales claro que ellos pueden traer cualquier problema a ti. No seas como la madre que dijo acerca de su hija, «¡Yo me temo que ella está saliendo con la gente equivocada. Pero si regresa embarazada, mas le vale que sepa que ella ya no es miembro de esta familia! ¡Se va de aquí!» Mi corazón sintió pena por su hija. Aunque ella estaba atravesando problemas normales de desarrollo y no se estaba revelando en ese tiempo, yo supe que si ella se metían en problemas algún día, ella no podría ir a con su madre. ¿Por qué? Porque su madre no era accesible.

- **Cuando los perdonas** - ¿Sabías que un niño siente la misma molestia en cuanto al mal comportamiento—culpabilidad—que los adultos. Cuando cometes un error, ¿qué es lo que más necesitas desesperadamente? Que la persona a quien ofendiste ponga sus brazos a tu alrededor y te diga «te perdono». Tu hijo necesita lo mismo. Cuando tu hijo sabe que te ha lastimado o decepcionado, él necesita que tú le demuestres que todavía lo amas, que sigues preocupándote por él, y que lo perdonas. Si haces eso, vas a hacer que sea más fácil para tu hijo entender y recibir el perdón de Dios.

La misión de toda tu vida no es castigar a tus hijos, sino llevarlos hacia la madurez.

Manera #7: Recuerda la ley de la siembra y la cosecha

Gálatas 6.7 lo declara bien, «No te dejes engañar, de Dios nadie se burla, pues todo lo que el hombre siembre, eso también segará». Enséñale a tus hijos la ley de las consecuencias—que por cada decisión, hay una consecuencia. Si haces eso, tus hijos van a aprender a ser orientados hacia el futuro. Ellos van a aprender a pensar, si hago eso hoy, esto va, o puede suceder mañana. Por ejemplo, si te acuestas con cualquiera, te arriesgas a contraer alguna enfermedad, a la paternidad, dolor emocional y pecado espiritual. Si no aprendes a trabajar y a ahorrar tu dinero, no vas a tener dinero cuando lo necesites.

El principio de siembra y cosecha es de mucha importancia para el éxito futuro de un niño en todas las áreas de su vida.

Manera #8: Sirve y piensa en otras personas

Desafortunadamente, nuestro mundo es tremendamente individualista. Todos están tratando de cuidar del número uno—incluso si eso significa usar y abusar de otros. Es por eso que quienes sirven a otros y piensan primeramente en los demás, realmente se destacan en nuestra cultura como modelos a seguir. Aun así, muchos tiene miedo de servir a otros por temor a que otros se aprovechen.

Mientras que caminó en la tierra, Jesús fue el modelo máximo de lo que es un siervo. Pero eso no quiere decir que Él era una alfombra de puerta o un debilucho que permitía que todos caminaran sobre Él, y que hicieran lo que les diera la gana con Él. En cambio, Él se mantuvo firme y fuerte a favor de lo que era justo. Él sirvió a otros porque se preocupada por ellos.

Así que sigue el modelo de Jesús. Enseña a tus hijos a pensar en los demás. Que se pregunten, ¿Cómo puedo ser de valor para otra persona? ¿Qué puedo hacer? ¿Cómo puedo ayudar? ¿Cómo puedo animar a esa persona?

¿Cómo puedo ayudar para que logre su sueño? Si tus hijos concentran sus energías en servir a otros, en animarlos, amarlos, y ayudarlos, ella van a tener vidas vibrantes y emocionantes.

Manera #9: Mantente alerta de la guerra espiritual

Hay una guerra constante llevándose acabo en el espíritu de cada niño: de hacer lo bueno, o hacer lo malo. Es por eso que es importante que los padres monitoreen lo que los hijos ven en la televisión, lo que leen, y lo que están aprendiendo en la escuela. Es por eso también que es imprescindible que los padres se involucren en una iglesia equilibrada que crea en lo que dice la Biblia. Eso hace que sea más fácil para tu hijo llegar a conocer a Jesucristo de una manera personal. Aunque no hay iglesia perfecta porque toda iglesia está compuesta por seres imperfectos, escoge una iglesia que presente el evangelio de una manera positiva y emocionante—y una que defienda la verdad de la Biblia.

Además, ten cuidado de quienes son los amigos de tus hijos. Cuando tus hijos lleguen a la edad de la pubertad, los amigos van a tener una gran influencia sobre ellos, más que tú. Como dice Proverbios 13.20 «El que anda con sabios será sabio, más el compañero de los necios sufrirá daño».

Manera #10: Muestra amor verdadero

Todos los padres saben que la disciplina es importante. El versículo más común que los padres escuchan acerca del entrenamiento de sus hijos está en Proverbios 22.6 «Enseña al niño en el camino en que debe de andar, y aun cuando sea viejo no se apartará de él». Sin embargo, el texto hebreo no garantiza que el niño nunca será rebelde. En lugar de eso, indica que el niño nunca se olvidará de su formación—siempre estará ahí como un recordatorio, como parte de su consciencia.

Efesios 6.4 dice a los padres que disciplinen a los hijos y les enseñen del Señor, pero no que no exageren y provoquen a ira que no es necesaria. Así que, sí, tú necesitas disciplinar, pero tiene que haber un balance. Los expertos dicen que por cada vez que disciplinas a un niño, ese niño necesita por los menos cinco expresiones de amor, calidez y afecto para contrarrestar la disciplina. Eso quiere decir que cada niño necesita cinco veces más apoyo, amor, aprecio, y ánimo, que disciplina.

Cuando se trata de mostrar amor por tus hijos, recuerda estas tres palabras:

- **Aprecio:** Dile a tus hijos lo mucho que aprecias lo que ellos son y lo que hacen. Si no se te hace fácil decirlo, aprende. Los niños necesitan aprecio constantemente.
- **Aprobación:** Muéstrale a tus hijos que te gusta lo que ellos hacen y que estás orgulloso de sus logros.
- **Afirmación:** Dile y demuéstrale a tus hijos que los amas como personas y que ellos son valiosos para ti.

Manera #11: Guía a tus hijos a Jesucristo

Mi esposa Amy habla con fluidez a audiencias de convenciones de negocios en todo el mundo acerca de su experiencia de cuando ella se convirtió. A la edad de tres años ella le dijo a su madre que quería a Jesús en su corazón. Con la instrucción de su madre, Amy se puso de rodillas a lado de su cama y pidió a Jesús que le perdonara todos sus pecados. Ella le pidió a Él que entrara en su corazón y fuera su Señor y amigo. Aunque ella tuvo que crecer en los caminos cristianos mientras fue madurando, Amy dice que ella entendió lo que estaba haciendo en ese momento.

Para que tu hijo pueda conocer a Jesús de una manera personal, tú también necesitas conocerle. En 1 de Corintios 11.1, el apóstol Pablo le dice a un grupo de cristianos antiguos, «Sed imitadores de mí, como también yo lo soy de Cristo». Como padre quizás te sientas muy mal e indigno de esa responsabilidad. Todos somos indignos. Pero con la ayuda de Dios, nosotros podemos hacerlo. Así que haz de 1 de Corintios 11.1 tu guía, tu versículo motivador como padre. Diles a tus hijos, «Sígueme, yo voy a tratar de seguir a Jesús».

Si eres cristiano, la alegría que vas a experimentar no será en esta tierra. Será en el cielo, algún día, cuando te encuentres con Dios porque elegiste aceptar la sangre de Cristo como expiación de tus pecados. Nada en el mundo es de gran importancia como dirigir a tus hijos hacia Cristo.

Conectándose poderosamente con los hijos

En el mundo caótico de hoy, en el cual la cultura está bombardeando a tus hijos con influencia negativa, ¿Cómo te conectas poderosamente con ellos? Prueba estos consejos:

Consejo #1: Sé positivo

Positivo—es una palabra que se usa demasiado, pero una actitud que no se usa demasiado. Si quieres atraer a tus hijos a tu manera de pensar y vivir, entonces trata de ser positivo, entrena para ser positivo, estudia para ser positivo, y ora para ser positivo. Entonces tus hijos también se convertirán en pensadores positivos.

Consejo #2: Sé placentero

Nadie quiere estar con un gruñón.

Cuando recientemente estaba en una tienda de galletas, el empleado de la tienda me dijo, «Su total es $3,51». Yo le entregué un billete de diez dólares, luego metí la mano a mi bolsillo y saqué cincuenta y un centavos. Claramente molesta porque ella tenía que esperar, ella me miró, agarró el efectivo, y lo estrelló en la caja registradora sin contarlo. Y toda esta ira debido a que le causé inconveniencia monetaria. Bien, ¿cómo me sentí acerca de esa tienda? Yo quiero comprar mis galletas en otro lado.

Aun en una situación difícil, siempre se puede ser cortés y educado. Una actitud placentera siempre te lleva lejos—ya sea la tuya o la de tu hijo.

Consejo #3: Sé persuasivo

Date cuenta que yo no dije, «sé combativo». Tú no estás yendo a una guerra. Tu propósito no es ganar un argumento, es ganar a un niño.

Consejo #4: Sé persuadido

Está convencido de lo que vas a decir es correcto – antes de hacerlo o decirlo. Y luego, si tú sabes que es correcto, sé determinante. No permitas que nadie te disuada de llevar a cabo la acción correcta o declaración.

El himno,«Yo sé a quien le he creído» es basado en 2 de Timoteo 1.12. En el inglés antiguo, el término «persuadido» significa estar internamente convencido hasta las entrañas de tu vida. Esa es la clase de persuasión de la que yo hablo. Si no estás tú mismo persuadido, ¿cómo puedes persuadir a tus hijos?

Consejo #5: Sé persistente

Ser persistente no significa que eres desagradable. Simplemente significa que no te das por vencido. Estás comprometido a ser amable, cortés, persistente para construir lo mejor en tu hijo.

Consejo #6: Sé preparado

Siempre haz tu investigación antes de abrir la boca y decirle a tus hijos algo importante. Lee libros o escucha CDs. Aunque esto toma tiempo (tiempo que quizás pienses que no tienes) estar preparado da como resultado grandes recompensas. Si sabes de lo que estás hablando, tus hijos van a estar más dispuestos a escuchar...y hacer lo que tú dices.

Consejo #7: Sé pacificador

Soluciona problemas por tus hijos. Trae paz a las partes en conflicto. Trata de solucionar conflictos entre miembros de familia cada vez que puedas. La Biblia dice, «Bienaventurados los que procuran por la paz, pues ellos serán llamados hijos de Dios» (Mateo 5.9).

Pero también date cuenta que tú no eres el Mesías. Tú no siempre vas a poder traer paz. A veces tus hijos tienen que solucionar sus problemas por sí solos.

Consejo #8: Sé justo

Nunca manipules a tus hijos ni les mientas. Nos los engañes ni les hagas trampa. Nunca pongas tu integridad en peligro. Los resultados de no ser justo y veraz pueden ser sumamente dañinos para los niños porque tu falta de equidad viola la confianza que tienen en ti.

Consejo #9: Sé paciente

Los niños son individuales y no siempre hacen las cosas en el período de tiempo que tú quieres que las hagan. En el proceso, sé paciente. Los niños florecen debajo de una mano amorosa y paciente. Cuando tus hijos te sacan de quicio, simplemente recuerda: tú también sacaste a alguien de quicio y fueron (espero) pacientes contigo. ¿Por qué no regresar el favor a tus hijos? Permíteles que crezcan a su manera y en su propio tiempo.

Consejo #10: Enfócate en las posibilidades

Cada niño tiene posibilidades—tú tienes que buscarlas. Tal ves estén enterradas en capas de fracasos, años de desilusiones, y montones de decepciones.

Pero no te des por vencido. Trabaja hasta que encuentres aunque sea una chispa de posibilidad en tu hijo, y luego sopla esa chispa a una llama vibrante. Si lo haces, la vida de tu hijo será cambiada para siempre.

Cuando recuerdes usar estos consejos en la vida de tus hijos, te vas a sorprender de los resultados. Te volverás más sensible a quienes son tus hijos, vas a entender mejor porqué ellos reaccionan de la manera que reaccionan, y vas comenzar a desarrollar una mejor relación con ellos, emocional y espiritualmente.

Dios te bendijo a ti como padre para reflejar el carácter Dios mientras crías a tus hijos. No minimices la responsabilidad ni eches a perder las oportunidades.

CAPÍTULO 3

Haciendo del matrimonio una prioridad

¿Cómo describirías tu matrimonio en una escala del uno (en la ruina) y diez (muy bueno?) ¿Tienes un matrimonio estupendo—lleno de emoción, maravilla, aventura, amor, generosidad, amabilidad, y respeto mutuo?

Si es así, considérate a ti mismo afortunado, y dale gracias a Dios. Pero también considérate a ti mismo excepcional.

Si muchas parejas contestaran la pregunta anterior honestamente, probablemente evaluarían su matrimonio en uno o dos niveles. Muchos matrimonios se han convertido en horribles campos de batalla de estrés, infidelidad, insatisfacción y abuso emocional, verbal y físico. Como resultado, esto deja a los cónyuges con heridas emocionales y a veces físicas que pueden tomar toda una vida superar y los hijos sufren un sentimiento de culpabilidad, como si ellos hubieran causado los problemas matrimoniales, así como también traición de parte de las personas en las que confiaban. Todos estos sentimientos pueden conducir a toda una vida de desarraigo—buscando la relación perfecta que parece no existir.

No hay duda que la familia se encuentra en un

tremendo bombardeo, pero no todo está perdido. Yo creo de todo corazón que no importa en qué situación se encuentre tu matrimonio ahora, tú puedes cambiar la situación, pero se necesita compromiso. Tú tienes que hacer de tu familia y tu matrimonio una prioridad. Te tienes que enfrentar contra la cultura que aprueba la infidelidad y el divorcio.

Recientemente leí un libro revelador, *The Abolition of Marriage* (La abolición del matrimonio) por Maggie Gallagher. Al principio uno piensa que el libro simplemente está diciendo «deshagámonos del matrimonio». En lugar de eso, la Sra. Gallagher hace declaraciones contundentes tales como esta:

> *Nuestra cultura divorciada enseña que lo que tú quiere se vuelve algo más importante de lo que es bueno para la gente que supuestamente amas e incluso gente de la cual eres responsable. Cuando los padres les demuestran a sus hijos que la familia no es, después de todo, lo más importante; que los deseos individuales son más importantes que los compromisos solemnes que forman la familia, la familia pierde su poder para mantener la lealtad de todos sus miembros.*

En esta declaración, la Sra. Gallagher da en el punto de lo que es el núcleo del matrimonio: la gran roca del compromiso. Tú debes demostrarle a tu cónyuge y a tus hijos que los deseos individuales no son tan importantes como los votos matrimoniales que forman la familia. Cuando comienzas a ser absorbido por satisfacer tus propias necesidades (por ejemplo, «yo quiero jugar golf los sábados, en comparación a, «qué querrán hacer mi esposa y mis hijos»), te convierte, en alguien egoísta y dominante. Si un miembro de la familia es egoísta, todos los miembros pierden.

¿Por qué hablar de matrimonio en un libro sobre paternidad? Porque es una verdad absoluta que los padres que se aman el uno al otro, y que se mantienen juntos en los tiempo difíciles, van a producir hijos más exitosos, felices y saludables, que podrán enfrentar el mundo adulto con confianza.

¿Pero cómo se encuentra una relación como ésta?

Mi esposa Amy y yo hemos estados casados por más de veinte fabulosos años. Eso no quiere decir que ha sido fácil y que no hemos tenido altas y bajas, pero en los momentos de fricción y preocupación por aquí y por allá, hemos disfrutado de una maravillosa intimidad.

Al inicio, conocí a Amy en la universidad, en Kentucky. Yo estaba tan enamorado de ella y quería que nuestra primera cita fuera perfecta. Así que planee tantas actividades como pude para la tarde—temía que Amy no estuviera lo suficientemente ocupada y que se aburriera. No quería que ella tuviera tiempo para pensar: ¿Cómo se me ocurrió salir con este muchacho? Así que jugamos minigolf, jugamos boliche, cenamos y después comimos postre.

Cuando estábamos de regreso al campus de la universidad ese día hermoso de junio, el sol comenzó a ponerse. Yo dejé escapar un suspiro de alivio, esperando no haber arruinado tanto nuestra cita y con la esperanza de que ella quisiera salir conmigo otra vez. Luego Amy me sorprendió. Movida por la belleza del ocaso, espontáneamente comenzó a cantar las palabras: «Te amo Dios. Yo elevo mi corazón a ti». Yo estaba impresionado. Ese simple acto de reverencia a Dios hizo un impacto poderoso en mi vida.

Desde ese momento, comencé a orar por Amy. No solamente sentía pasión y deseo físico por ella, sino también estaba emocionado por su personalidad, sus dones, su estilo e incluso más que eso, deseaba orar por ella. La dimensión espiritual en nuestra relación comenzó a crecer. La noche siguiente, me desperté a las 2 de la mañana y no podía dormir. Mientras caminaba por la salida de emergencia del dormitorio, sentí una gran necesidad de orar por Amy y lo hice, ahí mismo, en ese mismo momento. Como resultado de esa oración, comencé a sentir una conexión más cercana con ella. Lo mismo ocurrió en las siguientes cuatro noches y me empecé a preguntar qué estaba pasando. ¿Por qué Dios me seguía despertando para que rezara por Amy?

En algún momento de la siguiente semana, tuvimos nuestra segunda cita. Durante nuestra conversación, quedé boquiabierto al escuchar a Amy decir que ella se había estado despertando todas las noches a las 2 AM, con un sentimiento de que tenía que orar por mí. Ambos sentimos que Dios estaba trabajando en nuestra relación. Yo estaba emocionado porque incluso en ese tiempo sentí un afecto tan tierno y amor por Amy. Después de muchas desventuras en nuestras citas (una vez yo estaba hablando de manera expansiva, como lo hago normalmente y derramé leche y pizza sobre ella) nuestro amor creció. En octubre de ese año, le pedí que se casara conmigo. ¡Milagrosamente ella aceptó!

Nos casamos el siguiente año. Prometimos nunca perder la emoción por estar juntos y la pasión que sentíamos el uno por el otro cuando éramos novios y durante el período de nuestro compromiso. Deseábamos mantener esa cercanía de corazón—sin importar lo que enfrentáramos en la vida. Fue por eso que cuando recientemente fui a Nueva Zelandia y Australia, me sentí solo y vacío. Era la primera vez en seis viajes que no iba con Amy y la extrañé terriblemente. La amo tanto que quería estar ahí para ella, para cuidarla y escuchar la plática de su día y es difícil hacer eso al otro lado del océano. Así que en lugar de eso, me fui a caminar por un largo y devanado camino en Camber, Australia. Mientras pasaba por cientos de ovejas, árboles de goma gigantes y estanques que se sumergían en el día tan soleado, pensé en Amy y desee que ella estuviera ahí. Veintisiete años y dos niños después, me di cuenta qué tan intensamente y cuánto seguía amando a mi mujer. Ella verdaderamente es la otra mitad de mi alma. Juré de nuevo que siempre mantendré mi compromiso con mi mujer y mis hijos, no importa lo que cueste.

Sin embargo, en la sociedad de hoy—con esa actitud insensible hacia el adulterio—mantener un compromiso de matrimonio no es siempre fácil.

Los enemigos del matrimonio

Yo he descubierto que hay cinco enemigos a esta clase de compromiso:

Enemigo #1: Egoísmo

No hay rasgo humano más desagradable que el egoísmo, porque es el origen de la rebelión contra Dios. Todo empezó con Lucifer, el arcángel brillante y resplandeciente que decidió que quería hacerse cargo del Trono de Dios. En Isaías 14.14 él declaró: «Subiré sobre las alturas de la nubes, y me haré semejante al Altísimo». Según lo que he estudiado sobre la Biblia, parece que había una salvaje intensidad en su enfoque, incluso antes de convertirse en el Diablo. Cuando él se reveló contra Dios, fue echado del cielo—y se llevó consigo una cantidad de ángeles caídos.

Como resultado de su egocentrismo y su odio contra Dios, Satanás comenzó un programa de siglos para herir a Dios. Luego se dio cuenta que no podía lastimar a Dios, y probó otra táctica: Dios ama a la gente. Si yo lastimo a la gente, lo voy a lastimar a Él. Así que se abalanzó a la tierra y confrontó a Adán y Eva en el Jardín del Edén. Intentó contagiarlos con el mismo egocentrismo. Lamentablemente, su plan funcionó.

Debido a que cada uno de nosotros es hijo e hija de Adán y Eva, también somos tentados por el egoísmo. Muchos matrimonios se separan porque uno de los cónyuges, o ambos insisten en hacer las cosas a su manera. Cuando cedemos a vivir para nosotros mismos, inevitablemente enfrentamos argumentos, frecuentemente acerca de lo que no es justo y acusamos a nuestro cónyuge de no escucharnos. Sin embargo, existe una cosa importante que hay que recordar: ¿Qué hace que tu camino sea necesariamente correcto? Un matrimonio está compuesto por dos personas que desean trabajar juntas hacia un objetivo común.

Mi esposa y yo no tenemos una relación perfecta porque no somos personas perfectas. Ha habido tiempos en que nos hemos sentido distante el uno del otro, pero nos hemos preguntado: ¿Quiero realmente estar con esta persona? Ha habido momentos en que hemos estado enojados el uno con el otro, pero esos momentos han sido ocasionales y un momento ocasional no quiere decir que tenemos que renunciar a cada buen momento o recuerdo especial. Debido a que amo tremendamente a mi mujer, estoy decidido a no dejar que el egoísmo arruine nuestro futuro. Así que cuando tengo conflictos con ella, trato de detenerme, sentir humildad en mi corazón, disculparme y luego escuchar sin interrumpir. Cuando lo hago, es asombroso cómo Dios bendice nuestra comunicación. La mayoría de veces llegamos a una decisión mutua.

¿Está tu matrimonio plagado de egoísmo? ¿Las cosas se tienen que hacer a tu manera? ¿Pones mala cara cuando no consigues esto o aquello? Si es así, Dios te puede ayudar a cambiar tu hábito egoísta—un hábito que se llama pecado—y tú te puedes convertir en una nueva creación en Cristo. Como lo dice 2 de Corintios 5.17 «De modo que si alguien está en Cristo, nueva criatura es. Las cosas viejas pasaron, he aquí todas son hechas nuevas». Mientras Cristo comienza a cambiarte para que seas más como Él, te vas a dar cuenta que vas a ser liberado del egoísmo, que de otra manera te controlaría y dominaría tu matrimonio.

Enemigo #2: Medios de comunicación engañosos

Hoy en día estamos rodeados de medios de comunicación. No importa hacia dónde voltees, te encuentras con la Internet, los titulares del periódico, comerciales de televisión, anuncios de radio, películas, música que canta en voz baja amor fácil. No creas todo lo que ves y escuchas.

Por ejemplo, cuando la *Constitución de Atlanta* pasó una serie especial de televisión acerca del sexo, ellos determinaron que el 97% de todo el sexo en la televisión era fuera del matrimonio. Así que ¿qué comunica esto a los hijos, jóvenes y adultos que están en busca de amor? Eso destroza los lazos matrimoniales, convirtiendo el sexo en copulación anomalística de gente sin dimensión espiritual. Peor aún, ignora los parámetros que Dios puso para algo que Él llamó «bueno»—que el sexo debería de llevarse a cabo dentro de un compromiso matrimonial de amor seguro y que sea para siempre.

Además, los medios de comunicación presentan el divorcio como una salida fácil. Si no te sientes feliz o no te sientes realizado en tu matrimonio, simplemente puedes abandonar a tu marido o mujer, así que estarás libre para encontrar la «felicidad» y alguien que satisfaga tus necesidades. Un corresponsal de un medio de comunicación dijo una vez: «En los años 50s, la gente se quedaba unida por los hijos. ¡Qué razón tan estúpida! No eran felices; siempre estaban peleando. Así que ¿Por qué no divorciarse?» La opinión insensible de que el divorcio es bueno para ti, está arruinando tu cultura. Para ver los resultados, simplemente ve a tu alrededor y observa el mar de familias destruidas. Las familias están creyendo esta mentira que no proviene de Dios y como consecuencia destruye a los hijos.

No obstante, esa no es la manera de Dios. Él quiere que hagamos todo lo posible para cumplir con los votos del matrimonio que prometimos el día de nuestra boda. He aquí la verdad: estadísticamente, está demostrado que la única vez que el conflicto matrimonial es malo para los niños es cuando este conflicto es intenso, violento y prolongado. Si alguien te dice que necesitas el divorcio porque tú y tu cónyuge tienen una pelea de vez en cuando o porque no te sientes feliz por el momento, no escuches a esa persona. En lugar de eso, escucha a Dios, quien diseñó el matrimonio y la familia. Dios no ve el divorcio como una válvula de escape de un mal matrimonio o como el único camino a la felicidad.

No existe tal cosa como el buen divorcio. Cada

persona involucrada resulta lastimada de alguna manera. Esa es la razón por la cual la intención de Dios es que el voto matrimonial sea uno para siempre en esta tierra.

Enemigo #3: La idea de que los padres no son necesarios

Durante los pasados treinta años, ha habido gente que ha tratado de desprestigiar a la familia tradicional de padre-y-madre, pero la sabiduría de miles de años prueba que esta combinación es la mejor.

El plan de Dios de la familia está descrito en la Biblia, es para que los niños tengan a ambos, padre y madre ¿Por qué? Porque el niño necesita a los dos. El padre no está solamente en el hogar por su papel que juega en la economía, él es necesario para modelo de masculinidad, fuerza y liderazgo amoroso. Todas estas cualidades que los niños necesitan por separado tienen que ser representadas en la familia.

Las estadísticas muestran que si los niños no reciben un liderazgo masculino amoroso en su propia familia, ellos van a salir a la calle a buscarlo, particularmente en los primeros años de adolescencia. Esa es la razón por la cual un buen número de jovencitas en circunstancias sexuales promiscuas va en crecimiento. Cuando la niña no se siente cerca de su padre, o amada por él, busca en otro lado esa sensación de amor y pertenencia. Un hijo usualmente escoge rebelarse y convertirse en joven delincuente o a veces incluso se convierte en homosexual. Algunos científicos creen que ese «gene homosexual» no existe, esa homosexualidad no es heredada sino creada por el medio ambiente del niño. Con frecuencia, chicos que son separados de sus padres comienzan a tomar decisiones destructivas.

Enemigo #4: La cultura de divorcio

La tasa de divorcio en los Estados Unidos va en aumento. En la actualidad existen 40 millones de niños estadounidenses (entre edades de inicio de adolescencia hasta finales de adolescencia) de familias divorciadas. Y debido a que los medio hermanos(as) no son considerados 100% miembros de familia por un padrastro o madrastra, eso significa que 40 millones de niños americanos quizás estén experimentado crisis de identidad. Quizás ellos ni siquiera se sientan aceptados en su propio hogar. Y eso sucede cuando están llegando a la edad de la adolescencia, cuando el potencial para la rebelión y violencia es asombroso. Sociólogos, ministros del evangelio, rabinos, y otros profesionales, hombres y mujeres confiables que estudian este fenómeno se están preparando para lo que temen será una avalancha de problemas sociales que va a minimizar lo que hemos visto en el pasado.

¿Cómo podemos cambiar este problema social? Podemos empezar por honrar esos que permanece casados a largo plazo, en lugar de glorificar el divorcio. Maggie Gallgher, en el libro, *The Abolition of Marriage*, habla acerca del nacimiento del «divorcio romántico», tú preguntarás, ¿Qué es eso? Es la idea errónea que de alguna manera el divorcio es más romántico que el matrimonio. La idea es algo así: yo estaba simplemente tratando de aguantar en este matrimonio miserable, vacío, y aburrido, y de repente lo/la conocí. De repente los pájaros contaron, mi mundo se iluminó, y el amor renació en mi corazón. Lo que los que creen en este concepto no se ponen a pensar es que el amor puede renacer en el matrimonio si haces el trabajo. Pero pocos están dispuestos a pagar el precio.

Considera la película, *The Bridges of Madison County* (Los puentes del condado de Madison). Una de las razones por la cuales a mí no me gusta esta película es porque glorifica el adulterio, el cual Dios dice que es pecado. Sin embargo, el personaje principal, una mujer, permanece con su esposo al final. Ella sabía que divorciar a su marido iba romper su lealtad hacia él e iba a arruinar la vida de sus hijos. (Curiosamente, los grupos feministas parecen estar molestos con la película porque el personaje no deja a su marido).

Qué tan cierto es que cuando cierta manera de

pensar—como la idea del divorcio romántico—llega a ser parte de la sociedad, empieza a alimentarse a sí misma. Busca maneras de justificarse y protegerse a sí misma. Como resultado, muchas personas divorciadas tratan de presentar estudios para ocultar lo que ellos sospechan que estuvo mal en lo que hicieron.

Aquí yo tengo que decir que ningún matrimonio está en tan malas condiciones que Dios no pueda salvar. Nuestro Dios Todopoderoso es un Dios de milagros. Y si ambos cónyuges se vuelven a Dios por medio del Señor Jesucristo, Dios va a derramar su poder en su matrimonio y los va a transformar—si los esposos obedecen lo que Dios dice en su Palabra.

¿Pero qué pasa si el marido o la mujer no está de acuerdo en vivir los mandamientos de Dios? Entonces estás es un problema. Pero no significa que el divorcio es tu respuesta. Con excepción de situaciones peligrosas y abusivas, Dios dice no al divorcio. «Porque yo detesto el divorcio—dice el Señor, Dios de Israel—y el que cubre de iniquidad su vestidura—dice el Señor de los ejércitos —prestad atención, pues, a vuestro espíritu y no seáis infieles». Dios también dice que los hombres que no se mantienen fieles a sus esposas sufrirán las consecuencias de su pecado (ve Proverbios 5.18-23).

Pero, eso no significa que Dios te odia si estás divorciado o estás considerando el divorcio. Dios no está enojado ni es vengativo. No, Él es un Dios de amor, que mandó a su hijo, Jesucristo, a morir en la cruz por ti. Jesús se levantó de los muertos en victoria para que tú pudieras estar en el cielo con Él algún día si decides aceptar Su sacrificio por ti. Jesús caminó en esta tierra. Tú no tienes idea lo tierno que son sus pensamientos hacia ti, la manera que se preocupa por tu infelicidad, ansiedad, y depresión. Él sabe que el divorcio, en la mayoría de casos, no es la respuesta. Su anhelo es que tú no renuncies a tu matrimonio. Si buscas lo suficiente, tú todavía puedes encontrar algo bueno en tu cónyuge.

Así que en lugar de «seguir tu corazón», y salir de

tu matrimonio, ¿Por qué no sigues tu corazón hacia tu matrimonio? Revisa tus votos matrimoniales. Díselos a tu corazón. Dice la Sra. Gallagher, «La gente tiene que darse cuenta de nuevo del valor de un matrimonio lo suficientemente bueno. Nosotros hemos sido tan condicionados por lo medios del entrenamiento a creer que el matrimonio debe ser espectacular—como un espectáculo de fuegos artificiales todos los días. En cualquier oportunidad disponible tienes a tu disposición pasión romántica increíble...pero la mayoría de la gente no vive ni puede vivir así. Si lo hicieran, sería agotador.»

Ningún matrimonio es perfecto. Pero la mayoría son lo suficientemente buenos para que la pareja permanezca unida, disfruten el uno del otro, protejan a sus hijos, y envejezcan juntos. Simplemente porque tu matrimonio no es perfecto no quiere decir que tienes que renunciar a algo que todavía tiene algo bueno...y el potencial para formar la vidas de tus hijos para bien.

Si estás divorciado, tú puedes elegir no permanecer en la cultura del «divorcio romántico». Tú puedes hacer cualquier esfuerzo para ver a tus hijos (si la corte de familia te lo permite), ya sea o no que vivan contigo.

Enemigo #5: El mito del matrimonio terapéutico

¿Por qué te casaste? ¿Para que todas tus necesidades—sexuales, emocionales, románticas, etc.—fueran cumplidas? ¿Para que alguien estuviera contigo todo el tiempo satisfaciendo tus deseos? Si ese es el caso, tu matrimonio está en arenas movedizas. Si sientes que tus necesidades no están siendo satisfechas, entonces probablemente pienses que tienes todo el derecho de buscar alivio a esas necesidades en cualquier otro lugar. La verdad es que nadie se siente bien todo el tiempo, pero millones de americanos han decidido creer esta mentira de Satanás y anteponen su felicidad personal antes de lo que es mejor para sus niños.

La ironía es que entre más busques tu felicidad personal, ésta se vuelve más difícil de alcanzar. Entre más te enfoques en ti mismo y trates de sentirte bien, más difícil es sentirse bien. Entre más feliz trates de ser, más difícil es serlo, pero lo opuesto también es verdad: entre más dedicas tu vida a otros y das más sin esperar nada a cambio, entre más te sacrificas y trabajas para otros en lugar de hacerlo para ti, más grande va a ser tu bendición, tu gozo y felicidad. Entre más das, más fácil se vuelve dar. Esa es la manera de Dios y es mucho mejor. Si la sigues, siempre vas a ganar. Es por eso que enseguida vamos a hablar acerca de cómo construir tu relación a la manera de Dios para que desarrolles una cercanía y compromiso que será una alegría absoluta para tu corazón, una bendición y la fuente de seguridad para tus hijos.

Las recompensas del matrimonio

¿Qué se necesita para construir un buen matrimonio? Yo le dije a Amy al inicio de nuestro matrimonio: «Yo no quiero una relación ordinaria, quería una extraordinaria. Estoy dispuesto a trabajar y orar y dedicarme a cualquier requerimiento necesario para hacerlo».

¿Esto significa que nuestra vida ha sido perfecta? No. Nosotros hemos tenido problemas y dificultades, como la mayoría de las parejas casadas, pero existe una diferencia. En el umbral de nuestro compromiso—cuando las estrellas aún estaban en nuestros ojos—nos prometimos un cambio de vida y sacrificio el uno con el otro. Nosotros hicimos un juramento que sin importar lo que ocurriera, estábamos decididos a permanecer juntos toda la vida. Cuando dicho compromiso se hace para toda la vida, es asombroso lo que Dios puede hacer por medio de una pareja para cambiar el mundo para bien.

Problemas que destruyen un matrimonio y sus soluciones

Hace un tiempo atrás, yo estaba paseando por una tienda examinando su colección de música. Vi una gran variedad, incluyendo una bella y romántica Colección de Bodas, y luego las feas imágenes de los CDs, tales como la música de la banda sonora de la película *Mortal Kombat* (Combate mortal). Luego me llamó la atención, ¿cuántos matrimonios son como la Colección de bodas—dulces, cariñosos, románticos? ¿Cuántos son como las Combate Mortal—bajo una tensión constante, con palabras de ira, y echando fuera injurias e insultos?

¿Qué es lo que saca a un matrimonio de la «colección de bodas» (el día dichoso de la boda, lleno de romance, encaje blanco, velas encendidas y rostros sonriendo) hacia el *Combate Mortal,* (lo que muchos matrimonios llegan a ser en realidad, en su vida cotidiana)? ¿Y qué podemos hacer con estos problemas para revertirlos o cortarlos de raíz?

Problema #1: Una crisis de identidad

Después de que Amy y yo tuvimos nuestra breve luna de miel, de repente me sorprendió el terror. Caminando una vez solo en el campus de la universidad, me pregunté: ¿Qué he hecho? ¿Quién soy aparte de Amy? ¡Todo este pánico aun cuando sabía que amaba a Amy y que quería estar casado con ella!

Ahora bien, ¿es eso simplemente un trauma de post-luna de miel? No, porque muchas mujeres (y hombres, acerca de sus esposas) me han dicho: «Mi esposo me dejó porque de repente se dio cuenta que se había perdido de muchas cosas de la vida, así que me dejo a mí y a nuestros hijos. Él dice que se cansó del matrimonio y ya no quiere esa responsabilidad. Quiere irse a encontrarse a sí mismo. Dice que ya no me quiere—sino que quiere a alguien más».

En lugar de dejar que tu crisis de identidad los separe, úsala como una oportunidad para dejar que tu cónyuge vea en tu interior y que te ayude a resolver tus preguntas y tus inquietudes.

Problema #2: Desilución sexual

Muchos problemas en el matrimonio están relacionados con malentendidos de los géneros sexuales. Generalmente, una mujer no está condicionada para el sexo observando la apariencia física de su marido; ella es condicionada por la manera gentil con que la trata su marido y por la atmósfera de seguridad que él provee para ella. Así que si un hombre se queja conmigo: «Nosotros raramente dormimos juntos y cuando lo hacemos, es algo que ella simplemente hace a regañadientes», yo tengo que hacer la pregunta: «¿Cómo eres tú como esposo en el trato hacia tu esposa?».

La desilusión sexual puede causar desilusión seria en un matrimonio. Si ésta es tu situación, háblalo claramente con tu cónyuge y busquen ayuda, antes de que se separen más.

Problema #3: Disminución de seducción

Esto significa que ya no estás interesado en tu pareja. Ya no hay admiración en tu relación, y un frente ártico ha descendido en tu hogar. Ya no pareces preocuparte por las pequeñas facetas del romance.

Tu actitud hacia el romance es un barómetro de la salud de tu relación matrimonial. No olvides hacer las pequeñas cosas que mejoran el barómetro en tu hogar—una nota de amor para el almuerzo, una llamada telefónica, una sorpresa de entrega de flores o chocolates, simplemente para decir que te importa.

Problema #4: Soledad

¿No es esto extraordinario? Como persona casada, tú, supuestamente tienes que estar en la relación más íntima de todas las relaciones humanas y aun así sentirte solo. Dicha soledad es con frecuencia una señal de división íntima y un problema más profundo.

Mira a Mike y Joan, por ejemplo. Casados por siente años, tienen dos niños hermosos, pero ellos no habían dormido juntos por un año. Lo único que tenían en común era el odio del uno hacia el otro. Mike le dijo al consejero: «Mi esposa vive como un cerdo. Ella se queda en la cama hasta las 11 en punto y no hace nada para mejorar nuestra vida y nuestro hogar». Ella se quejó: «Él nunca quiere pasar tiempo conmigo, desde los seis años de matrimonio, cuando se ocupó tanto en el trabajo, yo me he sentido tan sola». La soledad de Joan la estaba llevando a la depresión y ella incluso batallaba para salir de la cama».

La buena noticia es que Mike y Joan buscaron ayuda y repararon su matrimonio y sus heridas emocionales. Si estás en una situación similar, tal vez sea tiempo para que tú también busques ayuda para descubrir la verdadera razón de tu soledad o la de tu cónyuge.

Problema #5: Injusticia

La injusticia no se trata de adulterio, se trata de engañar en compromisos en otras áreas. Por ejemplo, si el esposo promete: «Sí cariño, yo estaré ahí» y no se presenta, un creciente sentimiento de injusticia comienza a afectar el ambiente emocional del hogar. La esposa se vuelve resentida y luego el esposo se volverá amargado por el espíritu resentido de ella.

Así que para el ciclo de la injusticia antes de que comience, hagan lo posible por cumplir sus compromisos el uno con el otro y humildemente den una explicación cuando no puedan cumplir.

Problema #6: Manipulación

¿Estás realmente jugando con tu cónyuge en un campo que está al mismo nivel, lidiando directamente con él o ella?

En el pasado, cada vez que Amy y yo íbamos a un viaje, Amy quería parar en un hotel a medio camino de nuestro destino, pero yo nunca quería. Al inicio, era por razones de dinero, era demasiado tacaño para hacerlo. Luego, cuando tuvimos suficiente dinero, yo no lo hacía porque quería llegar del punto A al punto B lo más rápido posible, pero para Amy, ir de viaje era para relajarse, tomar las cosas con calma. No entendía que yo siempre le decía: «cariño, solamente nos faltan pocas millas». Una vez le prometí que íbamos a parar un par de horas a las cuatro de la tarde, pero yo no paré hasta que llegamos a nuestro destino, a las dos de la mañana. ¡Ya te imaginas lo infeliz que estaba Amy! Ha tomado años, pero finalmente aprendí. Ahora, si Amy dice: «Yo quiero parar en un hotel» me paro en el siguiente. Es un pequeño sacrificio con una gran recompensa: una esposa más feliz.

Si a ti no te gusta que te manipulen (¿y a quién gusta?) recordemos que lo mismo ocurre a los demás. A ellos tampoco les gusta que los manipulen.

Problema #7: Estrés

Quizá llegues a un período en tu vida (o tal vez ya estés ahí) donde no vas a poder lidiar con la vida de la forma que lo hiciste una vez. Tus responsabilidades parecen abrumadoras. Te preguntas si eres más lento, más callado o te estás desmoronando. El estrés está aumentando dentro de ti.

Si esto está pasando en tu vida, hazte cargo de ella. Averigua qué está causando el estrés, reajusta tus prioridades, habla con tu cónyuge y busca ayuda. El estrés puede dañar tremendamente la vida de tu familia.

Problema #8: Violencia

Una mujer con la cara hinchada se me acercó una vez y me preguntó acerca de la oportunidad de un negocio. Cuando yo le pregunté amablemente mientras estábamos hablando «¿Estás bien?». No pude evitar verle los moretones en las mejillas, ella dijo rápidamente: «Yo... yo tuve un accidente automovilístico», pero después de hablar con ella acerca de su vida en el hogar, supe que ese no era el caso. Rutinariamente, su esposo abusaba de ella y de los niños.

Yo solamente lo voy a decir una vez y lo voy a decir con fuerza—no hay ninguna razón para que golpees a tu esposa o a los niños. Si tú eres quien está recibiendo dicho abuso, vete a un lugar seguro inmediatamente. Si tú eres el abusador, humíllate y busca consejería para que te ayuden a controlar tus estados de ánimo violentos.

PROBLEMA #9: DESINTEGRACIÓN VERBAL

Cuando un matrimonio se debilita, por lo general, las charlas son las primeras en desaparecer. Las palabras del uno hacia el otro se convierten en volcanes verbales. Tú hablas negativamente de tu cónyuge con otros y le dices palabras poco amables en su cara.

¿Cómo detener esta situación? Piensa de esta manera: la Regla de Oro de Dios ha funcionado por años. ¿Por qué no tratar a otros de la manera que tú deseas que te traten? ¿Te gustaría que alguien hablara negativamente de ti con alguien más cuando tú no estás presente para defenderte? ¿Te gustaría que alguien estuviera siempre diciéndote lo que hay de malo en ti o que no vales nada?

Un amigo mío tuvo una buena sugerencia: Trata a tu cónyuge como si él o ella fuera algún huésped especial en tu casa.

PROBLEMA #10: «SHOCK» DE RECONOCIMIENTO

En algún punto de la relación, muchas parejas casadas se dan cuenta que ellos realmente no son felices con la persona con quien se casaron. Quizá pensaron que podían cambiar los hábitos después del matrimonio o que esa antigua herida o encanto de esa relación pasada no iba a salir a la superficie después de que se dijeran los votos matrimoniales.

¿Cómo puedes lidiar con dichos momentos de insatisfacción?

- No te enfoques en las cosas negativas de tu cónyuge. Recuerda, tú también tienes tus imperfecciones (aunque algunas veces te cueste admitirlas). En lugar de eso, enfócate en las cosas que tu cónyuge puede hacer, y luego ayúdale a él o a ella a que logre precisamente eso.
- Haz una lista de las razones por las que te casaste con tu cónyuge. ¿Qué disfrutas de esa persona?
- Pídele a Dios que te ayude a re-enfocarte en tu compromiso matrimonial. Compromete más, en lugar de menos, con tu cónyuge.

- Despierta la chispa romántica. Si el romance en tu matrimonio está declinando, haz cosas pequeñas para reavivar la llama del amor. Piensa en los tiempos cuando eran novios y las cosas que tu cónyuge disfrutaba.

Problema #11: Competencia

¿Te la pasas compitiendo con tu cónyuge—tratando de demostrar superioridad sobre él o ella? La competencia tiene la tendencia a crear rivalidad en lugar de crear una pareja energética y saludable.

Una verdadera sociedad está hecha de dos personas que hacen contribuciones únicas, quieren caminar el uno al lado del otro hacia un objetivo común. ¿Cuál es tu misión común en tu matrimonio? Háblalo con tu cónyuge y encuentra maneras de contribuir individualmente a ese objetivo.

Problema #12: Falta de imaginación

¿Se ha convertido tu matrimonio en algo aburrido? Si ese es el caso, ¿Por qué no leer un libro acerca de cómo mejorar tu matrimonio? Noventa por ciento de los libros acerca del matrimonio los leen las mujeres y a los hombres, lamentablemente, a menudo les falta imaginación en esta área. Así que, muchachos, ¿por qué no, como un compromiso para su relación, escuchen algún buen CD, lean un buen libro para mejorar su matrimonio? Eso les traerá dividendos para toda la vida.

Problema #13: Vacío espiritual

Algunas parejas están divididas por un océano espiritual que parece imposible de cruzar—quizás uno de los cónyuges es cristiano y el otro no. Deben de hablar de dichos «océanos» que separan el matrimonio.

Para mí, el momento más importante que cambió mi vida, fue cuando acepté a Cristo como mi Salvador. Ese momento me cambió; cambió la manera en el enfoque que daba a mis compromisos y tuvo un impacto en mi futuro matrimonio. ¿Dónde estás tú y tu cónyuge cuando se trata de fe? ¿Están unidos o las diferencias espirituales los separan?

Problema #14: Traición

Algunas personas me han hecho esta pregunta: ¿Cómo sabes si «has cruzado la línea» emocionalmente en la relación con algún compañero de trabajo, amigo o conocido? Ellos se preguntan si la relación está bien—siempre y cuando no incluya contacto sexual. Yo les digo que hay cuatro niveles de atracción sexual:

- **Nivel 1:** Tú te vuelves sexualmente consciente de otra persona y de una sensación de química. Esto no necesariamente representa problemas, porque es una reacción humana normal—incluso si estás felizmente casado con alguien mas.
- **Nivel 2:** Tú pasas de estar consciente de esa persona, a querer que esa persona te vea de una manera sexual. Tú quieres que él o ella aprecie tus atractivos, tu autoestima, tu ropa.
- **Nivel 3:** Tú avanzas a un «modo de persecución» —buscas conversaciones o pasar tiempo con esa persona.
- **Nivel 4:** Tú haces un compromiso con esa persona (ya sea verbal o no verbal) que te lleva a romper tus votos matrimoniales. Es aquí donde destruyes tu matrimonio, rompes el corazón de tu esposa y de tus hijos, avergüenzas a Dios, y rompes Sus leyes.

¿Cómo sabes si estás yendo hacia los problemas? Si tu relación con alguien más, además de tu cónyuge, va más allá del Nivel 1.

¿Porqué casarse?

Cada persona tiene su opinión de un día de bodas perfecto —incluyendo un compañero o compañera perfecta. Pero algunas veces no es tan perfecto como estaba planeado, y tu cónyuge no es tan perfecto como soñaste. Es por eso que, ya sea en tiempos buenos o en tiempos malos, tú tienes que saber a quién eliges para casarte.

Si alguien te preguntara porqué te casaste, ¿qué le contestarías? Aquí tienes diez objetivos principales para un buen matrimonio.

Objetivo #1: Intimidad - Intimidad es lo que Jesús quiso decir cuando Él dijo: «Por eso dejará el hombre a su padre y a su madre y se unirá a su mujer y juntos serán una sola carne» (Mateo 19.5). ¿Qué significa, «serán una sola carne?», se refiere no solamente a la unión sexual, sino también a una combinación profunda de dos personalidades. Son dos partes convirtiéndose en una sola.

En la sociedad de hoy, llegar a ser uno con otra persona no es tan fácil como suena, especialmente si creciste en una familia donde el patrón de intimidad era inexistente. Quizá cuando eras niño tus emociones fueron aniquiladas y ahora que estás casado, no estás seguro de cómo responder emocionalmente a tu cónyuge que siempre quiere abrazarte. Te congelas por dentro.

Esta situación es particularmente devastadora en las mujeres. Un estudio de cuatro mil adolescentes americanas que han tenido sexo explica el porqué. Cuando se les preguntó «¿Por qué dormiste con él o ella?» la mayoría de los hombres contestaron, «porque me gustó»; la mayoría de las jóvenes contestaron: «porque pensé que lo amaba y que él me amaba». Estas jovencitas no estaban en busca de sexo. En lugar de eso, las impulsó el hambre de intimidad. El Dr. Donald Joy está de acuerdo. Él dice que las mujeres anhelan mucho más la intimidad y por eso muchas veces se involucran en relaciones sexuales demasiado pronto, por lo tanto, esto arruina la progresión de la relación. Una relación saludable y normal se desarrolla por etapas: contacto visual, conversación, un toque amigable, caricias ligeras, etc. Si el sexo entra en escena demasiado pronto, el proceso de unión se interrumpe en ese momento y pocas parejas logran avanzar más allá de esa barrera. Por lo tanto, si llegan al matrimonio, es casi como si se estuvieran casando con un extraño. Todo lo que tienen en común es el ballet corporal que disfrutan, porque con frecuencia no tienen conexión espiritual, intelectual, emocional o psicológica.

La verdadera intimidad es mucho más que sexo—es una unión profunda que requiere compromiso sacrificio y amor verdadero. Es una conexión entre dos personas, dos corazones para toda la vida. Las mujeres la anhelan y los hombres la necesitan.

Objetivo #2: Compañerismo - Todos hemos conocido parejas que no solamente no se gustan, sino que les gustaría estar en diferentes continentes el uno del otro. Pero el primer objetivo del matrimonio es tener alguien con quien salir, con quien divertirse.

Objetivo #3: Comprensión - Todos nosotros anhelamos un alma gemela que logre llegar a nuestro corazón y nos entienda. Alguien que sea sensible y nos escuche y ya sea que esté o no de acuerdo en lo que hacemos o decimos, que entienda nuestras motivaciones en lugar de simplemente reaccionar.

Permíteme platicarte sobre una «explosión» que Amy y yo tuvimos seis meses después de casarnos. Yo estaba de camino a la escuela de postgrado y ella se dirigía a su clase de universidad, cuando tuvimos una tremenda pelea. Cuando estaba a punto de explotar, pensando: ¿Cómo puede ser que alguien pueda decir algo como lo que Amy acaba de decir? Me detuve en la entrada de nuestro pequeño apartamento. Respiré profundo, entré nuevamente y dije: «espera un minuto. Voy a suponer que no entendí lo que acabas de decir». Ninguno fue a clase. Nos sentamos en el piso y hablamos por tres horas. Poco a poco me di cuenta que ella no dijo lo que dijo para irritarme, sino que su sentir era diferente al mío. Eventualmente, llegamos a un acuerdo mutuo. Pero tomó tiempo, sensibilidad y que yo cerrara la boca el tiempo suficientemente para que ella explicara lo realmente quería decir. ¿Estás realmente escuchando y entendiendo lo que tu cónyuge quiere decir?

Objetivo #4: Diversión - Todos necesitamos a alguien con quien reír. Muchas parejas que vienen a mí para consejería me dice que ya no se divierten. Ellos no recuerdan la última vez que se rieron juntos.

El antiguo dicho es una poderosa verdad: la risa es un remedio infalible, y todo matrimonio necesita una dosis constante y saludable de ésta.

Objetivo #5: Romance - El romance tiene que ver con la manera en que se atraen el uno al otro. Yo uso la palabra deliberadamente porque es importante alimentar el autoestima del otro.

Así que, adelante—aumenta el ego de tu cónyuge. Solamente asegúrate de que no estás aumentando su ego falsamente—tú tienes que ser sincero en tus halagos. Cuando tus halagos son honestos y fluyen continuamente en tu hogar, tú creas una atmósfera perfecta para el romance.

Objetivo #6: Sexo - No hay tal cosa en la Biblia como un matrimonio sin sexo. Simplemente no existe. Échale un vistazo al libro *Cantar de los Cantares*—una glorificación del amor sexual y romántico en una relación matrimonial comprometida.

El sexo es una parte vital de una buena relación matrimonial. Pero muchas parejas luchan con desajustes debido a muchas causas—abuso del pasado, cansancio de itinerarios ocupados de trabajo, sentimiento de rechazo, alejamiento del cónyuge, daño psicológico, espiritual, emocional y físico.

Si tienen problemas en esta área, sean honestos el uno con el otro. Hablen de sus preocupaciones y busquen ayuda profesional donde la necesitan.

Objetivo #7: Apoyo - Todos nosotros anhelamos tener alguien que sea leal—alguien que nos dé apoyo cuando los tiempo son difíciles y cuando nos sentimos miserables.

Deslealtad—incluyendo insultos del uno hacia el otro, o bajarlo en presencia de otros—no tiene cabida en un matrimonio comprometido. Jamás. Así que hagan un pacto que nunca van a usar esas tácticas en su matrimonio.

Objetivo #8: Cooperación financiera - Juntos se pueden ayudar el uno al otro a construir un sueño—un futuro más grandioso del que pudieran tener separados. ¿Qué sueños tienen tú y tu cónyuge en el presente que pueden lograr por medio de la cooperación financiera?

Objetivo #9: Hijos - No todos quieren tener hijos. Algunas parejas tienen la confianza en su papel como profesionales y sienten que Dios no les ha llamado a tener hijos. Sin embargo, existen otras parejas que anhelan que los niños formen parte de su vida diaria, pero incluso para estas parejas, la espera puede ser dolorosa.

Nosotros tuvimos tremenda dificultad para concebir a nuestro segundo hijo. Amy y yo tratamos por cuatro años de tener otro bebé, después de que nuestra hija Allison nació.

Perdimos un bebé a los cuatro meses.

Una adopción fracasó la semana en que íbamos a viajar para ir a recoger al bebé y cuando el cuarto del bebé estaba a punto de llegar, en de un período de doce horas se desvanecieron nuestras esperanzas.

Luego, tres meses después de esa agonía, Dios nos dio un milagro—Amy quedó embarazada con nuestro hijo, Jonathan Dexter.

Objetivo #10: Nuevas tradiciones - Todo aquel que se casa trae a la familia algunas tradiciones a la relación. Cónyuges sanos pueden hablar de estas tradiciones, adoptar las que funcionan en la familia, y luego crear nuevas tradiciones familiares que son únicas para ellos.

Componentes básicos para un buen matrimonio

Ahora que hemos hablado de los problemas que pueden afectar tu relación, identificar algunas soluciones, y hablar de las razones para elegir una unión para siempre en esta tierra, concluiremos que con ocho componentes para un buen matrimonio. Ningún matrimonio puede prescindir de éstas. Con un poquito trabajo de tu parte, vas a cosechar tremendas recompensas—una esposa feliz, niños más alegres, y un ambiente del hogar más saludable. ¿Cuáles son estos componentes básicos?

Componente #1: Respeto - Esta es la base fundamental. Sin respeto, nada más va a funcionar en tu matrimonio. Trata a tu cónyuge con respeto en todo momento y en cualquier situación—incluso cuando quizás tu cónyuge no te muestre el mismo respeto.

Componente #2: Cortesía - Cortesía y buenos modales es la manera en que muestras respeto. Así que siempre recuerda ser una persona civilizada al momento de hablar. Trátense el uno al otro, no solamente de manera decente, sino amablemente. Siempre recuerda la Regla de Oro: Trata a otros como te gustaría que te trataran.

Componente #3: Confiabilidad - Haz siempre lo que prometiste. Sé una persona confiable y fidedigna. Si dices que vas a estar en casa para ayudar a los niños, entonces hazlo. Dicha confiabilidad es lo que forma el carácter ante los ojos de tu esposa y de los demás.

Componente #4: Estabilidad financiera - Según *Money Magazine*, las parejas casadas pelean por dinero más que por cualquier otra cosa. El dinero puede ser un gran divisor, pero no tiene que ser. Ambas personas pueden hablar abiertamente de sus opiniones sobre el dinero, tener un respeto saludable por el trasfondo del cada uno, y encontrar una solución mutua para gastar y ahorrar su dinero.

Componente #5: Unidad - Unión verdadera significa entusiasmo en lugar de andar a regañadientes o de mala gana—apóyense el uno al otro. Sé el porrista de tu cónyuge, échale porras a él o ella hacia la excelencia.

Componente #6: Ceder - Uno de los grandes enemigos del matrimonio es la testarudez. Un modo de pensar como este: *yo siempre lo he hecho de esta manera, así que simplemente se va a tener que acostumbrar.*

Siempre disponte a escuchar lo que tu cónyuge tiene que decir. Quizá te des cuenta, para tu sorpresa y beneficio de tu matrimonio, que vas a ser capaz de ceder en muchas cosas que pueden parecer poco para ti, pero que son muy importantes para tu cónyuge (cosas tales como ir a un viaje de campamento, incluso cuando no es tu idea de unas vacaciones, sino simplemente porque a tu cónyuge le encanta acampar).

A medida que ambos aprendan a ceder, habrán menos problemas grandes en los cuales sentirás que tienes que ponerte firme, pero en esos problemas más grandes, no dudes en hacerlo, particularmente si son problemas morales (tales como no reportar ingresos en tus impuestos). Puedes ejecutar dicha firmeza con integridad, honor y con semejanza a como Cristo lo haría. Puedes mostrarle a tu esposo o esposa que todavía le amas, pero que tienes que mantener ese principio divino en este caso en particular porque es lo que Dios dice que debe de ser.

Componente #7: Placer sexual - Cuando conoces bien el cuerpo de tu cónyuge, es fácil volverse mecánico, pero no olvides las bromas sexuales—la llamada telefónica, las notas, las flores, la bata de encaje. Esfuérzate por desarrollar un ambiente de romance y no siempre hagan el amor con la luz apagada. Como un hombre le dijo a su esposa: «A mí me gusta ver cuando te pones tu batas de encaje porque pienso en lo que está por venir. ¡Y me gusta quitártela!».

Es por eso que un consejero dio origen a lo que él llama: «Teoría del Encaje». Aquí está lo que él dice en relación a esto: «Hay momentos en que algo que parece tan ilógico e innecesario tiene que entrar en la dimensión sexual porque es como el encaje en un cuerpo. Tú no lo usas para mantenerte caliente, no lo usas para ir a trabajar, lo usas porque crea una atmósfera que es atractiva para la otra persona. La idea es traer de regreso un poco de encaje a la relación sexual conyugal.»

¿Qué tal te va a ti y a tu cónyuge en el arte del placer sexual? ¿Necesitas traer un poco de sentido de sutileza y romance a tu ecuación matrimonial?

Componente #8: Compromiso de por vida - Ya sea que estés casado por primera vez, o que hayas estado divorciado y ahora estés casado nuevamente, decide hacer de tu matrimonio un compromiso de por vida. Para los que han estado divorciados, mantenga en mente esta estadística: estadísticamente, tú tienes doble probabilidad de divorciarte del segundo matrimonio que del primero. Yo no digo esto para asustarte, sino para animarte a solidificar tu compromiso para que tu segundo matrimonio funcione.

Cuando camines por ese pasillo y estés a punto de casarte, no permitas que el «fuera», de divorcio entre en tus pensamientos. Haz un pacto con tu cónyuge, de que el divorcio nunca, en ninguna situación, sea una opción en tu matrimonio. Decidan juntos que van a estar comprometidos el uno al otro para toda la vida. A medida que construyas estos componentes matrimoniales y pidas a Dios su dirección todo los días—vas a estar sorprendido de las pequeñas maneras—y, yo confío, en gran manera —que Dios va a revitalizar tu matrimonio. ¡Simplemente prueba y verás!

CAPÍTULO 4

Los inhibidores y predictores del éxito

Cuando tú ves a un ganador, ¿no deseas saber cómo lo logró?

Yo sí. A mí siempre me han fascinado los logros. Mientras que entrevistaba a cientos de individuos y leía muchos libros, investigué el fondo del éxito. ¿Por qué? Porque quería saber acerca de ello. Quiero heredar esos mismos principios a mis hijos y todo aquel a quien conozca.

Por lo tanto ¿Qué hace que una persona que viene aparentemente de la nada, para vencer grandes obstáculos y ganar? ¿Qué hace que una persona tenga hambre de ser diferente, de ser especial, de sobrepasar sus propias expectativas? ¿Qué hace que una persona anhele sobresalir por encima de la manada y querer ser grande? Una vez leí esta declaración escrita por una persona sabia: «Recuerda: el único obstáculo es tu opinión de ti mismo. Si crees que eres débil y estúpido, lisiado o pisoteado, entonces lo serás.» Así que, en lugar de pensar en la discapacidad de tu hijo, anímalo a que se prepare para hacer lo mejor y de esa manera, lo va a lograr.

Un buen ejemplo es el jovencito que estaba afuera en el jardín de atrás trabajando vigorosamente para otro vecino. Mientras trabajaba, sonreía, reía a carcajadas y hablaba con todos los vecinos. No fue después de largo rato de nuestra conversación que me di cuenta que no tenía la mano izquierda. No la tenía—tal vez por un accidente o posiblemente debido a un defecto de nacimiento. Pero he aquí lo extraordinario: la pérdida de su mano izquierda no era incapacidad para él. Estudios de hombres y mujeres con incapacidades paralizantes muestran que aquellos que tienen actitud positiva, superan la incapacidad mucho más rápido que aquellos que no la tienen. Aunque tal vez no se recuperen por completo físicamente, recuperan sus vidas, y debido a que no están amargados o ensimismados en sí mismos, tal vez logren tener un gran impacto en el mundo.

Si alguien como este joven puede hacerlo o como Joni Eareckson Tada—quien quedó paralizado cuando joven en un accidente de clavados—puede hacerlo, ¿Por qué no tus hijos? Dios quiere usar sus vidas para su gran gloria y sus propósitos increíbles y Él dice que los va a ayudar en cualquier cosa que quiera hacer: «No por el poder ni por la fuerza, sino por mi espíritu» (Sacarías 4:6) Aunque Dios trabaja con debilidades, transmite a tus hijos que Él quiere lo mejor de ellos. Hagan lo que hagan debe ser para Su gloria, no para la de ellos.

Lo que no es logro

Una de las maneras en que puedes inspirar a tus hijos para alcanzar algo, es modelando logros para ellos. Pero primero ellos tienen que entender lo que no es un logro:

1.- Logros no dependen de la personalidad

Lo más probable es que cada persona en tu familia tiene diferentes combinaciones de temperamentos. Steven Pinker, quien escribe acerca de la capacidad mental y las personalidades, dice que las personalidades difieren en al menos cinco formas principales:

- Sociable (extrovertido) o reservado (introvertido)
- Constantemente preocupado (neurótico) o calmado y autosatisfecho (estable)
- Cortés y amable (que está de acuerdo) o grosero y sospechoso (antagonista)
- Cuidadoso (consciente) o descuidado (no directo)
- Atrevido (abierto) o no está de acuerdo (no es abierto)

Es importante recordar que los logros no dependen de la personalidad básica con que nacen los niños. Tus hijos pueden cambiar o moderar esas tendencias y adaptarse a ellas para lograr el éxito. Así que enséñales a que no se concentren en sus limitaciones, en lugar de eso, anímalos que se enfoquen en lo que ellos pueden hacer.

2.- El éxito y los logros no dependen de la educación o el coeficiente intelectual

El coeficiente intelectual evalúa la habilidad de tus hijos para tomar exámenes. No prueba si ellos van o no a ser exitosos en la vida. Recientemente, leí un estudio fascinante de personas que tenían coeficiente intelectual de 120 y arriba de 120, lo cual es un coeficiente muy alto, pero la mayoría de ellos estaban trabajando para personas que tenían un CI entre 100 y 105, personas que eran más agresivas, tenían mejor actitud y estaban más comprometidas a tomar riesgos que los que tenían los CIs más altos.

El famoso fundador de la mayor parte de la educación pública en el siglo XIX fue Thomas Arnold. Cuando en 1828, él se convirtió en el director de la escuela más famosa en Inglaterra, se dedicó a reorganizarla. Cuando ascendió de posición a un hombre de menor educación para una posición de liderazgo, uno de los profesores con educación superior se acercó a él con ira. «Te quiero informar que he estado aquí por veinte años. ¿No debería mi experiencia valer de algo?» El señor Arnold contestó: «Señor, usted no tiene veinte años de experiencia. Me temo que usted solamente tiene un año de experiencia y ha repetido eso veinte años».

No te sientas perturbado por las pruebas de coeficiente intelectual que ponen a tus hijos en una categoría. Cada niño puede tener éxito, sin importar su coeficiente intelectual.

Los hábitos del éxito

Hemos visto lo que no es el éxito. Ahora hablaremos acerca lo que se necesita para que tus hijos sean exitosos en lo que hacen y en lo que son. Nosotros lo llamamos «Marco de referencia DEPR».

D = Decisión o Firmeza de decisión

El éxito no es automático. No es algo que simplemente le sucede a tus hijos mientras van caminando por a vida. Tienen que perseguirlo. Deben comprometerse. Ningún logro grandioso ocurre sin que tomemos la decisión de perseguir un objetivo o un sueño.

Hay muchos que temen tomar decisiones porque temen a las consecuencias. ¿Y si hacen algo mal? Como resultado, se congelan de miedo y no logran hacer nada. Entonces, están a merced de los acontecimientos que ocurren a su alrededor.

Si tus hijos postergan sus decisiones de manera persistente porque no tienen la fuerza para ponerse de pie y tomar decisiones, entonces le dan el control a las fuerzas que se encuentran a su alrededor. Están indefensos ante la influencia de otros para que los manejen como títeres.

Otros niños son renuentes a tomar decisiones porque no quieren la responsabilidad, pero para poder crecer, tienen que aprender a tomar una acción decisiva. De otra manera, serán impotentes durante toda su vida, detrás de los que les quitan la responsabilidad.

¿Pero cómo pueden saber tus hijos si están tomando buenas decisiones? Ellos tienen que revisar la información por sí solos, en lugar de confiar en lo que otros dicen. De otra manera, van a tomar decisiones basadas en información errónea. Por lo tanto, pide a tus hijos que siempre investiguen los hechos, sin que ello provoque que pospongan la toma de decisiones.

E = Expectativas

Si quieres que tus hijos entiendan el éxito y los logros, entonces ellos necesitan altas expectativas de sí mismos. Ellos necesitan metas claras y específicas, y sueños de a dónde ellos quieren ir. Ellos tienen que esperar más de sí mismos todos los días.

¿Cómo funciona esto en mi propia vida? Cuando me levanto en la mañana, cito en mi interior esté versículo bíblico: «Este es el día que El Señor ha hecho; regocijémonos y alegrémonos en él» (Salmo 118:24).

Después digo: «Buenos días, Señor» porque deseo reconocer el control de Dios en mi vida.

Además, parafraseo otra cita: «Voy a esperar grandes cosas del Plan de Dios para mí hoy».

Esta rutina ayuda a energizar mi día. Me da una expectativa alegre de los resultados felices de Dios para mí cada día.

Samuel Johnson dijo que la esperanza es un buen desayuno porque te mejora durante el día. De esa manera me siento cada día, mientras hago mi rutina.

Por lo tanto, anima a tus hijos a pensar acerca de lo que verdaderamente quieren y tendrán el poder de lograr lo que desean.

P = Patrones

Para poder lograr esas expectativas, tus hijos necesitan hábitos saludables de éxito. Eso significa que ellos tienen que poder manejar su tiempo y dinero de ciertas formas y maneras predicibles. Eso les va a dar la libertad para construir sus vidas de tal manera que alcancen el éxito.

¿Por qué son tan importantes los patrones positivos? Porque éstos se convierten en hábitos profundamente arraigados que eventualmente van a gobernar su vida.

Esto es particularmente importante para tus hijos. Tienes que asegurarte que ellos aprendan cómo tener éxito. Entonces esos principios se convertirán en patrones de vida para ellos.

R = Resultados

Definitivamente, tu objetivo es obtener resultados. No tiene ningún sentido si dices que te vas a quedar en casa para pasar tiempo con tu hijo, si él o ella no estarán ahí cuando tú estés presente. Tu intento es inútil porque no va a tener resultados. La cuestión es alcanzar el objetivo, capturar el sueño, cumplir tu propósito.

Enseña a tus hijos a que busquen resultados para saber si están teniendo éxito o no. De otra manera, juntos busquen una estrategia, una manera en la que pueda tener éxito.

Inhibidores para el éxito

¿Alguna vez tu hijo ha arruinado algo, decide no volver a hacerlo y termina cayendo en la misma trampa? Si ese es el caso, esta sección te va a aclarar cuáles son los obstáculos para el éxito. Algunos obstáculos se van a aplicar a ambos, niños y adultos, algunos solamente a los adultos, pero mientras hablas con tus hijos —adolescentes y jóvenes adultos—acerca de estos obstáculos (a la edad apropiada) ayudas a tus hijos a vencerlos. Estos «elementos depresivos» pueden frenar a tus hijos a que busquen de todo corazón el éxito y los logros.

Inhibidor #1: Demandas financieras

Preocuparse por dinero puede comerse tu motivación, corroer tu confianza y agotar toda tu energía.

Lo creas a o no, este obstáculo de éxito parece afectar más a mujeres que a hombres. Cuando David Buss le envió un cuestionario acerca de dieciocho cualidades de un compañero, a hombres y mujeres de trece países—gente de todas razas y diferentes perfiles educativos—se sorprendió de los resultados. En casi todos los casos, las mujeres valoraban la capacidad de ganar altos ingresos más que los hombres y ellas tienen la tendencia a querer un tercio o un medio más de ingreso del que la mayoría de las familias (ya sea uno o dos ingresos) que puedan producir. Eso quiere decir que las mujeres ponen una tremenda presión en los hombres, especialmente si él es la única fuente de ingreso para crear seguridad financiera para la familia, pero esto no es porque las mujeres sean codiciosas. Es porque la seguridad es vital para ellas. Después de todo, así las diseñó Dios—desean seguridad para ambos, para ella y para sus hijos.

Eso significa que con frecuencia las mujeres son el impulso detrás de cada hogar. Aunque los hombres quieren tener éxito y tienen grandes sueños, con frecuencia, sus esposas son la principal motivación. Si el hombre reacciona a esta presión de manera negativa o rencorosa—culpando a su mujer por querer más, o a sus hijos por crear la necesidad de más ingreso—la familia sufre. Después de todo, Dios hizo a los hombres para proteger y proveer para sus familias y esa es su función principal. Por lo tanto, el hombre debería de usar los codazos de su mujer para encender la llama de su pasión por el trabajo e impulsarse hacia arriba. Podrá llegar a estar orgulloso del hecho de que puede cumplir las exigencias y ser la clase de hombre de quien una familia puede depender para satisfacer estas responsabilidades financieras.

Inhibidor #2: Retrasos financieros

Tus hijos sueñan con una ganancia financiera...pero no llega cuando ellos quieren. Sueñan con todas las cosas que van a poder hacer algún día, pero ese «algún día» nunca llega. Puede que comiencen a sentirse frustrados, incluso avergonzados frente a personas que conocían sus objetivos y planes.

Tus hijos pueden elegir. Pueden permitir que este retraso les desvíe o los agote o pueden convertirlo en un factor de motivación. Pueden reevaluar el por qué están en un período de retraso financiero y luego trazar un mapa de un plan para hacer algo al respecto.

Inhibidor #3: Deseos incumplidos

Estas esperanzas y deseos incumplidos pueden ser financieros o no, por eso están separados del Inhibidor #2. Si tus hijos están en una posición de tener sueños no realizados, deben echar un vistazo a estos sueños. ¿Son realistas? ¿O están tan lejos de la realidad que no pueden lograrlos? ¿Si son realistas, por qué no los están logrando? ¿Tus hijos no están dispuestos a pagar el precio? Si es así ¿Qué los está deteniendo?

Tener deseos incumplidos no es necesariamente algo malo. Si tú tuvieras todo lo que quieres, no tendrías ningún motivo para lograr algo. Esa es la naturaleza humana. ¿Por qué en lugar de eso, no animas a tus hijos a que se fijen metas para ellos mismos? Por ejemplo, si pueden alcanzar cierto nivel de logros, entonces pueden comprar un carro nuevo ellos mismos.

Premiarse uno mismo cuando logra algo no es un concepto no bíblico. Algunas personas lo confunden con «codiciar», pero la palabra «codicia» en el hebreo original del Antiguo Testamento literalmente quiere decir: «querer algo que alguien más tiene y nosotros no queremos que lo tenga». En otras palabras, si tu vecino tiene un Cadillac blanco, tú no quieres un Cadillac blanco, tú quieres el Cadillac blanco de él. Es por eso que codiciar es tan pecaminoso porque significa que quieres despojar a otros de algún bien, incluso si se lo han ganado de manera legítima.

Enseña a tus hijos que lidiar con deseos no satisfechos puede ser algo que motiva. Nos motiva a alcanzar algo en lugar de estar aburrido con la vida y tener deseos que no han sido satisfechos también nos ayuda a enfocarnos en Dios y lo que nos provee, en lugar de enfocarnos en nuestras propias debilidades. Como dice en Eclesiastés: «Si perseguimos posesiones tontamente, nunca vamos a estar satisfechos. Solamente Dios puede satisfacer nuestra alma».

Inhibidor #4: Deseos contradictorios

Todos hemos enfrentado deseos contradictorios. Digamos que te metes a un programa de salud porque quieres estar más saludable y quieres bajar de peso, pero luego ves una valla publicitaria promocionando una comida alta en calorías y sin más ni más, deseas consumir esa comida más que nada. ¿Qué está pasando? Estás respondiendo a un estímulo inmediato, en lugar de pensar en la meta a largo plazo.

Si tus hijos ceden a estos deseos contradictorios todo el tiempo, van a perder la disciplina. Eso los conducirá a ser débiles e indecisos, por lo tanto, enséñales que en lugar de ceder al deseo inmediato que está frente a ellos, deben determinar qué es más importante. En ese caso, deben ser lo suficiente disciplinados para seguir adelante.

Por ejemplo, un amigo mío con frecuencia está tentado a comer más de la cuenta. Así que cuando ha comido cierta cantidad en un restaurante, toma su vaso de agua y lo derrama en el resto de la comida. Eso hace que la comida se vea lo suficientemente desagradable al punto de que él no quiere tocarla, mucho menos comerla. Es un truco simple, pero lo ayuda a desarrollar el patrón correcto de reacción y disciplina cuando se trata de comida.

De una manera similar, esfuérzate para enseñar a tus hijos cómo se pueden entrenar para enfocarse en los objetivos a largo plazo que son importantes para ellos.

Inhibidor #5: Desilusión sexual y estrés

La desilusión sexual dentro del matrimonio ocurre por varias razones. Puede ser que las dos personas no tengan una relación de amor mutuo, respeto y confianza, los fundamentos de una relación sexual.

También puede ser que la presión del estrés financiero es tan grande que le roba al matrimonio la espontaneidad y la alegría. Debido a que la mujer necesita sentirse segura (y puede ser que resienta a su marido profundamente si él no provee esa seguridad financiera) es posible que no responda a su marido en tiempos como esos. Aunque quizás no lo diga en voz alta, quizá perciba que él no la está protegiendo o proveyendo para ella y sus hijos. Cuando ella está convencida que él provee para ella, que es bueno y que la ama, ella se mostrará más entusiasmada y sexualmente perceptiva hacia él.

Sin embargo, si las parejas no se dan cuenta de estas

respuestas innatas, pueden llegar a estar muy enojados por la falta de sexo en el matrimonio.

Si tus hijos se casan y descubren que el sexo no es tan gratificante como a ellos les gustaría que fuera, es posible que sea necesario mejorar otras cosas primero: su bondad hacia su cónyuge, mostrar respeto, consideración, su compromiso, su lealtad y fidelidad.

¿Cuál es la diferencia entre decepción y angustia? Angustia es cuando la situación sexual en el matrimonio de tus hijos se vuelve una crisis. Si tu hijos comparten alguna preocupación contigo, anima a ese hijo y a su cónyuge a buscar un consejero cristiano comprometido, quien les va a ayudar a trabajar juntos para solucionar el problema en lugar de empujarlos a que se separen y animarlos a que se vaya cada uno por su lado.

Inhibidor #6: Desilusión de la niñez

Esto es diferente para los varones que para las mujeres. Déjame explicar:

Muchos chicos crecen con lo que yo llamo «el síndrome del héroe». Ellos quieren ser el héroe de cada juego y en todos los eventos deportivos. Como resultado, descubren tarde en la vida que han puesto en peligro las cosas que realmente querían hacer y no son lo que querían ser. Se inclinan hacia logros de segunda o tercera categoría. Sienten frustración profunda, decepción y una tremenda ira. Se sienten perdedores porque no pudieron mantener esa imagen de héroe.

Con frecuencia las mujeres crecen con lo que yo llamo «complejo de Barbie». Ellas están muy embelesadas con la idea de glamour y cuando llegan a la adultez, se dan cuenta que nunca van a igualar la idea poco realista de la apariencia en la sociedad, especialmente cuando tienen esposo, hijos, hogar y un sinnúmero de responsabilidades que las agotan. Ya no son la Barbie en la que soñaban convertirse. Se resienten con quien ellas sienten que tiene la culpa de que se hayan convertido en alguien que no es como Barbie.

La verdad es que tus hijos tienen ahora la oportunidad de convertirse en verdaderos héroes y heroínas. Ellos pueden elegir llegar a ser verdaderos triunfadores, ignorando la falsa ilusión de heroísmo y del complejo de Barbie. Pueden convertirse en grandes hombres y mujeres que den a otros generosamente, que experimenten el éxito y que sean parte de una familia feliz y productiva.

Inhibidor #7: Fricción relacional

La escena es presentada una y otra vez en las escuelas en todo el país: tu hijo tiene un mejor amigo en quien confía. Le dice a ese amigo un secreto. El amigo lo traiciona y se lo dice a varios niños de la escuela. Tu hijo se siente avergonzado y enojado.

Este solamente es un ejemplo de la clase de fricción en la relación que tus hijos enfrentan cada día. Dicha fricción puede distraerlo del éxito. Necesita saber esto. En lugar de pelear o huir de dicha fricción, necesita tomarse un tiempo para enderezar esas relaciones. Necesita perdonar a la persona que lo lastimó—y además, tiene que pedir perdón a las personas a quienes hubiera lastimado.

Si los niños adoptan un patrón de conducta de huir de las relaciones con fricción, tanto ellos como otras personas involucradas, terminarán profundamente lastimadas a largo plazo. La fricción en la relación puede dar lugar a problemas en muchas otras áreas. ¿Por qué crees que muchos hombres y mujeres se vuelven alcohólicos? Con frecuencia es porque son infelices en la relación del hogar.

Fricción en la relación es una experiencia abrumadora en la vida. Un hombre que ha estado estudiando los matrimonios por varios años dice que él puede predecir con 97% de exactitud quién se va a divorciar. Una de las señales de divorcio que él da es cuando la fricción se vuelve común, cuando los insultos se convierten en algo que sucede todos los días. Es cuando uno o ambos cónyuges comienzan a sentirse degradados y el divorcio se convierte en la mayor probabilidad. La fricción con frecuencia ocurre debido al conflicto en la conversación.

Cuando tú estás resentido, haces comentarios sarcásticos y desagradables y a nadie le gusta que lo traten de esa manera. Así que no le permitas que tus hijos que te hablen de esa manera, ni a ti ni entre ellos. De otra manera, estás estableciendo un camino de relaciones con fricción que es probable que se extienda a sus vidas adultas.

Inhibidor #8: Distanciamiento relacional

Esta es diferente a la fricción, es el hecho de que la pareja está alejándose constantemente. Con frecuencia, es el resultado de una relación con fricción y uno o los dos cónyuges buscan logros en otras áreas para poder escapar de la relación. Los logros son algo que deberían disfrutar juntos como pareja, al punto que renueve su relación.

Enseña a tus hijos que las parejas que persiguen juntos un sueño son los que tienen más posibilidades de permanecer juntos. Si hacen algo juntos y se ayudan el uno al otro a tener éxito, entonces se complementan y se apoyan. En dichos casos, es absolutamente fenomenal lo que Dios puede hacer para bendecir tu matrimonio.

Inhibidor #9: Negligencia de los padres

En la sociedad de hoy, se daña a muchos niños porque sus padres aspiran a tener éxito, excluyéndolos a ellos. Estos niños se vuelven rebeldes y están enojados debido al descuido de parte de sus padres.

¿Qué tan importante es que nosotros como padres pasemos tiempo con nuestros niños? ¿Que hagamos a nuestros hijos parte de nuestra vida en lugar de que sean una distracción para nuestros logros?

Por lo tanto, juega pelota con tus hijos. Deja que martillen a tu lado. Permite a tu niño chiquito que lleve cosas de una habitación a otra contigo mientras estás reorganizando la casa.

Todos los niños quieren sentir que están haciendo algo importante y que están contribuyendo con la familia. Los niños son más felices cuando saben que son una parte vital de un equipo que escucha sus palabras y su corazón, que los entiende, y que trata de crear situaciones donde sus talentos pueden contribuir al sueño de la familia.

Sueña en grande, pero incluye a tus hijos en ese sueño. Toda la familia necesita sentir emoción por un propósito en común. Los niños necesitan saber que hay una razón por la cual existen, que Dios tenía un propósito específico en Su mente para ellos, incluso antes de que nacieran. El profeta Jeremías, en el Antiguo Testamento cita a Dios diciendo: «Antes que yo te formara en el seno materno, te conocí, y antes que nacieras, te consagré y te puse por profeta a las naciones» (Jeremías 1.5). Dios le dio a Jeremías un propósito y eso alimentó la pasión del profeta.

Tú puedes hacer lo mismo con tu familia. Pon atención al gran propósito de tu familia. Si lo encuentran juntos, va a transformar la vida de todos y la vida de tus hijos más adelante.

Inhibidor #10: Reacción inmadura a los agravios normales de la vida

La verdadera inmadurez es hacer algo porque en realidad no te das cuenta que estás cometiendo un error, pero la definición se ha mezclado en nuestra sociedad. Con frecuencia, decimos que las personas están actuando de forma inmadura cuando en realidad son inmaduras. Se comportan de manera testaruda y rebelde. Saben lo que están haciendo y aun así lo hacen. Esa no es inmadurez, es necedad.

Existen dos clases de errores: errores de la mente y errores del corazón. Si tus hijos comenten un error de la mente, pueden re-aprender. Otros pueden darles información y ayudar a desarrollar sus destrezas, pero solamente Dios puede corregir los errores del corazón, ya que eso se hace deliberadamente. Es un defecto en el carácter del niño. Finalmente, es rebelión contra Dios.

La vida siempre tiene sus altas y bajas. Dichas frustraciones son normales. Yo solía enojarme cuando las llantas de mi auto se desgastaban. ¿No es estúpido? Sí, pero aun así me enojaba. No quería gastar dinero para comprar llantas nuevas. Era yo quien decidía conducir mi auto por tantas millas y esas millas desgastaban las llantas de mi auto. Enojarme con las llantas era evidentemente una tontería, justamente como enojarse por tener que pagar impuestos es una tontería. Sucede cada año, así que mejor acéptalo y prepárate para hacerlo. ¿Por qué gastar tu preciosa y vital energía en ciertas cosas que de todos modos van a suceder?

Demasiadas personas están absortas por los problemas pequeños de la vida. Hacen sus «berrinches» compadeciéndose a sí mismos cuando tienen un problema con su auto o se enojan cuando alguien se les atraviesa en el tráfico.

Dichas reacciones desgastan tu cuerpo, tus emociones y te elevan la presión sanguínea y si respondes de esta manera a las tensiones normales de la vida, estás enseñado a tus hijos a reaccionar de la misma manera y eso desviará la energía que debe enfocarse a su verdadera búsqueda del éxito. Cada uno de nosotros tiene solamente cierta cantidad de energía y necesitamos usarla lo más astutamente posible.

Inhibidor #11: Definiciones erróneas del éxito

Muchas personas actúan como si para poder tener éxito en la vida tuvieran que dejar a sus familias en el polvo. Trabajan hasta tarde, no cenan con su familia, no asisten a los juegos de sus hijos y todo con la consigna de «ser exitosos», así no tendrán que trabajar de la misma forma más adelante. Sucede que dicha definición del éxito va a conducir a la persona a un fracaso personal y de relaciones.

Otros creen que para poder salir adelante tienen que engañar, mentir y confundir a las personas, pero tus hijos tienen que saber que Dios no bendice dichas acciones. ¿Por qué? Porque Dios nos llama a reflejar Su carácter en todas las áreas. Como resultado, mentir, engañar y otras acciones como esas, van a crear una culpabilidad que puede acompañarlos por el resto de sus vidas.

Inhibidor #12: Resentimiento

¿Alguna vez has pensado que no es justo que otros tengan más de lo que tú tienes?

Mientras que estaba en un salón haciéndome un corte de cabello, los empleados estaban viendo una novela en la televisión. Alcancé a echar un vistazo y vi que los personajes bellos ni siquiera trabajaban; solamente llegaban y recogían el dinero. Solo se ocupaban en sostener relaciones extravagantes. Incluso los anuncios estaban orientados a la belleza. No es de extrañar que las mujeres del salón comenzaron a hacer comentarios de lo injusta que es la vida y cómo ellas nunca conseguían lo que querían. Se rodeaban constantemente con mensajes de injusticia y resentimiento.

¿Qué clase de mensajes están absorbiendo tus hijos con lo que están viendo, escuchando, y leyendo?

Inhibidor #13: Crisis verdadera

Cuando viene una crisis verdadera—muerte, enfermedad, accidente automovilístico o bancarrota—tienes la obligación de enseñarles a tus hijos cómo lidiar con eso de manera honesta y apropiada. Recuérdales que no tienen que pelear solos. Pueden pedirle a Dios Su ayuda y que Su paz descienda sobre sus vidas. Acostúmbrate a que la oración sea un hábito durante tus propios tiempos de crisis y enséñales a tus hijos como trazar un mapa con un plan para manejar esas crisis reales.

Inhibidor #14: Agotamiento

El agotamiento no tiene que ser físico. También puede ser mental, espiritual, financiero o emocional. Muchos individuos están al borde del agotamiento todos los días. ¿Por qué? A veces es porque pelean batallas innecesarias. Se preocupan por cosas pequeñas. Algunos otros están pasando por un divorcio o tratando de poner su vida en orden en medio de los efectos del pecado.

En tiempos de agotamiento, recuerda volver a Dios, quien realmente te ama y se preocupa por tus necesidades.

Él quiere ayudarte. Yo sé esto personalmente, porque Dios ha cambiado mi vida. Él ha llevado a mi familia a través de muchas situaciones difíciles. Debido a que he elegido confiar en Jesucristo y aceptar Su muerte por mí en la cruz, tengo esperanza, incluso en los tiempos difíciles.

Dios quiere que también tú y tus hijos reconozcan Su mano en su vida. Si haces eso, no significa que Él va a hacer todo de la manera que tú piensas que se tiene que hacer. Él sigue siendo Dios y tiene su propósito final más allá de lo que nosotros remotamente podemos entender, pero todo lo que Él hace, está motivado por su amor por ti. Es por eso que Él envió a Su hijo a morir en la cruz por ti. Él te ama. ¿Te volverás a Él, te rendirás, le entregarás tu vida a Él?

Si anhelas pedirle a Jesús que entre en tu vida ¿Por qué no hacerlo ahora?

¿Por qué no animar a tus hijos a que lo hagan también?

Inhibidor #15: Percepción falsa del problema

Muchas personas tienen una falsa percepción de la «injusticia» de Dios. Ellos culpan a Dios por sus problemas y decepciones. Culpan a Dios por su divorcio y dicen que fue culpa de la otra persona, pero Dios no es quien causa estas cosas. Con frecuencia es la propia necedad de esa persona lo que arruina su vida. Es por eso que la única y verdadera respuesta es buscar conscientemente al único ser que puede ordenar tu vida nuevamente: el Dios de la Biblia. Según el Nuevo Testamento, Dios te ama. Él no está tratando de hacerte daño. Sin embargo, debido a que has actuado de una manera pecaminosa, es posible que estés cosechando las consecuencias negativas de tu pecado. Dios quiere entrar en el proceso y caminar a tu lado. ¿Abrirás tu corazón y le permitirás hacer eso?

Si comienzas una auténtica búsqueda de Dios para tus hijos, los encaminarás hacia una ruta segura de éxito para la vida.

¿Cómo sabes si tus hijos van a tener éxito? Existen diez indicadores de logros. Entre más fortifiquen estas cualidades, más es la probabilidad de que tengan éxito en la vida y la buena noticia es que tú les puedes enseñar a tus hijos a tener éxito con estas destrezas.

Diez predictores del éxito

¿Cómo sabes si tus hijos van a tener éxito? Existen diez indicadores de logros. Entre más exhiban tus hijos estas cualidades, más es la probabilidad de que tengan éxito en la vida. Y la buena noticia es que tú les puedes enseñar a tus hijos a tener éxito enseñándoles estas destrezas.

PREDICTOR #1: BUEN MANEJO DEL TIEMPO PARA OBTENER LOS RESULTADOS DESEADOS

Yo no conozco a nadie que haya logrado algo grande sin tener un buen manejo del tiempo. Esto no quiere decir que la vida de tus hijos tiene que ser excesivamente organizada y programar cada momento de día, pero ellos deben de saber cómo hacer malabares con el tiempo que tienen. Como lo dice el proverbio antiguo: «Todos tenemos la misma cantidad de tiempo en nuestra maleta. Algunos de nosotros simplemente somos capaces de meter más cosas que otros».

PREDICTOR #2: MANEJO DE DINERO PARA LOGRAR LIBERTAD

Eso significa que tus hijos controlan sus deudas. Si sus ingresos bajan, también sus gastos. Siempre que nosotros hemos estado financieramente apretados, yo he descubierto que solamente una parte del porqué fue la disminución de los ingresos, pero la otra parte fue porque no elegimos cambiar nuestros hábitos de consumo. Nosotros queríamos todo lo que deseábamos y al momento que lo deseábamos, así que pedimos dinero prestado para mantener nuestro nivel de gastos al mismo nivel en que lo hacíamos antes que nuestros ingresos disminuyeran. ¿El resultado? Terminamos con más presión financiera. Tristemente, tuvimos que atravesar ese ciclo más de una vez, antes de realmente aprender a disminuir nuestros gastos.

PREDICTOR #3: METAS CLARAS Y ORGANIZADAS

Quizás suena demasiado simple, pero para poder lograr algo, tus hijos tienen que saber hacia dónde están yendo.

PREDICTOR #4: DISCIPLINA

En primer lugar: un triunfador es puntual. Esto no significa que tu hijo va a ser un fracaso si llega tarde de vez en cuando, debido a una cuestión inevitable, pero llegar a tiempo, muestra que no solamente respetas el horario de otros, sino que también estás a cargo de tu propia vida.

En segundo lugar: un triunfador es confiable, da seguimiento a las cosas y cumple sus promesas. Confiabilidad es lo que los empleadores quieren de los empleados. Es lo que nosotros queremos de los políticos y líderes. Es lo que queremos de un marido y una mujer. Si él dice que me ama y que se va a casar conmigo ¿irá a cumplir? Ella dice que me va a ser fiel y que juntos vamos a construir un sueño y criar hijos. ¿En realidad quiere ella hacer eso?

PREDICTOR #5: ÉTICA DE TRABAJO BIEN ESTABLECIDO

Aunque mucha gente desearía que fuera de otra manera, nadie puede tener éxitos sin esfuerzo. Así que anima a tus hijos que traten de hacer lo mejor en cada tarea.

PREDICTOR #6: HABILIDAD EN EL TRATO PERSONAL

Tú puedes tener todas las metas, habilidades administrativas, disciplina y ética en el trabajo y aun así echar a perder tu vida. ¿Por qué? Tal vez porque no eres hábil en el trato con las personas. Si eres desagradable o insultas a otros, no vas a llegar muy lejos en la vida.

En los años cincuenta, los gerentes ejecutivos decían consistentemente que las destrezas de las personas no eran importantes. En lugar de eso, todo lo que tenías que hacer era decirle a la gente lo que tenía que hacer y esperar que lo hicieran. Si no lo hacían, los despedían. No parecía haber mucha sensibilidad hacia los trabajadores en el ambiente corporativo. Un gerente de alto nivel escribió, en respuesta a un estudio, que era mejor no ser sensible hacia la gente porque entonces te comenzaban a gustar. Si sentías compasión, no podías ser tan duro con ellos si necesitabas serlo.

Mucho ha cambiado en el mundo de hoy. Hoy en día, la importancia de la habilidad del trato con las personas es reconocida y no significa que los líderes con dichas habilidades no existían en los tiempos antiguos. Tenemos, por ejemplo, a Dwight Eisenhower, cuya gran habilidad era crear una situación donde gente—incluso aquellos con egos diferentes—pudieran trabajar juntos. Su tremenda habilidad, planeación y ejecución de la invasión del Día D en Normandía marcó el inicio del fin de la Segunda Guerra Mundial. En esencia, su habilidad de tratar con la gente salvó al mundo. ¿Quién sabe lo que tu hijo podrá hacer si le enseñas dicha habilidad?

Predictor #7: Ambición

Esos que llegan a ser exitosos deben de tener un deseo para tener éxito; ellos deben de tener el anhelo de mejorar constantemente. Y deben de tener un hambre profunda para mejorar sus vidas y la de otros.

Predictor #8: Equilibrio emocional

En su investigación de las emociones, Peter Slovene dice que tú tienes que tener cinco cosas para tener éxito:

- Conocer tus emociones. Entiende tu propia reacción. Tienes que saber lo que te hace enojar. Tienes que saber lo que te pone triste.
- Maneja tus emociones. Si entiendes tus emociones, tú puedes estar preparado para atajarlas cuando pasen, por así decirlo.
- Motívate a ti mismo con tus emociones. En lugar de dejar que tus emociones te incapaciten, úsalas para animarte para hacer algo bueno por el mundo.
- Reconoce las emociones de otros. Sé sensible; escucha a otros y respeta lo que ellos están diciendo y haciendo.

- Maneja adecuadamente las emociones de otros. En otras palabras, si alguien te grita, no reacciones de la misma manera gritando a quien te gritó. En lugar de hacer eso, averigua el origen del problema, y presenta una solución creativa.

Si tú no puedes controlar tu temperamento, ciertamente vas a tener una vida desequilibrada. Vas a ceder a los sentimientos y tristeza y les vas a permitir que te agobien. Y eso ciertamente va a bloquear tu éxito. Para poder realmente ser un individuo exitoso, tienes que llevar a cabo algo aunque no te sientas bien. Tú debes de perseguir tu sueño, incluso cuando estás decepcionado. Y tú deberías de ser sensible a las emociones de otros a lo largo del camino.

Enséñale a tus hijos la importancia de actuar, en lugar de reaccionar, y los vas a poner en el asiento del conductor de la vida.

Predictor #9: Carácter ético y moral

Aunque parece que hay gente sin carácter ético y moral que tiene éxito, observa con atención. Es posible que ellos hayan acumulado algo de poder, riqueza o influencia, pero con frecuencia su vida privada está en ruinas. Viven con temor, distanciados de su propia familia y con frecuencia mueren en soledad y agonía en el alma. Esto ciertamente no es éxito.

Predictor #10: Una actitud verdaderamente positiva

Nada es más importante para el éxito que una actitud positiva. No puedo enfatizar esto lo suficiente. Esa es la razón por la cual tus hijos necesitan alimentarse en una perspectiva positiva. Deben de hacerse acompañar con aquellos que son optimistas. El viejo proverbio es verdad: «Dime con quién andas y te diré quién eres».

¿Con qué clase de gente quieres que tus hijos se junten? Si los ayudas a elegir a sus compañeros—y su actitud—sabiamente, incluso cuando son niños pequeños, les vas a inculcar un ejemplo de éxito para toda la vida.

CAPÍTULO 5

Convirtiéndose en una persona exitosa

Yo he tenido el gran privilegio de trabajar con cientos de hombres y mujeres que empezaron desde abajo y terminaron en la cima. Lo más asombroso para mí en cuanto a su avance y logros es que ellos sabían muy poco cuando comenzaron a construir su negocio.

Uno de mis mejores amigos es un gran ejemplo de estas personas asombrosas. Él estaba involucrado en drogas y apenas podía subsistir como pintor de casas.

En un momento crucial de su vida, un amigo le mostró una oportunidad personal de negocios. El sueño de un futuro nuevo lo capturó, mientras comenzó a buscar un cambio de vida. En muy pocos años, tenía una relación con Jesucristo, una familia sólida y un negocio próspero y en crecimiento. Todo esto porque él eligió seguir los principios correctos del éxito.

Todos los padres anhelan que su o sus hijos tengan éxito. Desde el momento que arrullas al bebé en tus brazos, estás planeando, soñando y esperando que muchas cosas buenas sucedan en el futuro del niño, pero ese niño, al igual que mi amigo, sabe muy poco acerca de cómo ser exitoso.

¿Cómo puedes ayudar a promover esos momentos

cruciales en la vida de tu hijo? ¿Cómo puedes ayudar a tu hijo a convertirse en una persona exitosa en crecimiento?

Ocho rasgos claves para un individuo exitoso

Cuando Gene Landrum, quien ha sido autor de libros excelentes como, *Perfilando genios* y *Poder y éxito,* estudió individuos que son asombrosos en sus logros, descubrió siete rasgos. Yo agregué el número ocho.

Característica #1: Impulso

En un automovil, el tren de trasmisión es lo que impulsa a un vehículo a ir hacia delante, le da impulso. De manera similar, el impulso le da al triunfador energía y poder. Las personas que tienen ese impulso no son frágiles, no los pueden lastimar o herir fácilmente. No los sacude la desaprobación de otros. Cuando son derribados, no se dan por vencidos. Se levantan, se sacuden el polvo y siguen adelante. Por lo tanto, enseña a tus hijos cómo desarrollar resistencia—cómo deshacerse de los obstáculos; como un tanque remueve los estorbos que encuentra en el camino. Esto no significa que vayas a acribillar a la gente en la guerra, porque la ternura sigue siendo una cualidad importante, sino que significa que tienes que ser una fuerza que no se puede detener fácilmente.

Característica #2: Carisma

En el idioma griego, la palabra *charis* significa «don» o «dones», esto no significa que toda la gente exitosa tiene personalidades complacientes o son físicamente atractivos. Pero todos tienen la habilidad de comunicarse bien con los demás. Ellos tienen la habilidad de compartir sus sueños muy bien y otros les escuchan y son inspirados. Así que ayuda a tu hijo a desarrollar buenas habilidades de comunicación y una personalidad encantadora.

Característica #3: Toma riesgos

Muchas personas llegan al final de su vida y piensan en

todas las cosas que hicieron o que pudieron haber hecho. Aclárale a tus hijos que ellos no pueden lograr nada sin hacer cambios y tomar riesgos. Ellos no tienen que vivir con arrepentimiento. A la larga es mejor arriesgarse que pasar el resto de la vida deseando haberlo hecho.

Yo he oído decir que hay tres tipos de personas en el mundo: los que se arriesgan, los que van tras el desafío; cuidadores, quienes simplemente quieren cuidar de las cosas, pero no amplían sus límites; y los enterradores, que quieren tomar los sueños de los otros dos y enterrarlos. ¿Cuál de estos tres tipos es tu hijo? ¿Cómo lo puedes animar a que sea una persona que tome riesgos?

Característica #4: Naturaleza renegada

Esto no quiere decir que las personas exitosas no son rebeldes (aunque a veces sí lo son). Lo que quiere decir es que ellas están dispuestas a hacer las cosas de una manera diferente, para cambiar las reglas. A ellas les gustan las sorpresas.

Característica #5: Tenacidad

La gente de éxito puede ensartar los dientes en cualquier situación y no soltar hasta que ganan. Ellos tienen la habilidad de permanecer en la situación, no importa lo difícil que sea. Ellos tienen fuerza de voluntad que no se dan por vencidos.

Característica #6: Visión

Tu hijo necesita un propósito—y metas organizadas..

Característica #7: Trabajar duro

Gene Landrum estudió que cada persona exitosa, (y eso incluye gente de un período de más de quinientos años) trabaja fuerte. Eso demuestra que si quieres hacer algo significativo con tu vida, no puedes ser haragán.

Característica #8: Adaptabilidad

La flexibilidad es vital para el éxito. Si tienes que hacer las cosas de cierta manera para estar cómodo donde éstas, tú siempre vas a batallar.

Por ejemplo, cuando una mujer me dijo que tenía que estar en la cama a las 10:00 en punto cada noche o no se podía adaptar, yo supe que ella estaba en problemas, especialmente porque la carrera que había elegido incluía reuniones por las noches. Al ponerse a sí misma una regla tan estricta, ella estaba arriesgando su éxito futuro. ¿Qué tan adaptables son sus hijos?

Cuatro habilidades de manejo de vida para tus hijos

Ahora que ya sabes cuales son las características de una persona exitosa, ¿cómo puedes incorporarlas en la vida de sus hijos? Tienes que fomentar estas cuatro habilidades básicas:

Habilidad #1: Sé positivo a la hora de manejar tu tiempo

Para hacer que esta habilidad sea fácil de recordar, yo uso las letras de la palabra POSITIVO.

P = Prioridades

Algunas cosas son más importantes que otras. Si tú no puedes tomar las tareas y priorizarlas en cierto orden, no estás manejando tu tiempo de manera efectiva. A menos que priorices, puedes pasar mucho tiempo llevando a cabo las cosas que no son tan importantes. En lugar de especializarte en hacer las cosas insignificantes, especialízate en hacer las cosas importantes.

0 = Ordenado

Esto quiere decir que tienes un plan ordenado para ejecutar tus ideas. Tú sigues un sistema. Por ejemplo, yo siempre llevo un cuaderno de notas y un bolígrafo para apuntar las cosas que debo de hacer y luego le doy seguimiento a mi lista.

S = Simplicidad

Es posible que tengas un buen plan de manejo de

tiempo, pero si es demasiado complicado, muy detallado, o demasiado engorroso, te vas a cansar mucho y muy pronto, y vas a parar de hacerlo. Simple es siempre mejor.

I = Iniciativa

El propósito del plan de manejo de tiempo es permitirte a ti mismo controlar tu vida en lugar de dejar que otros o circunstancias externas (o tiranía de urgencia) te controlen a ti.

T = Tanteo

A medida que manejas tu vida todos los días, algunas estrategias van a funcionar, otras no. Así que adelante, prueba diferentes estrategias, pero siéntete libre para cambiar lo que no funciona para ti.

I = Industriosos

El propósito de este manejo de tiempo, es ayudarte a llevar a cabo más cosas y que te sientas bien con lo que estás haciendo. Dios ha creado dentro de cada uno de nosotros un deseo para ser industriosos.

V = Valioso

Cuando trabajas duro, tú deseas que ese esfuerzo represente algo. Tú quieres que sea valioso, no simplemente pérdida de tiempo.

O = Optimizar

El objetivo final del manejo de tiempo es extender y optimizar tu vida, extender y optimizar tu dinero, extender y optimizar tu influencia, y extender y optimizar quien eres.

Habilidad #2: Aprender a administrar a las personas

Existen tres principios básicos para administrar a las personas:

- **Libertad** - En lugar de ser exigente y controlador, dale libertad a las personas para que sean quienes son. Incluso si éstas personas son parte de tu familia, tú no eres su dueño. Al tratar de dominar a otros, solamente logras que se alejen. Al darles libertad, tú estás mostrando que respetas su identidad.

- **Flexibilidad** - Un libro humorístico que vi declaraba lo siguiente, «Los negocios serían grandiosos si no fuera por la gente». ¡Qué tan cierto es esto! Las personas son factores X – los elementos inesperados que cambian toda la ecuación porque ellos son impredecibles. Esa es la razón por la cual tienes que ser flexible, en lugar de ser rígido cuando trabajar con ellos.
- **Perdonar** - Hay veces que las personas te hacen algo malo o te insultan. Ellas te van a causar una gran dificultad. En esos momentos, uno tiente la tentación de decir, «bueno, te mereces todo lo que te pasa» y se volverse resentido y enojado. Pero la Biblia tiene una mejor manera. Efesios 4.26-27 dice (estoy parafraseando), «No dejes que el sol se ponga sobre tu ira porque si lo haces, le estás dando la oportunidad al mal para que cause estragos en tu vida». Si te permites a ti mismo continuar con la ira, contaminas tu espíritu con desechos tóxicos.

Sí, es posible que la gente te haya hecho cosas malas y terribles, pero si no los perdonas y sigues adelante con tu vida, te vas a convertir en un orgulloso propietario de tu prisión. Cuando perdonas, te convierte en una persona libre.

Algunas personas piensan equivocadamente que el perdón en un sentimiento. No, lo es. Es una decisión. Es algo que eliges deliberadamente para dar a otra persona — incluso cuando no se lo merece. Y lo puedes hacer. Porque Dios te ha perdonado a ti, tú puedes perdonar a otros. El Espíritu Santo dentro de ti te ayudará, dándote el poder de perdonar, incluso cuando crees que no es posible.

Habilidad #3: Adminístrate a ti mismo

Hay tres áreas personales que todos necesitan administrar:

- **Tu cuerpo** - Mi amigo Dexter Yager me dijo una vez, «El peor error que he cometido en mi vida descuidar los buenos principios de salud. Y he pagado el precio. Diez años atrás yo tuve un derrame cerebral que por poco me mata. Ahora yo sé que el ejercicio, descanso, manejo de estrés, tomar vitaminas, y comer comida saludable tiene sentido. Dichos hábitos me van a hacer bien a largo plazo.»
- **Tu mente** - Cuidadosamente controla las entradas de tu mente. Aliméntate con información positiva, conceptos piadosos, porque lo que echa raíces en tu mente eventualmente va a resultar en tu comportamiento.
- **Tu espíritu** - Sendas del espíritu son vital para una vida saludable.

Y como cristiano, yo creo con todo mi corazón que esas sendas solamente se pueden encontrar en la persona de Jesucristo. Yo no digo esto para ofenderte si no eres cristiano, sino porque es lo que yo he descubierto como una verdad en mi vida. Jesucristo realmente ha cambiado mi corazón y me ha dado un nuevo propósito para mi vida.

Habilidad #4: Administración del dinero

En el libro, *The Absolutes of Leadership*, Philip Crosby declara cuatro grandes cosas acerca del dinero:

- Es alimento, no medicina. En otras palabras, el propósito del dinero no es solamente levantar tu espíritu cuando estás desaminado. En lugar de eso, el propósito de éste es alimentar el propósito en tu vida, tus sueños, y tus logros.
- Es mejor saber cómo prevenir un problema, que saber cómo corregirlo. He dicho.
- Es sabio seguir la práctica de márgenes vitales. Para poder sentirse estable y seguro, tú tienes que tener suficiente dinero en el banco para no preocuparte; tienes que eliminar tu deuda.

- Se trata de sentido común. Así que úsalo. Nunca te metas en deudas que no puedas controlar; nunca gastes más dinero del que ganas.

Lo no-negociable del éxito y cómo reforzarlo

¿Cuáles son los no-negociables del éxito de tu hijo? Existen cuatro que tienes que inculcar en tus hijos:

No-negociable #1: Creer que vas a ganar

Mientras estaba leyendo una fascinante historia de grandes líderes militares, políticos y de negocio, yo descubrí algo que todos ellos tienen en común: su creencia personal de éxito. Debido a que ellos creen fuertemente, esa creencia positiva se convirtió en parte de su éxito. Napoleón fue solamente uno de dichos ejemplos.

No-negociable #2: Ser optimista

Nada puede tomar el lugar del optimismo. Una investigación de Seguros de Vida Metropolitano reveló que algunos de los individuos que pasaron el riguroso examen de la compañía de empleo tenían actitud negativa. Y una vez que habían sido empleados, ellos no tuvieron buen desempeño. Así que Metropolitan concluyó que, entre más optimista eres, mejor desempeño vas a tener. Pero pruebas adicionales los sorprendieron más adelante. Ellos decidieron ver qué podían hacer con los individuos con buena actitud que habían fallado el examen de entrada de la compañía. Cuando estos individuos fueron contratados, ellos superaron a todos los demás.

No-negociable #3: Perseguir una visión específica

Para poder tener éxito, tienes que tener—y perseguir un sueño en particular.

No-negociable #4: Aprender el valor de trabajar duro

Cuando quieres ver que algo suceda—que se cumpla tu sueño—vas a trabajar incansablemente. Tú no vas a descansar hasta ver más de ese sueño hecho realidad.

¿Cómo puedes animar a tus hijos a hacer estos «no-negociables» parte de su vida diaria? Si usas el recordatorio en tu propia vida, es más probable que tus hijos también los usen.

Recordatorio #1: Mantén una lista con un día de ventaja
Eso simplemente significa que escribes hoy lo que tienes que hacer mañana. Luego dale seguimiento al plan. No tiene que ser complicado; simplemente una lista escrita con garabatos.

Recordatorio #2: Elige tu actitud cada mañana
Tú eres el único encargado de tu actitud. Cada mañana cuando te levantas, tú tienes el poder de elegir si vas a ser positivo o negativo. Si eliges una actitud vibrante y llena de expectativas, va a ser una diferencia fenomenal en tu día (y también va a afectar a quienes que están a tu alrededor). Así que comienza tu día bien. Lee un libro positivo, toma un paseo calmadamente, ora, estudia la Biblia.

Recordatorio #3: Trágate la medicina mala primero
¿Alguna vez has pospuesto porque no te gustaba una tarea en particular? Quizás alguna llamada telefónica que tienes que hacer, o una factura que tienes que pagar. A esas cosas que odias hacer, yo les llamo «medicina mala». Tú la necesitas, pero no te gusta su sabor. Posponer la tarea solamente hace que parezca más larga. Así que haz tu «medicina mala» primero; y entonces el resto del día te vas a sentir recompensada.

Recordatorio #4: No juegues juegos con tus juegos ¿Tú sabes que eres más vulnerable cuando estás relajado? El sentido del humor especialmente, te ayuda a bajar la guardia. Te hace que rías de cosas que son trágicas y equivocadas, tales como la homosexualidad (algo que condena la Biblia). Es por eso que la recreación puede ser peligrosa. Date cuenta que cualquier tipo de recreación en la que estás involucrado, a la larga afecta tu estado mental y emocional. Así que aunque estés siendo entretenido, recuerda mantener la guardia en alto. Películas que hacen una broma del adulterio no son divertidas. El adulterio va arruinar tu vida, la vida de tu cónyuge y la vida de tus hijos.

Recordatorio #5: Coloniza correctamente tu mundo privado todos los días

¿Sabes que dentro del cerebro hay pequeños químicos y conectores eléctricos llamados sinapsis, y ellos «encienden» mensajes en tu cerebro? Si eres positivo y lees material positivo, tus sinapsis dispara respuestas positivas en tu cerebro. Si te rodeas con imágenes negativas, respuestas negativas son enviadas a tu cerebro. Así que ¿cómo quieres que sea impreso tu cerebro?

Por eso es tan importante llenar, incluso tus fantasías y tus sueños, con imágenes positivas. Como lo dijo una vez Dennis Kinlaw, profesor y ex presidente de Asbury College, «Ten cuidado como colonizas tu mundo privado, porque va a vivir contigo toda tu vida».

Si tus hijos siguen estos hábitos, si ellos operan con optimismo en lugar de elegir una perspectiva limitada, dudosa y de temor—ellos van a tener una vida fantástica, una vida mucho más emocionante de lo que se hayan imaginado. Y la mejor manera para empezar, es persiguiendo una relación con Dios, quien los hizo a Su semejanza. Lo que tus hijos creen acerca de sí mismos, de otros, y del mundo, va a impactar la manera en que vivan su vida.

Así que lo que yo quiero que hagas ahora mismo es creer algo de tus hijos. Cree que ellos van a ganar. Cree en que sus malos hábitos van a ser reemplazados con buenos hábitos. Cree que ellos van a tener una buena salud, mental, emocional y espiritual. Cree que ellos van a hacer cosas grandiosas. ¡Luego ve y ayúdales lograr hacer justamente eso!

CAPÍTULO 6

Entendiendo el comportamiento de tu hijo

Años atrás, recibí una llamada que se trataba de una oportunidad de negocios. No es la oportunidad en la que me involucré subsecuentemente, sino la manera en la que manejé la llamada me desconcertó en aquel momento. Aunque quien me llamó era cortés y no había levantado ninguna controversia, fue asombroso lo que sucedió cuando yo colgué el teléfono. De repente una furia volcánica me arrastró y yo agarré el teléfono y comencé a maltratarlo. Lo golpeé contra la pared, luché y lo llevé hasta el otro lado de la habitación y luego lo golpeé contra la mesa, luego contra el piso por aproximadamente dos minutos. Mientras yacía ahí en el agotamiento, el teléfono comenzó a sonar, mostrando que estaba descolgado. Y me pregunté, ¿qué fregados está pasando? ¿Por qué me comporté de esta manera después de dicha conversación telefónica? Normalmente yo no peleo con objetos inanimados.

Mientras que pensaba detenidamente y por medio de la oración examinaba el incidente, más tarde ese mismo día llegué a una conclusión: yo recibí la llamada durante un período en mi vida cuando estaba bajo una intensa tensión financiera. Estaba batallando para pagar por mi casa y mis autos y mi ingreso era limitado. Había acumulado mucha deuda. La presión era tan grande que incluso me despertaba durante la noche gimiendo y enfermo porque me había ido a la cama con temor de lo que mis finanzas iban a producir. Esta persona, de repente, sin saberlo, me había hecho un recordatorio gigante de la situación que yo mismo había creado. Mi reacción fue sacar toda mi frustración y hostilidad en el teléfono.

De manera difícil, descubrí que los factores escondidos influencian nuestro comportamiento y tus hijos también pueden caer presa de factores de estrés escondidos. Si de repente te preguntas si tu hijo se está transformando en un extraterrestre debido a su comportamiento sorprendente, existe ayuda. Juntos echemos un vistazo a la raíz del comportamiento humano.

Dos maneras de ver a las personas

Aunque han muchos puntos de vista de la humanidad, yo quiero abordar dos que son de vital diferencia que te van a afectar a ti y a tus hijos fuertemente: el punto de vista humanístico y el punto de vista cristiano.

Vista #1: Punto de vista humanístico (centrado en lo humano, no en Dios)

Existen cinco elementos básicos en el punto de vista humanístico:

- La gente es moralmente neutral. En otras palabras, ellas son como un nacimiento de borrón y cuenta nueva. Ellos son ni malos ni buenos, son moralmente vacíos.
- La vida es esencial y espiritualmente sin sentido. No existe una verdadera experiencia espiritual. Es algo producido a través de diferentes ideas, pensamientos, hormonas, reacciones y emociones, pero no existe una dimensión espiritual. No hay vida más allá de la existencia de esa persona en la tierra.

- La gente es ambientalmente controlada y producida. Tú eres esencialmente producto de tu ambiente social, psicológico, y familiar, así como también la combinación de respuestas y reacciones de esos ambientes. No existen elementos o factores que influyan más allá de tu ambiente. No hay Dios. Tú no tienes alma o espíritu. Tú solamente tienes tu existencia biológica.
- La gente es capaz de mejorar ilimitadamente por medio de la educación y el entrenamiento. Básicamente esto niega el concepto de pecado. ¿Por qué? Porque si no hay factor que influya en nosotros más allá de quienes y cómo somos es esta existencia actual, entonces obviamente la educación y el entrenamiento son nuestra única esperanza. La gran vergüenza de humanistas tradicionales en el siglo veinte ha sido su dificultad para explicar las guerras mundiales; Hitler, Mussolini, y Stalin; el genocidio de masas en Vietnam, Cambodia y Laos, y las tasas de criminalidad en nuestras ciudades. ¿Por qué? Porque tales eventos no se ajustan al punto de vista de la naturaleza humana—que los humanos están continuamente mejorando. Alemania, una vez la más ilustrada y educada nación en el mundo, fue instrumento para producir dos de guerras mundiales catastróficas y un salvajismo increíble con el holocausto judío.
- La gente no es nada más que animales avanzados. Esta declaración es basada en las teorías de la evolución, conocidas como Darwinismo. Justifica cualquier clase de comportamiento humano que podría violar las leyes reveladas por el Dios altísimo en a Biblia. ¿Por qué? Porque nosotros somos justamente parte del reino animal, un aborto realmente no importa. Si eliges vivir una vida homosexual, ¿qué importa? Existen cinco teorías básicas de la evolución. A la que más

atribuyen los humanistas es la teoría mecanicista, la generación accidental de la vida humana. Pero yo personalmente estoy convencido que se necesita más fe para creer en esa vida y toda su complejidad «simplemente sucedió» que creer que Dios nos hizo, porque hay muchas preguntas sin contestar en la teoría mecanicista. Más y más científicos también están expresando su escepticismo serio en estas teorías de la evolución porque existen grandes diferencias en estas teorías. No existe prueba científica concluyente de la teoría de la evolución, y aun así, las escuelas públicas la enseñan como una verdad. Es por eso que si encuentras un maestro que enseñe eso, tú deberías de desafiarlo firmemente a él o ella a para que por lo menos diga que es una teoría que no se ha probado.

VISTA #2: PUNTO DE VISTA CRISTIANO

El punto de vista cristiano de la humanidad se encuentra en los primeros tres capítulos de Génesis. En realidad explica que pasó a toda la raza humana después de que Dios la creó. En el Jardín del Edén, el primer hombre y la primero mujer le hicieron caso a la seducción de la serpiente. Satanás los engañó haciéndoles pensar que ellos podían ser como Dios. Y la humanidad ha estado en rebelión desde entonces. Es por eso que necesitamos un Mesías—un Salvador, Jesucristo—que viniera y nos rescatara de un dilema espiritual.

Existen cuatro elementos en este punto de vista cristiano sobre los humanos:

- Somos una creación agrietada. Somos creados por Dios, pero existe una grieta en esa creación debido a la rebelión pecaminosa. Aunque seguimos siendo Creación de Dios, la protección de la mano de Dios, la cual estaba en Adán y Eva en el jardín, ha sido removida.

- Nosotros fuimos hechos a la imagen de Dios, pero somos una imagen defectuosa. Eso quiere decir que si cada niño es hecho a la imagen de Dios, nosotros debemos de echarle otro vistazo al aborto. Una vez que un niño es concebido, ese niño es conocido por Dios, y tiene alma eterna según Salmo 139.13-16. Dios está presente en el cuerpo de la madre en el momento de la concepción. Salmo 139.16 dice: «Tus ojos vieron mi embrión y en Tu libro se escribieron todos los días que me fueron dados, cuando no existían ni uno solo de ellos». Sin embargo, debido a que somos criaturas pecaminosas, somos egoístas y capaces de hacer mucho mal.
- Nosotros merecemos el amor de Dios. 1 de Pedro 1.18-19 dice: «Sabiendo que no fuisteis redimidos de nuestra manera de vivir heredada de vuestros padres con cosas perecederas como el oro y la plata, sino con sangre preciosa, como la de un cordero sin tacha y sin mancha, la sangre de Cristo». Esto quiere decir que somos inmensamente valorados por Dios. No hay manera de calcular lo que valemos para Él, porque Él te ama lo suficiente como para mandar a Su Hijo para salvarte. Dios te ama como si fueras la única persona en la tierra.
- Nosotros somos dignos de recuperación. Debido a que Dios nos ama mucho y considera que somos valiosos, Él ha provisto una manera para «recuperarnos». 2 de Corintios 5.17 dice que esto pasa cuando te adentras en tener una relación personal con Jesucristo (ve también el capítulo 3 de Juan, donde a esto se le llama «nacer de nuevo»). Tú te conviertes en una nueva creación en Jesucristo. Todas las cosas viejas pasaron y todas son hechas nuevas. Él te da un nuevo corazón, haciéndote más como Él.

Si tú no aceptas el sacrificio de Cristo por ti, la parte espiritual tuya se queda muerta (ve Efesios 2). En caso que pienses que te puedes salvar tú mismo, Gálatas te lo aclara. Nadie puede ser justificado por medio de las obras o la religión. Solamente Jesús puede curar esa grieta en tu alma—por medio de Su muerte en la cruz.

Entender los cuatro elementos del punto de vista cristiano es tremendamente importante para ayudar a formar el comportamiento de tu hijo. Porque cada uno de nosotros es nacido de «creación pecaminosa», tu hijo va a ser afectado por las siguientes dinámicas.

Las claves del comportamiento de tu hijo

¿Te preguntas porqué tu hijo hace lo que hace? ¿Algunas veces te sorprende su comportamiento?

Para poder entender por qué tu hijo responde de la manera como lo hace, tienes que estar consciente de estas nueve claves del comportamiento humano:

Clave #1: Egocentrismo

Mucho de lo que hacen tus hijos es motivado por su propio egoísmo—se enfocan en sus propios deseos y excluyen los deseos de los demás (incluyendo los de Dios). Ser orientado a sí mismo no siempre es malo.

Quizás tengas interés propio en cosas que sientes que Dios quiere que hagas y eso no es necesariamente malo, siempre y cuando no comprometas los propósitos de Dios debido a lo que tú quieres. Sin embargo, el egoísmo es una determinación de hacer las cosas a tu manera, no importando nada más, incluso si eso conlleva usar a los demás en el camino.

Clave #2: Necesidades no satisfechas

Con frecuencia la gente reacciona de cierta manera debido a una necesidad en su vida que no ha sido satisfecha. Quizás un niño se aferra a su madre, o hace alguna rabieta porque su necesidad de amor no ha sido satisfecha. Un muchacho adolescente quizá comience a beber alcohol para olvidar sus problemas en casa. Las necesidades no satisfechas, a menos que trates con ellas, van a perseguir a tu hijo día y noche.

Clave #3: Símbolos de éxito

¿Por qué crees que los niños actúan de cierta manera? Porque con frecuencia se les muestra que el éxito está conectado con cierta imagen. Por ejemplo, yo recuerdo el banquero de mi pueblo, que era muy exitoso, rico, cortés, generoso y amable con los niños. Todos nosotros lo queríamos y queríamos emular su modelo. Lo más gracioso es que él vivía en una casa blanca grande con un gran porche frontal y ahora yo vivo en una casa así, aunque no es tan grande, ese hombre fue mi símbolo de éxito cuando yo era pequeño.

Pero el mismo principio funciona en lo negativo. Los niños quizás conecten el fracaso con cierta imagen y por lo tanto saquen esa persona de su vida con disgusto, incluso si esa persona en particular nunca les ha hecho nada. Quizá ellos no puedan entender esa reacción automática que viene de su interior, pero sin embargo está ahí.

Clave #4: Motivado por compañeros

El comportamiento de tus hijos tiene presión externa. Hay cosas que tú y otros esperan que un niño haga y su comportamiento es motivado a responder a esas presiones.

Cuando yo era pequeño, quería formar parte del club de niños de la calle donde vivía. Dos de mis amigos fueron conmigo, todos fuimos y preguntamos que si podíamos ser parte del grupo. ¡Pero otros niños se mofaron de nosotros y nos dijeron que nos desapareciéramos! Yo estaba herido, pero mis amigos estaban enojados. Después de mucho hablar, los otros dos chicos me convencieron a que los ayudara a destruir la casa club durante la noche. Mi padre y mi madre siempre me dijeron que respetara la propiedad, especialmente la de otra persona. Aunque yo sabía que esta era regla inflexible, ayudé destruir la mayor parte de la casa club esa noche. El siguiente día mi culpabilidad era masiva. A mí nunca se me ha olvidado la habilidad de otros niños para influenciar a un niño a hacer el bien o el mal. Motivación externa, especialmente por los compañeros, es una fuerza poderosa en la vida de los niños.

Clave #5: Culpabilidad y vergüenza

Muchas personas asumen que la culpabilidad y la vergüenza son la misma cosa, pero no es así. Tú te puedes sentir culpable por alguna cosa y decides hacerla nuevamente (por ejemplo, tener sexo con diferentes personas). Pero la vergüenza es diferente, ésta implica responsabilidad. Tú realmente te sientes mal por haber hecho algo y no quieres que vuelva a suceder.

Sentir vergüenza (si es el resultado de haber hecho algo malo, no falsa vergüenza, como muchos niños que han sido abusados sexualmente se siente) en realidad puede ser algo positivo. Puede motivar a tus hijos a cambiar. La culpabilidad también es buena cuando ayuda a alguien a dejar de hacer algo malo. Es un regalo de Dios para mostrarte lo importante que eres para Él y que estás yendo más allá de los límites de lo que Él tiene para ti. Esa es la verdadera culpabilidad legítima.

Pero también existe la culpabilidad falsa. Quizá la gente se condena a sí misma por años por algo que hicieron o algo que ellos hicieron y que ya pasó y tuvo su fin. Muchos cristianos viven en la realidad del perdón de Jesucristo, pero se siguen condenando por cosas que ocurrieron en el pasado. Una persona me dijo: «Yo sé que Dios me ha perdonado, pero yo no me he perdonado». Si tú crees esto, lo que en realidad estás diciendo es: el perdón de Dios no es suficiente, así que me voy a castigar a mí mismo por un tiempo o yo sé que tus intenciones son buenas, Dios, pero tú no entiendes que lo que hice fue muy malo. Esa clase de pensamiento se mofa del sacrificio que Cristo hizo por nosotros en la cruz para limpiarnos de todo pecado.

Enseña a tus hijos la diferencia entre la verdadera

culpabilidad y la falsa culpabilidad y asegúrate que ellos estén conscientes que el perdón de Dios no se gana. Es un regalo.

Clave #6: Venganza

Si está ocurriendo algo malo en la vida de tu hijo, tal vez esté siendo abusado en la escuela y va a liberar sus frustraciones en otras áreas. Quizás va a provocar una pelea con su hermano o va a comenzar a gritar por alguna declaración insignificante o va a arrancar la cabeza de la muñeca de su hermana. Date cuenta que un problema en un área se puede manifestar en otra. Psicológicamente, tu hijo tiene la necesidad de «venganza» por las cosas malas que se le han hecho a él o por algún tipo estrés que siente.

Sin embargo, eso no significa que tu hijo tenga que mostrar sus frustraciones de esa manera. Enseña a tu hijo cómo lidiar con los problemas de manera constructiva en lugar de actuar ciegamente con venganza.

Clave #7: Asociaciones negativas

Este es un temor de que eres en realidad como alguien a quien no te quieres parecer, así que evitas a esa persona, condenándola, enojándote con ella. ¿Por qué? Porque ves rasgos en esa persona que te recuerdan a ti mismo y temes que haya algo negativo en ti también. Esto sucede a menudo en los años de la adolescencia y se convierte en algo obviamente doloroso para los niños que se sienten fuera del círculo «interno».

Clave #8: trampas en cuanto a rendimiento

Los niños con frecuencia sienten la tensión de tratar de vivir a la altura de las expectativas de sus padres, maestros y compañeros. Con frecuencia caen en la trampa de rendimiento solamente para hacer felices a sus padres.

Clave #9: Malas influencias

Cuando tus hijos tienen contacto con otros niños que son mala influencia, no es de extrañar que tus hijos también se vayan a meter en problemas. En situaciones de consejería, muchas veces les he dicho a los padres que la clave para ayudar a su joven hijo, que está en una situación crítica, es sacar al muchacho del ambiente en el que se encuentra en esos momentos, lejos de su red social y atraerlo hacia influencias positivas y constructivas. Como lo dice Proverbios 27.17: «El hierro con hierro se afila y un hombre aguza a otro». Eso quiere decir que tus hijos son «aguzados» por las personas con quienes se relacionan, por las películas que ven, por las revistas que leen para bien o para mal.

Manejo del comportamiento de tus hijos

Aunque al final de cuentas cada niño es responsable por su propio comportamiento, hay cosas que quizá tu hijo hace que le impiden ser lo mejor que puede ser. Yo llamo a éstos «destructores del comportamiento».

Destructores del comportamiento

Destructor #1: El que habita en la bodega

Hay un consenso entre los profesionales de la salud y pastores de que cuando deliberadamente te aíslas, creas un sentido de soledad y oscuridad. En muchas maneras nuestra cultura es una cultura de aislamiento—nuestros hijos llegan de la escuela a la casa y se aíslan viendo televisión y jugando juegos en la computadora. Lo que tienen que hacer es involucrarse con otras personas. Claro, habrá momentos cuando se cansen de las personas y necesiten estar solos, pero Dios nos hizo para que estuviéramos asociados. Por lo tanto, anima a tus hijos a pasar tiempo con otros—incluso cuando se sientan incómodos, inseguros y con incertidumbre. Cuando ellos pasan tiempo con otros, van a salir del enfoque intenso en ellos mismos y van a comenzar a contribuir en la vida de otros.

Destructor #2: Dominación de culpabilidad

Demasiadas personas permiten que el remordimiento de las experiencias pasadas cuelgue como soga alrededor de su cuello. De lo que ellos no se dan cuenta es que debido al pecado que hay en el mundo, las cosas ocurren por razones lógicas. Un consejero cristiano cuenta una historia acerca de un cliente que fue víctima de abuso sexual cuando era niño por un miembro de su familia. Mientras le contaba la historia al consejero, él dijo: «Esto no debió haber pasado». «Oh, pero pasó», dijo el consejero. «Tú me has dado una descripción detallada de este miembro enfermo y disfuncional de tu familia. Debido a que estabas solo con él y que él era un pervertido sexual, tiene sentido que eso haya sucedido. Es un resultado lógico de haber estado solo con él en la habitación, pero eso no quiere decir que lo que pasó es justo y no es tu culpa haber estado en la habitación». Cuando te das cuenta que lo que ha pasado «debió» haber pasado, te liberas del dominio de lamentaciones.

Destructor #3: Agenda egocentrista

Las personas que siguen una agenda de ego, son los tiburones de la vida buscando sangre en cada situación. Deliberadamente eligen dar una mordida a otros para lucir mejor y más grandes. Eligen ser feroces—engañar, maniobrar y manipular para sus propias agendas de ego.

Destructor #4: Compromisos compulsivos

A los niños se les debe decir que nunca se tienen que sentir atrapados para hacer esto o lo otro. Se trata de elegir. Por ejemplo, un consejero me contó de Alan y Sandra. Ellos se casaron porque Sandra había quedado embarazada y Alan se sintió atrapado. Él no quería que ella tuviera un aborto y deseaba ayudarla a criar al niño, así que se casó con ella. Tal como se lo dijo al consejero mucho después: «Todos estos años, he tenido que hacer las cosas de la misma manera como me casé». ¿La repuesta del consejero? Estás equivocado. Tienes que darte cuenta del poder de tu elección. No tenías que casarte con ella. Pudiste haber elegido el aborto—aunque es malo—o la adopción.

Sin embargo, no lo hiciste. Has tomado decisiones a lo largo del camino». Una vez que Alan se dio cuenta que las cosas que estaba haciendo no habían sido forzadas o inevitables, se dio cuenta de su responsabilidad personal y comenzó a trabajar en su matrimonio. Cuando dejó de jugar el papel de víctima, su matrimonio comenzó a mejorar y Alan comenzó a crecer.

Destructor #5: Trastornos adictivos

Gente con trastornos adictivos continúan diciendo: no puedo evitarlo, pero también son un producto de sus decisiones.

Mira Kermit Roosevelt, uno de los hijos de Theodore Roosevelt tuvo tremendas oportunidades de viajar con su padre a Brasil para explorar áreas que nadie más había cartografiado. Él fue un gran luchador en la Primera Guerra Mundial y se casó con una bella mujer llamada Belle, pero durante la mediana edad, se volvió un borracho que cometió adulterio. Desperdició su dinero, convirtió a su amante en beneficiaria de su póliza de seguro de vida y en consecuencia se convirtió en un escándalo de su generación. Se pasó la vida diciendo que no podía evitar sus trastornos adictivos. ¡Claro que no pudo! Él hizo la elección de que fuera de esa manera.

Destructor #6: La tiranía del perfeccionismo

A veces no existe una manera correcta de hacer algo. Es posible que sea solamente preferencia personal. Yo no estoy diciendo que tus hijos no deben buscar la excelencia, pero comprometerse a ser continuamente perfecto es imposible, desgasta a las personas, aleja a otros, destruye su deseo de tener una vida feliz y crea estrés a su alrededor. Las personas no son perfectas cuando parecen serlo. Una verdadera perfección, además de la de Nuestro Dios Todopoderoso, es imposible. Por lo tanto, enseña a tus hijos que está bien no ser perfecto (tú puedes modelar esto, no esperando perfección de parte de tus hijos). La vida sigue su curso y aún puede ser exitosa.

Destructor #7: Desarrollando o cediendo a los patrones de error

No es suficiente entender los errores. Tienes que parar de cometerlos. Los errores hacen varias cosas:

1.- Conducen a cometer otros errores. Una vez compré un auto que no podía costear. Afectó mi presupuesto y por esa razón me atrasé en el pago de mi casa, lo cual hizo que me atrasara en otras cosas. Eso me metió en problemas con todo los demás porque compré en auto equivocado, en el momento equivocado, simplemente porque yo quería un auto nuevo. Un error alimenta a otro.
2.- Los errores pueden causar que malinterpretes tus experiencias, juzgar mal a otros y malinterpretarte tú mismo.
3.- Con frecuencia los errores de otros te hacen enojar porque te hacen recordar tus propios errores.

¿Cómo pueden tus hijos lidiar con errores de manera apropiada?

1.- Enfocándose en el futuro. Cuando tu hijo siente que «la regó», anímalo para que la siguiente vez lo piense bien. ¿Qué haría diferente la próxima vez para no sentirse de esa manera?
2.- Aprendiendo de ellos. Enséñale a tu hijo que él puede aprender de sus errores—es educación en proceso.
3.- Manteniendo el sentido del humor. Si aprendes a ver el humor en los errores de tus hijos, ellos también van a aprender a reírse de ellos.

El Dr. Arthur Freeman usa el enfoque IDEA para vencer sus errores:

I = Identificar el error
D = Definir el error
E = Evaluar y seleccionar la manera de proceder
A = Actuar. Aprender de los errores y seguir adelante

Destructor #8: Reacción desproporcionada

Esto quiere decir que tú puedes actuar totalmente fuera de proporción en cierta situación creando una reacción. Por ejemplo, digamos que dos niños están jugando afuera, cuando uno alcanza un juguete, el otro grita de rabia, le arrebata el juguete y empuja al otro con fuerza frotándole la nariz en el suelo. Al inicio quizás estés impresionado por la reacción del segundo niño, pero en situaciones como esas, usualmente existe otro factor (o varios) influyendo fuertemente la reacción del atacante. Tu papel es enseñar a tu hijo a que aprenda a batallar con dichas reacciones desproporcionadas y cómo adaptarse a patrones saludables. Enséñale a tu hijo a pensar, ¿Vale la pera reaccionar de esa manera a la ofensa antes de actuar?

Destructor #9: Ignorar factores de vulnerabilidad

Hay momentos cuando estás más vulnerable al pecado, a los errores y al mal juicio, especialmente cuando estás cansado y con mucha tensión nerviosa.

Ayuda a tus hijos—especialmente adolescentes y jóvenes adultos—a prender cómo mantener el ritmo de vida y poner atención a los factores de vulnerabilidad. Los Alcohólicos Anónimos usan el sistema de alerta HASC.

H = Hambriento
A = Airado
S = Solitario
C = Cansado

Enséñale estos síntomas a tus hijos, por su propio bien.

Destructor #10: Acumulación de estrés

Cada uno tiene límites diferentes de estrés. Los psicólogos usualmente evalúan el límite de estrés en una escala numérica del uno a cien. Lo que eso significa es que tú puedes manejar todo tipo de estrés de manera exitosa hasta que pasas tu límite de estrés. Ya que lo niños no están conscientes de su propio límite de estrés hasta que ataca, es importante que estudies a tus hijos. Averigua dónde está el límite de estrés de tus hijos y luego estudia cuidadosamente algunas maneras en que puedes proteger a tu hijo durante los momentos de estrés. Al hacer esto, ayudas a ese niño a adoptar patrones saludables para cuando sea adulto.

Destructor #11: Críticos inventados

Hay suficiente crítica a tu alrededor sin que tú crees la propia. Aquellos que caen en esta trampa usan mucho la palabra «todos» «Todos piensan que debiste haber hecho esto...». Enseña a tu hijo a que escuche solamente a la gente en quien confía, gente que tienen las mejores intenciones en su corazón, que vive de la manera que quiere vivir y que son firmes bíblica y espiritualmente.

Destructor #12: Repeticiones putrefactas

Todos tenemos una máquina mental que graba y en la que repetimos escenas negativas de nuestro pasado, pero si repites constantemente momentos desastrosos, nunca vas a poder escapar de ellos. Tienes que apagar la máquina, sacar el CD y comenzar a repetir los éxitos, las cosas buenas del pasado. ¿Están tus hijos adictos a su propia miseria? ¿Les encanta sufrir? ¿Te sientes culpable pensando que ellos tienen que sufrir constantemente por algo malo que hicieron? Enséñales el principio de ser perdonado y de dejar pasar las cosas.

Destructor #13: Parejas miserables

Cuando encuentras gente que es miserable y te apegas a ellos, suceden dos cosas: te adaptas a lo negativo de la otra persona y adoptas lo negativo de la otra persona. ¿Qué sucede? A la miseria le encanta la compañía.

Destructor #14: Conexión excesiva con otros

Esto sucede cuando llegas a ser tan comprensivo con otros que tu propia vida se convierte en un estrés emocional. Tus hijos necesitan desarrollar una empatía sana, juntamente con una distancia independiente o nunca van a poder asistir a otros. Van a estar continuamente agotados y arruinados.

Destructor #15: Mensajes codificados

En lugar de ser honesto con otros, algunas personas les dan mensajes en forma de códigos, como el niño que le da una bofetada a su madre solamente porque está cansado o un adolescente abrumado por la vida que se encierra en la habitación y rehúsa salir porque piensa que a nadie le importa lo suficiente como para escuchar, como resultado, se aleja más y más de su familia. Enseña a tus hijos a evaluar sus sentimientos y emociones para que ellos lo puedan verbalizar en lugar de dar mensajes en forma de código. Diles a tus hijos que si expresan sus sentimientos verbalmente, tú prometes escuchar. Cumple esta promesa.

Destructor #16: Personalización

Si la maestra le dijo a los compañeros de clase de tu hijo que algunos de ellos no habían estudiado y tu hijo pensó con pánico, ella está apuntado su dedo hacia mí, aunque yo si estudié, eso es tomar las cosas de manera personal. Personalizar significa que tú distorsionas el significado del momento. Tú le aumentaste a las cosas y las hiciste más grandes de lo que son. Tú asumes que si caminas por el pasillo y todos dejan de hablar, están hablando de ti. La personalización tiene raíces en inseguridades internas y puede ser una influencia mortal en la vida de tus hijos. Puede mantener a tu hijo atrapado en un ensimismamiento que va a dañar sus relaciones adultas.

Destructor #17: Hambre de simpatía

Algunas personas son tan dependientes de la aprobación de otros que parece que nunca desarrollan una personalidad saludable por su propia cuenta. Están demasiado ocupados tratando de que tú sientas pena por ellos. Siempre están tratando de lidiar con cierta clase de dolencia, una vida muy ocupada y llena de estrés o un acontecimiento catastrófico que haga su mundo rotar. Lo que dichas personas están realmente diciendo es: por favor mírame. Es importante que tus hijos sepan que no le van a caer bien a todos y que no tienen que depender de la aprobación de los demás.

Los constructores del comportamiento

Por lo tanto, ¿cómo puedes construir un comportamiento positivo en tus hijos? Enséñales estos diez constructores del comportamiento:

Constructor #1: Sé amigo de la realidad

Hazte amigo de los hechos. La vida es difícil a veces. Así que, en vez de pelear contra ella, acéptala y siga adelante. Esta es la base para una buena salud mental.

Constructor #2: Elige tu reacción

Enseña a tus hijos que las reacciones no son automáticas; se pueden controlar. Si tus hijos eligen actuar en lugar de reaccionar negativamente, van a estar en el asiendo del piloto de la vida.

Constructor #3: Desarrolla mentores mentales

Cuéntales a tus hijos acerca de personas que han modelado rasgos nobles y admirables, tales como Abraham Lincoln, un ejemplo de humildad, visión y sensibilidad o cuéntales acerca de Winston Churchill, un ejemplo de valor o Harry Truman, un ejemplo de firmeza o el apóstol Pablo, un ejemplo de pasión-al-rojo-vivo por el Señor Jesucristo. Háblales de la Madre Teresa, un ejemplo de servicio desinteresado o Billy Graham, un ejemplo de integridad o Ruth, un ejemplo de lealtad. Existen personas que se han vuelto representantes de ciertas cosas para mí. Cuando necesito inspiración para actuar de una manera noble, me obligo a mí mismo a pensar en estas personas. Ellos son mis mentores mentales.

Constructor #4: Sé motivado por las posibilidades

Enséñales a tus hijos que ellos tienen grandes razones para motivarse por la posibilidad. Ser positivo simplemente significa ser radiante, optimista y tener confianza en la vida. Por ejemplo, cuando Franklin Delano Roosevelt se dio cuenta que no iba a volver a caminar, eligió desarrollar una personalidad tan encantadora y tal destreza en la conversación que la gente se olvidaba por completo de su discapacidad. A él lo motivaba la posibilidad y llegó a ser presidente de los Estados Unidos.

Constructor #5: Enfócate en una misión

Anima a tus hijos a tener sueños grandes, metas grandes. Ayúdalos a descubrir su única misión que ha sido dada por Dios. De esa manera, tus hijos van a tener un propósito en la vida en lugar de estar a la deriva en nuestra cultura.

Constructor #6: Entiende, acepta y perdona

Aprende a aceptar el perdón de Dios por medio de Jesucristo y luego extiende el perdón a otros. Este es un principio grandioso de salud mental, devoción espiritual y patrones positivos de comportamiento.

Constructor #7: Sé sensato al tomar riesgos

Enséñales a tus hijos el balance entre riesgo e imprudencia. Sí, ellos van a querer tomar riesgos de aventura y emoción, pero necesitan además una base segura por dónde empezar.

Constructor #8: Impúlsate con dirección

Tus hijos necesitan saber hacia qué dirección están yendo, porque esa dirección va a determinar sus decisiones.

Constructor #9: Incluye a otros de manera equilibrada

Tus hijos necesitan gente en su vida. Necesitan, además, interacción positiva y balance que la comunicación con otras personas les puede dar.

Constructor #10: Obedece a Dios

Tus hijos deben aprender que la autoridad más grande en su vida es Jesucristo, quien murió por ellos y resucitó de los muertos. Es Dios quien hace que la vida funcione, cuyos principios hacen que la vida tenga significado. Pero sobre todo, enséñales que es el Espíritu Santo, quien vive dentro de ellos cuando deciden elegir el sacrificio de Jesús en la cruz. Con la ayuda del Espíritu Santo, podrán vivir una vida que agrade a Dios y ser consistentes con sus principios de comportamiento.

Sobre todo, enseña a tus hijos este secreto fundamental: Tu comportamiento depende de ti, al final, tú eres el único responsable. Tú no eres víctima de nadie. Si le aclaras este secreto a tus hijos, ellos van a bendecir a todos aquellos que estén a su alrededor en generaciones futuras.

CAPÍTULO 7

Entendiendo las emociones de tu hijo

Recientemente nuestro hijo de seis años, Jonathan, pasó dos noches perturbadoras sin poder dormir. Usualmente Jonathan es un chico feliz cuando descansa, pero en esta ocasión, estaba temeroso y en total incertidumbre. Cuando examinamos la situación, descubrimos que de alguna manera, desconocida para nosotros, él había visto caricaturas de monstruos y se había comenzado a preguntar si alguien o algo estaba compartiendo su habitación durante las noches.

¿Qué padres no han se han enfrentado con una variedad de emociones de sus hijos a quienes aman? Desde zapatear hasta gritos de entusiasmo, desde alegría hasta ira que se deja ver en las rabietas, los padres lo han visto todo. ¿Por qué las emociones de los niños oscilan de manera tan salvaje? Porque la mayoría de las emociones de tus hijos están basadas en emociones y sentimientos del momento.

Como escribe el psicólogo Arthur Freeman: «Con frecuencia el sentido común nos abandona cuando más lo necesitamos y a lo que nosotros llamamos "buen juicio" es inundado por una marea de emoción». Esto es particularmente cierto en los niños, quienes con frecuencia no tienen idea de cómo manejar sus emociones y ni siquiera están seguros de lo que son sus emociones.

Nosotros sabemos muy bien que las emociones de los niños influyen en su comportamiento. Es por eso que queremos dedicarle todo un capítulo al estudio de esas emociones—definirlas, entender las clases de emociones y luego ayudar a nuestros hijos a que aprendan a dominarlas antes que éstas los dominen a ellos.

¿Qué son las emociones?

¿Por qué nuestro sentido común a veces es barrido por las emociones? ¿Por qué es posible que nuestros hijos sean cegados por amor, intoxicados por la felicidad, paralizados por la ansiedad y asustados por sus ingenios?

A mí me encanta esta aclaración de la emociones, escrita por un investigador: «Esas emociones que te molestan, que te perturban o que te emocionan, no están guardadas en algún lugar en lo profundo, siempre agitándote. Las emociones son, de hecho, manufacturadas en el momento cuando ves la necesidad que tienes de ellas o sientes la necesidad de ellas. Tú las manufacturas con tu manera de pensar en cierta situación en particular. La Biblia dice: «Pues como piensa dentro de ti, así es» (Proverbios 23.7 LBLA). Ese investigador está en lo correcto: nuestras emociones son manufacturadas. Cuando olvidamos ciertas experiencias, las emociones se desaparecen. La emoción es producida cuando recordamos la situación.

¿De dónde vienen las emociones? Mientras que los científicos saben que las emociones son producidas por varios químicos en el cerebro, nadie entiende en su totalidad cómo funciona esto, pero efectivamente nosotros sabemos pocas cosas acerca de su naturaleza:

1.- **Las emociones son reacciones, no son iniciativas** - La experiencia viene primero, después la emoción.
2.- **Las emociones fluyen y menguan** - Toma el dolor, por ejemplo, si alguien a quien tú amas se muere, tal vez sientas ciclos de dolor como una marea fluyendo

y menguando. La oleada de emociones seguirá ahí cada vez, pero va a mermar conforme pasa el tiempo. Eventualmente vas a sentir sanidad de la herida. El decaimiento y el flujo de tus emociones es en realidad un mecanismo de defensa que Dios puso en la personalidad del ser humano. Si mantienes tus emociones altas todo el tiempo, eventualmente vas a colapsar de tensión.

3.- **Las emociones solamente tienen el poder que tú les das -** Tú no eres víctima de las emociones. Es por eso que nadie puede decir: «yo no pude evitar la manera en que reaccioné». Sí, tú pudiste haberlo hecho. Todos tenemos control sobre la manera en que respondemos a las emociones. Puede ser que nuestras emociones sean poderosas, pero no tenemos que permitir que nos controlen.

4.- **Las emociones no son confiables -** Nuestras emociones a veces cambian sin razón aparente. Éstas también quizás sean afectadas por trastornos biológicos tales como depresión clínica. Por lo tanto, nos son confiables como base de la conducta humana. Si tus hijos dependen de sus emociones, van a ser barridos en todas direcciones. Van a pasar su vida corriendo por todos lados, tratando de capturar sus emociones, las cuales están huyendo.

5.- **Las emociones pueden ser confundidas -** Pueden ser el resultado de pensamiento negativo y defectuoso, tal como: no le voy a caer bien. Como resultado, tu hijo tal vez actúe de manera inapropiada cuando está cerca de cierta persona, en cierto sentido, haciendo que su propia declaración se vuelva realidad debido a su comportamiento. Por lo tanto, enseña a tus hijos a no depender de sus emociones.

Los tipos de emociones

Existen cinco emociones negativas dominantes y cinco emociones positivas dominantes. Consideremos a las negativas primero:

Las emociones negativas

1.- El temor

El temor tiene la tendencia a ser específico. Tiene un objetivo—una persona o un objeto. Un psicólogo lo llama «implicación horror». Comienzas a amplificar cierta cosa específica o a una persona a quien le temes, hasta que crece a un tamaño monumental y amenaza tu equilibrio emocional y entonces el futuro se convierte en algo a que temer.

¿Cuál es la respuesta? Comunícale a tu hijo que él no tiene por qué temer. Sabías que hay más de trescientos versículos bíblicos donde Dios dice: «No temas. No tengas miedo». Yo creo que era porque Dios sabía lo mucho que lo necesitaríamos. ¿Quiere esto decir que debemos ignorar el temor? Ciertamente no.

Y es posible que haya ocasiones cuando, como padres, necesitemos tomar acción a favor de nuestros hijos. Por ejemplo, si tu hijo tiene miedo de caminar a la escuela porque un perro malo que anda suelto lo persigue cada mañana, tal vez sea hora que le ayudes a tu hijo a cambiar la ruta hacia la escuela (o hablar con el dueño del perro).

2.- La preocupación

La preocupación tiene la tendencia de ser más generalizada. Un psicólogo la llama, «el principio del catastrofismo». Esta es la creencia de que todo en tu vida eventualmente va a producir una catástrofe de cierta proporción.

¿Por qué sucede esto? Porque nos permitimos a nosotros mismos escribir guiones negativos en nuestras mentes. Creemos que en realidad no merecemos una bendición, favor o éxito, así que terminamos siguiendo el guión negativo que escribimos, hasta que a través de nuestra preocupación, producimos el resultado que temíamos.

El Dr. Arthur Freeman dice que siempre que tienes una preocupación—un pensamiento completo, debes inmediatamente parar y revisar ese pensamiento por lo que realmente significa. Luego analizar las posibles consecuencias. Pregúntate a ti mismo, ¿Qué real o lógicamente puede sucederme a mí? ¿Será que va a ser así de malo? ¿Cómo lo voy a manejar? Enseguida cuestiona la evidencia. Quizás sea algo erróneo.

A los tres puntos del Dr. Freeman, yo le agrego dos más: formula tu plan. En lugar de poner tu energía en la preocupación, ponla en la planeación de tu acción y confía en nuestro Dios amoroso. Si lees la Biblia, verás cómo la gente aprendió a confiar en Dios y cómo Dios nunca los decepcionó. ¿Por qué no hacer lo mismo por ti mismo? Ve a Dios con oración y pídele que te ayude.

3.- La ira

Existen dos clases de ira: la ira egocéntrica y la ira farisaica. Si tu hijo está enojado porque alguien lo ha tratado con crueldad e injusticia—su ira es legítima. Pero la ira egoísta ocurre cuando alguien o algo no cumplen con sus expectativas. Dios quiere que acabemos con esta clase de ira para que no gane control sobre nosotros (ver Efesios 4:26).

4.- La depresión

Hay diferentes formas de depresión. Hay momentos normales cuando tu hijo se va a sentir deprimido y desanimado debido a las circunstancias de la vida. Es posible que sepa exactamente por qué se siente deprimido. Tal vez esté deprimidos por causas físicas—mal estado de salud, enfermedad, o una dieta no balanceada. Existen causas de depresión clínica más grave que requiere ayuda profesional. Si tu hijo está batallando con depresión, busca ayuda de un profesional. Los padres sabios buscan la ayuda necesaria para ayudar a sus hijos a escapar del túnel de la depresión.

5.- El odio

Jesús dijo que si tú odias a alguien, estás cometiendo asesinato en tu corazón. Ahora bien, esto no quiere decir que Jesús esté diciendo que eres un criminal condenado y que deberías de morir por eso. No. Él dice que el asesinato comienza en el corazón; que no es malo odiar el pecado, injusticia y abuso, pero que es malo odiar a las personas.

El odio es un veneno que tu hijo no puede tener en su vida. Eso no solamente daña a la persona odiada, sino que además daña a la persona que siente odio.

Por lo tanto, enseña a tus hijos que si alguien los has lastimado o traicionado, tienen que pedirle a Dios que les ayude a perdonar a esa persona. Deben resolver la situación por su propio bien mental.

Cualquier emoción negativa puede también ser una táctica, un medio pervertido para que tu hijo se sienta especial. Si tu hijo ha desarrollado o está desarrollando una personalidad que alimenta estas cosas negativas, él en realidad quizás lo esté haciendo como un juego de poder para llamar atención, simpatía o algo más, pero ese es un intercambio que no vale la pena.

Las emociones negativas van dificultar su desarrollo como ser humano y van a evitar que disfrute la vida y que se acerque más a Dios.

Las emociones positivas

Por lo tanto ¿qué clase de emociones debe de desarrollar tu hijo?

1.- El deseo

Es una ambición, un interés para mejorar y avanzar. Es una motivación para querer aprender y saber más de lo que sabe actualmente.

2.- La confianza

Una sensación sana de ánimo y desafío por la vida. En lugar de estar destrozado y temeroso por las fricciones de la vida diaria, la persona segura de sí misma sigue hacia delante, sabiendo que él o ella puede lidiar con lo que está por venir.

3.- El entusiasmo

Muy pocas cosas se logran sin una oleada de emoción positiva. Como dice Norman Vincent, «El entusiasmo hace la diferencia».

4.- El regocijo

Esto quiere decir que estás contento y que disfrutas de tu trabajo, tu vida y quien tú eres.

5.- El amor

Estoy hablando del amor como un compromiso hacia alguien. Tú estás comprometido a mostrar afecto hacia ella, a ayudarla. Incluso a veces yendo en contra de tu propio egoísmo.

El capítulo que habla más de amor en la Biblia es 1 de Corintios 13. Es una expresión maravillosa de un compromiso de amor real—amor que edifica, anima, alienta y no destruye. Anima a tus hijos a que lo lean, particularmente durante los años de adolescencia.

Cómo ayudar a tu hijo a dominar su estado de ánimo

¿Cómo puedes ayudar a tus hijos a tus hijos a dominar sus estados de ánimo y sus emociones? Anímalos a hacer tres cosas básicas con sus emociones:

1.- Aceptarlas - Esto no quiere decir que las apruebes. Esto quiere decir que aceptas legítimamente una emoción como algo que realmente estás sintiendo. Identifica cuál emoción es. Por ejemplo, digamos que tu hijo está lanzando una rabieta porque tienen hambre. Debido a que estás en la autopista, no hay nada que puedas hacer en cuanto a su hambre. Tú le puedes decir a tu hijo (en lenguaje apropiado), «Cariño, yo sé que tienes hambre, yo también tengo hambre. Vamos a comer algo, pero será en x minutos antes de que podamos comer. Lanzar una rabieta no nos va a ayudar, porque no va a hacer que el auto vaya más rápido».

2.- **Entenderlas** - Esto quiere decir que evalúas de dónde vienen esas emociones. Si estás enojado ¿Por qué estás enojado? Por ejemplo, digamos que tu hijo patea con enojo a su hermana pequeña—sin razón aparente. Ayuda tu hijo a descubrir porqué él se comporta de esa manera. ¿Será que él está molesto porque su hermana tiene más atención que él? ¿O porque ha tenido un día difícil, está cansado y simplemente quiere arremeter contra alguien?

3. **Elige actuar en lugar de reaccionar** - Enséñales a tus hijos que en cualquier situación, pueden elegir actuar en lugar de reaccionar. Si entrenas a tu hijo a tener un patrón de conducta y decir, «Yo realmente estoy triste por...» en lugar de reaccionar a esa tristeza encerrándose en su cuarto a llorar, estará aprendiendo destrezas efectivas de cómo enfrentarse a la vida.

El Dr. Chris Thruman, un psicólogo cristiano, habla acerca de un plan excelente para lidiar con las emociones. Se llama la reacción **PREVA**. Aunque la redacción de estos conceptos quizás sea difícil de entender para un niño, te va a ayudar a ti. Como adulto, les puedes enseñar a tus hijos estos principios cuando tengan edad apropiada y en el nivel apropiado.

P = lo que **P**rovoca el evento (lo que pasó en realidad)
R = **R**eflexión (¿Qué hago ahora?)
E = Reacción **E**quivocada (la reacción no saludable)
V = **V**erdad (¡Un minuto, esto no es lo que quiero hacer!)
A = Reacción **A**certada (cuando cambias a esta acción, eso comienza a cambiar tus emociones)

Si les enseñas a tus hijos el programa **PREVA**, los vas a ayudar a convertirse en adultos saludables.

La importancia de una buena actitud

Todos lo hemos visto (o quizá haya sido tu hijo)—el niño

llorón en el supermercado que hace una rabieta por todo lo que no puede conseguir o el joven adolescente que se para con las piernas separadas y mala actitud escrita sobre su cara mientras sus padres le hablan.

Inculca en tus hijos a la edad más temprana posible la importancia de tener una buena actitud. Aquí tienes siete elementos cruciales:

Actitud #1: Elige ser positivo

Hace poco tiempo yo estaba en el estado de Illinois conduciendo una serie de seminarios. En medio de una sesión de una tarde, un hombre se puso de pie. Él procedió a criticarme bruscamente simplemente por sugerí que el pensamiento positivo se puede aplicar a los cristianos.

Permíteme dar respuesta a este argumento. Primero, pensamiento positivo es anti-bíblico. La Biblia tiene mucho que decir acerca del enfoque correcto en la vida—uno que es positivo y emocionante.

Segundo, no hay nada de anticristiano en un enfoque positivo en la vida. Pensamiento positivo no quiere decir que crees que nada puede salir mal o que crees que nunca vas a enfrentar angustia o desastre. Eso no quiere decir que tu cabeza esté enterrada en la arena. Tú te das cuenta que hay mucha maldad en el mundo, pero pensamiento positivo quiere decir que miras la vida directamente a los ojos, incluso cuando se torna difícil. Tú eliges creer en Dios y confiar en Sus principios. Tú no permites que el desastre y la tragedia te derroten.

Ayuda a tus hijos a acercarse a la vida con alegría, de una manera positiva que va a honrar a Dios y liberar el potencial en sus vidas. Luego, con la ayuda de Dios, ellos van a poder lograr lo que Dios quiere que logren ahora y en el futuro.

Nosotros siempre jugamos un juego llamado «Revisión de Actitud». Yo le dijo a Amy (con gran entusiasmo) «Revisión de Actitud», ella sonríe y dice (con gran entusiasmo) «¡Caramba, qué bien me siento!» Nosotros también hemos hecho esto con nuestros hijos, siguiendo el juego hasta que todos terminan carcajeándose. ¡Siempre funciona!

La actitud positiva puede cambiar tu panorama de la vida y lograr a tu alrededor cosas grandes, pero tienes que dejar esto totalmente en claro: el pensamiento positivo no te va a dar la entrada al cielo. Puede hacer que la jornada hacia allá sea más fácil, más feliz y más productiva de lo que de otro modo sería, pero no puede perdonar tus pecados. No puede cambiar tu vida. No te puede hacer diferente individual y espiritualmente; realmente no puede alterar la verdad en ti. El pensamiento positivo no puede hacer que estés bien con Dios. No es un sustituto de Jesucristo, el único camino hacia Dios. La única manera para tener paz en tu corazón es aceptando la muerte de Cristo en la cruz por ti y eligiendo caminar diariamente con él y su guía. La clave para una vida positiva es una relación vibrante, en crecimiento y personal con Jesucristo.

¿Cómo puedes llegar a conocer y seguir a Jesucristo? Primero, tú debes tomar una decisión clara de ser cristiano. Cuando escoges aceptar a Cristo como tu Salvador, él te cambia desde arriba hacia abajo, pero también debes optar por tener esperanza. Tú no te levantas un día en la mañana y de repente encuentras que todo en tu vida es positivo. No es así de simple, especialmente si tienes la tendencia a ver la vida de un modo sombrío. Debes aprender a enfocarte en la vida como un creyente, viendo las dificultades desde una perspectiva adecuada. Como lo dice Filipenses 4:8: «Por lo demás, hermanos, todo lo que es verdadero, todo lo que es digno, todo lo que es justo, todo lo puro, todo lo amable, todo lo honorable, si hay alguna virtud o algo que merece elogio, en eso meditad». Eso quiere decir que debes enfocarte en lo que está en la cima, en lugar de enfocarte en lo que está en el valle. Es lo opuesto a la manera humana de vivir.

Si ya eres cristiano, es incluso más importante que elijas ser positivo. No hay testigos de Jesucristo con un enfoque agrio, negativo y triste de la vida. ¿Quién en el mundo querría ser como Jesús sabiendo que conocerle a Él les haría sombríos y deprimidos? El pensamiento positivo es una tarjeta magnética de atracción a Dios—especialmente en un mundo que tiene la tendencia a producir negativismo.

Actitud #2: Evalue el ingreso diario

Esto quiere decir que tú y tus hijos deben de tener cuidado en qué clase de aporte absorben. Si quieres que tus hijos tengan un enfoque positivo y productivo de la vida, pero aun así se quejan de estar deprimidos, desanimados y que no tienen la energía que necesitan, es posible que estén absorbiendo el material equivocado. Películas, programas de televisión, libros y revistas pueden tener una influencia tremenda en la vida de los niños, para bien o para mal. Por lo tanto, escoge diariamente reforzamiento positivo.

La fuente diaria más importante de reforzamiento positivo es la Palabra de Dios, su comunicación con nosotros. Como lo dice Proverbios 13:20 «El que anda con sabios sabio será, más el compañero de los necios sufrirá daño». El compañero de los necios va a pagar el precio de un gran daño por su propia vida. Por lo tanto, observa a tus hijos ahora. ¿Son ellos compañeros de necios? ¿Consistentemente disfrutan de videos malos o juegos electrónicos malos? Si es así, monitorea más de cerca lo que ellos hacen. No dejes que sean compañeros de gente o cosas que los va a alejar de Dios y Sus principios.

Actitud #3: Practique vivir como termostato

Existe una diferencia entre un termostato y un termómetro. Un termómetro básicamente registra, en lugar de controlar la temperatura. El termostato regula la temperatura. Como cristiano, tú tienes que tomar la decisión deliberadamente de ser termostato en lugar de ser termómetro. Tú no debes de ser simplemente un termómetro espiritual, emocional y psicológico que mide la temperatura de la gente que está a tu alrededor, en otras palabras, cuando ellos están espiritualmente calientes, tú estás caliente; cuando están espiritualmente fríos, tú estás frío. En lugar de eso, debes de ser un termostato que ayuda a regular la temperatura de otros.

Por ejemplo, si alguien es malo contigo, no solamente irradies esa temperatura creciente de regreso a esa persona. En lugar de eso, sé un termostato que regula la ira antes de afectar a otros. Jesús le llamaba «poner la otra mejilla». Como influencia positiva en el mundo, tu hijo será como una brisa fresca soplando en un día con mucha humedad.

Por lo tanto, infórmales a tus hijos que a veces van a suceder cosas malas y que es posible que se sientan tristes o enojados, pero que hay una buena manera de tratar con esos sentimientos, que arremeter contra otros no es la manera.

Enséñales a tus hijos que ellos pueden tener buena actitud, incluso en tiempos difíciles. Hasta puedes hacer de eso un juego divertido. Cuando tus hijos comiencen a estar de mal humor, explícales que ellos están siendo un termómetro en lugar de ser un termostato. Haz que el aprendizaje de este principio sea algo divertido.

Actitud #4: Enfócate en tus oportunidades en lugar de tus incapacidades

En otras palabras, levántate, sacúdete el polvo y olvídate de las excusas. Tus desventajas solamente son desventajas si tú las ves de esa manera.

Yo fui a un seminario con un hombre joven que había sido el campeón líder del baloncesto americano, All-American, en el estado de Ohio. Pero el verano después que se graduó de la secundaria, tuvo un horrible accidente automovilístico. Como resultado, quedó cuadripléjico.

Al inicio se rebeló, se volvió amargado y resentido. Pero después su vida cambió completamente cuando conoció a Jesús. Ahora él está casado con una mujer maravillosa que lo ama y es capellán en un hospital para personas minusválidas de Cincinnati. Él ha llevado a docenas de personas a Cristo cada año—debido a que ellos son atraídos a Dios como resultado de ver la gracia de Dios en la vida de este hombre—incluso teniendo en cuenta su situación difícil.

Enseña a tus hijos que una discapacidad no debe evitar que se conviertan en lo que Dios quiere que sean, al menos que ellos lo permitan. Como lo dice Mateo 19.26 «Pero Jesús, mirándolos, le dijo: "para los hombres eso es imposible, pero para Dios es posible"». Eso es algo grandioso que tus hijos deben recordar cuando se sientan aplastados por algo que los deje sin esperanza.

Yo creo que la cruzada del Mar Rojo que permitió que los israelitas pasaran de esclavitud a seguridad, es un hecho histórico, no un cuento de hadas. Dios realmente envió un milagro para cuidar de sus hijos, así que diles a tus hijos que no hay un «mar rojo» en sus vidas que sea más grande que el Dios Altísimo y que no hay discapacidad que los pueda parar de hacer la voluntad de Dios.

Actitud #5: Domina tus estados de ánimo

Enseña a tus a que dominen sus estados de ánimo. Proverbios 16.32 dice, «Mejor es el lento para la ira que el poderoso y el que domina su espíritu, que el que toma una ciudad». Dominar tus estados de ánimo es un elemento vital para tener impacto positivo en la vida que Dios quiere que tengas. ¿Por qué? Porque si tus hijos solamente hacen lo que es correcto cuando sienten ganas, nunca lograrán nada. Tus hijos necesitan aprender control. Si ellos no controlan sus estados de ánimo, sus estados de ánimo los controlarán a ellos.

Actitud #6: Saca el provecho máximo de tu cuerpo

La Biblia enseña que eres una persona formada de cuerpo, mente y espíritu. Por lo tanto, lo que afecta una parte de ti afecto todo. Es por eso que los fundamentos de la buena salud son tan importantes. Como lo dice 1 de Corintios 6.19-20: «¿No sabéis que vuestro cuerpo es templo del Espíritu Santo, que está en vosotros, el cual tenéis de Dios, y que no os pertenece? Pues por precio habéis sido comprados; por tanto, glorificad a Dios en nuestro cuerpo y vuestro espíritu, los cuales son de Dios». Eso quiere decir que tú tienes que cuidarlo. Si pasa algo malo con tu cuerpo, va a afectar el resto de ti. Así que ten cuidado con tu peso, tu consumo de aire fresco, tu ejercicio y no comas en exceso debido a la presión, el rechazo de otros o el hecho de que no estés feliz con quiere eres. Si estás seguro en el amor de Dios y fuerza y eres una persona estable, tú no le tienes que probar nada a nadie.

Cada niño tiene algo que no le gusta de su cuerpo. Enséñale a no preocuparse por eso. En lugar de preocuparse, debe aceptarlo, aprovecharlo al máximo y enfocarse en las cosas que puede cambiar.

Actitud #7: Guarda tu lengua

Un pastor dijo una vez, «El secreto del éxito o fracaso está tan cerca de ti como tus propios labios». Si hablas de manera negativa de ti mismo, de otros, de tu trabajo, te vas a sentir derrotado. Así que pídele a tus hijos que se prueben a sí mismos. ¿Cómo se tratan cuando hablan de sí mismos? ¿Es con un lenguaje denigrante?

El libro de Santiago aclara que la lengua es un órgano tan pequeño, pero aun así puede encender un gran fuego. Puede ser usada para hacer algo muy bueno o algo muy malo.

Enséñales a tus hijos a que usen su lengua para hacer el bien. En lugar de hacer comentarios negativos acerca de otros, pueden aprender a decir cosas buenas y animar a otros que están a su alrededor.

Estos siete elementos de una buena actitud, en conjunto, encajan en una imagen gigante de una vida vibrante y exitosa, pero tus hijos tienen que saber que tomar la decisión de vivir una vida al máximo—siendo lo mejor para Dios—no es algo automático. Es tu decisión. Si decides seguir los principios de Dios para una vida positiva, vas a vivir una vida de pureza, justicia, compromiso y emoción y mejor aún, vas a impactar las vidas de otros. Ahora bien, eso es algo de lo que ambos, tú y tus hijos pueden estar emocionados.

Capítulo 8

En cuanto a disciplina

Si has luchado para saber cómo disciplinar a tu hijo, no eres el único. Los padres de todo el mundo se preguntan cuánto es demasiado y cuánto es muy poco. Se preguntan cómo pueden encontrar ese equilibro difícil de alcanzar para ayudar a sus hijos a controlar su comportamiento.

Yo recuerdo claramente la etapa que nuestra hija Allison atravesó a la edad de cuatro años. Una vez ella nos hizo una rabieta colosal en un centro comercial en Atlanta. Gritó tan fuerte que los empleados llamaron a los paramédicos porque pensaron que estaba enferma. La verdad era simple: estaba enojada porque no le permitimos que se quedara con un juguete en particular. Su rabieta en público era algo que Amy y yo no nos podíamos atrever a fallar. Si le hubiéramos comprado el juguete a Allison para que dejara de gritar, ella hubiera aprendido que hacer una rabieta en público era una manera efectiva para conseguir lo que quería.

Ejemplos como éste muestran que los niños necesitan disciplina al igual que los jardines necesitan cultivo. En ambos casos, el futuro está en juego. La década promiscua y permisiva de los años 60 ha demostrado la necesidad de un enfoque equilibrado para entrenar a los niños, uno que funcione bien. Como lo declara Proverbios 13.24: «el que escatima la vara odia a su hijo, más el que lo ama lo disciplina con inteligencia».

¿Qué clase de disciplina funciona mejor? Proverbios 22.6 dice: «Enseña al niño en el camino en que debe de andar y cuando sea viejo no se apartará de él». Este versículo no es un sábana de garantía que el entrenamiento en la niñez promete buenos resultados; en lugar de eso, nos anima, como padres, a encontrar la mejor opción en cuanto a temperamento para cada uno de nuestros niños y a que los eduquemos de acuerdo con ello.

Cuando educas tu hijo, eso quiere decir que lo guías o ayudas a su desarrollo deliberadamente con un propósito más grande en mente. La implicación es obvia: educación requiere no solamente un plan bien pensado, sino también un deseo de disciplinar, enseñar y controlar.

La disciplina es vital para la producción de un adulto maduro y responsable, pero en algunos círculos se ha ganado una mala reputación. Hace unos años atrás, en una evaluación ridícula de un reportero indudablemente parcial, el psicólogo y líder cristiano James Dobson fue acusado de promover abuso infantil encubriéndolo con lo que llamaba «disciplina infantil». Cualquiera que conoce al Dr. Dobson y su ministerio sabe que eso no es verdad. Sin embargo, la historia mostró la profunda diferencia entre en punto de vista bíblico y el enfoque liberal de la crianza de niños excesivamente permisiva.

El plan bíblico es claro y simple. Cuando amas a tus hijos de verdad, los educas, los disciplinas, los controlas y los guías. Si vas a hacer todo esto, hazlo con sensibilidad, amor profundo y apoyo.

Yo he iniciado este capítulo con una declaración cuidadosa acerca de prioridad bíblica de disciplinar y educar porque es importante para el futuro de tus hijos.

Ocho consejos que cada padre debe considerar

Si sólo tuvieras veinte minutos para leer algo antes de convertirte en padre, debería de ser esta sección. Te va a dar los ocho consejos más importantes de lo que puedes hacer para criar a tu hijo y logres que sea una persona piadosa y equilibrada.

Consejo #1: Haz todo con mucho amor y que sea obvio

Algunas personas trabajan con entrenadores personales que hacen maravillas con sus cuerpos. El entrenador explica que los músculos se vuelven fuertes después que han sido quebrantados por demandas físicas de ejercicios extenuantes. Cuando el músculo se mueve a las etapas de recuperación, es cuando empieza a desarrollarse a lo que pueden ser capaz de convertirse.

Esto es lo que sucede con tus hijos como resultado de la disciplina. Cuando les muestras amor inconfundible y afecto físico, cuando los abrazas y los acaricias y les das seguridad emocional, es como si sus «músculos» emocionales y espirituales se desarrollaran. Después de que el niño ha sido disciplinado, es un tiempo de alta-receptividad, así que debes de aprovecharlo al máximo.

Nuestro hijo Jonathan Dexter todavía está pequeño. Cuando Jonathan está claramente con necesidad de disciplina, nosotros se la damos. Luego damos seguimiento inmediatamente con un desbordamiento de amor y cuidado que cura las heridas emocionales del niño Jonathan. Es en ese momento de castigo que Jonathan está abierto a la enseñanza.

Esta clase de amor paga dividendos importantes en la vida y la estabilidad de tus hijos. Nunca permitas que tus hijos tengan la menor duda de que los amas. Demuestra el amor a tus hijos en cada oportunidad que tengas, especialmente cuando los acabas de disciplinar. Ese es el momento primordial para demostrarles afecto físico. Acarícialos y tranquilízalos y diles que aún les amas.

Consejo #2: Que la disciplina sea consistente e inevitable

Estudios sociológicos interesantes han demostrado que ciertos criminales son más afectados por la certeza de los castigos que por la severidad de éstos. Haz que tu disciplina siga los mismos principios.

Uno de los momentos más vergonzosos para un padre es cuando un padre frustrado y agobiado le dice al niño que haga algo y el niño lo ignora. El padre advierte al niño de un desastre inminente si la respuesta no es inmediata. El niño sigue sin moverse.

Luego el padre prueba una última solución—LA CUENTA REGRESIVA. «Te estoy advirtiendo», amenaza el padre «Si tengo que contar...de acuerdo. ¡UNO! ¡DOS! ¡TRES! «!No me hagas llegar a 5!» Mientras tanto, el niño sigue esperando, sin moverse y todavía en control.

Esta no es manera de enseñar a tus hijos respeto a la autoridad, o control personal. Todo lo que hace es impulsar a tu hijo a una «zona de malcriadez». Tú estás enseñando que la obediencia está parcialmente bajo el control suyo y a su discreción.

Amy y yo estamos convencidos que si no es inmediata, no es obediencia. No hay tal cosa como obediencia renuente. Por lo tanto, enséñales la tus hijos que hablas en serio. Tus instrucciones son para ser obedecidas rápidamente, sin cuestionar y sin quejarse.

Quizá estés preguntando: ¿produce esto un robot tonto cuya única respuesta es el cumplimiento al instante? ¡Claro que no! En lugar de eso, produce un niño equilibrado, respetuoso y bien portado que ha aprendido con la ayuda de Dios y tu entrenamiento a disciplinar sus impulsos egoístas que tiene por naturaleza.

Consejo #3: Ajusta la disciplina según la falta

Siempre ten como finalidad la proporción y balance. Como dice Efesios 6.4 «Y vosotros padres no provoquéis la ira a vuestros hijos, sino criadlos en la disciplina e instrucción del Señor».

Los niños tienen un radar interno que detecta la injusticia inmediatamente. Tu propósito en disciplinar y entrenar debería ser una respuesta adecuada que se ajuste a sus malas acciones. El castigo también debería ser apropiado para su edad, madurez y nivel de comprensión. Saber cómo disciplinar adecuadamente implica conocer muy bien a tu hijo.

CONSEJO #4: QUE LOS MODALES SEAN IMPORTANTES

Los buenos modales son una parte vital de la educación de tu hijo. Decir «por favor», «gracias» «de nada» es una señal de respeto hacia los demás, así que enseña a tu hijo a que siempre trate a otros con cortesía.

Mis hijos te pueden decir que un límite que yo no les permito que crucen es la falta de respeto a su madre. Mi padre nunca me permitió salirme con la mía cuando mostraba algo de falta de respeto hacia mi madre.

Tus hijos tienen que saber que la cortesía es un fundamento importante para el buen funcionamiento de sus relaciones, incluyendo la dinámica en su propia familia. Ellos necesitan saber que no hay nada de tonto o anticuado en ser un caballero o una dama. En la cultura en deterioro de hoy en día, los buenos modales van a separar a tus hijos dramáticamente de la mayoría de sus compañeros.

La mejor manera de asegurarse que tus hijos sepan cómo expresarse y actuar de una manera apropiada es darles ejemplo constante. Si muestras tú mismo buenos modales, vas a ver que es más fácil enseñar a tus hijos.

¿Y qué de la etiqueta? ¿Deberías educar a tus hijos para comportase correctamente en la mesa? ¿Comportamiento apropiado en un restaurante? ¿La manera correcta de reconocer un regalo o un mensaje telefónico? ¡Absolutamente sí! Esto no significa que todo lo divertido y espontáneo debería ser programado para estar fuera de ellos, pero que ellos deben sentirse cómodos en ambientes sociales diferentes. Esta es otra manera para que ellos se diferencien en un mundo que cada vez es más grosero y socialmente negativo.

Yo siempre recuerdo que los buenos modales y etiqueta aceptable son maneras de mostrar consideración a otras personas y que han sido comprobados con el tiempo. Cuando enseñas a tus hijos a ceder un asiento a alguien de mayor edad, estás enseñando a respetar la edad de las demás personas (así como también a frenar su propio egocentrismo).

Por lo tanto, ayuda a tus hijos a que estén en ventaja en la vida. Enséñales patrones de conducta de las personas que se preocupan de los demás y saben cómo mostrarlo.

Consejo #5: No «perfecciones» a tu hijo

El mundo está lleno de adultos neuróticos, inquietos e impulsivos que constantemente están «perfeccionados» por padres bien-intencionados. ¿Por qué? Porqué muchos padres confunden el compromiso por la excelencia con la compulsión de ser perfecto. Tú siempre debes animar a tus hijos a trabajar duro, a servir con excelencia y alcanzar sus metas y sueños. Pero no pongas sobre ellos una exigencia de perfección. De otra manera, ellos van a pasar la vida tratando de llegar a la altura de un estándar imposible establecido para ellos como niños.

El artista B.J. Thomas, intérprete de «Raindroops Keep Fallin' on my Head» (Gotas de lluvia caen sobre mi cabeza) cuenta su lucha por ser un buen jugador en las ligas de baseball Little League. Cuando bateaba él un juego, ponchó mientras su padre le estaba viendo. Thomas nunca se ha olvidado del disgusto de su padre que fue expresado en voz alta. Recuerda a su padre gritándole lo que todos podían oír: «¡Eres un perdedor!».

Cualquier niño que es avergonzado de tal manera, recuerda la humillación para toda su vida. Nunca se te olvide lo poderosas que son tus palabras para los corazones sensibles y las almas vulnerables de los niños. Si batallas para «perfeccionar» a tus hijos, piensa en esto: muchas veces los padres quieren que sus hijos cumplan los sueños que ellos mismos no pudieron cumplir y esa es mucha presión en un niño.

Siempre recuerda que lo que dices de tus hijos, los ayuda a formar su identidad y como se van a sentir de sí mismos. Como dice la Biblia en Santiago 3.5 «Así también la lengua es un miembro pequeño, y sin embargo, se jacta de grandes cosas. Mirad: ¡qué gran bosque se incendia con tan pequeño fuego». Tu ataque o apoyo verbal va a hacer mucho estableciendo o destruyendo a tus hijos. Así que asegúrate de que tus palabras ayuden, animen, construyan y guíen, en lugar de desgarrar o crear exigencias imposibles que nunca van a poder cumplir.

CONSEJO #6: MUESTRA DOMINIO PROPIO

Mientras realizaba una cruzada cristiana en Mississippi, me encontré con un hombre que respondió a una invitación a aceptar a Jesús como su Señor y Salvador. En una reunión de seguimiento, este hombre rudo admitió tener un temperamento explosivo que en ocasiones lo llevaba a cometer acciones desagradables. Cuando le expliqué que ahora el Espíritu Santo de Dios vivía en él y le iba a ayudar a controlar su violencia, el hombre sacudió la cabeza. «Pero mi temperamento no puede ser controlado. Soy irlandés».

A eso, yo le tuve que contestar sin rodeos: «Ser irlandés no es una excusa. Si le entrega su temperamento a Dios y le obedece, Él va a cambiar esa violencia en su vida».

Cuando se trata de tu comportamiento, no hay excusas. Tus hijos te están mirando.

¡Si no quieres que tus hijos consuman alcohol, no consumas alcohol!

¡Si quieres que tus hijos usen un vocabulario limpio, limpia tu propia boca!

¡Si quieres que tus hijos sean honestos, no engañes!

¡Si quieres que tus hijos trabajen duro, ten una ética buena de trabajo!

¡Si quieres que tus hijos tengan una relación vibrante con Jesucristo, modela eso!

¡Si quieres que tus hijos traten a su futura pareja con amor, compromiso, respeto y dignidad, muestra las mismas cualidades con tu cónyuge!

El papel más importante de un padre es ser buen modelo a seguir con un comportamiento que se asemeje al comportamiento de Jesucristo.

Consejo #7: Gánate a tus hijos a temprana edad

Los expertos dicen que los niños aprenden mejor a través de una combinación de demostración y comunicación. Las mentes de tus hijos son como esponjas, absorbiendo e imitando tus acciones e imitando tu perspectiva del mundo. Ellos miran afanosamente lo que tú haces cada minuto que estás con ellos. Así que ¿por qué no usar algo de tiempo cuando están juntos para inculcar características piadosas en tus niños lo más temprano posible? Lean juntos un versículo bíblico, oren juntos, hablen acerca de un mensaje de un video o libro. Educa a tus hijos con tu propio ejemplo a caminar con Dios y a amar a la gente. Es posible que no siempre veas evidencia de lo que les has enseñado, pero las semillas que siembras temprano crecen y se convierte en una gran cosecha.

Consejo #8: Ora por tus hijos todos los días

Todos hemos cometido errores, pero todos deberíamos estar de acuerdo con esto: nosotros necesitamos la gracia de Dios, Su ayuda e intervención en la vida de nuestros hijos más que de cualquier otra cosa.

Un ex-jugador de fútbol de la Universidad Auburn en Alabama, dice que las oraciones de su padre son lo que le protegieron espiritual y moralmente en un ambiente de tentación sexual. «Mi padre ora por mí todas las noches. Cada vez que era tentado a hacer algo malo, yo recodaba a mi padre encerrado en su habitación, orando por mí. Después de los entrenamientos tardíos en la escuela secundaria, yo caminaba cuidadosamente a mi habitación, pero siempre me detenía en la puerta de la habitación de mi padre, solamente para escuchar esas oraciones». Yo recuerdo a mi padre y mi madre orando por mí. La familia de Amy oraba por ella. Yo crecí con un abuelo y dos abuelas que oraban por mí diariamente.

Nosotros estamos convencidos que esas oraciones y las oraciones que hacemos constantemente por nuestros hijos son la razón por la cual Dios ha protegido y bendecido a nuestra familia.

Aquí tienes una oración directamente de la Biblia, que incorpora los conceptos básicos importantes para pedir a Dios Su bendición y presencia, confiando que Él nos protegerá, y rindiéndonos a su bondad. Esa oración fue hecha por un hombre llamado Jabes, cuya vida era como la vida de todos nosotros, necesitaba el toque de Dios. Así como Dios contestó la petición sincera de Jabes, Él va a contestar las oraciones que tú hagas por tus hijos.

«Había un hombre llamado Jabes que era más distinguido que cualquiera de sus hermanos. Él fue quien oró al Dios de Israel. «¡Oh, si en verdad me bendijeras, ensancharías mi territorio y tu mano estaría conmigo y me guardarías del mal para que no me cause dolor»! Y ¡Dios le concedió lo que pidió!». (1 Crónicas 4.9-10).

No existe ningún bien más grande que la oración que puedas hacer por tus hijos en el nombre de Jesús. ¿Por qué no comenzar hoy? Si ya lo estás haciendo por tu propia cuenta, haz que sea una parte consistente en tu vida. Tú nunca vas a saber los beneficios sorprendentes de dicha oración tan poderosa hasta que elijas orar por tus hijos todos los días.

CAPÍTULO 9

Enseñando a tu hijo acerca del dinero

Cuando nuestra hija Allison tenía nueve años, nosotros le quitamos todas sus prestaciones (siguiendo el consejo de un amigo cristiano cuya sabiduría financiera era respetada). Al inicio ella estaba angustiada, pero después se motivó a generar sus propios ingresos. Como sugerencia adicional que nuestro amigo nos dio, Allison comenzó su propio negocio diseñando y desarrollando lapiceros con colores brillantes y lemas de motivación. Para cuando ella llegó a la edad adolescente, su negocio estaba bien establecido y ella tenía su propio ingreso.

Se pueden imaginar nuestro orgullo como padres cuando ella comenzó—por su propia cuenta—a dar el diezmo y dar a causas cristianas en las que ella creía. Hasta el día de hoy, la lección que inició a temprana edad continúa impactando sus hábitos financieros.

¿Te preocupa el bienestar financiero de tus hijos? ¿Estás preocupado de que tengan suficiente dinero para cubrir todas sus necesidades y quizás algo de sus deseos? ¿Cómo puedes educar a tus hijos a respetar el dinero y usarlo sabiamente? Todo comienza contigo. La manera en que manejas tus finanzas va a ser el patrón que tus hijos van a estar propensos a seguir.

Sin embargo, hay buenas noticias: no importa cuál sea tu situación financiera en estos momentos, tú no tienes que ser genio para vivir en libertad financiera. Todo lo que necesitas es tener un enfoque básico y saludable hacia el dinero. Entonces no vas a sentirte sacudido ni vas a entrar en pánico cuando pase lo inesperado.

El significado del dinero

¿Cuál es tu punto de vista acerca del dinero? ¿Lo ves como un medio para un fin? ¿Cómo un fin en sí mismo o como algo más? Generalmente, el dinero representa para la mayoría de la gente una de la siguientes cinco cosas:

1.- Seguridad

Tener dinero significa que estás a salvo y protegido. El dinero es como un padre que te consuela.

2.- Poder

Tener dinero significa que tienes el poder para intimidar, influenciar y mover a otra gente a hacer lo que tú quieres que hagan.

3.- Aceptación social

Tener dinero significa que eres parte de «un todo». Eres aceptado socialmente y ahora puedes sentirte mejor.

4.- Maldad

Algunas personas usan el dinero como algo malo, sucio. En realidad, el dinero en sí no es malo, pero el abuso y amor al dinero (es decir, la búsqueda continua como fin en sí mismo). Existen tres malentendidos de que el dinero es malo:

- **El malentendido cristiano** - 1 de Timoteo 6.10 dice: «Porque el amor al dinero es la raíz de todos los males, por el cual, codiciándolo algunos, se extraviaron de la fe y se torturaron con muchos dolores». Algunos cristianos han hecho una cita errónea de este versículo diciendo que el dinero es malo, en lugar de decir que el amor al dinero es la raíz de todos los males. Si tienes dinero, eso no quiere decir que no puedas tener una vida espiritual saludable. Sin embargo, Jesús dijo muy claro que no puedes servir a Dios y al dinero. Él está en lo cierto. Tú solamente puedes servir a Dios y Él no se verá comprometido. Eso quiere decir que tú debes de mantener tu visión del dinero en una perspectiva apropiada, una herramienta que te fue dada por Dios para ser usada para Su honra y gloria.

- **El error socialista** - La creencia que el dinero crea pobreza. Estas personas creen que entre más dinero ganas, más lo arrebatas de alguien más. En otras palabras, que existe una cantidad limitada de dinero en el mundo, que tienes que restar de otros para agregar al tuyo, pero este punto de vista es incorrecto. En realidad, uno crea más riqueza y fuentes de trabajo usando más capital.

- **El error psicológico** - El error de pensar que el dinero te echa a perder como persona; te puede causar problemas (y visitas al psicoterapeuta). Te hace sentir ansioso y presionado y te da más responsabilidad que pesa en tus hombros. Sin embargo, tus problemas en realidad no provienen de tener dinero. En lugar de eso, los causa una dependencia excesiva del dinero y del amor al dinero, así como también quizás una incapacidad de confiar en un Dios amoroso a quien le importas.

5.- Una herramienta hacia la libertad financiera

Un punto de vista saludable acerca del dinero es verlo como una simple herramienta que provee seguridad, crecimiento y desarrollo para ti y para quienes amas. Es algo que intercambias por algo que necesitas. El dinero en sí es moralmente neutral, pero tenerlo significa que tienes libertad material. Date cuenta que yo no dije que te hace una persona materialista. Un materialista es alguien que adora lo material y eso, desde la perspectiva de Dios, es algo erróneo porque te desvía para adorarlo a Él. Es por esa razón que es importante mantener una perspectiva balanceada. Después de todo, Dios creó el mundo material (Génesis 1 lo declara) y lo llama «bueno» así que, ¿Por qué no disfrutarlo? Sin embargo, es importante recordar que después de todo, todos nuestros recursos pertenecen Dios para ser usados para sus propósitos. Si recordamos esto, vamos a mantener nuestra perspectiva correcta y no vamos a caer en una trampa financiera.

Evitando las trampas financieras

Mientras que iba en taxi al aeropuerto en Charlotte, Carolina de Norte, entablé una conversación con el joven conductor. Originario de Jamaica, él me dijo que había venido a Estados Unidos por un deseo de tener libertad financiera. Ahora él es dueño de su propio taxi y paga los estudios de su hija en una escuela cristiana. Él ve América como la tierra de las oportunidades sin fin. ¿No es este hombre un genio? No, él simplemente conoce los secretos de cómo ser financieramente libre. Yo estoy convencido de que todo se trata de actitud.

Yo enseño tres cosas acerca del dinero: «lo deseamos, hacemos alarde de tenerlo y a veces nos obsesionamos con él». Según muchos planificadores financieros prominentes, existen seis trampas financieras. ¿Cuáles son estas trampas?

Trampa #1: Gastas más de lo que ganas.

Trampa #2: Compras lo que ves primero en vez de buscar opciones. Este es el caso de esas personas que nunca quieren esperar ofertas o negociar descuentos.

Trampa #3: Continúas en el trabajo que no te gusta porque no tienes otra salida. Tus deudas son muy altas. Tus facturas de pago son muy grandes. Tus obligaciones son demasiado fuertes. No ves ninguna salida. Lo odias, pero no ves otra alternativa.

Trampa #4: Necesitas ayuda adicional. Para poder alcanzar el equilibrio, tú necesitas ayuda adicional—ya sea con dos o tres trabajos, regalos de tu familia, ayuda gubernamental y tarjetas de crédito. Estás atrapado, y nunca vas a poder salir libre hasta que el círculo de dependencia sea roto.

Trampa #5: Dependes de alguien más que cuide de ti. En lugar de necesitar solamente ayuda adicional (Trampa #4) te vuelves dependiente de alguien más. Por ejemplo, todavía vives en casa y tienes treinta años. Otras personas toman las decisiones por ti.

Trampa #6: Estás permanentemente confundido. La mayoría de las personas no saben cómo manejar las deudas que tienen y debido a que dejan que sus finanzas se salgan fuera de control, están permanentemente confundidos. Tus hijos tienen que saber que pueden echar mano y manejar sus finanzas. Ellos deben de elegir ser amigos del dinero para que no se les vaya sigilosamente y los apuñale por la espalda.

Confundido acerca del dinero

Como lo dijo Lewis Lapham, editor de la revista *Harper's* hace pocos años atrás: «¿Por qué la mayoría de nosotros nos sentimos tan pequeños ante la presencia del dinero?» Nos sentimos intimidados. No sabemos cómo manejarlo, cómo obtenerlo, cómo utilizarlo. Para poder obtener dinero tenemos que tener un trabajo. Es posible que nos encante nuestro trabajo, es posible que lo odiemos. Para muchas personas, su trabajo es una ruta diaria hacia la infelicidad. Ven el trabajo como un castigo. Gastan su energía por un cheque de pago, haciendo algo que les disgusta.

Una encuesta reciente a 4.126 ejecutivos de género masculino encontró que 48% de ellos sentían que su trabajo, donde pasaban mucho tiempo, era «vacío y sin significado». Como resultado, sus vidas estaban vacías y sin sentido. Yo creo que existen dos razones para que esos hombres tengas esa clase de resultado en su vida:

Una es *espiritual*. Para poder tener paz y ser tan feliz como se puede ser humanamente, tú debes hacer la paz con Dios por medio de Jesucristo como tu Salvador. Jesús dijo en Juan 14.27: «La paz os dejo, mi paz os doy, no os la doy como el mundo la da. No se turbe vuestro corazón, ni tengan miedo».

La otra razón es la *rutina regular*. Muchas personas están atrapadas en un trabajo común con ingresos limitados de deforman su autoestima. Ellos ven pocos resultados en su trabajo. Ni siquiera pueden ahorrar mucho para su jubilación. ¿Sabías que los ahorros de vida promedio de un hombre ciudadano americano de cincuenta años de edad es $2.300? No es de extrañar que estas personas anden en busca de ayuda del gobierno.

La gente necesita ayuda monetaria. El dinero es una tensión aterradora alrededor de su cuello. En una encuesta de Money Magazine a jóvenes, ellos esperaban que el sexo fuera el tema del que más hablan los recién casados. Pero, para su gran sorpresa, 37% dijo que era el tema del dinero y muy pocos sabían realmente lo que estaba sucediendo en su vida financiera y creían que tenían tres veces más del dinero del que realmente tienen. No es de extrañar que sus gastos sean tan altos y que cada día se eleven más.

Se pone peor si tienes un trabajo que no te apasiona. Entonces te tienes que ir en la noche a tu casa y atravesar un período de des-comprensión. En lugar de que tu trabajo sea algo que esperas hacer, no puedes esperar para escaparte e irte a casa, donde puedes participar de entrenamiento sin sentido. Cuando sucede esto noche tras noche, comienzas a sentirte deprimido. Dime: ¿el dinero que estás ganando en tu trabajo es suficiente compensación para eso?

Metas y temores financieros

¿Te gusta el dinero o le temes? La mayoría de las personas viven con un temor constante al dinero. Su vida diaria está dominada por un acreedor exigente invisible que siempre está moviendo un dedo en su cara. Éste está ahí siempre para recordarles de su fracaso. Simplemente pensar en el dinero los hace sentirse desanimados y odian ir al trabajo. Es un consumidor de energía porque ellos no desean hacerlo. Es simple: tu energía va hacia tus disgustos y lejos de tus gustos. Esto quiere decir que lo que te gusta hacer va a producir un alto nivel de energía y reacción, pero tu energía se va a reducir si repugnas lo que tienes que hacer. Así que si quieres sentirte energizado nuevamente y ser libre de temor, es importante que te muevas hacia la libertad financiera.

Tres metas financieras

La mayoría de las personas en América tienen tres metas financieras y valen la pena. Probablemente tú también las tengas:

- ***Pagar su casa*** - Es el sueño americano tener una vida libre de hipoteca.
- ***Proveer para la educación de sus hijos*** - Todos queremos estar seguros que tenemos las ventajas y las oportunidades que van a impulsar a nuestros hijos hacia un futuro positivo.
- ***Poseer suficientes ingresos para la jubilación*** - Estarías asombrado del número de individuos en este gran país que no se han preparado para el futuro. Muchos ni siquiera saben dónde empezar. Consecuentemente, viven en un temor constante y se preguntan, ¿Podré pagar mis facturas? ¿Vamos a ser dependientes del Bienestar Social y Medical del gobierno?

Tres temores financieros

Muchos americanos tienen además tres principales temores financieros—los cuales te detienen emocionalmente.

Funcionar con temor financiero es como una maldición en la vida. Nunca se aleja de tus pensamientos.

- ***El temor al desempleo -*** La gente tiene temor de perder su empleo y con razón. En los últimos doce años, los despidos y reducciones corporativas han sido una epidemia, particularmente en Estados Unidos. Un ejemplo es el administrador de nivel medio que ha estado en una compañía grande por veinte años. Cada vez que la compañía se reestructura, él se pregunta: ¿Entraré en el recorte? ¿Vives así con temor? En la cultura de hoy, no es suficiente ser competente, capaz y efectivo en el trabajo. Aun con eso, te pueden despedir.
- ***El temor de una enfermedad, incapacidad o lesión -*** ¿Te preocupas de ser afectado físicamente y que no podrás proveer financieramente para ti y tu familia?
- ***El temor de un colapso económico -*** Hoy en día la presión económica es enorme.

Malentendidos acerca del dinero

Si la gente tienes estos temores ¿Por qué se sigue resistiendo a ganar dinero? ¿Por qué tienen temor a ser llamados materialistas? Considera las siguientes razones que da la gente:

- ***Otros estarán celosos -*** Sí, quizá tengas razón en ese punto. Pero ¿van otros a controlar tu vida? Ellos no son los responsables de cuidar de tu familia.
- ***No tengo deseos de riqueza -*** ¿En verdad crees eso, o es simplemente una pantalla para parecer humilde frente a otros? Si Dios ha puesto en tu corazón que no debes perseguir el dinero, que debes de vivir una vida simple, entonces está bien. Tú estás haciendo lo que Dios te ha llamado a hacer, pero también date cuenta que pocos en el mundo son llamados a esta simplicidad.

- ***No es bueno poseer dinero*** - Pero lo triste es que los que tienen dinero son los que emplean al resto del mundo. Ellos ayudan a que esta sociedad sea estable. Ellos tienen poder e influencia. Si tienes dinero, puedes estar en el asiento del conductor para hacer lo bueno en este mundo.
- ***Es muy difícil tener dinero*** - Estas personas están totalmente felices con su propia posición; simplemente no quieren más. Temen que más dinero va a complicar sus vidas. Ahora bien, quizá estés en lo cierto si tú no eres un buen administrador u organizador, si permites que las cosas se salgan fuera de control. Sin embargo, la planeación puede eliminar complicaciones. Tener dinero requiere trabajo y no puedes ser haragán, pero muchos de los hombres y mujeres que conozco que producen gran riqueza les encanta hacer su trabajo.
- ***Consume mucho tiempo*** - Estas personas se preocupan de que les va a tomar mucho tiempo producir dinero, aunque se preocupan por pagar sus facturas, su casa, la educación de sus hijos y ahorrar para su jubilación. Por lo tanto, en lugar de ser proactivos y pensar en el futuro, viven su vida con temor del futuro.

Dinero—¿monstruo o amigo?

Recientemente, recibí una llamada de un pastor que quería mejorar su vida financiera, pero estaba preocupado de que su ambición fuera algo materialista. Él citó Filipenses 4.11: «No que hable porque tenga escasez, pues he aprendido a contentarme con cualquiera que sea mi situación».

¿Cómo respondí? Le dije que no hay nada malo en tener ambición—un hambre de conseguir logros, de tener éxito, es el motor que mueve la vida y produce el progreso que nos beneficia a todos. Yo creo que uno puede ser ambas cosas: ser ambicioso y ser feliz. La palabra contentamiento no significa una condición pacífica donde te acuestas, te das por vencido y dejas pasar la vida. En lugar de eso, es una actitud de asombro, reconocimiento de la grandeza de Dios, Su provisión, Su orden en tu vida. Tú estás agradecido por las cosas con las que te ha bendecido, pero no es malo tener hambre de más. Lo que es erróneo es la manera en que a veces corremos tras la riqueza como un fin y no como un medio para lograr lo que Dios quiere que hagamos.

¿Por qué hay un temor inmenso de materialismo en la iglesia moderna?

1. **Para cubrir el fracaso**

    Yo creo que algunas personas y organizaciones cristianas se oponen a los logros, acusando a aquéllos que tienen éxito, de materialistas simplemente porque tienen celos. Como pastor y líder de avivamiento de cruzadas, yo he visto que esto sucede una y otra vez.

2. **Por la desconfianza que tienen del éxito**

    La desconfianza que algunas personas tienen del éxito proviene de raíces en el abuso del éxito. Ellos han visto personas pasar por encima de otros y descuidar a su familia, destruir sus hogares o buscar otra pareja. Han visto el lado equivocado del éxito, así que no es de extrañar que ellos se sientan alarmados. En dichas circunstancias, es importante recordar que la gente «exitosa» que se ha comportado de tal manera, no ha demostrado una vida piadosa y nosotros no deberíamos seguir su ejemplo.

3. **Debido a la falta de comprensión del verdadero éxito**

    Eclesiastés 9:10 dice, «Todo lo que tu mano encuentre para hacer, hazlo según tus fuerzas...»: Tú puedes hacer cualquier cosa con todas tus fuerzas para la gloria de Dios. David era un gran rey, Abraham fue un gran hombre de riqueza e influencia y Job era probablemente el hombre más rico de su generación.

Tú puedes ser rico y hacer lo mejor que puedas y aún ser piadoso.

4. **Debido a una preocupación por la vida espiritual de uno mismo**

Algunos temen que el énfasis en los beneficios materiales, crecimiento y avance, vaya a producir carencia de crecimiento espiritual, pero no es necesariamente cierto. En la Biblia, José de Arimatea y Nicodemo, ambos eran hombres que tenían mucha riqueza y que buscaban a Jesús. Algunas de las mujeres que seguían a Jesús, aparentemente proveían grandes cantidades de dinero y recursos para Su ministerio. Sí, el dinero te puede robar tu vida espiritual, pero no necesariamente tiene que ser así. Cada uno escoge cómo va a manejar la tentación financiera.

La perspectiva bíblica

¿Qué dice la Biblia acerca del dinero? ¿Por qué no investigas por ti mismo los siguientes versículos?

- **Deuteronomio 8.18** - «Mas recuérdate de tu Señor porque Él es quien te da el poder para hacer riquezas, a fin de confirmar su pacto, el cual juró a tus padres». Hay dos cosas en este versículo: primero, la advertencia de no olvidarse de Dios. Segundo, que es Dios quien te da el poder o la habilidad para producir riqueza. Si la riqueza en realidad fuera algo malo o erróneo, Dios nunca hubiera dicho eso.
- **Deuteronomio 12.7** - «Allí también vosotros y vuestras familias comeréis en presencia del Señor vuestro Dios y os alegraréis en todas vuestras empresas en las cuales el Señor vuestro Dios os ha bendecido». Este versículo es la mismísima imagen de prosperidad. Da a entender que si sigues los caminos de Dios, Él te va a bendecir por eso.

- **Proverbios 3.9-10** - «Honra al Señor con todos tus bienes y con las primicias de tus frutos; entonces tus graneros se llenarán con abundancia y tus lugares rebosarán de mosto.»

- **Filipenses 4.18-19** - «Pero lo he recibido todo y lo tengo en abundancia; estoy bien abastecido, habiendo recibido de Epafrodito lo que habéis enviado: fragante aroma, sacrificio aceptable, agradable a Dios. Y mi Dios proveerá a todas vuestras necesidades, conforme a sus riquezas en gloria en Cristo Jesús». «Bien abastecido», quiere decir más que suficiente para tus necesidades. Significa que todo pertenece a Dios y ampliamente provee para todas tus necesidades.

Hoy en día, es imperativo que recuperemos este equilibro y dejemos la moda del materialismo, la creencia de que solamente en las cosas materiales puedes encontrar verdadera satisfacción en la vida. Si crees en el materialismo como tu dios en lugar de creer en Dios mismo, entonces estás cayendo en la trampa de la religión falsa.

Recuerda: la Biblia no está en contra de la riqueza; está en contra del abuso de la riqueza. No está en contra de lograr el éxito, a menos que éste se convierta en un sustituto de Dios en tu vida. ¿Por qué es malo? Porque Dios dice que no se debe tener otros dioses delante de Él. Si lo haces, vas a verter tu corazón, tu vida y tu energía en esos dioses y no vas a recibir alimento. Por lo tanto, si dedicas tu vida al avance material—casas, botes y autos—vas a pasar al hambre espiritual. ¿Cómo puedes evitar esto? Estando consciente de Dios todo el tiempo, no de ti, ni de tus posesiones. Entonces cualquier riqueza que obtengas estará en la perspectiva correcta.

Alexis Tocqueville, un noble francés que vino a América en 1835 a investigar esta joven nación, dijo: «Uno pensaría que el hombre que ha sacrificado a sus amigos, su familia y su tierra por convicciones religiosas, debería de estar absorto por completo en la búsqueda del tesoro que ha comprado a tan alto precio. Y sin embargo, uno se los encuentra buscando con casi el mismo celo, la riqueza material, o bien moral o ambas. Buscan el bienestar y la libertad en la tierra, así como la salvación en el Cielo». A mí me encanta esta cita, por su gran ejemplo de balance bíblico—una descripción de hombres y mujeres que creen en la Biblia, aman a Jesucristo, honran a Dios con todo lo que hacen y creen que pueden tener éxito.

Identidad financiera: tú y tu hijo

Para que puedas tener éxito financiero, tienes que estar consciente de tus propias tendencias personales. Yo llamo a esto «identidad del dinero». Existen cinco tendencias diferentes que puedes tener, o puede ser la combinación de varias de ellas.

1. El Debilucho - Tú no esperas hacer mucho más en cuanto a lo financiero porque piensas que eres alguien débil. Mentalidad: *yo simplemente no entiendo el tema de los números. Las finanzas no son para mí.* Prefieres salir huyendo de éstas y esconderte. No quieres arriesgar porque no crees que la situación pueda mejorar.

2. El Llorón - Piensas: *lo pude haber hecho, pero no lo hice por la culpa de fulanito* o simplemente: *la economía está muy mal ahora.* Prefieres quejarte que buscar oportunidades. Te ves a ti mismo como una víctima.

3. La Comadreja - Para la mayoría de la gente, la comadreja simboliza trampa. Tú piensas: *para poder salir adelante, voy a tener que engañar.* Quizás engañes al gobierno, a tu jefe o a alguien más para poder salir adelante. Proteges tus recursos porque temes que alguien te los vaya a quitar.

4. **El que gira la rueda** - Cuando llegas a cierto nivel de logros, te detienes porque sientes que te está yendo lo suficientemente bien y no quieres ir más allá de tus límites. No quieres producir más allá de lo que tus padres hicieron o más allá de cierto límite artificial que te ha sido impuesto (o que tú mismo te has impuesto).

5. **El Ganador** - Tú creces cuando hay una oportunidad y tienes energía sin límites. Esperas salir adelante en tiempos difíciles. Esperas tener éxito, ganar suficiente dinero para tu familia y tu futuro. Y eres disciplinado en la manera que gastas tu dinero.

Un llamado a la disciplina

La disciplina es un término clave cuando se trata de ganar y gastar dinero ¿por qué? Porque esos que fracasan en el manejo de su vida (incluyendo cómo gastan el dinero) fracasan porque les falta disciplina. Permíteme darte un ejemplo histórico. Aunque Samuel Taylor Coleridge fue una de las grandes mentes del siglo diecinueve, él era indisciplinado en lo personal. Incursionó en la vida universitaria, luego se enlistó en el ejército, salió del ejército, entró nuevamente a la universidad. Dio inicio a un diario intelectual llamado The Watchman (El Centinela) el cual fue publicado solamente diez semanas. Él expresaba a sus amigos libros en su cerebro, pero solamente escribió unos pocos poemas magníficos. Un autor escribe sobre él y dice: «Hizo grandes cosas en su mente y produjo tan poco».

Cuando se le pregunta a los consejeros qué sienten las personas cuando se ven arrasadas por una mala decisión de crédito, hacen una lista de lo siguiente: desesperación, vergüenza, opresión, temor, culpabilidad, confusión, frustración, impotencia, vulnerabilidad, ansiedad, resentimiento y amargura. ¿Es esa una descripción de la vida que quieres para tus hijos?

Esos mismos consejeros dice que cuando la gente logra estabilidad financiera, esas emociones negativas son reemplazadas por reacciones positivas: un sentimiento de contentamiento, satisfacción, sensación de logro y capacidad, seguridad en sí mismo, dirección en la vida, determinación, calma, equilibro, seguridad y certeza. ¡Qué contraste tan intenso y dramático, diferente al primero!

Se estima que la mayoría de los adultos americanos gastan del 30% al 100% más allá de sus recursos. Es ahí donde la deuda se convierte en algo inevitable. La deuda del consumidor se define como cualquier balance de dinero que debes después de seis días. «Estar de acuerdo en pagarle a alguien, usualmente a un extraño, pagar después por lo que quieres ahora». Decides, no porque puedas hacer la compra, sino porque que puedes hacer el pago. Está comprobado que esto se pone peor con el matrimonio—debido a un estado que los economistas llaman CCC—competencia de crédito del consumidor. Esto quiere decir que muchos cónyuges compiten entre sí por la cantidad que cada uno va a gastar. En otras palabras, si la mujer usa la tarjeta de crédito y se mete en deudas, el esposo cree que es justo gastar la misma cantidad que ella gasta y el ciclo nunca de detiene.

Liz (no es su verdadero nombre) conoce ese ciclo por experiencia propia. Debido a que a ella le disgusta mucho su trabajo, va de compras a la hora del almuerzo, gasta aproximadamente cincuenta dólares al día. Incluso siendo agente de crédito bancario y estar entrenada para pensar en el dinero, ella pensó: yo tengo un buen trabajo, así que puedo manejar esto y es mi recompensa por resistir al día. Hasta que se dio cuenta que sus pequeños viajes a hacer compras le estaban constando miles de dólares al mes, buscó a un asesor financiero para que la ayudara. Después de todo, su salario sin incluir impuestos, era solamente veinticinco mil dólares y sus viajes de compras la habían metido en una deuda de consumidor de diez mil dólares. Ella había sido seducida por el mercadeo, a comprar artículos sin los cuales ella «no podía vivir». Se tuvo que dar cuenta que gastarse su sueldo como recompensa para sobrevivir otra semana era una trampa colosal.

Ella no es la única que ha caído en esta trampa. Una vez nos tomó a Amy y a mí dos años para salir de deudas. Fueron dos años muy difíciles, pero fueron buenos años en muchos sentidos. Nos acercaron más el uno al otro, nos acercaron más a nuestros amigos y nos acercaron más a Dios.

Por lo tanto, diles a tus hijos que no tomen ese camino fácil del crédito. Quizás parezca flexible y fácil para meterse y acurrucarse, pero a largo plazo les hará daño. En lugar de eso, enséñalos a salir de deudas y a pagar el precio para ser financieramente libres. Es posible que te haya tomado largo o corto tiempo, pero ahora es el tiempo para cambiar tu manera de vivir y gastar.

El verdadero significado de la riqueza

¿Qué significa ser rico realmente? Diferentes personas lo definen de diversas maneras. Sin embargo, a mí me gustan estas dos definiciones maravillosas de un economista y planeador financiero:

1. **Ser rico es tener suficiente dinero para nunca más preocuparte de asuntos financieros** - Nunca más tienes que pensar ¿Cómo voy a hacer para pagar esto? ¿Hago malabares con dos facturas? Tienes libertad financiera.

2. **Ser rico es tener suficiente dinero para mantener el estilo de vida de tu elección sin tener que trabajar** - Esto no quiere decir que no trabajes, pero vas a trabajar porque quieres trabajar, porque te encanta hacer lo que haces. No porque estés atrapado en un trabajo que es un callejón sin salida.

No estoy diciendo que no vas a ser feliz si no tienes dinero. Si eres cristiano, obviamente tu verdadero gozo, alegría, y paz se encuentran en la relación que tienes con Jesucristo. Él es tu fuente. Él es el Dios de toda comodidad, según las escrituras. Él es un buen Pastor de las ovejas. Él es el Pan de Vida. Tú te alimentas de Él y tu corazón y tu alma están satisfechos. Él es el Agua de Vida. Tú bebes libremente de Él y te sientes satisfecho.

Pensar en el dinero no significa que estés obsesionado y absorto con las riquezas. Significa que eres lo suficientemente realista para darte cuenta que vives en un mundo material. Si piensas correctamente acerca del dinero y su propósito, entonces te vas a comportar correctamente y por medio del trabajo duro, vas a crear seguridad financiera y un futuro dorado para ti mismo. Incluso los puritanos, que influenciaron enormemente los primeros años de la República Americana, creían que la riqueza—lo que tú produces—era una expresión de gratitud a Dios. Era una expresión de tu administración de su creación. Además era una expresión de tu esfuerzo para contribuir a la comunidad en general. La riqueza era vista como un resultado natural del esfuerzo humano, la iniciativa y la intensidad y el trabajo no era visto como una carga o un mal innecesario que se debía evitar. El trabajo daba satisfacción y placer real. Había oportunidad para innovación, creatividad, curiosidad e incluso competencia. La propiedad era vista como una fuente de orgullo y progreso.

Es por eso que es importante que los niños sean animados a hacer todo lo que sea posible por ellos mismos. Por ejemplo, si le compras un auto a tu hijo ¿Cómo lo va a tratar? ¿Cómo un automóvil alquilado, o como una posesión muy valiosa? Pero si él tiene que trabajar para conseguir dinero para comprarlo ¿Cómo lo va a tratar? Si tus hijos están motivados a tener algo, ellos trabajaran más duro.

Enseñando al hijo a administrar el dinero

Yo solía hacer muecas cuando la gente hablaba del manejo de dinero. Yo pensaba: todo lo que necesitas hacer es ganar más dinero. Yo no pensaba que el problema era el manejo de dinero. Simplemente pensaba que no ganaba lo suficiente, pero desde entonces, he aprendido que si no puedes administrar veinte mil, no podrás administrar doscientos mil dólares.

Cuando Roy Kaplin del Instituto de Tecnología de Florida rastreó mil ganadores de lotería en un periodo de diez años, se sorprendió al descubrir que la mayoría de ellos eran infelices. Estaban aturdidos por su dinero recién descubierto; la mayoría de ellos no podían administrar su éxito financiero. ¿Por qué? Porque habían adquirido su dinero de una manera muy fácil. No habían trabajado para ganárselo, así que no se esforzaban para gastarlo de manera sabia.

¿Cómo puedes gastar dinero sabiamente? Existen tres secretos para manejar el dinero:

Secreto #1: Medición

Tom Peters, autor de *In Search of Excellence* (En Busca de la excelencia) dice que sólo lo que se mide se hace. En otras palabras, si no sabes lo que tienes, nunca lo vas a cuidar. Este es un principio importante, ya que la mayoría de la gente piensa que tiene más dinero que viene en camino, de lo que en realidad viene.

La mayoría de la gente cree que el secreto de la libertad financiera en esta generación, está en tener dos ingresos: ambos cónyuges trabajando. Pero ¿en realidad funciona? Muchas parejas no piensan en el costo oculto que puede acabar con el beneficio de tener un segundo ingreso y convertirlo en pasivo: la ropa de trabajo para encajar con la imagen de la compañía, más comidas fuera de casa, cuidado de niños, tintorería, servicio de limpieza para que puedas descansar el fin de semana, transporte para el trabajo, pago de impuestos más alto. Desafortunadamente, la respuesta no es tan simple como que el cónyuge simplemente pueda renunciar al trabajo y se quede en casa (aunque esa sería una opción a considerar).

El primer paso es averiguar cuánto gastas realmente y en qué. Así que mantén la cuenta de en qué gastas cada centavo que sale de tus manos. Cuando lo veas más adelante, esto va a revelar tu actitud en cuanto al dinero. Así que empieza con tus hijos a temprana edad. Una vez ellos comiencen a recibir dinero, un regalo de parte de la abuela, un trabajo adicional que hagan, por qué no ayudarlos a mantener un registro diario de sus gastos. Se van a sorprender de cómo cada centavo que ganan va sumando.

Secreto #2: Mapa de dinero

La mayoría de las persona gime cuando hablas con ellas de un presupuesto, pero el presupuesto, así tan negativa como suene la palabra para mucha gente, es simplemente un plan. Si quieres estar libre de deudas y tomar decisiones financieras sabias, tienes que determinar tu dirección financiera. Por lo tanto, la dirección financiera que hayas determinado te va a ayudar a saber cómo actuar. Por lo tanto, tú determinas tus sueños, tus objetivos y cuánto dinero necesitas o quieres para ser financieramente libre. Algunas personas lo escriben en columnas; otras lo ponen como diagrama o gráfica en papel, otros mantienen un registro en la computadora. No importa qué método elijas, simplemente hazlo y luego revisa el plan de vez en cuando.

Si enseñas a tus hijos cómo planear sus gastos, les vas a proveer un futuro financiero inteligente y libre de deudas. También les ayudará a eliminar el desorden que no les sirve y llegar adonde quiere llegar. De otra manera, el enredo de tomar decisiones puede abrumar a las personas jóvenes.

Secreto #3: Misión

Ningún plan de manejo de dinero va a funcionar a menos que tengas una misión, un propósito en la vida. Este es tu sueño más grande, lo que te pone erizo. Es lo que quieres lograr en la vida. Te motiva, te inspira y te ayuda a cambiar tus malos hábitos por buenos hábitos.

Si batallas para romper con hábitos antiguos, intenta estas cuatro maneras:

1. **Haz un compromiso público de cambiar** - Eso añade la dimensión de tener que entregar cuentas a alguien más. Estarás menos propenso a fracasar si te das cuenta que alguien te está controlando, deberás sostener lo que dijiste.

2. **Toma el primer paso** - Inmediatamente necesitas dar el primer paso hacia tus metas, no importa que tan pequeño sea, antes que pierdas la motivación.

3. **Repentinamente, sin pensarlo demasiado** - Después de que obtengas valor para tomar el primer paso, tienes que decidir: ¿quiero realmente cambiar este hábito? Si es así, tienes que hacerlo rápido y sin pensarlo. Esto significa que dejas de practicar esa conducta y no toleras ningún lapso. Esa es la única manera segura de cambiar tu vida.

4. **Construye un equipo de refuerzo** - No compartas tus decisiones con gente negativa que no es libre. En lugar de eso, rodéate con gente que te va a animar a seguir tus sueños, gente que ha solucionado un problema similar y que puede ser un punto de referencia para ti. Luego ve tras tu objetivo. No reduzcas la velocidad para que viejos hábitos se cuelen de nuevo.

La importancia de diezmar

Si eres cristiano, asegúrate de dar el diezmo y de enseñar a tus hijos sobre el diezmo. Dar el diezmo es la disposición de creer en Dios. Malaquías 3.10 dice, «Traed todos los diezmos al alfolí para que haya alimento en tu casa y ponme ahora a prueba en esto, dice el Señor de los ejércitos—si no abriré la ventana de los cielos y derramaré sobre vosotros bendición hasta que sobreabunde.» Tú puedes confiar que Dios—va a hacer lo que Él dice. Incluso si el mundo entero explota, tú puedes confiar en Dios y con su ayuda, tú vas a hacer mucho más con el 90 que lo que podrías hacer con el 100 por ciento. Después de todo, Él te creó a ti y Él es capaz de hacer cualquier milagro. Cada uno de tus suspiros le pertenece a Él de todos modos. Tú simplemente eres el administrador del dinero de Él y darle a él es un reflejo natural de tu amor por Él—y tu agradecimiento por lo que él está haciendo en tu corazón y en tu vida.

Dominando el dinero

¿No es aquí donde queremos que nuestros hijos lleguen? ¿Un lugar donde no se preocupen por el dinero? Para que tus hijos puedan completar su dominio del dinero, tienen que agregar estos siete principios en su vida:

#1: Que sus acciones siempre sobrepasen sus palabras

Si quieres tener control sobre el dinero, no te limites a hablar de él—hazlo. Deja de gastar dinero neciamente. Haz un plan para salir de deudas y luego cúmplelo. Construye un negocio.

#2: Vive en un mundo de metas

Tú has visto pequeñas bolas de cristal que dentro tienen nieve con escenas de cantantes, patinadores, etc. Cuando sacudes la bola, copos de nieve falsos giran en todo el interior. Imagínate vivir en ese mundo miniatura, rodeado por esa atmósfera. Así es en una atmósfera de metas. Tienes que construir una atmósfera imaginaria a tu alrededor que esté colmada de metas en lugar de copos de nieve, donde siempre los estés sacudiendo y ellos den vueltas a tu alrededor. Vive en un mundo orientado a objetivos y dirígete hacia ellos.

#3: Domina lo mundano

En lugar de involucrarte en inversiones de alto nivel, primero domina la mecánica de las finanzas diariamente: haciendo un balance en tu chequera, haciéndote cargo de tus impuestos, pagando tus facturas a tiempo, no gastando más allá de tus ingresos, apartando tu diezmo.

#4: Desarrolla fuerza sobre el sentimentalismo

A veces quieres gastar dinero porque tienes un deseo sentimental por cierto artículo. A veces yo caigo en esta trampa. Por ejemplo, cuando varias compañías presentaron ofertas para remodelar mi casa, tomé la primera propuesta, porque el caballero era muy amable. Luego me di cuenta que era dinero que me había costado ganar y que era el futuro de mi familia. Debí haber revisado las propuestas con más cuidado. Debido a que yo sé que soy débil en esta área, tengo que desarrollar más protección para mi persona y eso incluye no hacer ninguna promesa monetaria por teléfono.

#5: Sé motivado por los logros, y no por la desesperación

La desesperación no es motivación suficiente. Lo peor es que crea pánico y en el mejor de los casos simplemente te deja un sentimiento de alivio monetario mientras que te metes nuevamente en el mismo enredo. La desesperación es energía negativa y agotadora. Es una reacción a una situación. En lugar de reaccionar, decide actuar. Trabaja para cumplir tus objetivos, uno a la vez.

#6: Rompe con todos los códigos en tu vida

¿Sabías que muchos de nosotros nos hablamos a nosotros mismos en código? En realidad, es una manera elegante de mentirnos a nosotros mismos. La verdad es que yo no estoy en deuda. Puedo manejar esto. A mí me irá mejor el otro año. Pero la tarea de llegar a la libertad financiera no se llevará a cabo si las mentiras gobiernan nuestras vidas. ¿Cómo podemos romper con ese código? Diciéndonos la verdad. Entonces vamos a ser libres para hacer planes de acción.

#7: Declara guerra contra la esclavitud financiera

¿Cómo declaras la guerra?

Primero, necesitas una estrategia, un mapa de dinero. Tal vez digas, «Aquí está mi objetivo, mi sueño y aquí está el plan que tengo para llegar ahí». Si te vuelves demasiado introspectivo analizando todo el tiempo sin crear una oportunidad de acción, vas a quedarte paralizado y no vas a poder moverte hacia adelante. Por lo tanto, organiza tus objetivos a largo plazo.

Segundo: Necesitas estrategias. Las estrategias son detalles de día a día de cómo va a funcionar esa estrategia. Si te sientes desanimado y te preguntas si realmente lo puedes hacer, trata de ver hacia el futuro. Imagínate a ti mismo financieramente libre, cómo te vas a sentir, qué vas a hacer. Reúne apoyo a tu alrededor, gente que crea en ti y en lo que estás haciendo. Gente que seguirá creyendo en ti incluso si tu éxito toma mucho tiempo en llegar. Ninguna clase de éxito llega de la noche a la mañana.

Padres: pregúntense ustedes mismos esto, ¿Qué clase de vida me gustaría para mis hijos en diez o veinte años? Si ellos eligen tener dominio sobre su dinero, van a tener un glorioso futuro. Recuerda: si tus hijos logran libertad financiera, van a ser libres para continuar persiguiendo sus objetivos de toda la vida. Aunque acumular dinero no es el significado de la vida, interactuar con Dios, su pueblo y el dinero son necesarios para asegurar el futuro de tus hijos. Por lo tanto, enseña a tus hijos a no tener miedo ni sentirse intimidados por el dinero. Ellos no deben adorarlo. En lugar de eso, deben utilizarlo como una herramienta para el cumplimiento de sus sueños. Tú puedes ayudar a que eso suceda. ¿Por qué no adoptar una buena administración de dinero por ti mismo y comenzar a enseñarlo a tus hijos hoy?

Capítulo 10

Cuando tu adolescente quiere cortejar

Recuerdo muy bien una cita desafortunada que tuve en la Universidad. No conocía muy bien a la chica, pero era bonita y bastante divertida y eso me motivó a invitarla a salir. Para mí era un desafío. Yo era estudiante de primer año en la universidad y ella lograba ponerme nervioso. De hecho, me era muy difícil decir las palabras correctas para pedirle que saliéramos.

Cuando aceptó, planeé cuidadosamente esa cita—patinaje sobre hielo y muchas otras actividades. Pero llegada la fecha, estuvo terrible y la razón fue que yo era muy inmaduro y solamente pensé en mí. No supe como relacionarme con ella apropiadamente. Sabía bien lo que era sentirse atraído por alguien, quería cortejar, pero metía la pata. ¿Por qué mi cita fue tan mala? La razón fue porque no tenía ninguna guía básica, metas o la actitud para construir una relación saludable.

Si tu hijo es ahora un adolescente, su interés por el sexo opuesto está despertando, junto con todos los cambios biológicos en su propio cuerpo. En ocasiones las adolescentes se avergüenzan, en otras se emocionan. Su punto de vista en general atraviesa cambios tremendos. Y todos estos cambios pueden dirigirlas a una tremenda confusión. Es por eso que muchos adolescentes empiezan a cortejar por razones equivocadas.

Razones equivocadas para cortejar

Las malas decisiones pueden lastimar a tus hijos por el resto de sus vidas. Por eso es tan importante enseñarles a los hijos que como primer paso se debe tener sensibilidad para después entender que lo que hagan hoy afectará su futuro. Necesitarás estar a la delantera con tus hijos. Por ejemplo, Explícales porqué esperar para tener sexo es ser inteligente. Si tienen citas inteligentes, lograrán tener cimientos firmes para futuras relaciones y se asegurarán de que el matrimonio que tendrán algún día será maravilloso, bello, íntimo y satisfactorio – como Dios manda. ¡Esperar hasta el momento del matrimonio para tener sexo, es el plan de Dios y a tus hijos les evitará muchos dolores de cabeza si hacen lo correcto, pero lo más importante, complacerán a nuestro Padre Celestial!

¿Cómo podría saber tu hijo si es correcto invitar o no a cierta persona a salir? Primero, veamos cuáles son las motivaciones equivocadas para tener una cita amorosa con alguien.

Razón #1: Sexo

Tus hijos deberían saber que ir a una cita no significa que tienen o que deberían dormir con la persona. En esta sociedad de sexo demente, donde todos parecen acostarse con todos fuera del matrimonio todo el tiempo, parecería que el sexo es una parte natural para una cita, pero eso no es lo que Dios enseña. Sus leyes son claras: No sexo fuera del matrimonio. Él nos da este mandamiento para nuestro propio bienestar—para protegernos de las enfermedades de transmisión sexual, caos emocional y de la ruina espiritual. La vida no es como en las películas, donde aparentemente es muy normal dormir con diferentes personas sin herir los sentimientos de nadie y sin consecuencias subsecuentes.

Tristemente, incluso jóvenes cristianos y mujeres que

provienen de familias conservadoras pasan por esto. De acuerdo con Josh McDowell, un joven especialista, casi la mitad de la gente joven ha tenido sexo con alguien antes de cumplir los dieciocho años de edad y el resultado de los estudios sobre esta experimentación sexual origina destrucción emocional, embarazos no deseados, el trauma y estrés de recurrir al aborto y caos relacional. Tu cuerpo no se hizo para tratarlo como un juguete por ti o que alguien más juegue con él. Dormir con alguien más antes del matrimonio, privará de ese momento especial e íntimo de su relación con su futuro cónyuge.

Si tu hijo ya violó la ley de Dios y ha tenido sexo antes del matrimonio, aun con eso hay esperanza. Fomenta en tus hijos el pedir perdón a Dios y su ayuda para que sus pecados sean perdonados. Establece límites para que tus hijos no se vean tentados con este tipo de comportamiento nuevamente. Enséñales a tus hijos que Dios aun los ama, pero que puede haber consecuencias por sus acciones.

Razón #2: Prestigio

Lo ves todo el tiempo en las escuelas secundarias. Los niños quieren ser vistos con la persona adecuada. Saliendo con alguien en estos días es algo más que pasar tiempo con alguien sino no que ayuda a establecer el *estatus* de una persona. Si sales con la persona adecuada, dicen otros niños, «Wow, ¿te vi con ella? ¡Qué increíble!» El motivo de prestigio es una razón egoísta para encontrar pareja, y si esa es tu meta, sólo te harás daño a ti mismo ya la otra persona.

Razón #3: Necesidad

¿Cuántas veces has escuchado de sus hijos, «Pero todo el mundo lo está haciendo!» Muchos adolescentes que ni siquiera quieren salir con alguien lo hacen por sentido de obligación, porque es lo que «todo el mundo» hace. Ellos no quieren que nadie piense que son perdedores. Ellos no quieren sentir vergüenza, y no quieren que los demás piensan que no pueden conseguir una corteja, así que salen con alguien sólo por quedar bien con todos.

Todo lo antes mencionado son motivos equivocados para tener una cita—tienen poca visión y son egocéntricos. ¿Te gustaría saber cuál es el mejor ingrediente para una relación saludable? ¿El mejor de los secretos para un buen matrimonio? Contrariamente a la opinión popular, no es el amor, es la madurez. Por lo tanto, si tus hijos comienzan a tener citas por alguna de las razones antes descritas, siguen en un estado de egocentrismo, poca visión y por lo mismo, no están preparados para comenzar a tener citas. Hacerlo sería meterse en serios problemas.

Los objetivos correctos para cortejar

Tu hija se para frente a ti, pidiéndote permiso para salir con un chico. ¿Qué deberías decirle con respecto a cuáles son los objetivos correctos para salir con alguien? Dile que tenga en mente lo siguiente cuando considere salir con alguien. Los objetivos correctos para una cita son:

Objetivo #1: De honrar y glorificar a Dios

La verdadera forma de honrar a Dios con la atención que él merece es a través de entregarle nuestra vida. Significa que tus hijos deberán comportarse en sus citas amorosas, como si Jesús estuviera con ellos en persona, porque él lo está. De manera sobrenatural – Incluso aunque tus hijos no puedan verlo. Como dice Corintios 10:31: «En conclusión, ya sea que coman o beban o hagan cualquier cosa, háganlo todo para la gloria de Dios». Si son cristianos, su motivación será tener a Jesús, nuestro Señor siempre en nuestras vidas, incluyéndolo en las experiencias que se tengan al salir a una cita.

Objetivo #2: De ayudar a la otra persona a ser lo mejor que pueda ser

Si tu hijo adolescente sigue preocupado por él mismo, es porque no está pensando en la otra persona. En caso contrario, tu hijo adolescente pensará: «Wow, la amo porque ella me hace muy feliz». ¿Qué pasa entonces si él se casa con esa muchacha y despierta una mañana y se da cuenta que no es feliz? ¿Debería divorciarse? El amor no es condicional, no depende de lo que la otra persona pueda darte. El amor es una decisión. Deberías enfocarte en ayudar a la otra persona, concentrarte en las necesidades del otro, no en las propias. Si todas las citas amorosas se basaran en esto, no habría preocupación por el sexo extramarital o citas donde incluso se dan las violaciones.

OBJETIVO #3: DE AYUDARTE A SER UNA MEJOR PERSONA Y PREPARARTE PARA EL MATRIMONIO

Como punto importante para ayudar a otra persona a crecer, otra meta sería trabajar para incrementar la madurez y en las habilidades sociales, con la finalidad de desarrollar el hábito de llevarse de manera exitosa con un miembro del sexo opuesto. Tener una cita amorosa es una oportunidad de expandirse y enriquecerse de manera personal—aprender más acerca de ti mismo y como interactúas con otros. Tener una cita amorosa te enseñará que dar y recibir es imprescindible para una relación saludable—de eso se trata.

Seis características de una buena cita

Una vez que tus hijos entiendan la diferencia entre las motivaciones equivocadas y las metas adecuadas para una cita y sean capaces de distinguir entre unas y otras, entonces estarán listos para la siguiente pregunta: ¿Con qué clase de persona debo tener una cita?

Si eres cristiano, saldrás con el que algún día deberá ser tu esposo y ame a Jesús. Es la única forma de construir un matrimonio pleno de la mayor intimidad posible: mental, emocional, física y espiritual. Querrás un hogar donde ambos estén interesados en fomentar en sus hijos el conocimiento de Cristo. Un hogar donde Cristo este continuamente presente. Como dice en 2 Corintios 6:16: «Viviré con ellos y caminaré entre ellos. Yo seré su Dios y ellos serán mi pueblo».

Eso significa que cuando tus hijos se casen, la intención de Dios para con ellos, será el que se unan con alguien con quien puedan tener unidad espiritual, entrega mutua y compromiso con Jesucristo. Si los cristianos tienen citas con otros que no son cristianos, existe la gran posibilidad de que sus corazones vivan confundidos y terminen el matrimonio sin fe. Por eso es importante establecer normas con tus hijos adolescentes para que tengan citas con aquellos que compartan las mismas creencias. ¿Cuáles son las características específicas que tus hijos deberían buscar en alguien para tener una cita y en ellos mismos?

Característica #1: Alguien que te trate con respeto

Una adolescente me comentó que tuvo una cita con un chico de la escuela muy popular—a pesar de que sus padres no lo aprobaban. Le pedí que me platicara acerca de él. «Bueno, hace drogas, fuma marihuana, le gusta el "heavy metal" y es rebelde, pero es buena onda y todo mundo lo quiere.» Contestó con esfuerzo. Cuando le pregunté como la trataba, agachó la cabeza y dijo: «No del todo bien. Algunas veces se enoja, me calla y me da órdenes». Ahora ¿Por qué esa muchacha querría vincular su vida con un tipo que la trata con esa falta de respeto? La muchacha estaba imposibilitada por su propia inmadurez y su incapacidad de ver la verdad de que este tipo era malo para ella.

El respeto está en el centro de todo lo que es verdadero, amor maduro. Si no puedes respetar a una persona, no podrás tener una relación adulta de dar y recibir con ella. Solo puedes compadecerlo, sentir lástima por él y simpatía, pero sería un error si crees que lo amas, porque no tendrías la fortaleza y la madurez del amor que llenaría tu vida y el cual te ofrecería un matrimonio para siempre.

Anima a tus hijos a que se hagan esta pregunta: ¿Verdaderamente respeto el carácter de la persona con la que estoy saliendo en cita? Eso no significa que respetes lo bueno que es en el campo de futbol, lo bien que ella se ve o el gran carro que él tiene. ¿Respetas a la persona con la que estás saliendo como ser humano? ¿Tiene personalidad? ¿Es ella una buena trabajadora? ¿Maneja él bien sus finanzas? ¿Trata él a tu familia con cortesía? ¿Se dirige ella a las personas de una manera amorosa, o se burla de ellos a sus espaldas? ¿Piensa él que eres genial cuando hablas mal de otros?

Característica #2: Alguien con buenos modales

Significa que la persona con la que sales será atento, cortés y considerado—alguien que no te diga: «¡Cállate!». Muchos chicos hoy en día todavía piensan que es «macho» pisotear a la persona con la que salen y abofetearlas de manera verbal y física. Ese no es un comportamiento civilizado, es una barbarie. Los buenos modales nunca pasan de moda. Ten una cita con quien te escuche y considere tus opiniones de manera cuidadosa como lo haría consigo mismo.

Característica #3: Alguien que tenga estabilidad emocional

Si una persona tiene un temperamento violento, por el cual tengas que caminar con pies de plomo constantemente cuando estés con él o con ella, es un indicativo para poner distancia. ¿Por qué querrías pasar tu vida con alguien así? Tendrías siempre miedo de decir algo incorrecto. ¿Quieres pasar tu vida con alguien que hace pucheros y llora si no se hace lo que dice? Tus hijos no deberían tener citas con niños inmaduros.

Aquí hay una buena manera para que tus hijos evalúen sus citas potenciales. Verifica las cualidades de la persona con la que va a salir en las Escrituras. Gálatas 5:22 enlista las cualidades que deberán estar presentes, si el Espíritu Santo esta en control de uno y una de esas cualidades es el control.

Permíteme darte un ejemplo. Una joven le escribió a «Querida Abby» y dijo: «Estoy comprometida con este tipo que cuando no consigue lo que quiere, se enoja de tal forma que agarra lo que encuentra a su paso y lo patea tan lejos como puede» ¿Qué le contestó Abby? «Dile que deje de ser un niño o lo dejarás por alguien más». La respuesta de Abby fue un buen consejo. Es aceptable que un chico actúe así cuando están en los quince, pero ¿qué tal si te casas con él y continúa comportándose como un inmaduro? Casarte con el sería como tener tu propio infierno en la tierra.

¿Por qué muchos matrimonios terminan rápidamente en dolor y en divorcio? Porque no tienen estabilidad emocional. Porque las parejas son emocionalmente inmaduros, inestables y con falta de compromiso. La habilidad de mantener un compromiso a largo plazo es una extensión de madurez y de carácter.

Característica #4: Alguien que tenga un buen sentido del humor

No tengas citas con personas que sean demasiado serias y pesimistas que nunca se puedan reírse de la vida. Esos quienes se precian de tener buen humor viven más tiempo, son más felices y tienen vidas más plenas. Estas personas pueden ser capaces de reírse de sí mismos en lugar de vivir conscientes de lo penosas y embarazosas que puedan ser las cosas tontas que hacen. Las personas que son capaces de reír, son con las que se puede vivir más fácilmente. Disfrutan de la vida y se disfruta estar cerca de ellos.

Característica #5: Alguien con quien tengas muchas cosas en común

La expresión popular dice: «Polos opuestos se atraen» y si, se atraen, hasta cierto punto, pero verdaderos polos opuestos no necesariamente hacen una buena pareja. Si tú tienes una cita con alguien que es muy diferente de ti, entonces prepárate para disfrutar la novedad inicial y la emoción, pero la chispa puede desaparecer rápidamente. Las diferencias que podrían parecer pasajeras al estar conociéndose, a menudo terminan en enfrentamientos en el matrimonio. Sería mejor tener una relación a largo plazo con alguien que comparta tus creencias, intereses, sueños y actitudes. Por eso es importante enfocar tus citas en diferentes escenarios y situaciones. Necesitas visualizar como responden en diferentes funciones. Tanto más te enfoques en ellos, aprenderás a conocerlos mejor y entre más tengan en común, será mucho más fácil de construir cimientos de común acuerdo. Esto no significa que tú y la persona con quien estás saliendo, tengan que disfrutar las mismas actividades, pero sus más importantes creencias y sueños deberían coincidir.

Característica #6: Alguien que tenga un correcto entendimiento de los roles masculino y femenino apropiados

La Biblia es muy clara con respecto a que los hombres son llamados para ser líderes espirituales del hogar y la familia, pero eso no significa que los hombres deban de ser tiranos y pisoteen a las mujeres. Dios espera que los hombres ejerciten su liderazgo de forma equilibrada.

Eso significa que una chica no debería tener una cita con alguien a quien quiera dominar. ¿Por qué? Porque para sus adentros, ella lo hará sentir mal si se casa con él. Por el contrario, alienta a tu hija a que tenga una cita con un joven que sea un líder, que entienda lo que quiere financieramente, espiritualmente, personalmente, maritalmente y profesionalmente. Un joven que enfoque su fuerza en quien él es.

De la misma manera, dile a tu hijo que no debería tener una cita con una mujer que carezca de personalidad propia. Ella necesita ser fuerte por quien ella es también y estar dispuesta a realizarse como pareja con él para construir un sueño juntos.

Las mejores preguntas que sus hijos adolescentes deberían hacer con relación a tener una cita son:

- ¿Cómo será esta persona dentro de cincuenta años?
- ¿Podremos construir juntos un sueño?
- ¿Seguirá él/ella conmigo?
- ¿Será capaz él/ella de sacrificar su vida, si eso es lo que toca?
- ¿Será él/ella un mimado o un buen trabajador?
- ¿Me seguirá gustando él/ella si él/ella ya no fuera físicamente atractivo?

Quien posee esa clase de carácter, tus hijos deberían desarrollar un buen carácter, madurez y compromiso espiritual.

Entonces si tus hijos no tienen una cita con el tipo de persona que quieren, diles que se pregunten honestamente, ¿por qué no? ¿Es porque no soy la persona correcta? Si es así ¿Qué pueden hacer para cambiar? ¿Necesitan parar de gimotear o de llorar cuando las cosas no salen bien? ¿Necesitan desarrollar mejor sus habilidades con las personas? ¿Son posesivos y malcriados? ¿Necesitan desarrollar más habilidades de liderazgo? ¿Son tan desaseados que dan la impresión de que nada les importa o de que son holgazanes?

Si tus hijos toman en serio el atraer a la persona correcta, necesitarán desarrollar la habilidad de la disciplina y la ayuda de Dios para llegar a ser personas de Dios, quien será una buena pareja de otra persona de Dios.

Recomendaciones para salir en citas

Tus palmas comienzan a sudar. Tu «pequeña» de ahora dieciséis años, se para a la puerta a esperar a la persona con quien saldrá a su primera cita. ¿Qué le dirías?

Cuando llegue el tiempo de una cita, hay tres cosas que una muchacha y un joven deberán tener en mente y tener cuidado:

Recomendación #1: Cuida tus acciones

Debido a que muchos adolescentes están cambiando hormonalmente, ambos, chicas y jóvenes tienen la responsabilidad de conservar la pureza de sus actos. Esto significa minimizar las tentaciones al no ser seductores en la forma de vestir o de comportamiento, ser un líder moral y conservar el bienestar de la persona con la que planea salir.

Recomendación #2: Guarda tus afectos

Los adolescentes están bajo una tremenda presión, en ambos socialmente y a causa de su constante cambio de emociones. Deben saber proteger sus afectos y no deshacerse de ellos como algo que no vale la pena. Los deseos sexuales fuera de control traen muerte. Por eso tus hijos deben aprender a permanecer alejados de lugares donde hay influencias excesivamente sensuales o donde no hay presencia de los padres o de alguna figura con autoridad. De otra forma, se generará un potencial para los problemas.

Recomendación #3: Planifica tus sitas

No esperes solamente que una cita ocurra. Existen muchos elementos cuando de tiempo libre se trata para dar paso a que las pasiones físicas se aviven. Contrariamente a esto, organiza actividades que sean honrosas para Dios y que te ayuden a ti y a y a la persona con quien estás saliendo a adquirir madurez, habilidades sociales y relacionales y no seas de una sola dimensión, haciendo siempre lo mismo (como ir al cine o a comer pizza). Si haces eso, nunca realmente aprenderás a conocer a la otra persona. Es recomendable que conozcas a la otra persona en una diversidad de situaciones para que puedas obtener un juicio justo de las reacciones y carácter de la otra persona.

Si decides comenzar un noviazgo, es primordial llegar a conocer bien a la familia de la otra persona. Si quieres tener conocimiento de cómo él o ella podrían llegar a ser en el matrimonio, conocer a los padres es importante. Aunque es muy posible que él o ella no sean exactamente como son los padres, en general, tendrán características en común. Por lo tanto, Pon atención al comportamiento de la otra persona ¿Trata él/ella con respeto a los miembros de su familia? Solo recuerda que de la manera como trate a su familia, es como él o ella te tratará a ti si se casan y si ambos son cristianos, lo más importante será participar juntos en oración y el estudio de la Biblia.

Yo comencé a conocer de Jesucristo a los trece años, pero en realidad no había crecido espiritualmente hasta los quince, cuando comencé a tener mi primera cita y decidimos orar juntos. Al principio, me daba pena orar, pero lo hice porque desde entonces tenía el deseo de ser un líder espiritual. (Aunque se me dificultaba orar en voz alta y algunas veces la muchacha se quedaba asombrada cuando yo quería orar).

Cuando eres un líder, harás cosas que no te guste hacer, porque hacer lo correcto no es fácil. Estoy convencido que esas oraciones verdaderamente protegieron mi tiempo de noviazgos. Cuando oras con la persona que sales, es difícil atreverse a hacer algo incorrecto con él o ella, ya que se fija un tono espiritual de protección con la persona que sales. Por lo tanto, si eres cristiano ¿por qué no permitirle la entrada a Cristo en tu tiempo de noviazgo también? Jesucristo necesita estar presente en todos los momentos de tu vida—incluyendo el tiempo de romance y demás relaciones.

Sobre todo, asegúrate que tus hijos entiendan que las decisiones que tomen en el momento de una cita son decisiones importantes que impactarán enormemente su futuro. (Tristemente, cuantos adolescentes llegan a ser padres como resultado de una aventura amorosa en la primera cita ¿Nunca pensaron que esa jovencita podría salir embarazada?) Pero si sigues las normas de Dios y piensas en Él y en la persona con la que sales, la experiencia de tus citas será grandiosa. Más tarde, si te casas, tu matrimonio se enriquecerá porque supiste esperar el momento adecuado para tener sexo. ¡Vas en camino de un futuro maravilloso!

CAPÍTULO 11

La crianza de un joven lector

¿Porqué leer?

Mi madre me infundió un gran amor por la lectura. Cuando tenía cuatro años, me enseñó a leer. Como maestra de educación elemental, quien enseñaba en el cuarto de una casa-escuela, ella creía de todo corazón que leer era la forma para que los estudiantes escaparan de la pobreza que afligía los campos de carbón de la parte oriental de Kentucky.

Sembró en mí también un gran deseo por el conocimiento. A través de la lectura—decía ella—podría ir a dónde quisiera. Podría viajar a islas en el océano. Podría escalar montañas más allá de mi imaginación. Podría visitar personas de las que nunca supe antes y hacer cosas nunca antes imaginadas. Amaba las historias de mamá, ya que eran pletóricas de aventura y emoción.

Heredé ese mismo amor por la lectura a mis hijos y en el presente, ellos aman leer. Puedo ver que el hábito de la lectura les ha enseñado a desarrollar un vocabulario más amplio, mayor facilidad con la gente y habilidades de conversación efectivas, así como un conocimiento rico.

Siempre he creído en la lectura, de hecho, leo

aproximadamente cien libros al año. Esto no es porque soy un lector rápido. Leo a una velocidad aproximada de cuarenta páginas en una hora, pero busco mi tiempo de lectura por la noche, en la mañana y cuando tomo un vuelo.

Ha habido momentos en los que no supe que hacer y Dios estimuló mi memoria con una respuesta de un libro. Si tuviera que aprender todo lo que se necesita para ser exitoso en la vida a través de la experiencia directa e inmediata, me hubiera llevado mil vidas, pero los libros pueden infundirte la esencia del conocimiento de otros para que tú puedas aprender lo que ellos, sin tener que vivir sus vidas.

¿Tienes idea del tremendo potencial que tiene la lectura para transformar la manera como tus hijos actúan y piensan? Muy pocas cosas en la vida me emocionan más que leer debido a todo el conocimiento que se encuentra en los libros.

Algunas personas, como yo, aman abrir un libro y sumergirse en su información, pero otros encuentran la lectura como una terrible y penosa tarea. Para aquéllos de ustedes que aman el arte de la lectura, este capítulo aumentará su emoción y para aquéllos a los que no interesa esta actividad, espero que se sientan estimulados.

Para que te des cuenta que tan poderosa es la lectura, tienes que luchar a brazo partido para adquirir conciencia de que hay mucho de lo que no sabes, pero eso no significa que no puedes tener acceso a toda esta información. Si deseas que tu hijo tenga aventura en la vida, emoción sin par y las habilidades que se requieren para triunfar, esta es la única manera de lograrlo: Por medio de un programa de lectura tremendo, dinámico y que sea para toda la vida.

¿Por qué tu hijo debería adquirir el hábito de la lectura?

Razón #1: Para que tenga visión

Cuando tus hijos lean, tendrán «momentos de claridad» cuando se den cuenta exactamente de lo que necesitan en ese punto en particular de sus vidas. Por ejemplo, el libro de Philip Crosby: Los Absolutos del Liderazgo me alentó a pensar en lo que deseaba lograr en ciertos puntos de mi vida. Me ayudó a determinar con precisión quién quería ser y lo que necesitaba hacer. La vida es muy corta para juguetear. ¿De verdad puedes darte el lujo de no leer? A través de los libros, recibes ojeadas de ti mismo y te conviertes en una mejor persona, lista para poner en funcionamiento lo que acabas de aprender.

Razón #2: Para impulsarte hacia la acción

¿Por qué es tan importante? Porque hay tanto que afecta a tu hijo todos los días. Cada persona necesita algo para energizarse. No todo lo que leas será edificante. Algunas veces, lo que leas te va a hacer sentir incómodo, te frustrará con respecto a tu situación o te hará sentirte enojado contigo mismo, pero de cualquier manera, te impulsará hacia la acción. Si lees sobre gente que ha logrado hacer lo que tú sueñas lograr, te sientes motivado a perseguir tus propias metas.

Razón #3: Para mejorar tus habilidades

La lectura puede ayudar a tus hijos a aprender cómo manejarse en las situaciones de la vida. Por ejemplo, su tu hijo adolescente está sufriendo con sus relaciones con los compañeros, le ayudaría leer libros (ficción y no ficción) que le enseñen como otros han hecho funcionar los retos en sus relaciones. Si tus hijos adolescentes no son expertos acerca del manejo del dinero, harían bien en leer acerca de eso. Si deseas desarrollar habilidades de líder en tus hijos, aliéntalos a que lean libros acerca de personas que fueron verdaderos líderes en diferentes áreas tales como ciencia, medicina, educación, etc.

Razón #4: Para desarrollar conocimiento

Esto es diferente de solo adquirir información. El desarrollar tu conocimiento significa el ir más profundamente en un área en particular. Tú ya sabes acerca de esta área, pero necesitas mejorar en ella. Por lo tanto ¿Qué haces? ¿Tomas un seminario cada semana por un mes? ¿Hablas con alguien que ha logrado lo que tú deseas lograr? Si, puedes hacer esas cosas y además, puedes leer y desarrollar tu conocimiento paso a paso.

Razón #5: Para verte a ti mismo de una manera más exacta

La lectura te muestra a ti mismo como verdaderamente eres. Te da un espejo en el cual verte—ambos lados, el bueno y el malo. Sólo viendo la verdad acerca de ti mismo, te dará la facultad para construir una casa en un cimiento sólido.

Razón #6: Para desarrollar un instinto para lo que es cierto

Si tus hijos leen, desarrollarán un instinto por lo que es correcto y confiable. No los engañarán fácilmente con información y números. Por ejemplo, los medios de información pasaron los estudios sobre sexualidad de Alfred Kinsey, los cuales fueron conducidos entre 1940 y 1950, diciendo que él comprobó que el 10% de la población era homosexual. Sin embargo, el lector cuidadoso se dio cuenta que esa declaración de los medios era incorrecta puesto que la información de Kinsey estaba parcialmente basada en un incidente de actos homosexuales en prisiones.

Por lo tanto, enseña a tus hijos a desarrollar una sospecha saludable de lo que escuchan en los medios de comunicación. Jóvenes bien informados no serán fáciles de convencer.

Razón #7: Para mantener tu perspectiva

Si tus hijos están desilusionados porque no tienen buenas notas en la escuela, pueden leer acerca de otros niños que han experimentado los mismos problemas, pero lograron convertirse en adultos exitosos. La lectura ayudará a tus hijos a ver como otros han sobrevivido tiempos malos y les ayudará a darse cuenta que pueden trabajar con los problemas.

Razón #8: Para conseguir un modelo a seguir

Enseña a tus hijos a elegir lo que quieren leer tan

cuidadosamente como eligen a sus amigos. Lo que leen estará con ellos el resto de sus vidas. Va a poblar su mundo interior. A través de la lectura, tus hijos pueden llegar a intimar intelectualmente con grandes mentes. La gente acerca de la que leen, serán buenas o malas influencias. Ayuda a tus hijos a evaluar lo que leen al preguntarse: ¿Es este un buen modelo a seguir o no? ¿Querría yo a esta clase de persona como amigo?

Razón #9: Para crecer espiritualmente

Para crecer espiritualmente a través de la lectura, tu hijo deberá tener tres metas:

1.- Hacer que Dios sea real en su vida. Los libros pueden ayudar a los niños a acercarse al Señor. Por ejemplo, cuando tu hijo lee la Palabra de Dios, se alimentará espiritualmente ¿Por qué? Porque la Biblia no es solamente un documento humano. Es una guía creada sobrenaturalmente que alimentará su espiritualidad de maneras que no podrá hacerlo nada más.
2.- Para fortalecer en sus áreas débiles. Si tu hijo tiende a tomar decisiones rápidas sin pensar en ellas, hay ciertos recursos—el libro de Proverbios, por ejemplo —puede ayudar.
3.- Para fortalecer sus áreas fuertes. Si sabes que tu hijo ya es fuerte en cierta área ¿Por qué detenerse allí? ¿Por qué no reforzar sus músculos espirituales en esa capacidad también que tu hijo se convierta en un líder?

Obstáculos para la lectura efectiva

Si a tu hijo no le gusta leer, no está solo. Hay cinco razones por las cuales los chicos no leen:

Obstáculo #1: Ha sido forzado

A nadie le gusta hacer lo que le fuerzan a hacer. Por lo tanto, no atestes a tu hijo con la lectura. De lo contrario, vas a crear una imagen en su mente que leer es algo de lo que hay que huir, algo que hay que evitar y entonces tu hijo siempre pensará en ello en esos términos. La lectura ya no será divertida. Por el contrario, será un requerimiento, una responsabilidad.

Obstáculo #2: Ha sido expuesto a mucho material irrelevante

Asegúrate que tus hijos entienden que el tipo de lectura que están leyendo contiene algo práctico para sus vidas. Explícales porqué leer es tan importante, nunca una pérdida de tiempo. Construye un puente de información de libros para tu hijo.

No leí literatura de no ficción hasta que no cumplí quince años. Antes de eso, leí un montón de ciencia ficción y otras novelas. Amé cada segundo de ello. Entonces, una maestra de historia en la secundaria me animó a darme cuenta que las lecciones de historia me enseñarían cómo ser exitoso en la vida. Por ejemplo, cuando leí acerca de un general lidiando con uno de sus subordinados que trató de acosarlo, me di cuenta que necesitaba hacer eso yo también para detener a los acosadores. Eso es lo que yo llamo el construir un puente de la información para leer en tu vida práctica de todos los días.

Obstáculo #3: Ve la lectura como una acción para divertirse

Diles a tus hijos que la lectura no es algo que te evite hacer otras cosas. Por el contrario, te permite dar una mirada a hombres y mujeres que han logrado grandes cosas. Muchos de los grandes líderes de acción de todos los tiempos han sido hombres y mujeres que adoran leer. Toma a Abraham Lincoln por ejemplo. Citaba la Palabra de Dios frecuentemente, así como a Shakespeare y otros trabajos literarios. Los escritores de la Constitución y los hombres que ayudaron a Jefferson a redactar la Declaración de Independencia fueron hombres inmersos en la literatura de su tiempo y de generaciones anteriores. Por lo tanto, el ser un buen lector no te mantiene fuera de la acción, no te evita el ser un hacedor orientado.

El mundo de la mente es asombroso. ¿De dónde crees que provienen tus instintos de motivación? ¿De dónde viene tu acción? Viene de tu mente. Si tu mente no ha sido ricamente alimentada, ¿De dónde obtendrás tus habilidades y el conocimiento que necesitas para tomar acción? En lugar de que sea «una coladera de acción», la lectura es una forma de ganar conocimiento y las habilidades que empujarán a tus hijos hacia el tipo de acciones correctas.

Obstáculo #4: Tiene miedo de ser catalogado como «nerd»

Tus hijos pueden temer que otros los molesten si se meten tanto en los libros que los estereotipen como el tipo de noventa libras, de anteojos redondos de quien todos se burlan. Aunque tenga un cerebro grande, es pálido como un fantasma porque siempre está dentro. Es un fiasco en todas las áreas—especialmente en atletismo—excepto para la lectura.

Escucha las preocupaciones de tus hijos y después cuéntales acerca de grandes líderes como Teddy Roosevelt y Robert Louis Stevenson que no fueron otra cosa más que nerds. Recuérdales gentilmente los beneficios a largo plazo de leer mucho más allá de que los molesten temporalmente.

Obstáculo #5: Es intelectuamente un holgazan

En la sociedad de hoy, parece mucho más fácil encender el televisor y jugar un juego de video en lugar de leer, pero la lectura ayuda a los niños—quienes son naturalmente curiosos de todas maneras—a desarrollar una disciplina mental importante. Si tus hijos leen material desafiante, los convertirá en mejores pensadores y comunicadores. Les ayudará a desarrollar sus talentos. ¡Si leen los materiales correctos, conservarán su curiosidad natural de por vida y van a lograr mucho más!

Las zonas de peligro

¿Podría la lectura de tu hijo ser alguna vez un problema? Sí, hay algunas áreas de peligro, pero si los alertas, puedes ayudar a tu hijo a filtrar lo malo para encontrar lo bueno.

Peligro #1: La propaganda de la Nueva Era

¿Qué es lo que significa en realidad «Nueva Era»? Existen muchas variaciones, pero la filosofía Nueva Era generalmente incluye la creencia de que hay una fuerza universal que interconecta a todas las criaturas vivientes y que de alguna manera, necesitamos convertirnos en uno con esa fuerza. La filosofía de la Nueva Era también incluye la idea de la reencarnación—la idea de que estás conectado con el universo a través de una vida pasada y has renacido en forma diferente. Sin embargo, ese pensamiento es absolutamente falso. Hebreos 9.27 declara: «Está destinado que cada persona muera solo una vez y que después de eso, llegue el juicio». Con esas contundentes palabras, la Biblia rechaza la idea de la reencarnación.

Enseña a tu hijo a que sospeche de libros que lo alejen de la dependencia de Dios, intenta hacerlo pensar que puede encontrar todas las respuestas en su interior, o hacerlo pensar que puede conectar con el místico «poder del universo».

Peligro #2: Una sexualidad no sana

Cualquier libro que aliente la pornografía o el sexo extramarital debilitará la moral de tus hijos. Si les permites a tus niños leerlo, estás construyendo un conflicto interno y tentación potencial para ellos cuando sean mayores. Sé un buen ejemplo para tus hijos. No leas tales libros y no les permitas leerlos tampoco.

Peligro #3: Historia re-escrita por razones políticas

Explícales a tus hijos que esa historia es solo historia y no debería ser reformada por motivos de la agenda política de alguien. Tus hijos necesitan estar alerta de los libros que re-escriben la historia y que dicen lo que el autor quiere decir, en lugar de que reflejen con exactitud lo que realmente ocurrió.

Peligro #4: Declaraciones dramáticas que no tienen fundamento

Enséñales a tus hijos a ser cautelosos con libros que hacen declaraciones de condenación sin fundamento. Anímalos, en lugar de eso, a que busquen los hechos reales.

PELIGRO #5: LIBROS QUE DEPRIMEN TU ESPÍRITU

Cuando entras a una librería o biblioteca, puedes escoger sobre una gran variedad de libros. Algunos son positivos, edificantes. Otros son negativos, violentos y feos. Aun cuando necesitamos estar conscientes de cosas tales como condiciones de vida terribles, injusticias a través de la historia y demás para ayudar a cambiar nuestro mundo, no deberíamos permitir que esa literatura nos deprima. La Biblia dice que debemos encontrar esperanza en Cristo—aún en un mundo que parece sin esperanza.

Si tus hijos luchan con el desaliento, aliéntalos a que sigan el antídoto de la Biblia «Concentra tus pensamientos en lo que es verdadero, honorable y correcto. Piensa acerca de cosas que son puras, adorables y admirables. Piensa acerca de cosas que son excelentes y vale la pena alabar (Filipenses 4.8).

PELIGRO #6: LIBROS QUE NO TE AYUDEN A DESARROLLAR TU POTENCIAL

Enseña libros a tus hijos que los impulsen a luchar y a lograr lo mejor, en lugar de libros que retraten personajes que no desarrollan su potencial.

PELIGRO #7: LECTURA ANTI-BÍBLICA

Aunque algunos creen que es bueno leer libros que contengan perspectivas diferentes de la tuya, demasiado de este tipo de lectura puede ser nociva para tus hijos. Si están constantemente bombardeados por fuentes que violan los principios bíblicos, se van a confundir. El leer «el otro lado» para obtener suficiente información para clarificar su posición es una cosa; el habitar en esos libros es otra. El alimentarse con libros que niegan lo que la palabra de Dios enseña tendrá un efecto negativo en tus hijos.

Buenos libros para leer

Si estás buscando libros grandiosos, permíteme hacerte estas sugerencias:

Para el desarrollo del carácter

Cuando yo era joven, amaba leer libros de Edgar Rice Burroughs. Este hombre que escribió la colección de Tarzán, influenció el desarrollo de mi personalidad ¿por qué? Por cuatro razones:

1. Sus héroes siempre se manejaban bajo bases de honor—todo el tiempo, sin excepción. Nunca eran egoístas. Siempre hacían el bien, por el simple hecho de ser correcto.
2. Sus héroes y heroínas siempre mostraron valentía. No eran cobardes. No eran la clase de cobardes de «corre por tu vida», sino hombres y mujeres de gran carácter.
3. Sus héroes eran recursivos aún en los momentos más oscuros, siempre había alguna manera para un héroe o heroína para discernir como salir de algún problema. Siempre podían ganar sino se daban por vencidos.
4. Sus héroes siempre eran corteses con las mujeres. Las mujeres en los libros de Burroughs siempre tenían agallas, no eran pusilánimes. Los hombres cuidaban y protegían a las mujeres. En una escena, Jane despierta en su choza de paja en la jungla, después de una violenta tormenta. Cuando se asoma, ve que Tarzán ha dormido en la puerta de la choza para protegerla todo el tiempo. Cuando leí eso, tenía doce años y pensé «¡Wow!». Esa es la manera de tratar a las mujeres. Cuando hay una oportunidad de tener sexo fuera del matrimonio, los héroes de Burroughs siempre la destruyen. Nunca me han abandonado los principios de estos libros.

Para un crecimiento cristiano

Amo leer el libro de Proverbios de la Biblia porque no hay un libro más exitoso en el mundo. Billy Graham lee los libros de Salmos y de Proverbios cada mes.

¿Por qué la gente se siente tan atraída por el Libro de Proverbios? Porque tiene un efecto positive en ti.

Te enseña cómo vivir la vida, tomar decisiones, hacer frente a momentos difíciles y trabajar en las relaciones. Cuando te alimentas de la Palabra de Dios, de manera sobrenatural te dirigirá, te transformará, te dará poder y energía.

Otros libros cristianos también han tenido un efecto tremendo en mí. El libro de Henry Clay Morrison Santa Cruzada me afectó tanto que solía pedirle a Dios todos los días que me hiciera como él – un hombre de gran valor y habilidad que no comprometería el evangelio. He absorbido la autobiografía de Charles Spurgeon y me he identificado con su lucha de ambición egoísta vs. Obediencia a Dios. El libro de J.I. Packer Conociendo a Dios es uno de los pocos libros que he leído dos veces.

Las biografías de tres hombres: Billy Graham, Dwight L Moody y John Wesley formaron una imagen para mí de cómo ser un hombre de Dios.

A.W Tozer y E.M. Bounds me introdujeron al poder de la oración y la intrepidez espiritual. Estos son solo unos cuantos libros que han influenciado mi vida. Por lo tanto, introduce a tus chicos a edad temprana en la Biblia y otros buenos libros cristianos que les ayudarán a esculpir sus almas y transformar sus mentes.

Excelentes recursos

LITERATURA (PARA NIÑOS DE 8 AÑOS EN ADELANTE)

- Cualquier obra de G.A. Henty
- *Las crónicas de Narnia* (la serie), por C.S. Lewis
- *El furgón de los niños* (la serie), por Gertrude Chandler Warner
- *La aventura de los chicos Cooper* (la serie), por Frank Peretti
- *Abby y las aventuras de los Mares del Sur* (la serie), por Pamela Walls
- *Diarios de Marte* (la serie), por Sigmund Brouwer
- *Elizabeth Gail* (la serie), por Hilda Stahl
- *Dejado atrás: Los niños* (la serie), por Jerry B. Jenkins y Tim LaHaye

Historia y Literatura (para niños mayores de 14 años)

- Sobre el origen de los EE.UU.: *George Washington's War: The Saga of the American Revolution,* por Robert Leckie
- Acerca de la Segunda Guerra Mundial: *Delivered from Evil,* por Robert Leckie
- *The Rise of Theodore Roosevelt,* por Edmund Morris
- Biografía de Robert E. Lee: *Lee,* por Douglas Southall Freeman
- *Modern Times: The World from the Twenties to the Nineties,* por Paul Johnson
- *Intellectuals,* por Paul Johnson

Matrimonio y familia (para padres)

- En cuanto al hogar, relación conyugal, niños, adolescentes: cualquier obra por Dr. James Dobson
- Sobre tu cónyugue: *Lo que él necesita, lo que ella necesita,* por Willard Harley
- Cómo obtener victoria sobre la depresión: *Happiness Is a Choice,* por Frank Minirth y Paul Meier
- Cómo mejorar tu vida sexual: *El placer sexual,* por Ed y Gaye Wheat
- *Men and Marriage,* por George Gilder

Negocios (para padres)

- *Self-Made in America,* por John McCormack
- Sobre las fuerzas económicas que afectan los EE.UU.: *The Great Reckoning,* por William Rees-Mogg y James Davidson
- Sobre Libre Empreza: *Wealth and Poverty,* por George Gilder
- Sobre mentalidad positiva: *The Greatest Discovery,* por Earl Nightingale
- *Everything I Know at the Top I Learned at the Bottom,* por Dexter Yager y Ron Ball

PERIÓDICOS

- *American Spectator*
- *National Review*
- *The Washington Times*

A CLASSIC GUIDE TO WORLD LITERATURE (PARA PADRES)

- *The New Lifetime Reading Plan,* por Clifton Fadiman y John Major

A CLASSIC GUIDE TO WORLD LITERATURE (PARA NIÑOS MAYORES DE 14 AÑOS)

- *The Thirty-Nine Steps, Greenmantle, Mr. Standfast,* y *The Three Hostages,* por John Buchan
- *The Coral Island,* por R.M. Ballantyne
- *King Solomon's Mines,* por H. Rider Haggard
- *Beau Geste,* por P.C. Wren
- *The Prisoner of Zenda,* por Anthony Hope
- Especialmente para niñas: cualquier obra por Grace Livingston Hill
- Especialmente para niñas: La serie *Anne of Green Gables,* por Lucy Maud Montgomery

Los grandes medios de cambiar tu mundo son por medio de convertirte en lector. Va a enriquecer tu vida, alimentará tu corazón, desarrollará tu espíritu y te motivará a la acción. Cuando leas las cosas correctas, no basura, te vas a sorprender de la gran diferencia que hará en tu vida y en la de los que están a tu alrededor.

¿Estás dispuesto a comprometerte al hábito de la lectura por el resto de tu vida? ¿Enseñarás esto a tus hijos? Si es así, puede que tus hijos alguna vez estén solos, pero nunca se sentirán solos. Siempre contarán con un buen libro como excelente compañía.

CAPÍTULO 12

Para padres y futuros padres

¿Por qué un capítulo especialmente para hombres y muchachos? Porque en la sociedad de hoy, cuando los papeles del hombre son minimizados o ridiculizados, es más importante que nunca que los muchacho entiendan cómo ser modelos piadosos. Aunque parece como si estuviera pasando por alto a las mujeres y niñas, yo creo que este capítulo también es importante para ellas. Así como los muchachos necesitan saber esta información, las niñas necesitan entender a los muchachos y saber qué están buscando en una joven.

¿Cuáles son los secretos de las fortalezas del hombre? ¿Cómo debe el hombre relacionarse apropiadamente con su esposa y sus hijos? ¿Cómo puede mantenerse al día con sus responsabilidades? ¿Cómo puede hacer malabares para cumplir con las necesidades emocionales de su esposa y sus hijos financiera y emocionalmente y con el cuidado de sus padres que están envejeciendo? Eso puede ser abrumador.

Y aun así, vale la pena. Qué tan crucial pueden ser los padres para el bienestar de sus hijos y el ajuste a su vida adulta.

Cuando yo llevé a mi padre de setenta años a su examen

médico de rutina del corazón (mi padre tuvo un leve ataque al corazón a principios de sus cincuenta) nosotros no esperábamos ninguna sorpresa. No obstante, cuarenta minutos después, el doctor nos dijo que mi padre estaba extremadamente enfermo. Tres de sus arterias tenían serios bloqueos y debían repararlas inmediatamente. Aunque mi madre tiene una maravillosa y dinámica relación con Cristo, ella estaba temblando. La siguiente mañana, mi padre tuvo, no triple, sino cuádruple cirugía del corazón. Fue ahí donde me tomó de sorpresa: un día mi padre iba a morir y fue allí donde me di cuenta de verdad qué tan importante era este hombre en mi vida.

Nuestro mundo está lleno de ejemplos de niños, cuyos padres no tomaron sus responsabilidades como padres de una manera seria. Por ejemplo, toma el controversial caso de la figura de deportes Dennis Rodman. Yo me encontré una interesante historia del propio libro de Rodman que explica cómo se convirtió en lo que es.

Cuando él tenía cinco años, su padre abandonó a la familia, pero antes de dejarlos, le dijo a los niños: «Me voy para estar con otra mujer. Ella va a ser mi esposa y voy a ser el padre de sus hijos. Tu madre ya no va a ser mi esposa, y yo ya no voy a ser tu padre».

Mientras que el pequeño Rodman veía salir a su padre en un auto, algo se rompió dentro de su corazón. Salió corriendo aturdido a la calle detrás del auto y comenzó a golpearlo. Gritó, «¡Papi, regresa!». Pero su padre siguió manejando sobre la calle transitada. Cada vez que el auto paraba por el tráfico o en una señal de alto, Rodman corría de nuevo y golpeaba la puerta. Pero su papi no le puso atención y nunca regresó. Como resultado, Rodman pasó el resto de su niñez sin un patrón real de lo que hace un hombre.

Sin embargo, niños adultos dañados emocionalmente no están fuera del alcance del milagroso poder de Dios, revelado por medio de Jesucristo en la Biblia.

Muchos hombres hoy en día luchan. Se sienten agotados, destrozados por las responsabilidades en conflicto. Sus emociones corren por diez o veinte direcciones. Están frustrados porque sus sueños no se han hecho realidad. Aunque tratan con energía, las facturas se siguen acumulando y las responsabilidades siguen creciendo y ellos se desesperan por el miedo. La presión los está aplastando. Se sienten abandonados.

Según la definición de inglés antiguo, eso significa que básicamente se han dado por vencidos. Su energía se ha terminado y algunos de ellos son simplemente un fracaso. Todo lo que han intentado se ha venido abajo y no saben qué camino tomar en este momento. Se han metido en un túnel sin salida y hasta que entiendan lo que les está deteniendo, no podrán tener éxito.

Obstáculos para el éxito

¿Cómo puedes lidiar con sentimientos de frustración? Puedes aprender a entender los obstáculos para poder encontrar maneras de vencerlos en la mayor medida posible. Los obstáculos no te tienen que aplastar o agotarte completamente. No tienen que ralentizar en lo que has progresado o paralizar tu futuro. Sin embargo, para que tus hijos puedan entender esto, tienen que ver esa mentalidad y trabajo en acción en la vida de sus padres.

Obstáculo #1: Los extremos de la terquedad

¿Tienes esos rasgos de terquedad? ¿Te rehúsas de decir que estás equivocado, incluso cuando lo estás? Si haces eso, no estás solo. Ciertamente es parte de mi familia y bueno, yo soy una prueba viviente. De hecho, he lastimado mi relación matrimonial con Amy en algunas ocasiones. Incluso cuando he sabido que ella ha estado en lo correcto, yo me «he puesto mis moños» y me he rehusado a darme por vencido. Muchas veces, he tenido que ponerme de rodillas y renunciar a mi estúpida terquedad. He necesitado la ayuda poderosa de Dios por medio del Espíritu Santo para que me libere de eso. En ocasiones, él ha permitido que caiga por mi propia estupidez y es justamente lo que he necesitado para darme cuenta de lo que estaba haciendo.

La terquedad puede ser extremadamente irracional. Si eres testarudo, haces cosas simplemente porque quieres que se hagan de cierta manera—incluso si ese proceso no tiene sentido. Por ejemplo, tú solamente pagas una cantidad pequeña del total de una factura que debes. La siguiente vez sigues pagando la misma cantidad. Gradualmente la cantidad de la factura solamente se vuelve más grande y la compañía exige pagos más altos. ¿Por qué deberías de estar sorprendido si te manda a colección? Para empeorar las cosas, probablemente te va a tomar varios años para reparar tu historial de crédito y lo más importante, tu terquedad no agrada a Dios.

Asegúrate que tus hijos sepan que apretar los dientes y determinar que cierta cosa se haga (o no se haga) de cierta manera solamente para mortificar a otros, a largo plazo solamente termina lastimándolos a ellos.

Obstáculo #2: El problema masculino para probarse a sí mismos

¿Cuántos adolescentes, jóvenes adultos e incluso hombres mayores de edad hacen cosas estúpidas para probar que ya son hombres y ya no soy niños? Todos los hombres luchan de alguna manera con la necesidad de probar su hombría. Una vez, con el fin de probarle a algunos muchachos que yo era fuerte, me metí en el bosque durante el invierno sin abrigo, sin guantes, ni gorro y terminé dos semanas en cama enfermo, atrasándome en varios proyectos importantes y críticos y arruinando por completo mi itinerario. Además, creé trabajo extra para mi esposa Amy, quien tuvo que cuidarme.

No todo lo que queremos probar es problemático. En ocasiones es legítimo. Por ejemplo, veamos a Theodore Roosevelt. Él creció siendo físicamente débil, asmático, y con problemas de visión. Cuando era un joven, tuvo que enfrentar a varios muchachos tiranos que lo golpearon al punto de dejarlo casi sin sentido, pero en lugar de traumatizarlo, la situación le energizó. Tuvo la determinación de que iba a construir su cuerpo para nunca más volver a ser objeto de esa clase de abuso. Como resultado, él se convirtió en un individuo físicamente poderoso.

Así que examínate a ti mismo. ¿Estás tratando de probar tu virilidad? Si este es el caso ¿Cuáles son los resultados? Si te estás exigiendo demasiado solamente para probar tu valor, vas a poner en peligro a otros con tu imprudencia y vas a poner tu cuerpo en confusión. Yo recuerdo que mi padre se abrió la camisa para mostrarme una incisión masiva en su pecho, producto de una cirugía de corazón y me dijo, «Nunca permitas que eso te pase a ti. Ten cuidado con tu salud».

Obstáculo #3: Debilidad emocional

¿Batallas para controlar tus emociones? ¿Estás siempre descargando tu mal humor?

Una de las responsabilidades de ser un adulto es ser disciplinado. Esto significa hacer las cosas que debes hacer, incluso cuando no tienes ganas de hacerlas. ¿Pasas de un estado de ánimo a otro y esperas a que otros se acomoden continuamente a tus cambios de ánimo? o ¿Disciplinas tus emociones?

Obstáculo #4: Dominio físico

Lo voy a decir sin rodeos: no hay ninguna excusa para que abuses físicamente a otros. Quizás digas: «Bueno, él me provocó» o «El muchacho me faltó al respeto». Esa no es excusa para que uses tu fuerza física para lastimar a otros.

Mientras Amy y yo estábamos manejando sobre la carretera Interestatal 75 pasando por Tennessee un hermoso día, nos entristeció ver un caso de abuso justo frente a nosotros. Mientras el tráfico disminuía la velocidad debido a una construcción, una camioneta blanca venía detrás de nosotros, casi pegada a nuestro auto. La pareja de la camioneta estaba teniendo una discusión. De repente, el hombre se inclinó y comenzó a golpear a la mujer con el puño. Ella gritó y él comenzó a darle una lección con su dedo en su propia cara. Cuando ella se dio la vuelta, como para huir del abuso, él la alcanzó y rompió su blusa hasta que ella solamente quedó en ropa interior. Así que ahí estaba esa pobre mujer, varada en el tráfico, sosteniendo desesperadamente los pedazos de su ropa. Se acurrucó en una esquina de la camioneta y comenzó a llorar amargamente. Cuando de repente el tráfico comenzó a avanzar, perdimos de vista la camioneta. Pero estábamos tan sorprendidos de la ira de este hombre y su trato monstruoso hacia la mujer.

No hay ninguna excusa para que un hombre muestre un comportamiento tan indignante. Supuestamente, él debe de proteger a la mujer, cuidar de ella y amarla. Él es responsable ante los ojos de Dios a nunca maltratarla. Él debe amar a su mujer con un amor incondicional y de sacrificio.

Obstáculo #5: Distanciamiento sexual

Cuando piensas en distanciamiento sexual, quizás pienses que es frigidez sexual. Pero no es de eso de lo que yo estoy hablando aquí. Yo estoy hablando de un hombre que simplemente no se relaciona románticamente con su mujer. Él quiere sexo, pero es sus términos. Si ella no responde a él inmediatamente, se vuelve frío. Cuando él consigue el sexo que quiere, la abandona y la descuida, nunca piensa ni aborda las necesidades y sentimientos de ella y cuando él no quiere sexo, simplemente se aleja de ella. Él no pasa tiempo con ella desarrollando su relación. No se comunica románticamente con ella. Simplemente la usa para satisfacer sus deseos y necesidades.

Obstáculo #6: Desvíos sexuales

Cuando un hombre se desvía sexualmente de su mujer, se está desviando hacia el infierno, a una locura y destrucción y locura espiritual. Si necesitas prueba de esto, simplemente da un vistazo a los titulares. Hablan de hombres y mujeres que viven una vida sin Dios, vidas moralmente vacías, que destruyen a su familia e hijos. Cualquier hombre que toma una desviación sexual, está optando por una vida que eventualmente lo matará espiritual, moral y físicamente y va a destruir a su mujer e hijos que Dios le ha confiado.

El adulterio es una de esas desviaciones, pero existen otras, incluyendo la homosexualidad y la pornografía. La Biblia dice que cualquier otra clase de relación sexual que no sea con tu mujer es errónea; es pecado.

Obstáculo #7: Demostración de falta de respeto

Existen dos maneras de mostrar falta de respeto:

- Ser abiertamente crítico y verbal y avergonzar a alguien.
- Descuidar a alguien y no pasar tiempo con él o ella.

La primera forma de mostrar falta de respeto es obvia. Todos pueden ver el resultado de ésta (un miembro de familia o amigo amargado) y el tipo de clima que se crea en el hogar. No obstante, la segunda manera de mostrar falta de respeto es más insidiosa: el descuido: Esto quiere decir que ignoras las necesidades de la otra persona. Tú no lo/la escuchas, no pasas tiempo con ella y no conversas con él o ella.

Ambas clases de falta de respeto le comunican a la persona que a ti simplemente no te importa. Por lo tanto, pregúntate: ¿Qué diría mi familia acerca de la manera como lo trato? ¿Muestro respeto o falta de respeto con mis palabras y acciones?

Obstáculo #8: Enojo descontrolado

No hay excusa para explotar de ira frente a tu familia o alguien más, por ningún motivo. No es una muestra de fuerza viril, es una muestra de debilidad. Es falta de disciplina emocional que rasga las entrañas de la familia y causa un daño tremendo.

Incluso de los que saben que los amas, van a tener cuidado si les gritas. Yo tengo una relación muy buena con mi hija Allison, pero recuerdo una ocasión el año pasado cuando yo me enojé mucho y le grité. Aunque fui y pedí disculpas, le pedí que me perdonara, pude ver el dolor en sus ojos días después. Eso realmente me humilló. Tomó muchos días para que yo pudiera recuperar la «preciosidad» de la relación que teníamos previamente. Así que ahora, aún más, yo le pido a Dios que me ayude a controlar mi genio frente a mis hijos.

Nadie es un modelo de virtud, pero en lugar de decir: «Bueno, a veces simplemente pierdo los estribos», pídele a Dios ayuda. Si le has entregado tu vida a Jesucristo, él va a satisfacer tus necesidades poderosamente. Como lo dice en Gálatas 5.22-23,25 «Mas el fruto del espíritu es amor, gozo, paz, paciencia, benignidad, bondad, fidelidad, dominio propio, contra tales cosas no hay ley».

Obstáculo #9: Desvíos de agenda

Un hombre con frecuencia tiene agendas divergentes que lo separan de su familia, su responsabilidad y compromiso principal. Cuando digo «agendas divergentes» no me refiero a un trabajo regular. Más bien, me refiero a que algunas veces nosotros los hombres comenzamos a desarrollar nuestro propio mundo y nos olvidamos de conectarnos con nuestra familia. Por lo tanto, terminamos jugando golf con un colega del trabajo cuando nuestros hijos necesitan que estemos en casa. Vamos a jugar raquetball en lugar de llevar a cenar a nuestra esposa. Esto no significa que no hagas cosas para divertirte, simplemente significa que parte de tener una familia significa que sacrifiques un poco de tu tiempo libre y lo pases con ellos.

Obstáculo #10: Entretenimiento excesivo

¿En qué pasas el tiempo? ¿Vas de actividad en actividad, esperando que dicho entretenimiento haga feliz a tus hijos? Si es así, quizás estés enfangado en un patrón de entretenimiento excesivo. El entretenimiento es bueno. Te ayuda a relajarte y disfrutar de las cosas buenas que Dios te ha dado, como la habilidad de reír a carcajadas, pero también puedes llegar a tener demasiado de una sola cosa.

La cantidad de entretenimiento no es el único problema. Los americanos también luchamos con un espiral ascendente de la calidad de entretenimiento. Por ejemplo ¿La película o programa de televisión que estás viendo está ayudando a ti y a tus hijos a ser más piadosos? ¿Es moralmente sospechoso y pleno de tentación sexual? Lo que observas, se arraiga no solamente en tu cerebro, sino en la mente de tus hijos y también las acciones.

Obstáculo #11: El molino de los rencores

¿Están los resentimientos latentes en el fondo de tu corazón? ¿Vives pensando en los males pasados y esperas cobrar venganza? Si es así, esos rencores te van destruir.

Para poder ser libre de rencores, vas a tener que arrancarte ese veneno. Eso quiere decir que si la gente te insulta, te pone en vergüenza o te causa dificultades, debes aprender a lidiar con tu ira—antes de que se convierta en una úlcera en tu alma. A veces eso significa ir con la otra persona y hablar con ella amablemente y con honestidad.

Aquí está lo que la Biblia dice acerca de guardar rencor: «Airaos pero no pequéis; que no se ponga en sol sobre vuestro enojo». Ese es un buen lema para todos, especialmente en esta época de violencia.

Obstáculo #12: Conflicto conversacional

¿Has estado cerca de alguien que siempre está queriendo tener conflicto? ¿Alguien que siempre tiene algo negativo que decir? ¿Qué dice algo que parece bien en la superficie pero es algo tenso, en el fondo es una respuesta negativa?

¿Alguien que piensa que el desastre está acechando a la vuelta de la esquina?

Éstas no son las únicas maneras de crear conflicto en la conversación. Tú también puedes hacerlo al discutir por todo o intentar imponer, obstinadamente, tu propio punto de vista, sin importar nada más. Crear este tipo de conflicto le robará la tranquilidad a tu hogar, el ambiente cómodo que Dios ha predestinado. Por lo tanto, antes de abrir la boca, mide tus palabras. Evalúa lo que estás a punto de decir y la manera como lo vas a decir.

Obstáculo #13: Violencia verbal

Puedes tener conflicto en una conversación de manera tranquila o indirecta, pero regularmente, la violencia verbal en el siguiente paso. Abres la boca y echas fuera lenguaje que golpea a quien lo está recibiendo. Presionas a los demás, los alteras y los pruebas para ver cuánto pueden aguantar. De hecho, tú actúas como el acosador en el área de juegos.

Hay un dicho: «Los palos y las piedras me van a romper los huesos, pero las palabras jamás me lastimarán». Sin embargo, este dicho es totalmente falso. A veces las palabras lastiman a quienes más amas. Piensa en los últimos siete días. ¿Qué clase de ambiente comunicativo has creado en tu hogar? ¿Es de violencia verbal y tensión?

Cualquier insulto puede ser problemático y las intenciones son peor. Eso quiere decir que conoces los puntos débiles de los miembros de tu familia e intencionalmente los haces enojar para lastimarlos. (Si los hombres se dieran cuenta de lo mucho que sus palabras lastiman a sus esposas, tal vez sabrían por qué a veces sus esposas responden fríamente en lo sexual).

Los hijos necesitan disciplina amorosa y los insultos no deben ser parte de la disciplina. La disciplina construye al niño y lo sitúa en el camino correcto. Insultar al niño destruye su autoestima y puede afectar su futuro en gran manera.

Obstáculo #14: Generador de celos

Los celos significan que siempre estás controlando a los demás, incluso si no tienes razón para hacerlo. Eres posesivo y sofocante y ejerces control emocional sobre los pensamientos y acciones de otros. Eres celoso del tiempo que pasan con otras personas porque quieres controlar cada parte de su vida.

Mostrar celos no te va a acercar a esa persona. Te va a forzar a separarte y resentir a todos los que estén a tu alrededor.

Obstáculo #15: Vacío espiritual

Si estás espiritualmente vacío, cualquier cosa puede arrasarte y tomar el lugar de Dios en tu vida. Por ejemplo, no hay nada malo con ser apasionado en la conversación, pero si tu pasión por conservar árboles es más importante que tu relación con Dios, tienes un problema. Estás reemplazando al Dios verdadero del universo por otra «religión».

Enseña a tus hijos a que Dios es el único que verdaderamente puede entender tus necesidades básicas.

Lo que realmente necesitan los hombres

¿Deseas entender mejor a tu hijo mientras está en crecimiento? ¿Deseas saber qué lo conduce a hacer las cosas que hace? Para poder entender a tu hijo, que un día se va a convertir en hombre, es importante estar consciente y entender las necesidades que impulsan al hombre, especialmente en una sociedad que tiende a hacer todos los papeles de «género neutro». Aquí están los fundamentos que yo he aprendido en mi experiencia personal (sólo pregúntale a mi esposa).

Necesidad #1: Alcanzar excelencia

No puedes engañarte. Sabes cuando has hecho tu mejor esfuerzo y cuando no. Cada vez que trabajas, te sacrificas y alcanzas la excelencia, sientes ese orgullo de logro y emoción en tu corazón. Ganes o pierdas, diste todo lo que tienes y eso despierta energía, emoción y compromiso en ti. Sin embargo, cada vez que no das lo mejor que puedas, algo se marchita dentro de ti. Es por eso que algunas personas se sienten agotadas, tristes y frustradas. No se han esforzado lo suficiente. No han dado lo mejor de ellos.

Necesidad #2: De ser admirado

Se han escrito muchos libros acerca de las diferencias entre hombres y mujeres. Estos libros revelan que las mujeres, principalmente, tienen la tendencia a estar más conscientes de las emociones, tanto propias, así como las de aquéllos que están alrededor de ellas. Se preocupan de cómo sus acciones y palabras afectan a otros. Ellas realmente despiertan esa suavidad en la sociedad, que de otra manera quizás no existiría.

Al hombre, sin embargo, lo impulsa, principalmente, la necesidad de sentir su ego enaltecido. Y al decir esto, no me refiero al egoísmo, orgullo o arrogancia. Un hombre necesita ser admirado y respetado. Si no lo es, su masculinidad se ve amenazada. Eso quiere decir que lo peor que puedes hacer es avergonzarlo, humillarlo y dañar su ego. Él anhela ser admirado por sus logros y su productividad. Los niños anhelan lo mismo.

Necesidad #3: De demostrar productividad

Un hombre necesita ver resultados de su productividad. Necesita saber que ha logrado la excelencia. Aunque quizás ciertas personas que estén a su alrededor lo admiren por ello (necesidad 2) él también quiere ver los resultados productivos de su trabajo en su familia. Es por esa razón que a veces un hombre tiene la determinación de construir un hogar para su familia y está preocupado por la clase de auto que conduce. Esos son resultados visuales de lo que el hombre en realidad ha logrado con el trabajo que ha desarrollado.

Necesidad #4: De proteger

El hombre tiene necesidad de proteger a quienes ama. Eso quiere decir que cada hombre necesita la oportunidad de proteger a su familia en todas las formas posibles.

Recientemente, hablé con una viuda cuyo esposo había construido un negocio tremendo. Ella me dijo con lágrimas en los ojos cuánto lo extrañaba y lo amaba. Debido a que ambos son cristianos, ella sabe que lo verá de nuevo en el cielo, pero además compartió conmigo lo importante que era para ella el hecho de que él la había dejado protegida financieramente. La protegió hasta donde pudo, incluso después de su muerte.

Necesidad #5: De resolver problemas

A la mayoría de los hombres, de forma innata les encanta solucionar problemas.

Yo recuerdo una vez que nuestra casa necesitaba muchas reparaciones. Planeé el tiempo de dos semanas para que los trabajadores se encargaran de toda la lista, pero eso no fue exactamente lo que sucedió.

Los trabajadores dijeron que vendrían pero nunca se presentaron o lo echaron todo a perder. Nos cortaron las líneas telefónicas tres veces por equipos diferentes, que no tenían idea de lo que hacían.

Al principio, estaba incrédulo, luego me frustré y me enojé. Me sentí deprimido. Después de todo, yo había tomado dos semanas de descanso para encargarme de estos problemas y sentía que me estaba golpeando la cabeza contra la pared. Mi actitud negativa comenzó a contagiar a mi familia.

Cuando me di cuenta de lo que estaba pasando—que mi familia necesitaba que solucionara los problemas en lugar de volverme yo mismo el problema—mi actitud cambio totalmente. Mi nivel de energía comenzó a subir y vislumbré el proceso como un reto.

El famoso Dwight Eisenhower, quien hizo un trabajo increíble coordinando a los Aliados para la Invasión de Normandía, Francia, el 6 de junio de 1944, es un buen modelo a seguir para solucionar problemas. Aunque organizar toda la invasión fue una gran tarea que algunos pensaban que era imposible, él lo logró. ¿Cómo? Enfocando el problema como un reto, como una oportunidad para solucionar las aflicciones de los demás.

Eso fue exactamente lo que yo hice con la situación de las reparaciones en mi casa. Al final de la prueba ¿saben lo que recibí de mi esposa? Admiración y alivio de que los problemas habían sido resueltos.

Por lo tanto, en lugar de que los problemas te golpeen el rostro, úsalos como combustible para convertirte en una persona con habilidades para resolver problemas.

Necesidad #6: Realización sexual

Los hombres—incluso esos que están felizmente casados, comprometidos a Cristo y moralmente limpios—tienen construidas antenas sexuales. Eso quiere decir que siempre están alertas a las oportunidades sexuales, incluso si no están tratando de detectarlas.

¿Cómo trata el hombre con esto? Quizás él elija actuar por sus instintos, convirtiéndose, en esencia, en un depredador sexual que se aprovecha de otra persona o bien puede elegir los caminos de Dios—puede canalizar esos deseos para satisfacer las necesidades de su esposa.

Es importante que cuando sientas esa vulnerabilidad sexual o disponibilidad de otra mujer que no sea tu esposa, nunca la pongas en práctica.

De hecho, debes escapar de esa situación lo más pronto posible. No caigas en la trampa de alagar a otra mujer por su apariencia, porque si haces eso, es posible que estés creando esa disponibilidad sexual que no debería existir.

Sí, el hombre tiene necesidades sexuales, pero éstas deben ser canalizadas apropiadamente. ¿Cuáles son las necesidades sexuales del hombre?

- **El hombre necesita una salida para su virilidad**

En otras palabras, un hombre necesita una esposa que lo anime a expresar su masculinidad, su emoción con el sexo.

- **Un hombre desea placer**

Necesita disfrutar el placer sexual y tener una compañera lo que disfrute.

- **Un hombre necesita que lo necesiten**

Necesita saber que excita a su mujer y que ella desea su unión. Esta excitación mutua es una gran bendición y un beneficio para su vida juntos.

- **Un hombre necesita variedad**

Esto quiere decir que el hombre disfruta el cambio de ritmo, por ejemplo, no tener sexo en la misma habitación todas las noches o siempre en la misma posición.

- **El hombre necesita frecuencia**

Los hombres están estructurados físicamente a tener sexo frecuentemente. Una esposa sensible va a entender este elemento biológico de su esposo y abrazará la oportunidad para satisfacer sus necesidades.

Necesidad #7: De diseñar el futuro

Tiene que ser capaz de vislumbrar el camino y tener metas y sueños que se pueden alcanzar.

Necesidad #8: De tener alguien para guiar

Un hombre necesita niños, alguien a quien pueda guiar. Un día, estando en un aeropuerto, vi a una niña aferrándose a su padre. Ella no quería que se fuera, pero él le dijo: «Te amo cariño, me gustaría quedarme, pero ya no vivo aquí». El egoísmo de los adultos que se divorcian está destrozando a los niños y eso tiene que parar.

Todas las parejas van a tener problemas de vez en cuando, pero creo que con la ayuda de Dios, se pueden solucionar. No hay problema para el cual Dios no pueda tener una solución, si ambos tienen el deseo de ser obedientes a Él, amarse el uno al otro y comprometerse a los principios de Su Palabra. Cuando te casas con alguien, la intención de Dios es que sea para siempre en esta tierra.

Para los que han pasado por un divorcio, no intento hacerlos sentir culpables. Dios te perdona y te ayuda si te vuelves a Él y le pides que te ayude. Lo que estoy diciendo es que tienes la oportunidad de tener un nuevo comienzo, de hacerlo correctamente la segunda vez. Lo que construyes en tus hijos o alguna persona a quien estés guiando es vital y tu contribución es única.

Necesidad #9: De tener amigos

En otras palabras, un hombre necesita pasar tiempo con otros hombres para tener amistad a través de juegos, pasatiempos y actividades. No puede sobrevivir como unidad aislada. Necesita otros hombres que sean confiables, que puedan confiar en él y que le dirán la verdad.

Necesidad #10: De ser competitivo

Un hombre tiene cierta necesidad de competencia positiva. Aunque algunos hombres son obviamente más competitivos que otros, todo hombre necesita cierto nivel de competencia saludable. Sin embargo, es importante mantenerla saludable, positiva y alegre, en lugar de permitir que se vuelva personal y muy intensa. La competencia saludable no significa que quieras ganar a cualquier precio. No significa que no puedas ser feliz a menos de que ganes. En lugar de eso, la competencia saludable afina tus destrezas.

Necesidad #11: De ser un líder espiritual

Un hombre necesita tener la oportunidad de ser líder espiritual. En su libro, *Men and Marriage* (Los hombres y el matrimonio) George Gilder escribe que 80% del tiempo los niños adquieren los valores morales y espirituales de parte de su padre, en lugar que de su madre. Aunque eso no minimiza para nada la importancia del papel de la madre, ciertamente es una prueba de que los padres son los líderes espirituales de la familia, ya sea que quieran serlo o no. Por lo tanto, sino acercas a tus hijos a Dios, los alejas.

Los ladrones de la masculinidad

Ya examinamos los obstáculos en el camino de la hombría y estudiamos profundamente las necesidades de un hombre. ¿Pero qué es lo que evita que un hombre se convierta en lo que está destinado a convertirse? Echemos un vistazo a «los ladrones de la masculinidad». Hasta que no lo hagamos, no vamos a encontrar los verdaderos secretos de la fuerza del hombre.

Ladrón #1: La medida de la memoria

Esto es cuando no se puede estar a la altura de alguna

memoria del pasado en cuanto a desempeño o expectativas. ¿Recuerdas el sueño de tu niñez, de lo que querías convertirte cuando fueras adulto? Aunque algunas de esas expectativas quizás hayan sido necias e irrealistas, aun así duele cuando no puedes estar a la altura. ¿Cómo reaccionas? Quizás lanzando tu ira contra alguien más o hundiéndote en la depresión.

¿Cómo peleas contra este ladrón? Olvida el pasado. A cambio, piensa en lo que vas a hacer ahora. Eso es lo que en realidad cuenta. Observa objetivamente lo que tienes para estar agradecido ahora y luego haz lo que tengas que hacer para poder desempeñarte bien en el presente y puedas almacenar una experiencia excelente de vida.

Ladrón #2: Un «vacío de rendimiento» en tu vida

Esto va más allá de la medida de la memoria. No es solamente un recuerdo de lo pensabas que ibas a hacer; es en realidad el entendimiento de que en realidad nunca has estado a la altura de tu potencial. Existe un hueco entre tu potencial (por ejemplo, como músico habiloso) y tu actuación (mediocre, porque no practicas).

Sin embargo, si nunca has puesto a prueba ese potencial, nunca vas a tomar ningún riesgo. No tomar riesgos significa que tu vida será fácil y segura, pero lo más probable es que no sea tan satisfactoria como quieres que sea.

Ladrón #3: Enojo por un padre con defectos

Seamos realistas—todos los padres tienen defectos. Quizás tu padre era distante, nunca estuvo física y emocionalmente cerca. Tal vez tu madre nunca te demostró amor o te gritó y se equivocó en los asuntos que afectan negativamente la forma en que se comunica tu familia. Como resultado, quizá tu familia completa ha sufrido. Quizás esta dinámica estuvo presente en tu niñez y tienes poco o ningún control sobre ello. Eso ya pertenece al pasado. Ahora es ahora. Como adulto, eres responsable de tu propia vida. Eso quiere decir que eres responsable de encontrar la manera de detener esos patrones de relación y convertirlos en patrones positivos en la vida de tu propia familia. No será fácil, pero es posible con la ayuda de Dios y de un buen consejero cristiano.

Ladrón #4: Repercusiones financieras negativas

Digamos que has tomado varias decisiones financieras negativas y ahora estás experimentando un contragolpe. Sigues enojado porque las cosas no salieron bien. En el fondo sabes que eres el único culpable, pero es difícil admitirlo. Por lo tanto, acarreas mucha ira, resentimiento y amargura hacia la vida y hacia cualquiera que esté teniendo éxito en las áreas que tú no lo lograste.

En lugar de considerarte una víctima, da pasos hacia la solución. Generalmente, hay maneras de salir de eso si tienes el deseo de trabajar fuerte y cambiar tus hábitos de gastos.

Ladrón #5: Desilusión física

A medida que envejeces, tu cuerpo se vuelve más flojo y coopera menos. ¿Sabes por qué solía enojarme? Porque me estaba poniendo más pesado y flácido. La razón es simple. A mí me encanta comer y mi abuela tiene un restaurante. Yo quería tener mi pastel y también comérmelo, pero descubrí que no podía consumir todas las calorías sin ponerme flácido, especialmente sin hacer ejercicio. Mi solución fue comer menos, hacer ejercicio con regularidad, correr y hacer sentadillas. Entre más envejezco, se hace más difícil. Simplemente así es la vida, he aprendido a aceptar este hecho, en lugar de gastar energía emocional en ello.

¿Estás enojado por algo que no puedes cambiar ahora, antes que sea más tarde? ¿Necesitas corregir tu punto de vista de ti mismo en esas cosas que no puedes cambiar?

Ladrón #6: Decepción sexual

Tal vez estás enojado porque tu vida sexual no ha sido lo que has deseado, pero ten cuidado. Pregúntate: ¿por qué estoy decepcionado? ¿Es porque estás comparando a tu esposa con situaciones sexuales no naturales—gente de la televisión que ha sido retocada en las películas o en las portadas de las revistas? Si es así, la estás equiparando a situaciones de erotismo excesivo que están destinadas a atizar la lujuria. Ninguna mujer en la vida real puede estar a la altura de dichas imágenes.

Sin embargo, si tu esposa no responde sexualmente, hablen del porqué ella no está respondiendo. Evita las acusaciones, está listo a escuchar. ¿Será porque siente que no la respetas? ¿Es debido a heridas y abuso en su pasado lo que la detiene de disfrutar sexo contigo? ¿Porque no se siente cómoda con cierta expresión sexual de tu parte?

En la mayoría de los casos, la decepción sexual tiene solución: mejora la comunicación con tu esposa.

Ladrón #7: Encuentras errores frecuentemente

¿Tiendes a criticar y encontrar errores en todas partes? Si es así, el ambiente a tu alrededor siempre será negativo. Si alimentas esa negatividad y aumentas más lo negativo, estás enfangado en un círculo y sientes que no puedes salir.

Pero recuerda esto: Tu actitud no es el resultado de tus circunstancias; es tu elección.

Ladrón #8: Oposición de tus hijos

Básicamente esto quiere decir que no te llevas bien con tus hijos. Ellos son irrespetuosos contigo. Un hombre sabio va a examinar las razones: ¿Será porque reaccionas de forma exagerada o los conduces a la ira cuando los disciplinas?

Los padres necesitan pasar tiempo con sus hijos, crear una atmósfera de respeto y comunicación y cuando se presente la situación, ellos pueden lidiar con ésta de una manera que ayude a tus hijos a cambiar, en lugar de crecer enojados.

Pídele ayuda a Dios para amar a tus hijos, ser lo más positivo posible y crear o recrear una relación que tenga un balance de amor y disciplina.

Ladrón #9: Desajuste masculino

¿Alguna vez has sentido como que no coincides con la imagen de lo que un hombre debería de ser? ¿Te sientes como que no has logrado lo suficiente o que no eres lo suficientemente fuerte o resistente? ¿Te sientes siempre culpable, inferior, inadecuado o débil?

Si es así, primero pregúntate a ti mismo: ¿Estoy proyectado una imagen de hombría que es poco realista? Si te sientes como debilucho porque no puedes hacer frente a menos que duermas por lo menos seis horas, es hora de evaluar tu proyección de lo que un hombre debe de ser y hacer.

Segundo, si estás siendo realista, reconoce tu debilidad y decide qué vas a hacer al respecto. Como dice un dicho antiguo de boxeo: «a veces te golpean y te noquean y no puedes hacer nada. Pero te puedes levantar; sí puedes hacer eso».

Básicamente existen doce tipos de hombres y una persona puede ser la combinación de varios de ellos.

- **Casanova** - Sexualmente obsesionado, un depredador buscando una presa en lugar de amor. De este tipo abunda en Hollywood—el amante, el playboy. De hecho, el imperio de Hugh Hefner está construido con esta imagen.
- **Cavernícola** - Áspero, tosco y abusivo. Totalmente insensible, gruñe hasta para comer y luego se arrastra de nuevo a su cueva y termina el día. Se da un fin de semana libre y luego comienza de nuevo a actuar como un cavernícola—emocionalmente perturbador y físicamente amenazante.
- **Oruga** - Se arrastra por la vida. Es débil y no quiere defender nada, simplemente se arrastras. Muchos se paran sobre las orugas.
- **Repugnante** - No es agradable. Es injurioso y manipulador. Es engañador y mentiroso.
- **Chiflado** - Es inestable—loco y poco confiable.

- **Camaleón** - Cambia constantemente de un estado de ánimo a otro y de situación a situación. Trata de reflejar cualquier actitud en la que se encuentra. No tiene ninguna base de carácter real.
- **Controlador** - tiene que estar en control. Tiene que tener la razón; tiene que tener la última palabra.
- **Incoloro** - Es debilucho, incoloro y vacío. No tiene opinión; cualquier cosa que quieran hacer los demás está bien. No tienes fuego, ni energía dinámica. Es templado. Va por la vida sin ninguna convicción hacia nada.
- **Conspirador** - No se puede confiar en él porque siempre está tratando de engañar a la gente. Su sonrisa dice una cosa, pero tiene una agenda totalmente diferente detrás de esa sonrisa. Siempre está conspirando.
- **Comprometedor** - Compromete sus valores morales para conseguir lo que quiere. Hace cualquier cosa para salirse con la suya.
- **Aplastante** - Aplasta los sueños, esperanzas, expectativas y autoestima de los demás. Sabotea el impulso y el éxito de otros. Deja tragedia en su camino.
- **De primera clase** - Uno debe de esforzarse para ser esta es la clase de hombre. Hombre que es verdaderamente un hombre, quien es excelente cuando tiene que ser excelente. Que es fuerte, valiente y heroico, pero siempre lleno de amor y sensibilidad, particularmente hacia esos que son más débiles que él. Esta clase de hombre se controla, paga sus facturas y cuida de su familia. Él crea un ambiente de seguridad en su hogar, obedece a Dios y ama a la gente. Sabe cómo ganar, trabajar y tener éxito.

¿Cómo puedes ayudar a tu hijo a que se convierta en un hombre de esta clase? Vamos a compartir los secretos enseguida.

Los secretos para criar hijos varones

¿Qué deberías de enseñarle a tu hijo en cuanto a convertirse en alguien grandioso? Aquí tienes dieciséis secretos para compartir con él:

Secreto #1: Esté a cuentas con Dios

Como cristiano, yo creo que Dios ha revelado que Jesús es El Mesías y que Jesús murió en la cruz y resucitó de entre los muertos. Él en verdad es el Camino hacia Dios. Cuando eliges rendir tu vida a Él, vas a sentir una paz tremenda y libertad.

Secreto #2: Siga un líder

Encuentra un gran hombre a quien puedas seguir. Evalúa cómo hace lo que hace, luego imita su caminar. De esa manera, tú también te convertirás en un gran hombre.

Por ejemplo, a mí siempre me ha encantado leer acerca de John Wesley, el gran hombre de Dios que encabezó el avivamiento metodista en siglo dieciocho en Inglaterra. Aunque Wesley medía cinco pies dos pulgadas y no era físicamente fuerte, era valiente. Una vez cuando fue atacado por una multitud que quería matarlo, él miró a cada persona cara a cara y les preguntó: «¿Alguna vez les he hecho daño? El resultado fue que la multitud se alejó.

Otros hombres grandiosos que me han influenciado han sido: Billy Graham, Ronald Reagan y Theodore Roosevelt.

Encuentra unos pocos hombres moralmente rectos que te inspiren y aprende a adaptar sus secretos de éxito en tu propia vida.

Secreto #3: Aliméntate de «alimento varonil»

Para poder convertirte en una persona fuerte, necesitas consumir literatura positiva, incluyendo la Biblia. Por lo tanto, anima a tus hijos a leer sobre héroes verdaderos que tienen moral, valor y fuerza; que dan su vida por lo que es correcto.

Secreto #4: Mantente puro sexualmente

El Diablo es inteligente. Él sabe que si te desvías hacia la tentación sexual, eso te va a robar lo que puedas llegar a ser. Él siempre está trabajando, planeando destruirte, animándote a que uses de forma errónea el regalo de Dios, el sexo.

Por lo tanto, diles a tus chicos que el sexo en sí no es malo. Fue creado por Dios como enlace maravilloso entre un esposo y una esposa. Piensa en esto como el agua vivificante, una gran bendición, pero el sexo fuera del matrimonio es destructivo. Es como agua furiosa de una inundación fuera de control.

Permitir que el sexo tome control de tu vida en un contexto equivocado (fuera del matrimonio) va a destruir tu fuerza. Te va a comprometer y hacerte caer.

Esto quiere decir que aquellos que han sucumbido al sexo fuera del matrimonio están perdidos para siempre. La Biblia dice en 1 Juan 1.7-9 «más si andamos en la luz, como Él está en la luz, tenemos comunión los unos con los otros, y la sangre de Jesús, Su hijo, nos limpia de todo pecado. Si decimos que no tenemos pecado, nos engañamos a nosotros mismos y la verdad no está en nosotros. Si confesamos nuestros pecados, Él es fiel y justo para perdonarnos nuestros pecados y para limpiarnos de toda maldad». Es posible que hayan consecuencias como resultado de tu pecado: SIDA y otras enfermedades de trasmisión sexual y paternidad fuera del matrimonio, por nombrar algunas, pero el sexo no es algo que no pueda ser perdonado; Dios puede limpiar tu corazón nuevamente.

Secreto #5: Desempéñate al máximo nivel

Trabaja duro, a medida de tu capacidad. Ten la expectativa de que vas a tener éxito, y puedes ser como el pequeño motor en el libro infantil que continúa diciendo: «Yo creo que puedo, yo creo que puedo»… y cumplió su meta.

Secreto #6: sé honesto

Nunca mientas, engañes, manipules o robes. Vive siempre

con honestidad en tu corazón, incluso cuando pienses que nadie te está observando.

Secreto #7: Ora

Entiende y cree en el poder de la oración para cambiar vidas. Cosas maravillosas pasan en la vida de una familia cuando un hombre y una mujer oran juntos.

Secreto #8: Nutre tu naturaleza

Desarrolla las características dadas por Dios. Si tu naturaleza es solucionar problemas, hazlo. Si eres un líder innato, entonces dirige.

Secreto #9: Aprenda ser lógico

En lugar de que te dejes llevar por tus emociones, aprende a pensar bien las cosas. Evalúa cuidadosamente lo que escuchas y lo que te dicen. No te limites a creer lo que dicen los medios de comunicación.
Piensa por ti mismo. Ser lógico no garantiza que vas a tomar decisiones buenas o correctas todo el tiempo, pero ciertamente vas a tener más éxito que si no piensas de esa manera.

Secreto #10: Ten un espíritu generoso

Enseña a tus hijos a dar sin tener la expectativa de recibir algo a cambio. No siempre seas tan protector de tus pertenencias y no siempre te protejas a ti mismo. La Biblia dice que si tú das «...den y se les dará: se les echará en el regazo una medida llena, apretada, sacudida y rebosante, vaciarán en vuestro regazo. Porque con la medida con que midáis, se os volverá a medir» (Lucas 6.38).

Secreto #11: Sé cortés

Los chicos necesitan aprender lo básico de la cortesía en la vida—ser amable y cortés, no ser grosero ni malhablado. Las buenas costumbres son la demostración de respeto y educación en la sociedad y mejoran la vida para los demás.

Secreto #12: Aprende a perdonar

Jesús dice que si no perdonas a otros, no vas a ser perdonado. Por lo tanto, enseña a tus hijos a perdonar verdaderamente en lugar de hacerlo de mala gana. Perdonar a alguien no quiere decir que permitirás ser golpeado o acosado continuamente. En lugar de eso, quiere decir que no albergas un espíritu amargado y rencoroso. Este secreto va a mejorar el bienestar emocional de tus hijos.

Secreto #13: Ama los principios de Dios

Para que tus hijos puedan amar las leyes de Dios, primero tienen que conocerlas, así que ayúdalos a investigar la Biblia. El libro de Proverbios es especialmente poderoso, lleno de sabiduría para la vida diaria.

Secreto #14: Sigue las prioridades de Dios

Si tus hijos conocen y siguen las prioridades de Dios para manejar dinero, para dar, trabajar, etc., se van a convertir en adultos que funcionan bien, balanceados y exitosos.

Secreto #15: Sé fuerte en tiempos de adversidad

Cuando los tiempos son difíciles, sé más fuerte. Cuando las cosas sean difíciles, sé más fuerte. Enseña a tus hijos que ellos necesitan ser—y pueden ser—valientes en situaciones difíciles. ¿Cómo pueden aprender esto? ¡Observándote!

Secreto #16: Sé agradecido

Como lo dice la canción: «Cuenta tus bendiciones, cuéntalas una por una. Cuenta tus bendiciones, ve lo que Dios ha hecho». Enseña a tus hijos el lado «de gratitud» de la vida y te vas a sorprender de cómo va a cambiar su perspectiva (o la tuya).

Si enseñas a tu hijo sobre posibles obstáculos para su éxito, adviértele lo que necesitan los hombres (y cómo pueden satisfacer estas necesidades correcta o incorrectamente). Modela para él las acciones y palabras de un hombre saludable y bien balanceado, y comparte con él los secretos para una vida de éxitos. ¡Lo ayudarás a estar en el camino de convertirse en un gran hombre!

Capítulo 13

Una palabra final de parte de Ron

Me encontraba con mi amigo John, disfrutando una de las mejores pizzas que he comido, cuando John se inclinó hacia mí y pidió ayuda con sus hijos. Él quería algo específico, no sugerencias. Después de pensarlo un poco, le di una lista de verificación para seguir. Aquí está la lista, con algunas modificaciones.

1.- La piscina de los compañeros

Cuando el padre de Franklin D. Roosevelt perdió a su esposa, buscó otra novia únicamente en un lugar: en la aristocracia del Valle del Río Hudson del cual él formaba parte. Él cortejó a una mujer en sus veintes, casi treinta años más joven que él y eventualmente se casó con ella. Esta nueva esposa, Sara, se convirtió en la madre de FDR. James Roosevelt cumplió este plan porque él quería continuar su vida con una mujer que compartiera sus creencias y sus sentimientos. Este era en realidad un mecanismo intrínseco para aumentar las posibilidades de éxito y las de sus hijos. Se movió dentro de una piscina específica de compañeros. Tú debes hacer lo mismo por tus hijos.

La mejor piscina de compañeros para ti, es una

dinámica basada en la Biblia activa. Un grupo bien organizado de jóvenes en la iglesia. Debes asistir a una iglesia:

- Que levante a Jesucristo como Señor y Salvador.
- Que predique y enseñe la Biblia como la Palabra de Dios, sin comprometerla.
- Que tenga un ambiente donde es obvio que el Espíritu santo está activo.
- Que vea que la gente viene a Cristo con regularidad.

Esta iglesia debe tener un grupo de niños para tus hijos que sea espiritualmente vivo, activo y positivo.

Estos grupos van a hacer que sea mucho más fácil para tus hijos encontrar una conexión con amigos cristianos que van a formar paredes de protección para ellos.

Las investigaciones demuestran que el grupo de compañeros de tus hijos tiene una enorme influencia en ellos. Debes de controlar esto.

Yo recomiendo mucho, que adicionalmente a un grupo de jóvenes cristianos:

- Le des escuela en el hogar a tus hijos o los envíes a una escuela privada. Nosotros le dimos escuela en casa a nuestra hija y estamos dándole escuela en casa a nuestro hijo. Somos felices como familia unida y nuestros hijos están muy bien educados y en parte es porque les estamos dando escuela en casa. Es una manera muy efectiva de sacar a tus hijos de la cultura de la juventud negativa y egoísta que llena muchas de nuestras escuelas públicas.
- Si tus hijos escogen universidad, que escojan una universidad cristiana conservadora. Las probabilidades de que tu hijo o hija conozca a su futuro cónyuge en la universidad son muy altas. En una universidad cristiana, no solamente les dan una educación con perspectiva bíblica, los sumergen en una piscina muy profunda de amigos cristianos de los cuales pueden buscar la/el compañero de vida. Nada es más importante que su futuro, aparte de su relación con Jesucristo.

2.- La actitud lo es todo

Nuestra hija ha tenido un negocio desde que tenía nueve años - «Positive Pencils International». Ella se ha financiado por años, por medio de la venta de bolígrafos con consignas de su propio diseño. Uno de los bolígrafos más populares de Allison dice: «La actitud lo es todo». Tus hijos deben de vivir de acuerdo a estos principios todos los días.

Nosotros le enseñamos a Allison y le estamos enseñando a Jonathan dos elementos importantes que siempre estén bajo su control: actitud y disposición de ánimo.

En nuestra casa hay tres reglas (especialmente para mamá y papá):

- No hay quejas ni protestas. Punto.
- No hay malos humores. El mal humor no es una opción.
- «Estoy aburrido» no es parte de nuestro vocabulario. Si estás aburrido, hay tareas extras y trabajos a tu disposición inmediatamente.

3.- La importancia del lenguaje

Esto significa dos elementos verbales no negociables.

- No malas palabras. Palabras groseras y vulgares son una marca de las personas no-civilizadas, insensibles y sin inteligencia. Enséñales a tus hijos que ellos no son de esa clase y de deben de demostrarlo.
- Cortesía y buenos modales. La manera más rápida de sobresalir es sonar como un individuo de calidad. «Sí, señora», «No, señor», «Sí, señor», «Por favor», «Gracias», «De nada», deben de convertirse en algo natural para tus hijos, tanto como el aire que respiran.

4.- Gana la batalla por el cuerpo

- •Habla de sexo a la edad apropiada y en una manera positiva que esté centrada en Dios.

A mí me ayudó tremendamente a la edad de once años, el que mi madre sensible respondiera mis preguntas sexuales sin ningún tipo de bochorno o burla. Ella escuchaba, me decía la verdad, e incluso mantuvo un sentido del humor divertido y alegre. Mi padre reforzó esto con información más específica cuando yo era mayor. Mi educación sexual provino de padres sólidos quienes me dieron respuestas honestas e información. Debido a esto, yo no tuve la tentación de lanzarme y «sumergirme en una cuneta» por información equivocada y experiencias equivocadas. Hasta el día de hoy, tengo un punto de vista cristiano bueno y bien equilibrado del sexo (solamente para matrimonios-sin opción) que ha alegrado y bendecido mi matrimonio.

- Enseña la importancia de la limpieza y la higiene. Esto incluye de todo, desde tomar la ducha hasta una higiene dental.
- Evita sustancias peligrosas que amenacen tu salud. No bebas alcohol, no consumas drogas y no fumes. Enseña a tus hijos a que se mantengan alejados de estas malas elecciones que son contra la salud.
- Enséñales la alegría y libertar de la actividad y buena condición física. Esto va a formar una buena base de bienestar que va a proteger su vida.

5.- Ética de trabajo

Nada se lleva a cabo a menos que tú lo hagas. Los resultados no suceden por si mismos a menos que tú te los ganes. No enseñes a tus hijos a ser haraganes y desenfrenados. Si ellos saben cómo trabajar, van a tener 75% del ingrediente del éxito. Aquí tienes dos maneras de formar sus hábitos de trabajo:

- Enséñales el orden. Mucho del estrés adulto ocurre debido al desorden, una manera desorganizada de vivir. Enséñales a tus hijos el poder protector de una buena capacidad de organización. Deben tender su propia cama,

guardar sus juguetes y limpiar después de cada comida. Ponlos en ventaja hacia el éxito con la disciplina personal.
- Enséñales puntualidad. Enséñales a respetar el tiempo y de esa manera, los vas a enseñar a respetar la vida. La puntualidad muestra respeto hacia las demás personas. Créeme, la gente se dará cuenta de tus hijos y los va ayudar a tener éxito.

6.- Administración del dinero

Nosotros ya hemos hablado de esto en un capítulo anterior. Simplemente observa este resumen:

- Ahorra dinero
- Gasta sabiamente
- Invierte
- Elimina deudas
- Da
- No juegues juegos de azar. Es demasiado arriesgado y no enseña ética de trabajo en cuanto al dinero.

7.- Disfruta solamente del entretenimiento que te enriquezca

Las películas, libros, música, revistas y televisión deberían de enriquecer, informar, y construir tu vida. El entretenimiento debe ser divertido, pero nunca hacer más difícil para ti o para tus hijos la obediencia a Dios.

8.- El egoísmo es la muerte de la felicidad

Educa a tus hijos a temprana edad a ser generosos y útiles, no solamente a querer tomar más. Esta es la base del éxito y la felicidad.

9.- Lectura

Así como escribe el autor más vendido Charlie «Tremendo» Jones: «Lectores son líderes y líderes son lectores». He dicho.

10.- Escritura

Enseña a tus hijos a que se expresen en papel. Esto va a disciplinar y desarrollar su mente como ninguna otra cosa. Además los va a colocar en una posición para influenciar la cultura - ¡Necesitamos eso!

11.- Poder espiritual

Existen cuatro elementos esenciales:

- Guía tu hijo a tener una relación personal con Jesucristo.

- Enseña a tu hijo a orar—a hablar con Dios en lenguaje simple y sincero.

- Enseña a tu hijo a leer y estudiar la Biblia. Realmente es la Palabra de Dios. Herramientas buenas como *La Biblia para niños* y *La Biblia a día*, ayudan mucho.

- Enseña a tu hijo «evangelismo amigable». Entrénalos para contarles a sus amigos de su mejor amigo, Jesús, de manera positiva y natural.

12.- Identidad

Mi familia ha vivido en la misma ciudad, en el este de Kentucky por nueve generaciones. Yo crecí con padres, abuelos y tatarabuelos. Estuve rodeado de tías, tíos y primos. Mi identidad en las familias Ball y Laffety ha sido clara desde que yo recuerdo. Quizás no tengas una amplia red de relaciones familiares, pero aun así puedes dar a tus hijos un fuerte sentido de identidad familiar.

Hubo veces en que estuve tentado a hacer algo malo o estúpido y me detuve porque tuve un sentimiento extraño de lo que yo soy en realidad. Soy dueño de mi propio negocio debido a que la mayoría de los miembros de mi familia—mi círculo de identidad—son propietarios de negocios. Yo siempre me sentí especial porque soy parte de una familia especial, una familia específica. Haz todo lo puedas para darles eso a tus hijos.

13.- Legado

Esto es simple y necesario. Deliberadamente, debes transmitir a tus hijos las ideologías, los valores y las tradiciones que han formado tu vida. Si esas ideologías, valores y tradiciones no han sido cristianos hasta hoy en día, entonces entrega tu propia vida al señorío de Jesucristo y comienza a enseñar esas ideologías, valores y tradiciones. Ese es el mayor servicio que puedes darle a tus hijos.

14.- La relación sorprendente entre la ropa y la imagen personal

El Museo de Londres a menudo imparte clases que da a los visitantes una breve experiencia en una obra de teatro. Una mujer con quien me encontré recientemente describió la clase a la que asistió.

El elenco fue escogido entre las personas que fueron al museo ese día. Cuatro de ellos estaban vestidos pobremente, jóvenes tatuados con actitud negativa o defensiva. Estaban inseguros de sus papeles, eran maleducados y cooperaban muy poco. El instructor los engatusó para que hicieran un esfuerzo y se los llevó a una habitación para que se disfrazaran.

En breve regresaron, se les asignaron partes sencillas y practicaron poco. Durante las dos siguientes horas, ocurrió una transformación inesperada. Estos jóvenes difíciles de tratar comenzaron a convertirse en la persona en la que estaban disfrazados. Un muchacho engreído y malhablado que estaba vestido de sacerdote, se convirtió en alguien amable y solidario. Un hombre joven que estaba encorvado cuando llegó, ahora era un príncipe seguro y parado rectamente. Una muchacha joven, vestida con un traje de una dama educada y gentil, se comportó con amabilidad, estilo y consideración. Uno por uno, cada joven se fundió en una identidad representada por el papel adquirido en la obra.

Después de pocas horas, ninguno de los jóvenes quería entregar las prendas de vestir que le habían revelado a él o ella una posible nueva dirección en la vida.

La ropa y la apariencia básica de tu hijo o adolescente es una parte vital de su autoconocimiento general.

¿Qué hacen los pantalones flojos y arrugados y las camisas mal fajadas por la imagen? El efecto tiene más influencia psicológica de lo que te imaginas. El descuido te puede conducir a hábitos de holgazanería. La dejadez puede conducir a poca capacidad de enfoque y malos hábitos mentales. Ropa desaliñada puede conducir a hábitos indisciplinados en general. Y ¿Qué pasa con la elección de cierta apariencia o moda en particular (aretes, tatuajes, citas obscenas en las prendas de vestir, etc.) como una declaración de rebeldía? Yo creo que esto es una puerta de entrada para la derrota. La rebeldía hacia la autoridad de los padres es especial y profundamente condenada en la Biblia: «Hijos: obedeced a vuestros padres en el Señor, porque esto es justo» Efesios 6.1.

Con frecuencia tus hijos quieren encajar en cierto grupo y usar ropa o marcas en el cuerpo como una entrada, pero si el grupo en sí es rebelde, tú debes ayudar a tu hijo a encontrar un grupo diferente que refuerce los estándares de comportamiento bíblico.

Nuevamente hablando de la vestimenta, la apariencia que tus hijos muestran al mundo exterior va a lograr dos cosas: apoyar la imagen de quienes ellos creen que son y va a validar a las otras personas que ellos parecen ser. Enséñales a ser limpios, bien organizados y agradables en apariencia y van a construir una imagen personal que va a aumentar las probabilidades de éxito y logros.

15.- El secreto del logro excepcional

Recientemente leí una declaración escrita en 1920 por una mujer que escribió consejos a una joven amiga. Siendo ella misma muy educada y exitosa, había estudiado numerosas personas de alto rendimiento, buscando un elemento común que estuviera presente en cada uno de los individuos analizados. Todos habían tenido impacto en algún negocio, entretenimiento, ciencia o artes. Lo que a ella le pareció asombroso fue que de las varias y diferentes personalidades, trasfondos, talentos y experiencias, de todos los componentes solamente tenían en común uno: el deseo de ser poco convencional. Cada triunfador tenía el deseo y la determinación de ir contra la multitud y sobresalir como pionero de nuevas ideas.

Al mismo tiempo, que enseñas a tus hijos el peligro de la rebeldía, asegúrate que aprendan además el deleite de la verdadera individualidad. Anima a tus hijos a perseguir creatividad y originalidad con vigor y enfoque. Ayúdales a temprana edad a aprender a romper el molde del pensamiento poco inspirador, a salir «fuera de la caja» del pensamiento convencional siempre-lo-hemos-hecho de esta manera.

A inicios de los años 50s, una pequeña empresa trató de ganarse una posición en Illinois. Los dueños escogieron una ciudad pequeña, pero les informaron que no eran bienvenidos. Nadie de la comunidad quería sus negocios. Ellos batallaron y persistieron, con éxito gradual. A inicios de 1960, buscaban expandirse, pero en cada banco donde solicitaron les negaron el préstamo. Para los años 70s, ya eran la más grande y exitosa compañía de su clase en la historia del comercio mundial. Hoy en día todos han escuchado hablar de McDonald's. Tuvieron éxito debido a la combinación de trabajo duro, administración hábil y una dosis de un ingrediente secreto que ya hemos descubierto— el deseo de ser atrevido, diferente y poco convencional.

En el siglo dieciocho en Inglaterra, John Wesley conmocionó a la gente de ese tiempo predicando de Jesucristo al aire libre a miles de personas, después de que le habían dicho que no era bienvenido en los edificios de las iglesias tradicionales. Él fue atrevido, diferente y poco convencional.

Billy Graham en el siglo veinte, creó un enfoque audaz de informarle a gente acerca de Jesucristo por medio de la radio, TV y grandes «cruzadas» reuniendo a miles de personas. Él tuvo éxito, con la bendición de Dios, siendo atrevido, diferente y poco convencional.

Este es un patrón de influencia, efectividad aun mayor para tus hijos. Enséñales siempre a obedecer a Dios, pero nunca tener temor de ser diferentes para poder llevar a cabo el trabajo. Invención e innovación tienen que nacer de nuevo en cada generación. Permíteles nacer de nuevo en tu hogar y familia hoy.

16.- La familia que come juntos...

Durante la segunda parte de los 90s, se realizó un estudio extenso de la vida en familia. Los resultados fueron publicados en 2001. El hallazgo más sorprendente fue que en las familias que comían juntas por lo menos cinco noches por semana, las probabilidades de que los niños se metieran en problemas eran solamente del 2%. Una mirada más cercana a la información reveló que los padres que comían con sus hijos estaban también involucrados en otros aspectos de la vida de ellos. Fue esa participación lo que protegió y animó a los niños.

Tus hijos saben si deseas pasar tiempo con ellos o simplemente estás respondiendo porque tienes obligación o sientes culpabilidad. Tu influencia para lo bueno está construida en la decisión de tener un papel activo y feliz en la vida de tus insustituibles, inmensos, inmensurable propios hijos. Qué mejor manera de mostrar amor sólido que darles tu recurso más valioso—tu tiempo.

¿Cuál es entonces la conclusión de esta lista de comportamiento recomendado?

Toda la vida está compuesta de componentes básicos de decisiones diarias. Los comportamientos de un niño son en gran parte creados por las acciones que tú tomas.

Tus hijos te necesitan. Dales lo que hace a un ser humano magnífico—una madre y un padre que los guíe a tener una relación con Jesucristo y quien los ame, los críe, los guíe y los prepare para la vida. Lograrás el éxito con tus hijos más allá de la gran expectativa que te hayas creado. ¡ADELANTE!

Una palabra final de parte de Ron